ABBY AND THE
BACHELOR COP

MA

All the characters in this book have no existence outside the imagination of
the author, and have no relation whatsoever to anyone bearing the same name
or names. They are not even distantly inspired by any individual known or
unknown to the author, and all the incidents are pure invention.

First published in Great Britain 2011
by Mills & Boon, an imprint of Harlequin (UK) Limited,
Eton House, 18-24 Paradise Road, Richmond, Surrey TW9 1SR

© Marion Lennox 2011

ISBN: 978 0 263 88873 7

23-0411

Harlequin (UK) policy is to use papers that are natural, renewable and
recyclable products and made from wood grown in sustainable forests. The
logging and manufacturing processes conform to the legal environmental
regulations of the country of origin.

Printed and bound in Spain
by Blackprint CPI, Barcelona

Marion Lennox is a country girl, born on an Australian dairy farm. She moved on mostly because the cows just weren't interested in her stories! Married to a 'very special doctor', Marion writes Medical Romances as well as Mills & Boon Romance (she used a different name for each category for a while—if you're looking for her past Mills & Boon Romances, search for author Trisha David as well). She's now had over eighty romance novels published.

In her non-writing life Marion cares for kids, cats, dogs, chooks and goldfish. She travels, she fights her rampant garden (she's losing) and her house dust (she's lost).

Having spun in circles for the first part of her life, she's now stepped back from her 'other' career, which was teaching statistics at her local university. Finally she's reprioritised her life, figured what's important, and discovered the joys of deep baths, romance and chocolate.

Preferably all at the same time!

With huge thanks to the wonderful Kelly Hunter,
who gave me Kleppy, to the fabulous Anne Gracie,
and to all the Maytoners, whose friendship
brings my stories to life.

To Radar, who was Trouble. I look back on every
moment with laughter and with love.

CHAPTER ONE

IF YOU couldn't be useful at the scene of an accident, you should leave. Onlookers only caused trouble.

Banksia Bay's Animal Welfare van had been hit from behind. Dogs were everywhere. People were yelling at each other. Esther Ford was having hysterics.

Abigail Callahan, however, had been travelling at a safe enough distance to avoid the crash. She'd managed to stop before her little red sports car hit anything, and she'd done all she could.

She'd checked no one was hurt. She'd hugged Esther, she'd tried to calm her down and she'd phoned Esther's son who, she hoped, might be better at coping with hysterics than she was. She'd carried someone's crumpled fender to the side of the road. She'd even tried to catch a dog. Luckily, she'd failed. She wasn't good with dogs.

Now, blessedly, Emergency Services had arrived. Banksia Bay Emergency Services took the shape of Rafferty Finn, local cop, so it was definitely time for Abby to leave.

Stay away from Raff Finn.

It wasn't past history making her go. She was doing the right thing.

She tried to back her car so she could turn, but the crowd of onlookers was blocking her way. She touched her horn and Raff glared at her.

How else could she make people move? She did not need to be here. She looked down at her briefcase and thought about the notes inside that she knew had to be in court—now. Then she glanced back at Raff and she thought… She thought…

She thought Rafferty Finn looked toe-curlingly sexy.

Which was ridiculous.

Abby had fallen for Raff when she was eight. It was more than time she was over it. She *was* over it. She was so over it she was engaged to be married. To Philip.

When Raff had been ten years old, which was when Abby had developed her first crush on him, he'd been skinny, freckled and his red hair had spiked straight up. Twenty years on, skinny had given way to tall, tanned and ripped. His thick curls had darkened to burned copper, and his freckles had merged to an all-over tan. His gorgeous green eyes, with dangerous mischief lurking within, had the capacity to make her catch her breath.

But right now it was his uniform that was causing problems. His uniform was enough to make a girl go right back to feeling as she had at eight years old.

Raff was directing drivers. He was calm, authoritative and far more sexy than any man had a right to be.

'Henrietta, hold that Dalmatian before it knocks Mrs Ford over. Roger, quit yelling at Mrs Ford. You drove into the dog van, not Mrs Ford, and it doesn't make a bit of difference that she was going too slow. Back your Volvo up and get it off the road.'

Do not look at Raff Finn, she told herself. Do not.

The man is trouble.

She turned and tried again to reverse her car. Why wouldn't people move?

Someone was thumping on her window. The door of her car swung open. She swivelled and her heart did a back flip. Raff was standing over her—six foot two of lethal cop. With dog.

'I need your help, Abby,' he growled and, before she could react, there was a dog in her car. On her knees.

'I need you to take him to the vet,' Raff said. 'Now.'

The vet?

The local veterinary clinic was half a mile away, on the outskirts of town.

But she wasn't given a chance to argue. Raff slammed her car door closed and started helping Mrs Ford steer to the kerb.

There was a dog on her knee.

Abby's grandmother had once owned a shortbread tin adorned with a picture of a dog called Greyfriars Bobby. According to legend—or Gran—Bobby was famous for guarding his master's grave for almost fourteen years through the bleakest of Edinburgh's winters. This dog looked his twin. He was smallish but not a toy. His coat was wiry and a bit scruffy, sort of sand-coloured. One of his ears was a bit floppy.

His eyebrows were too long.

Did dogs have eyebrows?

He looked up at her as if he was just as stunned as she was.

What was wrong with him? Why did he need to go to the vet?

He wasn't bleeding.

She was due in court in ten minutes. Help.

What to do with a dog?

She put a hand on his head and gave him a tentative pat. Very tentative. If she moved him, maybe she'd hurt him. Maybe he'd hurt her.

He wiggled his head to the side and she tried scratching behind his ear. That seemed to be appreciated. His eyes were huge, brown and limpid. He had a raggedy tail and he gave it a tentative wag.

His eyes didn't leave hers. His eyes were…were…

Let's cut out the emotion here, she told herself hastily. This dog is nothing to do with you.

She fumbled under the dog for the door catch and climbed out of the car. The dog's backside sort of slumped as she lifted him. Actually, both ends slumped.

She carried him back to Raff. The little dog looked up at her and his tail still wagged. It seemed a half-hearted wag, as if he wasn't at all sure where he was but he sort of hoped things might be okay.

She felt exactly the same.

Raff was back in the middle of the crashed cars. 'Raff, I can't…' she called.

Raff had given up trying to get Mrs Ford to steer. He had hold of her steering wheel and was steering himself, pushing at the same time, moving the car to the kerb all by himself. 'Can't what?' he demanded.

'I can't take this dog anywhere.'

'Henrietta says it's okay,' Raff snapped. 'It's the only one she's caught. She's trying to round up the others. Come on, Abby, the road's clear—how hard is this? Just take him to the vet.'

'I'm due in court in ten minutes.'

'So am I.' Raff shoved Mrs Ford's car another few feet and then paused for breath. 'If you think I've spent years getting Wallace Baxter behind bars, just to see you and your prissy boyfriend get him off because I can't make it…'

'Cut it out, Raff.'

'Cut what out?'

'He's not prissy,' she snapped. 'And he's not my boyfriend. You know he's my fiancé.'

'Your fiancé. I stand corrected. But he's definitely prissy. I'll bet he's sitting in court right now, in his smart suit and silk tie—not like me, out here getting my hands dirty. Case for the prosecution—me and the time I can spare after work. Case for the defence—you and Philip and weeks of paid preparation. Two lawyers against one cop.'

'There's the Crown Prosecutor…'

'Who's eighty. Who sleeps instead of listening. This'll be a no-brainer, even if you don't show.' He shoved the car a bit further. 'But I'll be there, whether you like it or not. Meanwhile, take the dog to the vet's.'

'You're saying you want me to take the dog to the vet's—to keep me out of court?'

'I'm saying take the dog to the vet's because there's no one else,' he snapped. 'Your car's the only one still roadworthy. I'll radio Justice Weatherby to ask for a half hour delay. That'll get us both there on time. Get to the vet's and get back.'

'But I don't do dogs,' she wailed. 'Raff…'

'You don't want to get your suit dirty?'

'That's not fair. This isn't about my suit.' Or not very. 'It's just… What's wrong with him? I mean… I can't look after him. What if he bites?'

Raff sighed. 'He won't bite,' he said, speaking to her as if she were eight years old again. 'He's a pussycat. His name's Kleppy. He's Isaac Abrahams' Cairn Terrier and he's on his way to be put down. Put him on your passenger seat and Fred'll take him out at the other end. All I'm asking you to do is deliver him.'

It was twelve minutes to ten on a beautiful morning in Banksia Bay. The sun was warm on her face. The sea was glittering beyond the harbour and the mountain behind the town was blue with the haze of a still autumn morning. The sounds of the traffic chaos were lessening as Raff's attempts at restoring order took effect.

Abby stood motionless, her arms full of dog, and Raff's words replayed in her head.

He's Isaac Abrahams' Cairn Terrier and he's on his way to be put down.

She knew Isaac or, rather, she'd known him. The old man had lived a mile or so out of town, up on Black Mountain where…well, where she didn't go any more. Isaac had died six weeks ago and she was handling probate. Isaac's daughter in Sydney had been into the office a couple of times, busy and efficient in her disposing of Isaac's belongings.

There'd been no talk of a dog.

'Can you get your car off the road?' Raff said. 'You're blocking traffic.'

She was blocking traffic? But she gazed around and realised she was.

Somehow, magically, Raff had every other car to the side

of the road. Raff was like that. He ordered and people obeyed. There were a couple of tow trucks arriving but already cars could get through.

There was no problem. All she had to do was get in the car—with dog—and drive to the vet's.

But…to take a dog to be put down?

'Henrietta should do this,' she said, looking round for the lady she knew ran the Animal Shelter. But Raff put his hands on his cop hips and she thought any minute now he'd get ugly.

'Henrietta has a van full of dogs to find,' he snapped.

'But she runs the Animal Shelter.'

'So?'

'So that's where he needs to go. Surely not to be put down.'

Raff's face hardened. She knew that look. Life hadn't been easy for Raff—she knew that, too. When he was up against it…well, he did what he had to do.

'Abby, I know this dog—I've known him for years,' he told her, and his voice was suddenly bleak. 'I took him to the Animal Shelter the night Isaac died. His daughter doesn't want him and neither does anyone else. The only guy who loves him is Isaac's gardener, and Lionel lives in a rooming house. There's no way he can keep him. The Shelter's full to bursting. Kleppy's had six weeks and the Shelter can't keep him any longer. Fred's waiting. The injection will be quick. Don't drag it out, Abby. Deliver the dog, and I'll see you in court.'

'But…'

'Just do it.' And he turned his back on her and started directing tow trucks.

He'd just given Abigail Callahan a dog and she looked totally flummoxed.

She looked adorable.

Yeah, well, it was high time he stopped thinking Abby was adorable. As a teenager, Abby had seemed a piece of him—a part of his whole—but she'd watched him with condemnation for ten years now. She'd changed from the laughing kid she used to be—from his adoring shadow—to someone he no longer liked very much.

He'd killed her brother.

Raff had finally come to terms with that long-ago tragedy—or he'd accepted it as much as he ever could—but he'd killed a part of her. How did a man get past that?

It was time he accepted that he never could.

What sort of name was Kleppy for a dog?

He shouldn't have told her its name.

Only she would have figured it. The dog had a blue plastic collar, obviously standard Animal Welfare issue, but whoever had attached it had reattached his tag, as if they were leaving him a bit of personality to the end.

Kleppy.

The name had been scratched by hand on the back of what looked like a medal. Abby set the dog on her passenger seat—he wagged his tail again and turned round twice and settled—and she couldn't help turning over his tag.

It was a medal. She recognised it and stared.

Old Man Abrahams had done something pretty impressive in the war. She'd heard rumours but she'd never had confirmation.

This was more than confirmation. A medal of honour, an amazing medal of honour—hanging on the collar of a scruffy, homeless mutt called Kleppy.

Uh-oh. He was looking up at her again now. His brown eyes were huge.

Six weeks in the Animal Shelter. She'd gone there once on some sort of school excursion. Concrete cells with a tiny exercise yard. Too many dogs, gazing up at her with hope she couldn't possibly match.

'The people who run this do a wonderful job,' she remembered her teacher saying. 'But they can't save every dog. If you ask your parents for a pet for Christmas you need to understand a dog can live for twenty years. Every dog deserves a loving home, boys and girls.'

She'd been what? Thirteen? She remembered looking at the dogs and starting to cry.

And she also remembered Raff—of course it was Raff—patting her awkwardly on the shoulder. 'Hey, it's okay, Abby. There'll be a fairy godmother somewhere. I reckon all these dogs'll be claimed by tea time.'

'Yeah, probably by your grandmother,' someone had said, not unkindly. 'How many dogs do you have, Finn?'

'Seven,' he'd said and the Welfare lady had pursed her lips.

'See, that's the problem,' she said. 'No family should have more than two.'

'So you ought to bring five in,' someone else told Raff and Raff had gone quiet.

You ought to bring five in. To be put down? Maybe that was what Philip would think, Abby decided, though she couldn't remember Philip being there. But even then Philip had been a stickler for rules.

As were her parents.

'We don't want an abandoned dog,' they'd said in horror that night all those years ago. 'Why would you want someone else's cast-off?'

She needed to remember her parents' advice right now, for Isaac Abrahams' cast-off was in her car. Wearing a medal of valour.

'Move the car, Abby.' Raff's voice was inexorable. She glanced up and he was filling her windscreen.

'I don't want...'

'You don't always get what you want,' he growled. 'I thought you were old enough to figure that out. While you're figuring, shift the car.'

'But...'

'Or I'll get you towed for obstructing traffic,' he snapped. 'No choice, lady. Move.'

* * *

So all she had to do was take one dog to the vet's and get herself to court. How hard was that?

She drove and Kleppy stayed motionless on the passenger seat and looked at her. Looking as if he trusted her with his life.

She felt sick.

This wasn't her responsibility. Kleppy belonged to an old guy who'd died six weeks ago. His daughter didn't want him. No one else had claimed him, so the sensible, humane thing to do was have him put down.

But what if…? What if…?

Oh, help, what she thinking?

She was getting married on Saturday week. To Philip.

Nine days.

Her tiny house was full of wedding presents. Her wedding gown was hanging in the hall, a vision of beaded ivory satin. She'd made it herself, every stitch. She loved that dress.

This dog would walk past it and she'd have dog hair on ivory silk…

Well, that was a dumb thing to think. For this dog to walk past it, he'd have to be in her house, and this dog was headed to the vet's. To be put down.

He looked up at her and whimpered. His paw came out and touched her knee.

Her heart turned over. Nooooo.

It took five minutes to drive to the vet's. Kleppy's paw rested against her knee the whole time.

She pulled up. Kleppy wasn't shaking. She was.

Fred came out to meet her. The elderly vet looked grim. He went straight to the passenger door. Tugged it open.

'Raff rang to say you were coming,' he said, lifting Kleppy out. 'Thanks for bringing him. Do you know when the rest are coming?'

'I… Henrietta was trying to catch them. How many?'

'More than I want to think about,' Fred said grimly. 'Three months from Christmas, puppies stop being cute. Not your call, though. I'll deal with him from here.'

Kleppy lay limp in Fred's arms. He looked back at her.

The paw on her knee…

Help. Help, help, help.

'It'll be quick?'

Fred glanced at her, brows snapping. Abby had gone to school with Fred's daughter. He knew her well. 'Don't,' he said.

'Don't what?'

'Think about it. Get on with your life. Nine days till the wedding?'

'I…yes.'

'Then you've enough on your plate without worrying about stray dogs. Not that you and Philip would ever want a dog. You're not dog people.'

'What…what do you mean?'

'Dogs are mess,' he said. 'Not your style. You guys might qualify for a goldfish. See you later, love. Happy wedding if I don't see you before.'

He turned away. She could no longer see Kleppy.

She could feel him.

His eyes…

Help. Help, help, help.

She was a goldfish person? She'd never even had a goldfish.

A paw on her knee…

He reached the door before she broke.

'Fred?'

The vet turned. Kleppy was still slumped.

'Yes?'

'I can't bear this,' she said. 'Can you…can you take him in, check him out for damage and then give him back to me?'

'Give him back?'

'Yes.'

'You want him?'

'He's my wedding present to me.' She knew she sounded

defiant but she didn't care. 'I've decided. How hard can one dog be? I can do this. Kleppy is mine.'

Fred did his best to dissuade her. 'A dog is for life, Abigail. Small dogs like Kleppy live for sixteen years or longer. That's ten years at least of keeping this dog.'

'Yes.' But ten years? That was a fact to give her pause.

But the paw...

'He's a mutt,' Fred said. 'Mostly Cairn but a bit of something else.'

'That's okay.' Her voice was better, she decided. Firmer. If she was adopting a stray, what use was a pedigree?

'What will Philip say?'

'Philip will say I'm crazy, but it'll be fine,' she said stoutly, though in truth she did have qualms. 'Is he okay?'

Fred was checking him, even as he tried to dissuade her. 'He seems shocked, and he's much thinner than when Isaac brought him in for his last vaccinations. My guess is that he's barely eaten since the old man died. Isaac found him six years back, as a pup, dumped out in the bush. There were a few problems, but in the end they were pretty much inseparable.'

Inseparable? The word suddenly pushed her back to the scene she'd just left. To Raff.

Once upon a time, she and Raff had been inseparable, she thought, and inexplicably there was a crazy twist of her heart.

Inseparable. This dog. The paw...

'He looks okay,' Fred said, feeding him a liver treat. Kleppy took it with dignified politeness. 'Just deflated from what life's done to him. So now what?'

'I take him home.'

'You'll need food. Bedding. A decent chain.'

'I'll stop at the pet store. Tell me what to get.'

But Fred was glancing at his watch, looking anxious. 'I'm urgently needed at a calving. Tell you what, you'll be seeing Raff again in court. Raff'll tell you what you need.'

'How did you know…?'

'Everyone knows everything in Banksia Bay,' Fred said. 'I know where you're supposed to be right now. I know Raff's had the case set back half an hour and I hear Judge Weatherby's not happy. He's fed up with Raff though, not you, so chances are you'll get Baxter off. Which no one in Banksia Bay will be happy about. But hey, if your fees go toward buying dog food, then who am I to argue? Get Baxter off, then talk to Raff about dog food. He gets a discount at the Stock and Station store.'

'Why?'

'Because Raff has one pony, two dogs, three cats, two rabbits and, at last count, eighteen guinea pigs,' Fred said, handing her Kleppy and starting to clear up. 'His place is a menagerie. It's a wonder he didn't take this one but I guess even Raff has limits. He has a lot on his plate. See you later, love. Happy wedding and happy new dog.'

CHAPTER TWO

SHE couldn't go to the Stock and Station store now. That'd have to wait until she'd talked to Raff. Still, Kleppy obviously needed something. What? Best guess.

She stopped at the supermarket and bought a water bowl, a nice red lead with pictures of balls on it and a marrowbone.

She drove to the courthouse and Kleppy lay on the passenger seat and looked anxious. His tail had stopped wagging.

'Hey, I saved you,' she told him. 'Look happy.'

He obviously didn't get the word *saved*. He sort of... hunched.

What was she going to do with him while she was in court?

She drove her car into her personal parking space. How neat was this? She remembered the day her name had gone up. Her parents had cracked champagne.

It was a fine car park. But...it was in full sun.

She might not be a dog person but she wasn't dumb. She couldn't leave Kleppy here. Nor could she take him home—or not yet—not until she'd done something about dog-proofing. Her parents? Ha! They'd take him right back to Fred.

So she drove two blocks to the local park. There were shade trees here and she could tie him by her car. Anyone passing would know he hadn't been abandoned.

She hoped Kleppy would know it, too.

She gave him water and his bone and he slumped on the ground and looked miserable.

Maybe he didn't know it.

She looked at him and sighed. She took off her jacket—her lovely tailored jacket that matched her skirt exactly—and she laid it beside Kleppy.

He sniffed it. The paw came out again—and he inched forward on his belly until it was under him.

Her very expensive jacket was on dirt and grass, and under dog. Her professional jacket.

She didn't actually like that jacket anyway; she preferred less serious clothes. She was five foot four and a bit…mousy. But maybe lawyers should be mousy. Her shiny brown hair curled happily when she let it hang to her shoulders but Philip liked it in a chignon. She had freckles but Philip liked her to wear foundation that disguised them. She had a neat figure that looked good in a suit. Professional. Lawyers should be professional.

She'd given up on *professional* this morning. She was so late.

Oh, but Kleppy looked sad.

'I'll be back at midday,' she told him. 'Two hours, tops. Promise. Then we'll work out where we go from here.'

Where? She'd think of something. She must.

Maybe Raff…

There was a thought.

Fred had said Raff had a menagerie. What difference would one dog make? Once upon a time, he'd had seven.

Instead of advice, maybe she could persuade him to take him.

'You'd like Rafferty Finn,' she told Kleppy. 'He's basically a good man.' Good but flawed—*trouble*—but she didn't need to go into that with Kleppy.

But how to talk him into it? Or Philip into the alternative?

It was too hard to think of that right now. She grabbed her briefcase and headed to the courthouse without looking back. Or without looking back more than half a dozen times.

Kleppy watched her until she was out of sight.

Heart twist. She didn't want to leave him.

It couldn't matter. Her work was in front of her and what was more important than work?

What was facing her was the case of The Crown versus Wallace Baxter.

Wallace was one of three Banksia Bay accountants. The other two made modest incomes. Wallace, however, had the biggest house in Banksia Bay. The Baxter kids went to the best private school in Sydney. Sylvia Baxter drove a Mercedes Coupé, and they skied in Aspen twice a year. They owned a lodge there.

'Lucky investments,' Wallace always said but, after years of juggling, his web of dealings had turned into one appalling tangle. Wallace himself wasn't suffering—his house, cars, even the ski lodge in Aspen, were all in his wife's name—but there were scores of Banksia Bay's retirees who were suffering a lot.

'It's just the financial crisis,' Wallace had said as Philip and Abby had gone over his case notes. 'I can't be responsible for the failure of overseas banks. Just because I'm global…'

Because he was global, his financial dealings were hard to track.

This was a small case by national standards. The Crown Prosecutor who covered Banksia Bay should have retired years ago. The case against Wallace had been left pretty much to Raff, who had few resources and less time. So Raff was right—Philip and Abby had every chance of getting their client off.

Philip rose to meet her, looking relieved. The documents they needed were in her briefcase. He kept the bulk of the confidential files, but it was her job to bring day to day stuff to court.

'What the…?'

'Did Raff tell you what happened?'

Philip cast Raff a look of irritation across the court. There was no love lost between these two men—there never had been. 'He said you had to take a dog to the vet, to get it put down. Isn't that his job?'

'He had cars to move.'

'He got here before you. What kept you? And where's your jacket?'

'It got dog hair on it.' That, at least, was true. 'Can we get on?'

'It'd be appreciated,' the judge said dryly from the bench.

So she sat and watched as Philip decimated the Crown's case. Maybe his irritation gave him an edge this morning, she thought. He was smooth, intelligent, insightful—the best lawyer she knew. He'd do magnificently in the city. That he'd returned home to Banksia Bay—to her—seemed incredible.

Her parents thought so. They loved him to bits. What was more, Philip's father had been her brother Ben's godfather. They were almost family already.

'He almost makes up for our Ben,' her mother said over and over, and their engagement had been a foregone conclusion that made everyone happy.

Except… Except…

Don't go there.

She generally didn't. It was only in the small hours when she woke and thought of Philip's dry kisses, and thought why don't I feel…why don't I feel…?

Like she did when she looked at Rafferty Finn?

No. This was pre-wedding nerves. She had no business thinking like that. If she so much as looked at Raff in that way it'd break her parents' hearts.

So no and no and no.

Raff was on the stand now, steady and sure, giving his evidence with solid backup. His investigation stretched over years, with so many pointers…

But all of those pointers were circumstantial.

She suspected there were things in Philip's briefcase that might not be circumstantial.

Um…don't go there. There was such a thing as lawyer-client confidentiality. Even if Baxter admitted dishonesty to them outright—which he hadn't—they couldn't use it against him.

So Raff didn't have the answers to Philip's questions. The

Crown Prosecutor didn't ask the right questions of Baxter. It'd take a few days, maybe more, but even by lunch time no one doubted the outcome.

At twelve the court rose. The courtroom emptied.

'You might like to go home and get another jacket,' Philip said. 'I'm taking Wallace to lunch.'

She wasn't up to explaining about Kleppy right now. Where to start? But she surely didn't want to have lunch with Wallace. Acting for the guy made her feel dirty.

'Go ahead,' she said.

Philip left, escorting a smug Wallace. She felt an almost irresistible urge to talk to the Crown Prosecutor, tell him to push harder.

It was only suspicion. She had no proof.

'Thanks for taking Kleppy.' Raff was right behind her, and made her jump. Her heart did the same stupid skittering thing it had done for years whenever she heard his voice. She turned to face him and he was smiling at her, looking rueful. 'Sorry, Abby. That was a hard thing to ask you to do this morning, but I had no choice.'

Putting Kleppy down. A hard thing…

'It was too hard,' she whispered. The Crown Prosecutor was leaving for lunch. If she wanted to talk to him…

She was lawyer for the defence. What was she thinking?

'Hey, but you're tough.' Raff motioned to the back of the courtroom, where Bert and Gwen Mackervale were shuffling out to find somewhere to eat their packed sandwiches. 'Not like the Mackervales. They're as soft a touch as any I've seen. They lost their house, yet you'll get Wallace off.'

'Raff, this is inappropriate. I'm a defence lawyer. You know it's what I do.'

'You don't have to. You're better than this, Abby.'

'No, I'm not.'

'Yeah, well…' He shrugged. 'I'm going to find me a hamburger. See you later.'

Uh-oh. Maybe she shouldn't have snapped. Definitely she

shouldn't have snapped. Not when there was such a big favour to ask.

How to ask?

Just ask.

'You couldn't cope with another dog, could you?' she managed and he stilled.

'Another…'

'I couldn't,' she whispered. 'I can't. He's still alive. Raff, he…he looked at me.'

'He looked at you.' Raff was looking at her as if she'd just landed from Mars.

'I couldn't get him put down.'

Raff was carrying papers. He placed them on the nearest bench without breaking his gaze. He stared at her for a full minute.

She didn't stare back. She stared at her shoes instead. They were nice black shoes. Maybe a bit high. Pert, she thought. Pert was good.

There was a smudge on one toe. She considered bending to wipe it and decided against it.

Still silence.

'You're keeping Kleppy?' he said at last.

She shook her head. 'I'm…I don't think it's possible. I'm asking if you could take him. Fred says you have a menagerie. One more wouldn't…wouldn't be much more trouble. I could pay you for his keep.'

'Fred suggested…' He sounded flabbergasted.

'He didn't,' she admitted. 'I thought of it myself.'

'That I'd take Kleppy?'

'Yes,' she whispered and she thought that she sounded about eight years old again. She sounded pathetic.

'No,' he said.

She looked up at him then. Raff Finn was a good six inches taller than she was. More. He was a bit too big. He was a bit too male. He was a bit too…Raff?

He was also a bit too angry.

'N…No?'

'No!' His expression was a mixture of incredulity and fury. 'I don't believe this. You strung out a dog's life in the hope I'd take him?'

'No, I…'

'Do you know how miserable he is?'

'That's why I…'

'Decided to give him to me. Thanks, Abby, but no.'

'But…'

'I'm not a soft option.'

'You have all those animals.'

'Because Sarah loves them. Do you know how much they cost to feed? I can't go away. I can't do anything because Sarah breaks her heart over each and every one of them. Don't you dare do this to me, Abby. I'm not your soft option. If you saved Kleppy, then he's yours.'

'I can't…'

'And neither can I. You brought this on yourself. You deal with it yourself.' His voice was rough as gravel, his anger palpable. 'I need to go. I didn't get breakfast and I don't intend to miss lunch. I'll see you back in court at one.'

He turned away. He strode to the court door and she chewed her lip and thought. But then she decided there wasn't time for thinking. She panicked instead.

'Raff?'

He stopped, not looking back. 'What?'

Sometimes only an apology would do. She was smart enough to know that this was one of those times. Maybe a little backtracking wouldn't hurt either.

'Raff, I'm very sorry,' she said. 'It was just a thought—or maybe it was just a wild hope—but the decision to save Kleppy was mine. Asking you was an easy option and I won't ask again. But, moving on, if I'm to keep him… I know nothing about dogs. Fred didn't suggest you take him, but he did suggest I ask you for help. He said you'll tell me all the things I need to care for him. So please…'

'Please what?'

'Just tell me what I need to buy at the Stock and Station store. I have a meeting with the wedding caterers after work, so I need to do my shopping now.'

'You're seriously thinking you'll keep him?'

'I don't have a choice.'

He was facing her now, his face a mixture of incredulity and…laughter? Where had laughter come from? 'You're keeping *Kleppy?*' He said it as if she'd chosen Kleppy above all others.

'There's no other dogs out there?' she said, alarmed, and he grinned. His grin lit his face—lit the whole court. Oh, she knew that grin…

Trouble. Tragedy.

'There's thousands of dogs,' he said. 'So many needing homes. But you have to fall for Kleppy.'

'What's wrong with Kleppy?'

'Nothing.' He was still grinning. 'I take it you haven't told Philip.'

'I… No.'

'So where's Kleppy now?' His grin faded. 'You haven't left him in the car? The sun…'

'I know that much,' she said, indignant. 'I took the car to the park and I tied him to a nice shady tree. He has water and feed. He even has my jacket.'

'He has your jacket.' He sounded bemused, as if there was some private joke she wasn't privy to.

'Yes.'

'And you've tied him up…how?'

'I bought a lead.'

'Please tell me it's a chain.'

'The chains looked cruel. It's webbing. Pretty. Red with pictures of balls on it.'

'I don't believe this.'

'What's wrong?'

But she didn't have a chance to answer. Instead, he grabbed

her hand, towed her out of the courthouse—practically at a run—and he headed for the park.

Dragging her behind him.

Kleppy was gone.

Her pretty red lead was chewed into two pieces—or at least she assumed it was chewed into two pieces. One piece was still tied to the tree.

Her jacket lay on the ground, rumpled. The water bowl was half empty. Apparently chewing leads was thirsty work. The marrowbone wasn't touched.

No dog.

'He doesn't like being confined, our Kleppy,' Raff said, taking in the scene with professional care.

'You know this how?' *He'd chewed through a lead?*

'It's always been a problem. I'm guessing he'll make tracks up to the Abrahams place, but who knows where he'll end up in the meantime.'

'He'll be up at Isaac's?'

Isaac lived halfway up the mountain at the back of the town. Raff was looking concerned. 'It is a bit far,' he admitted. 'And from here… It'll be off his chosen beat.' He raked his hair. 'Of all the stupid… I don't have time to go look for a dog.'

'I'll look for him.'

'You know where to look?'

'Do you?'

'Backyards,' he said. 'Never takes the fastest route, our Kleppy.' He raked his hair again. Looking tired. 'I need lunch. If I'm not back in court at one then Baxter'll definitely get off. You need to do this, Abby. I can't.'

Look for a dog all afternoon… 'Philip'll kill me.'

'Then I guess the wedding'll be off. Is that a good thing?'

Raff spoke absently, as if it didn't bother him if her wedding was at risk. As indeed it didn't. What business was it of his to care about the wedding? What business was it of his to even comment on it? She opened her mouth to say so, but suddenly his gaze focused, sharpened. 'Is that…?'

She turned to see.

It was—and the change was extraordinary.

When she'd left him two hours ago, Kleppy had looked defeated and depressed. When he'd crawled onto her jacket he hadn't had the energy to even rise off his stomach.

Now he was prancing across the park towards them, looking practically jaunty. His rough coat was never going to be pretty. One of his ears flopped down, almost covering his eye. His tail was a bit ragged.

But they could see his tail wagging when he was still a hundred yards away. And, as he got closer…

He had something in his mouth. Something pink and lacy. What the…?

'It's a bra,' Abby breathed as the little dog reached them. She bent down and the dog circled her twice, then came to her outstretched hand. He rubbed himself against her leg and his whole body shivered. With delight?

He was carrying the bra like a trophy. She touched it and he dropped it into her hand, then stood back as if he'd just presented her with a cheque for a million dollars. His body language was unmistakable.

Look what I've found for you! Aren't I the cleverest dog in the world?

She dropped the bra and picked him up, hugging him close. He wriggled frantically and she put him back down. He picked up the bra again, placed it back in her hand and then allowed her to pick him up—as long as she kept the bra.

His meaning couldn't be plainer. 'I've brought you a gift. You appreciate it.'

'You've brought me a bra,' she managed and she felt like crying. 'Oh, Kleppy…'

'It could just as easily have been men's jocks,' Raff said. He lifted the end of the bra that was hanging loose. There was a price tag attached. 'I thought so. He's a bit small to rob clothes lines, our Kleppy. This has come from Main Street. Morrisy Drapers are having a sale. This will have come from the discount bin at the front of the store.'

Had it? She checked it out. Cop and lawyer for the defence, standing in the sun, examining evidence.

Pink bra. Nylon. White and silver frills. About an E Plus Cup. Room for about three of Abby.

'Very…very useful,' Abby managed.

'You'll need to pay for it.'

'Sorry?'

'It's theft,' Raff said, touching the bra's middle with a certain degree of caution. It was looking a bit soggy. 'He never hurts anything. He hunts treasures; he never destroys them. But they do get a bit…wet. Taking it back and apologising's not going to cut it.'

'Will they know he's stolen it?'

'He's not a cat burglar,' Raff said gravely, though the sides of his mouth were twitching. 'Dog burglars don't have the same finesse. He's a snatch and grab man, our Kleppy. There'll be a dozen people on Main Street who'll be able to identify him in a line up.'

'Oh, my…' And then she paused. Kleppy.

Kleppy was a strange name but she'd hardly had time to think about it. Now… 'Kleppy. Oh…'

Raff looked like a man starting to enjoy himself. 'Got it,' he said, grinning. 'And there's another reason you're not offloading this mutt onto me. This is a dog who lives to present his master with surprises. No dead rats or old bones for his guy. It has to be interesting. Expensive is good. One of a set's his favourite. Isaac gave up on him long since—he just paid for the damage and got on with it. So now here's Kleppy, deciding you're his new owner. Welcome to dog ownership, Abigail Callahan. You're the proud owner of Banksia Bay's biggest kleptomaniac—and also the littlest.'

A kleptomaniac… Kleppy.

She stared at Raff as if he was out of his mind. He gazed back, lips twitching, that dangerous smile lurking deep within.

She was about to present her fiancé with a kleptomaniac dog?

'I don't believe it,' she managed at last. 'There's no such thing.'

'You want to know how I know this dog?' He wasn't even trying to disguise his grin. 'I'd like to say I'm personally acquainted with every dog in Banksia Bay but, even with Sarah's help, I can't manage that. Nope, I'm acquainted with Kleppy because I've arrested him.'

'Arrested…'

'I've caught him red-handed—or red-pawed—on any number of occasions. The problem is that he doesn't know how to hide it. Like now. He steals and then he shows off.'

'I don't believe it.'

'You've already said that.'

'But…'

'That's why no one wants him,' he said, humour fading. 'He's always been a problem. Henrietta's had to be honest with everyone who came to the Shelter looking for the ideal pet. He isn't ideal. Isaac paid out on Kleppy's behalf more times than I can say. He's hidden stuff and he's been accused of stealing himself. Isaac never cared what people thought of him, which was just as well, as there's been more women's underwear end up at his house than you can imagine. He burned most of it—what choice did he have? Can you imagine wandering the town saying who owns this G-string? But he loved Kleppy, you see.' The smile returned. 'Like you will.'

'I… This is appalling.'

'I told you to get him put down.'

'You know I'm a soft option.' Anger hit then, fury, pure and simple. 'You know me, Raff Finn. You put this dog in my car because you knew I wouldn't be able to have him put down. You know I'm a soft touch.'

'Now how would I know that?' he said softly. 'I haven't known you for a very long time, Abby. You've grown up. You've got yourself engaged to Philip. The Abby I knew could no sooner have married Philip than fly. You're a lawyer engaged in getting Wallace Baxter off. A lawyer doing cases like that—of course you can get a dog put down.'

His gaze met hers, direct, challenging, knowing he was calling a bluff she couldn't possibly meet.

'You still can,' he told her. 'Put Kleppy in the car and take him back to Fred. You've made his last hours happy by giving him the freedom for one last hoist. He'll die a happy dog.'

You still can.

Say something.

She couldn't think of a thing to say.

She was hugging Kleppy, who had a pink bra somehow looped around his ears.

She still hugged Kleppy.

What Raff was saying was sensible. Very sensible. There were too many dogs in the world. She'd done her best by this one. She'd let him have a happy morning—if indeed Raff was right and Kleppy did enjoy stealing.

But he was certainly a happier dog now than he'd been when she'd first met him. He was warm and nuzzly. He was poking his damp nose against her neck, giving her a tentative lick.

His backside was wriggling.

Take him back to Fred? No way.

She'd always wanted a dog.

Philip would hate a dog.

Her marriage suddenly loomed before her. Loomed? Wrong word, but she couldn't think of another one.

Philip was wonderful. He was her rock. He'd looked after her and her family for ever. When Ben had died he'd held her up when her world seemed to be disintegrating.

Philip was right for her. Her parents loved him. Everyone thought Philip was wonderful. If she hadn't married him…

She *hadn't* married him, she reminded herself. Not yet. That was the point.

In nine days she'd be married. She'd move into the fabulous house Philip had bought for them, and she'd be Philip's wife.

Philip's wife would never bring home a kleptomaniac dog. She'd never bring home any sort of dog. So, if she wanted one…

She took a deep breath and she knew exactly what she'd do. Her last stand... Like it or leave it, she thought, and she sounded desperate, even to herself. But she had made up her mind.

'I'm keeping him.'

'Good for you,' Raff said and the twinkle was back with a vengeance. 'Can I be there when you tell Philip?'

'Get lost.'

'That's not kind. Not when you need help to buy what Kleppy needs.'

'I'm starting to get a very good idea of what Kleppy needs,' she said darkly. 'An eight-foot fence and a six-foot chain.'

'He'll mope.'

'Then he'll have to learn not to mope. It's that or dead.'

'You'll explain that to him how?'

'You're not being helpful.'

'No,' he said and glanced at his watch. 'I'm not. I need a hamburger and time's running out before court resumes. You want a list?'

'No. I mean...' The afternoon suddenly stretched before her, long and lonely. Or not long and lonely for her. Long and lonely for the little dog squirming in her arms. Her thief. 'I do need a list. I also need a chain.' She hesitated. 'But I can't leave him here. This morning was only two hours. This afternoon's four at least before I can collect him.'

'So take him home.'

'I can't.' It was practically a wail. She caught herself. Fought for a little dignity. 'I mean...it's not dog-proof. I need an hour or so there to get things organised.'

'That's fair enough.' He paused, surveyed her face and then decided to be helpful. 'You want me to ask Sarah to help?'

Sarah. Her eyes widened. Of course. Sarah loved dogs. And... Maybe her first suggestion was still possible. Maybe...

'No,' Raff said before she opened her mouth. 'Sarah's not taking ownership of another dog and if you ask her I'll personally run you out of town. I mean that, Abby.'

'I wouldn't ask her.'

'No?'

She managed a twisted smile, abandoning her last forlorn hope.

'No.'

'Good, then,' he said briskly, moving on. 'But she'll enjoy taking care of him this afternoon. Kleppy'll be tired after his excursion. We have a safe yard. The other dogs are quiet—they won't overwhelm him—and you can come by this evening and pick him up.'

Go back to Raff's? She couldn't imagine doing that. But Raff was moving on.

'It's a good offer,' Raff said. 'Take it or leave it, but do it now. If you accept, then I'll lock this convicted thief in my patrol car and take him out to Sarah. I may even do it with lights and sirens if it means getting back to court on time. You can take my list and go buy what you need and get back to court on time as well. Or I leave you to it. What's it to be, Abby?'

'I...' She was starting to panic. Go out to Raff's tonight? To Raff's? She hadn't been there since...

'Unless you have another friend you can call on?' he suggested, and maybe her emotions were on her face. Definitely her emotions were on her face.

'All my friends work,' she wailed.

'Then it's Sarah. Tonight, and you *will* collect him.' That irrepressible grin emerged again. 'Hey, you have a dog. What a wedding gift. To you and to Philip, one kleptomaniac dog. Happy wedding.'

He drove out to Sarah with Kleppy beside him and he found the smile inside him growing. Somewhere inside, the Abby he'd once known and loved was still there.

Once upon a time she'd loved him.

That had been years ago. A teenage romance. Yes, they'd felt as if they were truly, madly, deeply, but they were only kids.

At nineteen he'd headed off to Sydney to Police Training College. Abby had been stuck in Banksia Bay until she finished school, and she'd needed a partner for her debutante ball.

He still remembered the arguments. 'You're my boyfriend. How can I have anyone else as my partner? Why can't you come home more often so we can practice?'

And more... 'You and Ben are totally obsessed with that car. Every time you come home, that's all you ever think about.'

They were kids. He hadn't seen her need, and she hadn't seen his. Philip had been home from university; he'd agreed to partner her for her ball and Raff was given the cold shoulder.

They'd been kids moving on. Changing.

They had changed, he conceded, only just now he'd seen a glimpse that the old Abby was still in there. Feisty and funny and gorgeous.

But still...unforgiving, and who could blame her?

He'd forgiven himself. He didn't need Abigail Callahan's forgiveness. He couldn't need it.

If only she wasn't adorable.

CHAPTER THREE

THE afternoon was interminable. The case was boring—financial evidence that was as dry as dust.

The courtroom was as dry as dust.

She couldn't think of a way to tell Philip.

All afternoon she was aware of Raff on the opposite side of the courtroom. He was here this afternoon to present the police case. Thankfully, he wouldn't be here for the rest of the week. He was called away twice, for which she was also thankful, but he wasn't called away for long enough.

He was watching her.

He was waiting for her to tell Philip?

He was laughing at her. She knew he was. The man spelled trouble and he'd just got her into more.

Trouble? One small dog, easily contained in a secure backyard. How hard could this be?

So tell Philip.

There was lots of time. The police case went on for most of the afternoon—tedious financial details. She and Philip both knew it back to front. There were gaps while documents were given to the jury. She had time to tell him.

Philip would be civilised about it. He'd never raise his voice to her, especially not in a courtroom. But still...

She couldn't.

Across the court, Raff still watched her.

Finally the court rose. Raff crossed the courtroom and Abby panicked. *Don't say anything.*

'You guys okay?' he asked, and anyone who didn't know him would think it was simply a courtesy question. They wouldn't see that lurking laughter. *Trouble*.

'Why wouldn't we be?' Philip demanded, irritated. He disliked Raff—of course he did. He showed no outright aggression—simply cool, professional interaction and nothing more.

'It's getting close to your wedding,' Raff said. 'No last minute nerves? No last minute hitches?'

'We need to go,' Abby said, feeling close to hysterics. 'I have a meeting with the caterers in half an hour.'

'I bet there's lots of stuff you need to do.' Raff's voice was sympathy itself. 'Messy things, weddings.'

'Not ours,' Philip snapped. 'Everything's under control. Isn't that right, sweetheart?'

'I…yes.' Just go away, Raff. Get out of our lives. 'Are you coming to the caterers with me, Philip?'

'I can't.' Philip turned a shoulder on Raff, excluding him completely. 'My dad and my uncles are taking me out to dinner and bowling. A boys only night. I thought I told you.'

He had.

'That sounds exciting,' Raff said, mildly interested. 'Bowling, huh. I guess I won't be untying you naked from in front of the Country Women's Association clubrooms at dawn, then.'

'My friends…'

'Don't do wild buck's nights,' Raff said approvingly. 'I guessed that. You'll probably be home in bed by eight. So you're alone tonight, Abby? Organising caterers on your lonesome. And anything else you need to do.'

'Could you please…' she started and then stopped, the impossibility of asking another favour—asking him to bring Kleppy home—overwhelming her.

'Nope,' Raff said. 'Not if you're about to ask me anything that involves the wedding. Me and weddings keep far away from each other.'

'We're not asking you to be involved,' Philip snapped. 'Abby can cope with the caterers herself. Ready to go, sweetheart?'

'Yes,' she managed and allowed Philip to usher her out of the court.

She should have told Philip then. She had ten minutes while Philip went over the results of the day, what they needed to do to strengthen their case the next morning, a few wedding details he'd forgotten to cover.

Philip was a man at ease with himself. It was only when Raff was around that he got prickly and maybe…well, that did have to do with their past. Raff had messed with Philip's life as well as hers.

Philip was a good man. He was looking forward to his wedding. His father and his uncles were taking him out for a pre-wedding night with the boys and he'd enjoy it.

She didn't want to mess with that until she must, even if it did mean delaying telling him about Kleppy; even if it meant going to Raff's alone. Maybe it'd be better going alone. Going with Philip… It could make things worse.

'Come round tonight after bowling,' she told him, kissing him lightly on the lips. Her fiancé. Her husband in nine days. She loved him.

And if he was a bit dull… He'd had his days of being wild, they all had, before life had taught them that caution was good.

'We should get a good night's sleep,' he said.

'Yes, but there are things we need to discuss.' He'd like Kleppy when he saw him, she decided. Kleppy of the limpid eyes, wide and brown and innocent.

She should change his name. To Rover? Rover was a Philipish name for a dog.

But Kleppy suited him.

'What do we need to discuss?' he was asking.

Say it.

No. Introduce him to Kleppy as a done deal.

'Just…caterers and things. I don't want to make too many decisions on my own.'

He smiled and kissed her and she had to stop herself from thinking dry and dusty. 'You need to have more self-confidence. Make your own decisions. You're a big girl now.'

'I...yes.'

'Anything you decide is fine by me.'

'But you will drop by?'

'I'll drop by. Night, sweetheart.' And off he went for his night with the boys. His dad and his uncles. Bowling. Yeeha!

And that was the type of thinking that was getting her into trouble, she decided. So cut it out.

Philip was a lovely man. He was handsome. He was beautifully groomed. They'd had a very nice holiday last year—they'd gone to Italy and Philip had had four suits made there. They were lovely suits. He'd also had two briefcases made—matching ones, magnificent leather, discreetly initialled and fitted out to Philip's specifications. She'd only been mildly irritated when he'd decreed—for the sake of the briefcases—her surname would be his.

What was the issue, after all? She was to be his wife.

But buying suits and briefcases had taken almost half of their holiday.

Cut it out!

It was just... Raff had unsettled her. This whole day had unsettled her.

'So go home and organise your house for one small dog, then go organise caterers,' she told herself. 'Oh, and pay for Kleppy's stolen goods. Just do what has to be done, one step at a time.'

And then go out to Raff's?

Aargh.

She could do this.

She could visit Rafferty Finn.

She could do it. One step at a time.

The rest of the afternoon was full, but Abby and her dog were front and centre of his thoughts. He shouldn't have offered to bring Kleppy home. Not this afternoon. Not ever.

He didn't want her coming here.

After dinner, Raff washed and Sarah wiped, while Sarah told him about her day, the highlight of which had been minding Kleppy.

'He's a sweetheart,' his sister told him, her face softening at the thought of the little dog. 'He's so cuddly. Why does he love his bra?'

'He's a thief. He likes stealing things. He's a bad dog.' He found himself smiling at the thought of strait-laced Abigail Callahan having to front up and pay for stolen goods.

Maybe it wasn't a good idea to keep thinking of Abby. Not like this.

She was Philip's fiancée. Anything between them was a distant memory. It had to be.

But Sarah was looking doubtful. She looked down at Kleppy, snoozing by the fire, his bra tucked underneath him. 'He doesn't look bad. He's really cute and Abby's very busy. Are you sure Abby wants him?'

Raff hardened his heart. 'I'm sure.'

'And Abby's coming tonight?'

'Yes.'

'Abby's my friend.'

She was. The tension of the day lessened a little at that. No matter what lay between Raff and Abby, no matter how much she hated seeing him, Abby had always been Sarah's friend.

They'd all been best friends at the time of the accident. Ben and Raff. Abby and Sarah. Two big brothers, two little sisters. Philip had been in there, too. A gang of five.

But one car crash and friendship had been blown to bits.

In the months that followed, no matter that Abby had loathed Raff so much that seeing him made her cry, she'd stuck by Sarah. She'd visited her in Sydney, despite her parents' disapproval, taking the train week after week to Sydney Central Hospital and then later to the rehabilitation unit on North Shore.

Back home, Sarah's friends had fallen away. Acquired brain injury was a hard thing for friends to handle. Sarah was still

Sarah, and yet not. She'd struggled with everything—relearning speaking, walking, the simplest of survival skills.

They'd come so far. She could now almost live independently—almost, but not quite. She had her animals and their little farm Raff kept for her. She worked in the local sheltered workshop three days a week, and twice a week Abby met her after work for drinks.

Drinks being milkshakes. Two friends, catching up on their news.

Raff would pick Sarah up and she'd be happy, bubbly about going out with her friend—but Abby would always have slipped away from the café just before Raff was due. Since the accident, Abby had never come back to their farm. She'd never talked to Raff unless she absolutely must, but she'd never taken that anger out on Sarah.

'I'm glad Abby's coming tonight,' Sarah said simply. 'And I'm glad she's getting a dog. Abby's lonely.'

Lonely? Sarah rarely had insights. This one was startling. 'No, she's not. She's getting married to Philip.'

'I don't like Philip,' Sarah said.

That was unusual, too. Sarah liked everyone. When Philip met her—as of course he did because this wasn't a big town—he was unfailingly friendly. But still... In the times when Raff had been with her and they'd met Philip, Sarah's hand had crept to his and she'd clung.

Was that from memories of the accident?

The accident. Don't go there.

'There's nothing wrong with Philip,' he told Sarah.

'I want Abby to come,' Sarah said, wiping her last pot with a fierceness unusual for her. 'But I don't want Philip. He makes me scared.'

Scared?

'The man's boring,' Raff said. 'There's nothing to be scared about.'

'I just don't like him,' Sarah said and, logical or not, Raff felt exactly the same.

* * *

She didn't want to go.

She must.

She gazed round her little house with a carefully appraising eye. She'd hung her wedding dress in the spare room and she'd packed away everything else she thought a dog might hurt.

She'd bought a dog kennel for outside and a basket for inside.

She'd bought a chain for emergencies but she didn't intend using it. Her back garden was enclosed with a four-foot brick fence, and she'd checked and rechecked for gaps.

She had dog food, dog shampoo, flea powder, worm pills, a dog brush, padding for his kennel and a book on training your dog. She'd had a quick browse through the book. There was nothing about kleptomania, but confinement would fix that.

She'd take him for a long walk every day. Kleppy might sometimes be lonely, she conceded, but surely loneliness was better than the fate that had been waiting for him.

And if he was lonely… She might sneak him into the office occasionally.

That, though, was for the future. For now, she was ready to fetch him. From Raff.

So fetch him. There's not a lot of use staring at preparations, she told herself. It's time to go claim your dog.

It was eight o'clock. Philip's night out would be over by ten and she had to be back here by then.

Of course she'd be back. Ten minutes drive out. Two minutes to collect Kleppy and say hi to Sarah. Ten minutes back.

Just go.

She hadn't been out there since…

Just go.

'When will she be here?'

'Any time soon.'

He shouldn't care. He shouldn't even be here. There was bound to be something cop-like that needed his attention at the station—only that might look like he was running, and Rafferty Finn wasn't a man who ran.

'She never comes here.'

'She likes going to cafés with you too much.'

Sarah giggled, hugging Kleppy close. This place was pretty relaxed for a dog. The screen door stayed permanently open and the dogs wandered in and out at will. The gate to the back garden was closed, but Kleppy seemed content to be hugged by Sarah, to watch television and to occasionally eat popcorn.

Raff watched television, too. Or sort of. It was hard to watch when every sense was tuned to a car arriving.

The Finn place hadn't changed.

The moon was full but she hardly needed to see. She'd come here so often, to the base of Black Mountain, that she knew every bend. As kids, she and Ben had ridden their bikes here almost every day.

This had been their magic place.

Her parents had disapproved. 'The Finns,' her mother had told them over and over, 'are not our sort of people.' By that she meant they didn't fit into her social mould.

Abby and Ben didn't care.

Old Mrs Finn—everybody called her Gran—had been the family's stability. Gran's husband had died long before Abby had known her, and it was rumoured that his death had been a relief, for the town as well as for Gran. After his death, Gran had quietly got on with life. She ran a few sheep, a few pigs, a lot of poultry. Her garden was amazing. She seemed to spend her life in the kitchen and her baking was wonderful.

Abby barely remembered Raff and Sarah's mother, but there had been disapproving whispers about her as well. She'd run away from home at fifteen, then come home unwed with two small children.

She'd worked in the local supermarket for a time. Abby had vague memories of a silent woman with haunted eyes, with none of the life and laughter of her mother or her children.

She'd died when Abby was about seven. Abby remembered little fuss, just a family who'd got on with it. Gran had taken over her grandchildren's care. Life had gone on and the Finns were still disapproved of.

Abby and Ben had loved it here. They had always been welcome.

And now? She turned into the drive but her foot eased from the accelerator.

'You're always welcome.' She could remember Gran saying it to her, over and over. She remembered Gran saying it to her after Ben's death. As if she could come back here…

She had come back. Tonight.

This is only about a dog, she told herself, breathing deeply. *Nothing else. The past is gone. There's no use regretting—no use even thinking about it. Go get your dog from Raff Finn and then get off his land.*

Raff never meant…

I know he didn't, she told herself. Of course he didn't. Accidents happened and it was only stupidity.

Could she forgive stupidity?

Ben was dead. Why would she want to?

He saw her stop at the gate. It was after eight—would Philip have finished his wild night out? Would she have him with her?

Maybe that was why they'd stopped. Philip would be doing his utmost to stop her keeping Kleppy.

Would she defy him? She'd need strength if she was going to stay married to Philip. She'd need strength not to be Philip's doormat.

But the thought of Abby as a doormat made him smile. She'd never been a doormat. Abby Callahan was smart, sexy, sassy—and so much more. Or…she had been.

She'd followed him round like a shadow for years. He and Ben had scoffed at Abby and Sarah, the little sisters. They'd teased them, and had given them such a hard time. They'd loved them both. Until…

Until one stupid night. One stupid moment.

He closed his eyes as he'd done so many times. Searching for a memory.

Summer. Nineteen years old. Home from Police Training College. Ben home from university. They'd spent weekend after weekend tinkering with a car they were trying to restore. Finally they'd got it started, towards dusk on the day they were both due to go back to the city. They were pumped with excitement. Aching to see it go.

They couldn't take it on the road—it wasn't registered—but up on Black Mountain, just behind Isaac Abrahams place, there was a cleared firebreak, smoothed for access for fire trucks.

If they could get it out there, they could put it through its paces.

He remembered loading the car on the trailer behind Gran's ancient truck, Ben's dad watching them in disapproval. 'You should be home tonight, Ben. Your mother's expecting you.'

'We need to see this working,' Ben had told him and Mr Callahan had left in a huff.

Sarah was watching them, wistful. 'Can I come?'

'There's not enough room in the truck.'

'What if Philip brings me?'

'Sure. Bring Abby.'

'You know Abby's mad at you—and she's not talking to Philip, either.'

But neither Ben nor Raff were interested. They were only interested in getting their car going.

And it worked. Up on the mountain, he remembered Ben driving, yahooing, both of them high as kites. Months of work paying off.

He remembered getting out. Swapping drivers. Thinking it was too dark to be on this track, and it was starting to rain. Plus Ben had to get back to have dinner with his parents.

But Ben saying, 'We have lights. If I can cope with Mum being fed up, you can cope with a bit of rain. Just do one turn to see for yourself how well she handles.'

Then…nothing. He'd woken in hospital. Concussion. Multiple lacerations. Broken wrist and broken ankle.

All he knew of the accident was what was written in the official reports.

Philip had driven Sarah onto the track to find them. He'd turned off the main road onto the firebreak, and ventured just far enough down the break to reach the crest...

Philip had been the only one uninjured. His recall was perfect, stark and bleak.

Raff had burst over the crest on the wrong side of the road, driving so fast he was almost airborne. Philip had nowhere to go. Both drivers swerved, but not fast enough.

Both cars had ended up in the trees. The rain and the mess from the emergency vehicles had washed the tracks away before the authorities could corroborate Philip's story. Raff couldn't be prosecuted—but he had punishment enough. He'd killed his best mate and he'd destroyed his sister. He missed Ben like he'd miss a twin—an aching, gut-destroying loss. He'd lost a part of Sarah that could never be restored.

His grandmother had died six months later.

And Abby?

Facing Abby had been the hardest thing he'd had to do in his life. The first time he'd seen her...she'd looked at him and it was as if he was some sort of black hole where her heart used to be.

'I'm sorry,' he'd said and she'd simply turned away. She'd stayed away for ten years.

Her brother was dead and sometimes Raff wished it could have been him.

Which was dumb. Who'd take care of Sarah, then?

Let it go.

Go greet Abby. And Philip?

Abby and Philip. Banksia Bay's perfect couple.

CHAPTER FOUR

RAFF was waiting on the veranda and Abby felt her breath catch in her throat. She came close to heading straight back down the mountain.

What was it with this man? She was well over her childhood crush. She'd decided today that it was the uniform making him sexy, but he wasn't wearing a uniform now.

He was in faded jeans and an old T-shirt, stretched a bit tight.

He looked good enough to…

To get away from fast.

He was leaning idly against the veranda post, big, loose-limbed, absurdly good-looking. He was standing with crossed arms, watching her walk towards him. Simply watching.

His eyes said caution.

She didn't need the message. Caution? She had it in spades.

'Where's Kleppy?' she asked, and she knew she sounded snappy but there wasn't a thing she could do about it.

'Phil's still on his wild night out?'

'Cut it out, Raff.'

'Sorry,' he said. Then he hesitated and his eyes narrowed. 'Nope. Come to think of it, I'm not sorry. Why are you marrying that stuffed shirt?'

'Don't be insulting.'

'He's wealthy,' Raff conceded. 'Parents own half Banksia Bay. He's making a nice little income himself. Or a big income.

He's already bought the dream home. He's starting to look almost as wealthy as Baxter. You guys will be set for life.'

'Stop it,' she snapped. 'Just because he's a responsible citizen…'

'I'm responsible now. Maybe even more responsible than you. What have you got on Baxter that I don't know about?'

'You think Philip and I would ever do anything illegal?'

'Maybe not you. Philip, though…'

'I don't believe this. Of all the… I could sue. Give me my dog.'

'Sarah has your dog,' he said and stood aside, giving her no choice but to enter a house she'd vowed never to set foot in again.

He was standing on the top step of the veranda. He didn't move.

She would not let him make her feel like this. Like she'd felt as a kid.

But her arm brushed his as she passed him, so slightly that with anyone else she wouldn't have noticed.

She noticed. Her arm jerked as if she'd been burned. She glowered and stomped past and still he didn't move.

She pushed the screen door wide and let it bang behind her. She always had. It banged like it always banged and she got the same effect… From the depths of the house came the sound of hysterical barking. She braced.

When she'd been a kid and she'd come here, the Finns' dog pack would knock her over. She'd loved it. She'd be lying in the hall being licked all over, squirming and wriggling, a tadpole in a dog pond, giggling and giggling until Raff hauled the dogs off.

When she didn't end up knocked over she'd felt almost disappointed.

She was bigger now, she conceded. Not so likely to be knocked over by a pack of dogs.

But there weren't as many dogs, anyway. There was an ancient black Labrador, almost grey with age. There was a pug, and there was Kleppy bringing up the rear. Wagging his tail. Greeting her?

She knelt and hugged Kleppy. He licked her face. So did the old Labrador. The pug was young but this one…she even remembered the feel of his tongue. 'Boris!'

'Abby!' Sarah burst out of the kitchen, her beam wide enough to split her face. She dived down onto the floor and hugged her friend with total lack of self-consciousness. 'Abby, you're here. I've made you honey jumbles.'

'I…great.' Maybe she should get up. Lawyer on floor hugging dog…

Boris was licking her chin.

'Boris?' she said tentatively and she included him in the hug she was giving Kleppy.

'He is Boris,' Raff said and she twisted and found Raff was watching them all from the doorway. 'How old was he when you were last here, Abby?'

'I… Three?'

'He's fourteen now. Old for a Labrador. You've missed out on his whole life.'

'That's not all I've missed out on,' she whispered. 'How could I ever come back?' She shook her head and hauled herself to her feet. Raff made an instinctive move to help, but then pulled away. Shook his head. Closed down.

'But you will stay for a bit,' Sarah said, grabbing Abby's hand to pull herself up. Movement was still awkward for Sarah; it always would be. 'I've told the dogs they can have a honey jumble each,' she told Abby. 'But they need to wait until they've cooled down. You can't take Kleppy home before he's had his.'

'I could take it with me.'

'Abby,' Sarah said in a term of such reproach that Abby knew she was stuck.

How long did honey jumbles take to cool?

Apparently a while because, 'I've just put them in the oven,' Sarah said happily. 'I made a lot after tea but Raff forgot to tell me to take them out. They went black. Even the dogs didn't want them. Raff never forgets,' she said, heading back to the kitchen. 'But he's funny tonight. Do you think it's because you're here?'

'I expect that's it,' Abby said, trying desperately to find something to say. Babbling because of it? 'Maybe it's because I'm a lawyer. Sometimes police don't like lawyers 'cos they ask too many questions.'

'And sometimes they don't ask enough,' Raff growled.

'Meaning…'

'Baxter…'

Oh, for heaven's sake… 'Leave it, Raff,' she said. 'Just butt out of my life.'

'I did that years ago.'

'Well, don't stop now.' She took a deep breath. 'Sarah, love, I'm in a rush.'

'I know you are,' Sarah said and pushed her into a kitchen chair. 'You sit down. Raff will make you a nice cup of tea and we'll talk until the honey jumbles are ready. But don't yell at Raff,' she said disapprovingly. 'Raff's nice.'

Raff was nice? Okay, maybe a part of him was nice. She might want to hate Raff Finn—and a part of her couldn't help but hate him—but she had to concede he was caring for Sarah beautifully.

The twelve months after the crash had been appalling. Even her grief for Ben hadn't stopped Abby seeing the tragedy that was Sarah.

She'd lain unconscious for three weeks and everyone had mourned her as dead. At one time rumour had it that Raff and Gran were asked to stop life support.

At three weeks she'd woken, but it was a different Sarah.

She'd had to relearn everything. Her memory of childhood was patchy. Her recent memory was lost completely.

She'd learned to walk again, to talk. She coped now but her speech was slow, as was her movement. Gran and Raff had brought her home and worked with her, loved her, massaged, exercised, pleaded, cajoled, bullied…

When Gran died Raff had taken it on himself to keep on going. For over a year he hadn't been able to work. They'd lived on the smell of an oily rag, because, 'She's not going into care.'

With anyone else the community would have rallied, but not with the Finns. Not when Raff was seen as being the cause of so much tragedy.

How he'd managed…

If the accident happened now the community would help, she thought. Somehow, in the last years, Raff had redeemed himself. He was a fine cop. He'd cared for Sarah with such love and compassion that the worst of the nay-sayers had been silenced. She'd even thought…it was time she moved on. Time she learned to forgive.

But over and over… He'd killed Ben.

How could she ever be friends with him again?

She didn't need to be. She simply chose to be distant. So she sat in Raff's kitchen while Sarah chatted happily, showing her the guinea pigs, explaining they'd had too many babies and that Raff had told her they had to sell some but how could she choose?

Smelling honey jumbles in a kitchen she loved.

Knowing Raff was watching her.

She found her fingers were clenched on her knees. They were hidden by the table. She could clench them as much as she wanted.

It didn't help. This place was almost claustrophobic, the memories it evoked.

But Raff was watching her and how Raff was making her feel wasn't a memory. This was no childhood crush. It was like a wave of testosterone blasting across the table, assaulting her from every angle.

Sarah was laughing.

Raff wasn't laughing. He was simply watchful.

Judgemental? Because she was marrying Philip?

Why shouldn't she marry Philip? He was kind, thoughtful, clever.

Her fallback?

Um…no. He was her careful choice.

She'd gone out with Philip before Ben had died, just for a bit, when the boys had left home, Raff to the Police Training College, Ben to university.

Philip had left for university, too, but he'd caught glandular fever and come home for a term.

She'd needed a date for her debutante ball and was fed up with Raff being away, with the boys being obsessed with their junk-pile car when they did come home.

Philip had the most wonderful set of wheels. He had money even then. But he wasn't Raff.

She'd made her debut and she'd found an excuse to break up. The decision wasn't met with regret. Philip had immediately asked Sarah out.

Maybe if the accident hadn't happened… Maybe Sarah and Philip…

Where was she going? Don't even think it, she decided. They were different people now.

Philip especially was different. After the crash…he was so caring. Whenever she needed him, he was there. He'd encouraged her to take up law as well. 'You can do it,' he'd said. 'You're bright, organised, meticulous. Do law and we'll set up the best law firm Banksia Bay's ever seen. We can care for our parents that way, Abby. Your parents miss Ben so much. We can be there for them.'

And so they were. It was all working out. All she needed to do was avoid the judgement on Raff's face. And avoid the way Raff made her…feel.

How could he bear her here?

One night, one car crash.

And it stood between him and this woman for ever.

How could she marry Philip?

But he knew. It was even reasonable, he conceded.

Philip was okay. Once he'd even been a friend. Yes, the man made money and Raff did wonder how, but that was just his nasty cop mind. Yes, he took on cases Raff wouldn't touch with a bargepole. If he got Baxter off...

He would get him off, but Raff also knew a portion of Philip's fee would end up as a cheque to the pensioners Baxter had ripped off. Not all of it—Philip was careful, not stupid with his charity—but the town might end up being grateful. Baxter would think he was great as well.

It was only Raff who'd feel ill, and maybe that was part of ancient history as well. If Philip hadn't been there that night...

How unfair was that?

'Tell us about your wedding dress,' he said, and Abby shot him a look that was both suspicious and angry.

'You want to know—why?'

'Sarah would like to know.'

'I'm going to the wedding,' Sarah said and pointed to the invitation stuck to the fridge. 'You should come, too. Did you get an invitation? Where did you put it? Raff's coming, too, isn't he, Abby?'

'I'm on duty that day,' Raff told her before Abby was forced to answer. 'We talked about it, remember? Mrs Henderson's taking you.'

'It'd be more fun if you were there.'

No, it wouldn't, Raff thought, but he didn't say so. He glanced at his watch. 'I reckon they'll be cooked, Sares.'

'Ooh,' Sarah said, happily distracted. 'My honey jumbles. I could make you some more for your wedding present, Abby. Does Philip like honey jumbles?'

'Sure he does,' Abby said. 'Who wouldn't?'

Honey jumbles. A big cosy kitchen like this. Dogs.

Would Philip like honey jumbles?

Maybe not.

Abby ate four honey jumbles and Sarah beamed the whole time, and how could a girl worry about how tight her wedding dress was going to be in the face of that beam?

Sarah wasn't the only one happy. This morning Kleppy had

been due for the needle. Tonight he was lying under her chair licking the last of Sarah's honey jumbles from his chops.

And Sarah's beam, and Kleppy's satisfaction, and Raff's thoughtful, watchful gaze made her feel…made her feel…

Like she needed to leave before things got out of hand.

She needed to go home to Philip. To tell him she had a dog.

'What's wrong?' Raff asked and he sounded as if he cared. That scared her all by itself. She pushed her chair back so fast she scared Kleppy, which meant she had her dog in her arms and she was at the door before she meant to be.

She hadn't meant to look like she was rushing.

She was rushing.

'Will you take some jumbles in a bag?' Sarah asked and she managed to calm down a little and smile and agree. So Sarah bagged her some jumbles, but she was holding Kleppy, she didn't have a hand free, which meant Raff carried her jumbles down to the car while she carried her dog.

Kleppy was warm and fuzzy. His heart was beating against hers. He was a comfort, she thought, and even as she thought it he stretched up and licked her, throat to chin.

She giggled and Raff, who'd gone before and was stowing her jumbles onto the back seat, turned and smiled in the moonlight.

'Dogs are great.'

'They are,' she said and felt happy.

'Philip will be okay with him?'

Why must he always butt into what wasn't his business? Why must he always spoil the moment?

'He will.'

'So you'll tell him tonight.'

'Of course.'

'I wish you luck.'

'I won't need it.'

'No?'

'Butt out, Finn.'

'You're always saying that,' he said. 'But it's not in my power to butt out. It's my job to intervene in domestic crises. Stopping them before they start is a life skill.'

'You seriously think Philip and I would fight over a dog?'

'I'm thinking you might fight for a dog,' he said softly. 'The old Abby's still there somewhere. She'll fight for this dog to the death.'

'And how melodramatic is that?'

'Melodramatic,' he agreed. 'Call the police emergency number if you need me.'

'Why would I possibly need you?'

'Just offering.' He was holding the passenger door wide so she could pop Kleppy in.

'You know Philip wouldn't...'

'Yeah, I know Philip wouldn't.' He took Kleppy from her and laid him on the passenger seat. 'You're giving him honey jumbles and Kleppy. Why wouldn't the man be delighted?'

'I don't know when I hate it most—when you're being offensive or you're being sarcastic.'

'Maybe they're the same thing.'

'Maybe they are. I wish you wouldn't.'

'No, you don't,' he said softly. 'It helps you keep as far away from me as you want. Isn't that right, Abby?'

'Raff...'

'It's okay, I understand,' he said. 'How could I fail to understand? What you're doing is entirely reasonable. I only wish your second choice wasn't Philip.'

'He's not my second choice. He's my first.'

'That's right,' he said, sounding suddenly thoughtful. 'I forgot. You went out with Philip when you were seventeen. For two whole months and then you dumped him. Don't those reasons hold true now?'

'I can't believe you're asking me...'

'I'm a cop. I ask the hard questions.'

'I don't have to answer.'

'Meaning you can't.'

'Meaning I don't need to. Why are you asking this now?'

'I've hardly had a chance until now. You back off every time you see me.'

'And you know why.'

'I do,' he said harshly and she winced and thought she shouldn't have said it. It was too long ago. The whole thing... It was a nightmare to be put behind them.

'Yes, Philip and I broke up when I was seventeen,' she managed. 'But people change.'

'I guess we do.' He paused and then said, almost conversationally, 'You know, once upon a time we had fun. We even decided we loved each other.'

They had. Girlfriend and boyfriend. Inseparable. Raff had shared her first kiss. It had felt... It had felt...

No. 'We were kids,' she managed. 'We were dumb in all sorts of ways.'

He was too close, she decided. It was too dark. She should be back in her nice safe house waiting for Philip to come home. She shouldn't be remembering being kissed by her first boyfriend.

'I loved kissing you,' he said and it wasn't just her remembering.

'It didn't mean...'

'Maybe it did. There's this thing,' he said.

'What thing?' But she shouldn't have asked because, the moment she had, she knew what he was talking about. Or maybe she'd known all along.

This thing? This frisson, an electric current, an indefinable thing that was tugging her closer...

No. She had to go home. 'Raff...'

'You really want to be Mrs Philip Dexter? What a waste.'

'Leave it!'

'Choose someone else, Abby. Marrying him? You're burying yourself.'

'I am not.'

'Does he make you sizzle?'

'I don't...'

'Does he? You know, I can't imagine it. Good old Philip,

knocking your socks off. Are you racing home now to have hot sex?'

'I don't believe I'm hearing this.'

'You see, it's such a waste,' he said, and suddenly he was even closer, big and bad and dangerous.

Big, bad and dangerous? Certainly dangerous. His hand came up and cupped her chin, forcing her to look up at him, and her sense of danger deepened. But she couldn't pull away.

'I wouldn't mind if it wasn't Philip,' he told her and she wondered if he knew the effect he was having on her. She wondered if he could sense how her body was reacting. 'I've known since Ben died that nothing could bring back what was between you and me. But there are men out there who could bring you alive again. Men who'd like Kleppy.'

'Philip will like Kleppy.'

'Liar.'

He was gazing down into her eyes, holding her to truth.

She should break away. She *could* break away, she thought wildly. He was only holding her chin—nothing more. She could step back, get into the car and drive home.

To Philip.

She could. But he was gazing down into her eyes and he was still asking questions.

'So tell me he makes you sizzle.'

'I...'

'He doesn't, does he?' Raff said in grim satisfaction. 'But there are guys out there who could—who could find out what you're capable of—what's beneath your prissy lawyer uniform. Because you're still there, somewhere. The Abby I...'

He paused. There was a moment's loaded silence when the whole world stilled. *The Abby I...*

She should push away. She should...

She couldn't.

She tilted her face, just a little.

The moment stretched on. The darkness stretched on.

And then he kissed her. As inevitably as time itself, he kissed her.

She couldn't move. She didn't move. She froze. And then…

Heat. Fire. The contact, lips against lips, was a tiny point but that point sizzled, caught, burned and her whole body started heating. Her face was tilted to his but he had no need to hold her. It was as if she was melting against him—into him.

Raff…

He broke away, just a little, and his eyes blazed in the moonlight. 'Abby,' he said and it was a rough, angry whisper. 'Abby.'

'I…'

'Does he do this?' he demanded. He snagged her arms and held them behind her but this was no forceful hold. It was as if her arms might get in the way, could interfere, and nothing must. Nothing could.

She was paralysed, she was burning, but she couldn't escape. She didn't want to escape. What was between them… It sizzled. Tugged as if searching for oxygen.

He was watching her in the moonlight, his eyes questioning. She wouldn't answer. She couldn't.

She was being held by Raff. A man she'd once loved.

She found herself lifting herself, tiptoe.

So her mouth could meet his again.

This morning she'd fantasised about Raff Finn. Sex on legs. But this…

If she'd expected anything it was a kiss of anger, a kiss of sexual tension, passion, nothing more. And maybe it had started like that. But it was changing.

His kiss was tender, aching, even loving. It was as unexpected as ice within a fire, heating, cooling, sizzling all at once. She'd never felt anything like this—she'd never known sensations like this could exist.

Raff.

He'd released her hands and they were free to do as she willed. Her will was that her hands were behind *his* back, drawing him closer, for how could she not want him close?

Sense had flown. Thoughts had flown. There was only this man. There was only this need.

There was only now.

Raff.

Did she say his name?

Maybe she did, or maybe it was just a sigh, deep in her throat, a sound of pure sensual pleasure. Of taking something she'd never dreamed she could have. Of sinking into the forbidden, of the longed for, of a memory she'd have to put away quite soon but not yet, please, not yet.

Oh, but his mouth… Clever and warm and beguiling, it was coaxing her to places she had no business going, but she wanted, oh, she wanted to be there. She was helpless, melting into him, degree by achingly wonderful degree.

He was irresistible.

She was…appalled.

Somehow, she had to break this. Her head was screaming at her, neon danger signs flashing through her sensual need. No!

'No!' It came out a muffled whisper. If he didn't hear…if he ignored it, how could she say it again?

Did she want him to hear it?

But he did, he had, and the wrench as he put her away from him was indescribable. He let her go. He stepped back from her and his eyes in the moonlight were almost as dazed as hers.

But then his face hardened, tightened, and she knew he was moving on.

As she must.

Her mother's voice… *Keep away from the Finn boy. He's trouble.*

He surely was. She was kissing him nine days before her wedding. She was risking all—for the Finn boy?

'I…'

'Just go, Abby,' he said and she didn't recognise his voice. It was harsh and raw and she could even imagine there was pain. 'Get out of here. You know you don't want this.'

'Of course I don't.'

'Then take your dog and go. I'll see you in court.'

Of course she would. She'd see him and he'd be back to being the local cop and she'd be a lawyer sitting beside her fiancé, trying to pretend tonight had never happened.

But it had happened. The feel of his mouth on hers was with her still.

She caught herself, gasped and thumped down into the driver's seat before she could change her mind.

'That was ridiculous,' she managed. 'How…how dare you…?'

'You wanted it as much as I did.'

'Then we're both stupid.'

'We are,' he said gravely. 'We were. But heaven help us, Abby, if we're stupid still.'

CHAPTER FIVE

ABBY drove home in a daze. She felt ill. The feel of Raff's mouth on hers wouldn't go—it felt as if her lips were surely bruised and yet she knew they couldn't be.

There had been tenderness in his kiss. It hadn't been one-sided. He hadn't been brutal.

It had been a kiss of…

No. Don't even think about it.

Kleppy put out his paw in a gesture she was starting to know. Giving comfort as well as taking it. The feel of him beside her was absurdly comforting.

Almost as if he was a little part of Raff…

And there was a dopey thing to think. The whole night had been dopey, she thought. Stupid, stupid, stupid. Imagine if she ever thought there could be anything between herself and Raff. Imagine the heartbreak.

Her heart clenched down. No! Just because the man was a load of semi-controlled testosterone… Just because he had the ability to push her buttons…

She turned into her street and Philip's car was out the front. Her heart sank.

Philip, she told herself. Not a load of semi-controlled testosterone. A good, kind man who'd keep her happy—who'd keep her safe.

I might get tired of safe, she whispered to herself and then she let herself open her mind to the rush of memory that was

Ben and she felt the concept of safe, the need for safe, close around her again. Safe was the only way.

'Hi,' she said, climbing from the car. 'The buck's night finished early, then?'

'Hardly a buck's night.' He took her hands and kissed her and she had to stop herself from thinking *dry as dust.* 'Just my dad and uncles and cousins.'

'Why aren't you having a buck's night?'

'Tonight was enough,' Philip said contentedly. 'I'm busy right up to the honeymoon. Where have you...'

But then he paused. Inside the car, Kleppy had stirred and yawned and whimpered a little.

'What's that?'

Deep breath. 'It's Kleppy.'

'Kleppy?'

'He's my dog,' she said and she had a really good shot at not sounding defensive. Maybe she even succeeded. 'You know Raff gave me a dog this morning and asked me to take him to be put down? I couldn't. He's Isaac Abrahams' dog, he needs a new home and I've decided to keep him. Sarah's been looking after him for me.'

There was no need to mention Raff again. 'So we have a dog,' she said and she surprised herself by sounding cheerful. 'Philip, meet Kleppy. Kleppy, meet Philip. I just know you two are going to be best of friends.'

He didn't like it, but she wouldn't budge; she didn't budge and finally he conceded.

'It'll have to sleep outside.'

'*He,* not *it.*'

'He'll have to sleep outside,' he conceded—no mean concession.

'Okay,' she said with her fingers crossed behind her back. He could sleep outside for a little, she thought, until Philip got used to the idea and then she could sort of sneak him in. And for the next nine nights he could sleep inside at her place.

'And what about our honeymoon?'

'I'll get Mrs Sanderson to feed and walk him.'

'She'll charge.'

'We can afford it.'

'I don't want Eileen Sanderson snooping in our backyard.'

'I'll figure something else out, then. But you'll love him.'

'If you want a dog, then why don't we get a pure-bred?' he asked, checking Kleppy out with suspicion.

'I like Kleppy.'

'And Finn dumped him on you.'

'It was my decision to keep him.'

'You're too soft-hearted.'

'I can't do a thing about that,' she admitted, knowing the hurdle had been leaped and she was over the other side. 'You want to come in for coffee and get acquainted with our new pet?'

'I have work to do. I'm not confident about tomorrow.'

He would be confident, Abby knew, but he'd still go over his notes until he knew them backwards. And once again she wondered—why had he come back to Banksia Bay? He was smart, he was ambitious, he could have made serious money in the city.

'I came back for you,' he'd told her, over and over, but she knew it was more than that. He spent time with her parents. He worked at the yacht club where Ben had once sailed. Every time a challenge occurred that might draw him to the city, he looked at it with regret but he still turned back to Banksia Bay.

She kissed him goodnight and carried Kleppy inside, thinking every time she laid down an ultimatum Philip caved in.

This dog or no wedding?

This dog.

'He loves me,' she told Kleppy, sitting down on the hearth rug and allowing her scruffy dog to settle contentedly on her knee. 'He'll take you because he loves me.'

But she'd seen Philip's ruthless behaviour in court. He could be ruthless. He'd never liked dogs.

Why didn't he just say no?

'I'm so lucky he didn't,' she whispered and she hugged

Kleppy a bit tighter and then gazed towards the spare room door. Her wedding dress lay behind.

She was lucky?

Of course she was.

She was gone and Raff stayed outside, staring sightlessly into the moonlit night.

Abby Callahan.

Right now there was nothing in the world he wanted but Abby Callahan.

Oh, but there was. Inside, Sarah would be snuggling into bed, surrounded by dogs and cats, dreaming of the day she'd just had—her animals, her honey jumbles. Her big brother.

He loved Sarah.

He also loved this place. He loved this town. But love or not, he'd leave if he could. To stay in this place with so many memories…

To stay in this place and watch Abby married…

But leaving wasn't an option. He'd stay and he wouldn't touch her again. Tonight had been an aberration, as stupid as it was potentially harmful. He didn't want to upset Abby. It wasn't her fault she was the way she was.

It was his.

He was thirty years old and he felt a hundred.

He hardly needed to see her again before the wedding. His participation in the Baxter trial was almost over. He'd given the prosecutor all the help he could manage, even if it wasn't enough to convict the guy. There might be another couple of times he was called to the stand, but otherwise he could steer well clear.

So… He'd drop Sarah off at the church next Saturday, pick her up afterwards and it'd be done.

Abby Callahan would be married to Philip Dexter.

Abby spent until midnight making Kleppy hers. She bathed him and blew him dry with her hairdryer. He was never going to be a beautiful dog, but he was incredibly cute—in a shambolic kind of way. He was a very individual dog, she decided.

He tolerated the hairdryer.

He ate a decent dinner, despite his pre-dinner snack of honey jumbles.

He investigated her bedroom as she got ready for bed. And, curiously, he fell in love with her jewellery box.

It was a beautiful cedar box with inlaid Huon pine. Philip's grandfather had made it for her when she and Philip had announced their engagement. She loved its craftsmanship and she also loved the wood's faint and beautiful perfume, stronger whenever she opened it.

She also loved Philip's grandpa, she thought, as she removed Kleppy's paw from where it had been resting proprietorially on the box. His woodwork was his passion. He'd made these beautiful boxes for half the town. 'It'll last for hundreds of years after I'm gone, girl,' he'd told her and she suspected it would.

Philip's grandpa was part of this town. Philip's family. Her future.

More people's happiness than hers was tied up in next week's wedding. That should make her feel happy, but right now it was making her feel claustrophobic. Which was dumb.

'Do you like the box or the jewels?' she asked Kleppy, deliberately shifting her thoughts. She opened the lid so he could see he couldn't make millions with a jewel heist.

Kleppy nosed the trinkets with disinterest, but looked longingly at the box. He sniffed it again and she thought it was its faint scent he liked.

'No!' she said and put it further back on the chest.

Kleppy sighed and went back to his bra. The bra she'd paid for and given to him. Yes, he shouldn't benefit from crime but today was an exception.

He made a great little thief.

He slept on her bed, snuggled against her, and she loved it. He snored. She loved his snore. She didn't even mind that he slept with his bra tucked firmly under his left front paw.

'Whatever makes you happy, Klep,' she told him, 'but that's the last of your loot. You belong to a law-abiding citizen now.'

One who needs to stay right away from the law.

From Raff.

Don't think of Raff. Think of the wedding.

Some hope. She slept, thinking of Raff.

She woke feeling light and happy. For the past few weeks she'd woken with the mammoth feeling that her wedding was bursting in on her from all sides. Her mother was determined to make it perfect.

It was starting to overwhelm her.

But not this morning. She loved that Kleppy woke at dawn and stuck his nose in her face and she woke to dog breath and a tail wagging.

It was lucky Philip wasn't here. He'd have forty fits.

He wouldn't mind being here. Or rather…he'd be happy if she was *there*. As far as Philip was concerned, she was wasting money having her own little house when he already had a wonderful house overlooking the sea.

Her parents had said that, too. When she'd moved back to Banksia Bay after university they'd welcomed her home and even had her bedroom repainted. Pink.

She had a choice. Philip's house or her old bedroom.

But her grandparents had left her a lovely legacy and this little house was her statement of independence. As she let Kleppy outside to inspect her tiny garden she thought how much she was going to miss it.

Philip's house was fabulous. She'd been blown away that he could afford to build it, and it had everything a woman could possibly want.

So get over it.

She left Kleppy to his own devices and went and checked on her wedding dress—just to reassure herself she really was getting married.

She should be excited.

She was excited. It was a gorgeous dress. It was exquisite. It had taken her two years to make.

The pleasure was in making it. Not in wearing it.

This was dumb. She felt a cold spot on her leg and there was Kleppy, wagging his tail, bright-eyed and bushy-tailed. Looking hopefully at the front door.

Looking for adventure?

'I'll take you round the block before I go to work,' she told him. 'And I'll come home at lunch time. I'm sorry, Klep, but you might be bored this morning. I can't help it, though. It's the price you've paid for me bailing you out of death row.

'And I'm going to be in court this morning, too,' she told him as he looked doleful. 'You're a lawyer's dog and I'm a lawyer. I'm a lawyer with a gorgeous, hand-beaded wedding dress and you're a lawyer's dog with a new home. We need to be grateful for what we have. I'm sure we are.'

She was grateful. It was just, as she left for work and Kleppy looked disconsolately after her, she knew how Kleppy felt.

Raff wasn't in court.

Of course he wasn't. He didn't need to be. He was a cop, not a prosecutor, and he had work to do elsewhere. He'd given his evidence yesterday. Philip wouldn't call him back but she'd sort of hoped the Crown Prosecutor would.

There were things the Crown Prosecutor could ask...

It wasn't for her to know that or even think that—*she was lawyer for the defence*—and it also wasn't for her to have her heart twist because Raff wasn't here.

She slid into the chair beside Philip and he smiled and kissed her and then said, 'Second thoughts about the dog? He really is unsuitable.'

This was what would happen, she thought. He'd agree and then slowly work on her to come round to his way of thinking.

He wasn't all noble.

'No, and I won't be having any,' she said.

'Where is he now?'

'Safely in my garden.' Four-foot fence. Safe as houses.

'He'll make a mess.'

'I walked him before I left. Walking's good. I'm going to do it every morning from now on. Maybe you can join us.'

'Gym's far better aerobic exercise,' he said. 'You need a fully planned programme to get full cardiac advantage. Walking's...'

She was no longer listening.

Her morning had begun.

It was very, very boring.

The hands on the clock moved at a snail's pace.

How bored would Kleppy be?

How bored was she?

Malcolm, the Crown Prosecutor, should do something about his voice, she thought. It was a voice designed to put a girl to sleep.

Ooh, Wallace looked smug.

Ooh, she was bored...

Lunch time. All rise. Hooray.

And then the door of the court swung open.

All eyes turned. As they would. Every person in the room, with the possible exception of Wallace and Philip, was probably as bored as she was.

And suddenly she wasn't bored at all. For standing in the doorway was...Raff.

Full cop uniform. Grim expression. Gun at his side, cop ready for action. At his side—only lower—was a white fluff ball attached to a pink diamanté lead. And in his arms he was carrying Kleppy.

'I'm sorry, Your Honour,' he said, addressing the judge. 'But I'm engaged in a criminal investigation. Is Abigail Callahan in court?'

Of course she was. Abby rose, her colour starting to rise as well. 'K...Kleppy,' she stammered.

'Could you come with me, please, Miss Callahan?' Raff said.

'She's not going anywhere,' Philip snapped, rising and putting his hand on Abby's shoulder. 'What the...'

'If she won't come willingly, I'm afraid I need to arrest her,' Raff said. 'Accessory after the fact.' He looked down at his feet, to where the white fluff ball pranced on the end of her pink diamanté lead. A lead that led up to Kleppy's jaw. Kleppy had a very tight hold. 'Abigail Callahan, your dog has stolen Mrs Fryer's peke. You need to come now and sort this out or I'll have to arrest you for theft.'

The courtroom was quiet. So quiet you could have heard a pin drop.

Justice Weatherby's face was impassive. Almost impassive.

There was a tiny tic at the side of his mouth.

Raff's face was impassive, too. He stood with Kleppy in his arms, waiting for Abby to respond.

Kleppy looked disgusting. He was coated in thick black dust. His tail was wagging, nineteen to the dozen.

In his mouth he held the end of the pink lead and his jaw was clamped as if he wasn't going to let go any time soon.

On the other end of the lead, the white fluff ball was wagging her tail as well.

'He was locked in my backyard,' Abby said, eyeing the two with dismay.

'My sharp investigative skills inform me that the dog can dig,' Raff said, shaking Kleppy a little so a rain of dirt fell onto the polished wood of the courtroom door. 'Will you come with me, please, ma'am?'

'Just give the dog back to whoever owns it,' Philip snapped, his hand gripping Abby's shoulder tightly now. 'Tie the other one up outside. Abigail's busy.'

'Raff, please…' Abby said.

'Mrs Fryer's hopping mad,' Raff said, unbending a little. 'I've waited until court broke for lunch but I'm waiting no longer. You want to avoid charges, you come and placate her.'

She glanced at Philip. Uh-oh. She glanced at Justice Weatherby. The tic at the corner of his mouth had turned into a grin. Someone was giggling at the back of the court.

Philip's face looked like thunder.

'Sort the dog, Abigail,' he snapped, gathering his notes. 'Just get it out of here and stop it interfering with our lives.'

'Right this way, ma'am,' Raff said amiably. 'The solicitor for the defence will be right back, just as soon as she sorts her stolen property.'

Abby walked out behind Raff, trying to look professional, but she didn't feel professional and when she reached the outside steps and the autumn sun hit her face she felt suddenly a wee bit hysterical. And also…a wee bit free?

As if Raff had sprung her from jail.

Which was a dumb thing to think. Raff had attempted to make her a laughing stock.

'I suppose you think you're funny,' she said and Raff turned and looked at her, and once again she was hit by that wave of pure testosterone. He was in his cop uniform and my, it was sexy. The sun was glinting on his tanned face and his coppery hair. He was wearing short sleeves and his arms… They were twice as thick as Philip's, she thought, and then she thought that was a very inappropriate thing to think. As was the fact that his eyes held the most fabulous twinkle.

Her knees felt wobbly.

What was she doing? She was standing in the sun and lusting after Raff Finn. The man who'd destroyed her life…

She needed to get a grip, and fast.

'You're saying Kleppy dug all the way out of my garden?' she snapped, trying to sound disbelieving. She *was* disbelieving.

'You're implying I might have helped?' Raff said, still with that twinkle. 'You think I might have hiked round there and loaned him a spade?'

'No, I…' Of course not. 'But the fence sits hard on the ground. He'd have had to go deep.'

'He's a very determined dog. I did warn you, Abigail.'

'Why don't you just call me ma'am and be done with it,' she snapped. 'What am I supposed to do now?'

'Apologise.'

'To you?'

He grinned at that and his whole face lit up. She'd hardly seen that grin. Not since… Not since…

No. Avoid that grin at all costs.

'I can't imagine you apologising to me,' he said. 'But you might try Mrs Fryer. I imagine she's apoplectic by now. She rang an hour ago to say her dog had been stolen from outside the draper's. I did think we were looking at dog-napping—she'd definitely pay a ransom—but we have witnesses saying the napper was seen making a getaway. It seems Kleppy decided to go find another bra and found something better.'

She closed her eyes. This was not good, on so many levels.

'You caught him?'

'I didn't have to catch him,' he said, and his smile deepened, a slow, smouldering smile that had the power to heat as much as the sun. 'I found the two of them on your front step.'

'On my…'

'He seems to think of your place as home already. Home of Abby. Home of Kleppy. Or maybe he was just bringing this magnificent gift to you.'

Oh, Kleppy.

She stared at her scruffy, kleptomaniac, mud-covered dog in Raff's arms. He stared back, gazing straight at her, quivering with hope. With happiness. A dog fulfilled.

Why did her eyes suddenly fill?

'Why…why didn't you just take Fluffy back to Mrs Fryer?' she managed, trying not to sniff. *She had a dog.*

'Watch this.' He set Kleppy down and tugged the diamanté lead, trying to dislodge it from Kleppy's teeth.

Kleppy held on as if his life depended on it.

Raff tugged again.

Kleppy growled and gripped and glanced across at Abby—and his appeal was unmistakable. *Come and help. This guy's trying to steal your property.*

Her property.

Raff released him. The little dog turned towards her, his

whole body quivering in delight. She stooped and held out her hand and he dropped the lead into it.

Oh, my...

She was having trouble making herself speak. She was having trouble making herself think. This disreputable mutt had laid claim to her.

She should be horrified.

She loved it.

'You could have just taken Fluffy off the other end of the lead,' she managed.

'Hey, your dog growled at me,' Raff said. 'You heard him. He could have taken my hand off.'

'He was wagging his tail at the same time.'

'I'm not one to take chances,' Raff said. 'I might be armed but I'm not a fast draw. Too big a risk.'

She looked up at him, big and brawny and absurdly incongruous. Cop with gun. He'd shoot to kill?

'You don't have capsicum spray?' she managed.

'Lady, you think this vicious mutt could be subdued by capsicum spray?'

She ran her fingers down the vicious mutt's spine. He arched and preened and waggled his tail in pleasure.

The fluff ball moved in for a back scratch as well.

She giggled.

'Abigail...' It was Philip, striding down the steps, looking furious.

Philip. Dignity. She scrambled to her feet and the dogs looked devastated at losing her.

'I'm just settling the dogs down,' she managed. 'Before Raff takes them away.'

'Before *we* take them away,' Raff said. He motioned to his patrol car.

'You can cope with this yourself, Finn,' Philip snapped.

'No,' Raff said, humour fading. He lifted Kleppy in one arm and Fluff Ball in the other. 'You cope with getting Wallace off,' he told Philip. 'Abigail copes with the dogs.'

'I need...'

'You're getting as little help as I can manage to get that low life off the hook,' Raff snapped. 'Abigail, come with me.'

She went. Raff was not giving her a choice, and she knew Mrs Fryer would be furious.

Behind her, Philip was furious but right now that seemed the lesser of two evils.

She sat in the front of Raff's patrol car with two dogs on her knee and she tried to stare straight ahead; to think serious thoughts. She still wanted to giggle.

'Kleppy should be in the back,' Raff said gravely. 'A known criminal.'

'You've accused me of being an accessory. Why don't you toss me in the back as well?'

'I like you up front,' he said. 'You do my image good.'

'I need dark glasses,' she said, glowering. 'Carted round town in a police car.'

'You will keep a kleptomaniac dog. It might well push you over to the dark side. Spoil that good-girl reputation. Send you into the shadowy side, like me.'

Her bubble of laughter faded at that. He'd spoken lightly, but there was truth behind his words.

The shadowy side...

Raff's grandfather and then his mother had given the family a bad name. A drunk and then a woman who'd broken society's rules... If Raff's mother had had the strength to defend herself, to ride out community criticism, then maybe it would have been different but she'd been an easy target. The family had been an easy target.

Raff, though... He had defended himself. He'd come back here after the accident, he'd made a home for Sarah, he'd looked on community disdain with indifference.

Did it hurt?

It wasn't anything to do with her, she thought, but, as they pulled up outside Louise Fryer's, she watched the middle-aged matron greet Raff with only the barest degree of civility. It must still hurt.

After the accident… There'd been no trial.

She remembered the investigators talking to her parents. There'd been insufficient evidence to charge him.

'Is Raff denying it?' That had been Abby, whispering from the background. She barely remembered those appalling days after the crash but she did remember that. She did remember asking. 'What does Raff say?'

'He can't remember a thing,' the investigator told her. 'His blood alcohol's come back zero and frankly that's a surprise. He was just a stupid kid doing stupid things.'

'Our Ben wasn't stupid,' her mother said hotly.

'Led astray, more like,' the investigator said and the fair part of Abby, the reasonable part, thought no, Ben hadn't been wearing his seat belt. It wasn't all Raff's fault.

He'd been stupid. He had been on the wrong side of the dirt road and he'd been speeding.

He'd killed Ben and injured his sister.

Maybe that was enough punishment for anyone. The authorities seemed to think so. Even though her parents wanted him thrown in jail, it had simply been left as an accident.

Raff had come back as the town cop, he'd cared for his sister and he'd worked hard to rid himself of that bad boy reputation. For the most part he now had community respect, but there were those—her parents' friends…people with long memories… He was still condemned.

Louise Fryer, coming out now with her mouth pursed into a look of dislike, was one of the more vocal of the condemners.

'Haven't you found her yet?' Her voice was an accusation. 'I've had five phone calls. People have seen her. Don't you know how valuable she is?'

Abby was trying to untangle leads to get out of the car.

'You don't care,' Mrs Fryer said. 'We need a decent police presence in this… Oh…'

For, finally, Abby was out. She set Fluff Ball on the ground. Fluff Ball headed over to Mrs Fryer.

But… Uh-oh. Kleppy was out of the car and after his prize. He grabbed the lead and Fluff Ball stopped in her tracks.

Fluff Ball looked at Mrs Fryer, then looked at Kleppy. She wagged her pompom and proceeded to check out Kleppy's rear.

'She'll catch something… Get it away…' Louise was practically screeching.

Abby sighed. She picked up both dogs and tucked them firmly under her arms. 'Thank you, Kleppy, but no,' she said severely. She took the lead from Kleppy and handed over Fluff Ball.

And finally Mrs Fryer realised who she was. 'Abigail!'

'Hi, Mrs Fryer.'

'What are you doing here?'

'My dog stole your dog.'

'Your dog?' Louise's eyes were almost popping out of her head. 'That's never your dog.'

'He is. His name's Kleppy. He's lovely but I've only had him for a day so he's not exactly well trained. But he will be.' Just as soon as she installed fences down to bedrock.

'Has this man foisted him onto you?' Her glare at Raff was poisonous.

'No.' Not exactly. Or actually…yes. But that was what the woman was expecting her to say, she thought. Raff Finn— town's bad boy. One of *those Finns*.

Capable of anything.

Which was what she thought, too, she reminded herself, so why was she standing here figuring out how to defend him?

'He didn't foist…' she started.

'Yes, I did,' Raff said before she could get any further. 'Have you forgotten already? I definitely foisted. And that's exactly what you'd expect of someone like me, isn't it, Mrs Fryer? And here I am, messing up your front garden. But it's okay. Your dog's been restored. Justice has been done so I can step out of your life again. If you'll excuse me… Abby, when Mrs Fryer's given you a nice cup of tea so you can both recover from your

Very Nasty Experience, could you walk back to court yourself, do you think?'

'I…' She stared at him, speechless. He gave her his very blandest smile.

'I bet Louise wants to hear all about the wedding preparations. She'll be invited, though, won't she?'

'Yes,' Louise said, a bit confused but mostly belligerent. Her dislike for Raff was unmistakable. 'Of course I am. I'm a friend of dear Philip's mother.'

'There you are; you're practically family.' Raff's gaze met hers and there was laughter behind his eyes—pure trouble. 'All it takes for you to be friends for life is for your two dogs to bond, which they're doing already. Me, I have other stuff to do. Murderers and rapists to chase.'

'Or the police station lawn to mow,' Abby snapped and then wished she hadn't.

'I was just saying that to Philip's mother the other night,' Louise said. 'Old Sergeant Troy used to keep the Station really nice.'

'Yeah, but he wasn't a Finn,' Raff said. 'The place has gone to hell in a handbasket since I arrived. Did you think of the lawn yourself, Abigail, or did Philip mention it? A tidy man, our Philip. But enough. Murderers, rapists—and lawn!' He sighed. 'A policeman's lot is indeed a tough one. See you ladies later. Have a nice cup of tea.'

He turned and walked away. Louise put her hand on Abby's arm, holding her back.

The toad. Raff Finn knew she wouldn't be able to get away from here for an hour.

'Make sure you plant some petunias when you're finished,' Abby called after him. 'It'd be a pity if we saw our police force bored.'

'Petunias it is,' he said and gave her an airy wave. 'Consider them planted. In between thefts. How long till the next snatch and grab?' He shook his head. 'Keep off the streets, Abigail, and keep a tight hold on that felon of yours. Next time, I might have to put you up for a community corrections order. The pair of you might find yourself planting my petunias for me.'

CHAPTER SIX

ABBY didn't go back to court. Philip phoned to find out where she was and she decided she had a headache. She did have a headache. Her headache was wagging his tail and watching as she dog-proofed her fence.

According to the Internet, to stop foxes digging into a poultry pen you had to run wire netting underground from the fence, but flattening outward and forward, surfacing about eighteen inches from the fence. The fox would then find itself digging into a U-shaped wire cavity.

That meant a lot of digging. Would it work when Kleppy The Fox was sitting there watching?

'Don't even think about it,' she told him. 'Philip's being very good. We can't expect his patience to last for ever.'

Philip.

She was expecting him to explode. He didn't.

He arrived to see how she was just after she'd finished cleaning up after fence digging. They were supposed to be going out to dinner. Two of Philip's most affluent clients had invited them out to Banksia Bay's most prestigious restaurant as a pre-wedding celebration.

When Abby thought of it her headache was suddenly real—and, surprisingly, she didn't need to explain it to Philip.

'You look dreadful,' he said, hugging her with real sympathy. 'White as a sheet. You should be in bed.'

'I…yes.' Bed sounded a good idea.

'Where's the mutt?'

'Outside.' Actually, on her bed, hoping she'd join him.

'You can't keep him,' Philip said seriously. 'He's trouble.'

'This morning wasn't his fault.'

'You don't need to tell me that,' Philip said darkly. 'The dog might be trouble but Finn's worse. It's my belief he set the whole thing up. Look, Abby, the best thing would just be for you to take the dog back to the Animal Shelter.'

'No.'

He sighed but he held his temper.

'We'll talk about it when you're feeling better. I'm sorry you can't make tonight.'

'Will you cancel?'

'No,' he said, surprised. 'They'll understand.'

Of course they would. They'd hardly notice her absence, she thought bitterly. They'd talk about their property portfolios all night. Make some more money.

'What will you eat?' he asked, solicitous, and she thought she wouldn't have to eat five courses and five different wines. Headaches had their uses.

'I'll make eggs on toast if I get hungry.'

'Well, keep up your strength. You have a big week ahead of you.'

He kissed her and he was off, happily going to a wedding celebration without her.

The moment the door shut behind him, her headache disappeared. Just like that.

Why was she marrying him?

Uh-oh.

The question had been hovering for months. Niggling. Shoved away with disbelief that she could think it. But, the closer the wedding grew, the bigger the question grew. Now it was the elephant in the room. Or the Tyrannosaurus Rex. What was the world's biggest dinosaur?

Whatever. The question was getting very large indeed. And very insistent.

Philip was heading to a dinner she'd been dreading. He was anticipating it with pleasure.

Worse. Philip's kiss meant absolutely nothing. Last night…
Raff's kiss had shown her how little Philip's kisses did
mean.

And worse still? She'd almost been wanting him to yell at
her about Kleppy.

How had she got into this mess?

It had just…happened. The car crash. Philip, always here,
supporting her parents, supporting her. Interested in everything
she was doing. Throwing himself, heart and soul, into this
town. Throwing himself, heart and soul, into her life.

She couldn't even remember when she'd first realised he
intended to marry her. It was just sort of assumed.

She did remember the night he'd formally asked. He'd proposed at the Banksia Bay Private Golf Club, overlooking the
bay. The setting had been perfect. A full moon. Moonbeams
glinting on the sea. The terrace, a balmy night, stars. A des-
sert to die for—chocolate ganache in the shape of a heart,
surrounded by strawberries and tiny meringues. A beautifully
drawn line of strawberry coulis, spelling out the words 'Marry
Me'.

But there'd been more. Philip had left nothing to chance.
The small town orchestra had appeared from nowhere, playing Pachelbel's *Canon*. The staff, not just from the restaurant
but from the golf club as well, crowding into the doorways,
applauding before she even got to answer.

'I've already asked your parents,' Philip said as he lifted the
lid of the crimson velvet box. 'They couldn't be more pleased.
We're going to be so happy.'

He lifted the ring she now wore—a diamond so big it made
her gasp—and slid it onto her finger before she realised what
was happening. Then, just in case she thought he hadn't got it
completely right, he'd tugged her to her feet, then dropped to
his knees.

'Abigail Callahan, would you do me the honour of becoming
my wife?'

She remembered thinking—hysterically, and only for the
briefest of moments—what happens if I say no?

But how could she say no?

How could she say no now?

Why would she want to?

Because Rafferty Finn had kissed her?

Because Raff made her feel...

As he'd always made her feel. As if she was on the edge of a precipice and any minute she'd topple.

The night Ben died she'd toppled. Philip had held her up. To tell him now that she couldn't marry him...

What was she thinking? He was a good, kind man and next Saturday she'd marry him and right now she was going to sit in front of the television and stitch a last row of lace onto the hem of her wedding gown. The gown should be finished but her mother and Philip's mother had looked at it and decreed one more row.

'To make everything perfect.'

Fine. Lace. Perfect. She could do this.

She let Kleppy out of the bedroom. He seemed a bit subdued. She gave him a doggy chew and he snuggled onto the couch beside her.

She'd washed him again. He was clean. Or clean enough. So what if the occasional dog hair got on her dress? It didn't have to be that perfect. Life didn't have to be that perfect.

Marriage to Philip would be okay.

The doorbell rang. Kleppy was off the couch, turning wild circles, barking his head off at the door.

He hadn't stirred from his spot on her bed when Philip had rung the bell. Different bell technique?

She should tuck Kleppy back in her bedroom. This'd be her mother. Or Philip's mother. Philip would have reported the headache, gathered the troops. It was a wonder the chicken soup hadn't arrived before this.

Her mother would be horrified at the sight of Kleppy. She'd just have to get used to him, she decided. They'd all have to get used to him. The chicken soup brigade.

But it wasn't the chicken soup brigade.

She opened the door. Sarah was standing on her doorstep holding a gift, and Raff was right behind her.

See, that was just the problem. She had no idea why her heart did this weird leap at the sight of him. It didn't make sense. She should feel anger when she saw him. Betrayal and distress. She'd felt it for ten years but now... Somehow distress was harder to maintain, and there was also this extra layer. Of... hope?

She really didn't want to spend the rest of her life running into this man. Maybe she and Philip could move.

Maybe Raff should move. Why had he come back to Banksia Bay in the first place?

But Sarah was beaming a greeting—Raff's sister—Abby's friend—and Abby thought there were so many complexities in this equation she couldn't get her head around them. Raff was caught as well as she was, held by ties of family and love and commitment.

His teenage folly had killed his best mate. He was trapped in this judgemental town, looking after the sister he loved.

For ten years she'd felt betrayed by this man but she looked at him now and thought he'd been to hell and back. There were different forms of life sentence.

And he'd lost...her?

He'd never had her, she thought fiercely. She'd broken up with him before the crash. If she even started thinking of him that way again...

The problem was, she was thinking. But the nightmare if she kept thinking...

Her parents...Philip... The way she felt herself, the aching void where Ben had been...

She was dealing with it. She had been dealing with it. If only he hadn't kissed her...

'You're home,' Sarah said. She was holding a silver box tied with an enormous red ribbon. 'You took ages to answer. Raff

said you probably weren't home. He said you'd be out gall…
gall…'

'Gallivanting?'

'It's what I said but I guess that's the wrong word,' Raff
said. 'You wouldn't gallivant with Philip.'

She ignored him. She ignored that heart-stopping, dare-you
twinkle. 'Hi, Sarah. It's lovely to see you. What do you have
there?'

'We're delivering your present,' Sarah said. 'But Raff said
you'd be out with Philip. We were going to leave it on the
doorstep and go. But I heard Kleppy. Why aren't you out with
Philip?'

'I had a headache.'

'Very wise,' Raff said, the gleam of mischief intensifying
in those dark, dangerous eyes. 'Dinner with the Flanagans? I'd
have a headache, too.'

'How did you know we were going out with the Flanagans?'
She sighed. 'No. Don't tell me. This town.'

'Sorry.' Raff's mischief turned to a chuckle, deep and
toe-curlingly sexy. 'And sorry about the intrusion, but Sarah
wrapped your gift and decided she needed to deliver it
immediately.'

'So can we come in while you open it?' Sarah was halfway
in, scooping up a joyful Kleppy on the way. But then she faltered. 'Do you still have a headache?' Sarah knew all about
headaches—Abby could see her cringe at the thought.

'Abby said she *had* a headache,' Raff said. 'That's past tense,
Sares. I reckon it was cured the minute Philip went to dinner
without her.'

'Will you cut it out?'

'Do you still have a headache?' he asked, not perturbed at
all by her snap.

'No, but…'

'There you go. Sares, what if I leave you here for half an hour
so you can watch the present-opening and play with Kleppy?
I'll pick you up at eight. Is that okay with you, Abby?'

It wasn't okay with Sarah.

'No,' she ordered. 'You have to watch her open it. It was your idea. You'll really like it, Abby. Ooh, and I want to help you use it.'

So they both came in. Abby was absurdly aware that she had a police car parked in her driveway. That'd be reported to Philip in about two minutes, she thought. And to her parents. And to everyone else in this claustrophobic little town.

What was wrong with her? She loved this town and she was old enough to ignore gossip. Raff was here helping Sarah deliver a wedding gift. What was wrong with that?

Ten minutes tops and she'd have him out of here.

But the gift took ten minutes to open. Sarah had wrapped it herself. She'd used about twenty layers of paper and about four rolls of tape.

'I should use you to design my police cells,' Raff said, grinning, as Abby ploughed her way through layer after layer after layer. 'This sucker's not getting out any time soon.'

'It's exciting,' Sarah said, wide-eyed with anticipation. 'I wonder what it is?'

Uh-oh. Abby glanced up at Raff at that and saw a shaft of pain. Short-term memory... Sarah would have spent an hour happily wrapping this gift, but an hour was a long time. For her to remember what she'd actually wrapped...

There was no way Raff could leave this town, she conceded. Sarah operated on long-term memory, the things she'd had instilled as a child. A new environment...a new home, new city, new friends... Sarah would be lost.

Raff was as trapped here as she was.

But she wasn't trapped, she told herself sharply, scaring herself with the direction her thoughts were headed. She loved it here. She loved Philip.

She was almost at the end. One last snip and...

Ooooh...

She couldn't stop the sigh of pure pleasure.

This was no small gift. It was a thing she'd loved for ever.

It was Gran Finn's pasta maker.

Colleen Finn had been as Irish as her name suggested. She was one of thirteen children and she'd married a hard drinking bull of a man who'd come to Australia to make a new start with no intention of changing his ways.

As a young bride, Gran had simply got on with it. And she'd cooked. Every recipe she could get her hands on, Irish or otherwise.

Abby was about ten when the pasta maker had come into the house. Bright and shiny and a complete puzzle to them all.

'Greta Riccardo's having a yard sale, getting rid of all her mother's stuff.' Gran was puffed up like a peahen in her indignation. 'All Maria's recipes—books and books—and here's Greta saying she never liked Italian food. That's like me saying I don't like potatoes. How could I let the pasta maker go to someone who doesn't love it? In honour of my friend Maria, we'll learn to be Italian.'

It was in the middle of the school holidays and the kids, en masse, were enchanted. They'd watched and helped, and within weeks they'd been making decent pasta. Abby remembered holding sheets of dough, stretching it out, competing to see who could make the longest spaghetti.

Pasta thus became a staple in the Finn house and it was only as she grew older she realised how cheap it must have been. With her own eggs and her home grown tomatoes, Gran had a new basic food. But now…

'Don't you use this any more?' she ventured, stunned they could give away this part of themselves, and Raff smiled, though his smile was a little wary.

And, with the wariness, Abby got it.

She remembered Sarah as a teenager, stretching dough, kneading it, easing it through the machine with care so it wouldn't rip, making angels' hair, every kind of the most delicate pasta varieties.

She thought of Sarah now, with fumbling fingers, knowing what she'd been able to do, knowing what she'd lost.

'We don't use it any more,' Sarah said. 'But we don't want

to throw it away. So Raff said why don't we give it to you and I can come round and remind you how to do it.'

'Will you and I make some now?' she asked Sarah before she could stop herself. 'Can you remember how to make it?'

'I think so,' Sarah said and looked doubtfully at her big brother. 'Can I, Raff?'

'Maybe we could both give Abby a reminder lesson,' Raff said. 'As part of our wedding present. If your headache's indeed better, Abigail?'

Both? Whoa. No. Uh-uh.

This was really dumb.

The police car would be parked outside for a couple of hours.

'You want me to drive the car round the back?' he asked.

She stared at him and he gazed straight back. Impassive. Reading her mind?

This was up to her. All she had to do was say her headache had come back.

They were all looking at her. Sarah. Kleppy.

Raff.

Go away. You're complicating my life. My wedding dress is right behind that door. My fiancé is just over the far side of town.

Sarah's eyes were wide with hope.

'I guess it'll still get around that my car was round the back for a couple of hours,' Raff said, watching the warring emotions on her face. 'Will Dexter call me out at dawn?'

'Philip,' she said automatically.

'Philip,' he agreed. Neutral.

'He won't mind,' she said.

'I'd mind if I was Philip.'

'Just lucky you're not Philip,' she said and she'd meant to sound snarky but she didn't quite manage it. 'Why don't you go do what you need to do and come back in a couple of hours?'

'But Raff likes making pasta, too,' Sarah said and Abby looked at his face and saw...and saw that he did.

There was a lot of this man to back away from. There was a lot about this man to distrust. But watching him now… It was as if he was hungry, she thought. He was disguising it, with his smart tongue and his teasing and his blatant provocation, but still…

He'd just given away his grandmother's pasta maker. He'd given it to her.

She'd love it. She'd use it for ever. The memories… She and Sarah, Raff and Ben, messing round in Gran's kitchen.

If it wasn't for this man, Ben would still be here.

How long did hate last?

For the last ten years, every time she'd looked at Raff Finn she'd felt ill. Now… She looked at Sarah and at the pasta maker. She thought of Mrs Fryer's vitriol. She thought that Ben had been Raff's best friend. Ben had loved him.

She'd loved him.

She couldn't keep hating. She just…couldn't.

She felt sick and weary and desperately sad. She felt… wasted.

'Hey, Abby really isn't well,' Raff said and maybe he'd read the emotions—maybe it was easy because she was having no luck disguising them from herself, much less from him. 'Maybe we should go, Sares, and let her recover.'

'Do you really have a headache?' Sarah put her hand on her arm, all concern. 'Does it bang behind your eyes? It's really bad when it does that.'

Did Sarah still have headaches? Did Raff cope with them, take care of her, ache for his little sister and all she'd lost?

Maybe she should have invited Raff to her wedding.

Now there was a stupid thing to think. She might be coming out the other side of a decade of bitterness but her parents… they never would. They knew that Raff had killed their son, pure and simple.

Philip would never countenance him at their wedding. Her parents would always hate him.

Any bridges must be her own personal bridges, built of an

understanding that she couldn't keep stoking this flame of bitterness for the rest of her life.

They were watching her. Sarah's hand was still on her arm. Concerned for her headache. Sarah, whose headaches had taken away so much…

'Not a headache,' she whispered and then more strongly, 'it's not a headache. It's just… I'm overwhelmed. I loved making pasta with you guys when I was a kid. I can't believe you're giving this to me. It's the most wonderful gift—a truly generous gift of the heart. It's made me feel all choked up.'

And then, as Sarah was still looking unsure, she took her hands and tugged her close and kissed her. 'Thank you,' she whispered.

'Raff, too,' Sarah said.

Raff, too. He was watching with eyes that were impassive. Giving nothing away.

He'd given her his grandmother's pasta maker.

He'd killed her brother.

No. An accident had killed Ben. A moment of stupidity that he'd have to pay for forever.

She took a deep breath, released Sarah, took Raff's hands in hers and kissed him, too. Lightly. As she'd kissed Sarah.

On the cheek and nothing more.

She went to release him but he didn't release her. His hands held for just a fraction of a second too long. A fraction of a second that said he was as confused as she was.

A fraction of a second that said there could never be idle friendship between them.

No longer enemies? But what?

Not friends. Not when he looked at her like… Like he was seeing all the regret in the world.

She had to do something. They were all looking at her—Raff, Sarah and Kleppy. Wondering why her eyes were brimming—why she was standing like a dummy wishing the last ten years could disappear and she could be seventeen again and Raff could be gorgeous and young and free and…

And she needn't think anything of the kind. In eight days she was marrying Philip. Her direction was set.

Eight days was all very well, but what about now?

Now she closed her eyes for a fraction of a second, gave herself that tiny respite to haul herself together—and then she put on her very brightest smile.

'Let's make pasta,' she said, and they did.

CHAPTER SEVEN

HE SHOULDN'T have given the pasta maker away if it made him feel like this.

This was a bad idea and it was getting worse.

He was sitting at Abby's kitchen table watching Sarah hold one end of the pasta dough as Abby fed it through the machine. Watching it stretch. Watching Sarah hold her breath, gasp with pleasure, smile.

Watching Abby smile back.

He could help—Sarah kept offering him a turn—but he excused himself on the grounds that all Abby's aprons were frilly and there was no way Banksia Bay's cop could be caught in a rose-covered pinny.

But in reality he simply wanted to watch.

He'd forgotten how good it was to watch Abby Callahan.

Had she forgotten how to be Abby Callahan?

For years now, he'd never seen her with a hair out of place. Now, though, she was wearing faded jeans, an old sweatshirt smudged with flour, bare feet.

He remembered her in bare feet.

Abby. Seventeen years old. She'd laugh and everyone laughed with her. She could tease a smile out of anyone. She was a laughing, loving girl.

She'd been his girlfriend and he'd loved it. They just seemed to…fit.

But then they'd grown up. Sort of.

One heated weekend. Angry words. The car. The debutante ball. Incredibly important to teenagers.

Abby had started dating Philip. She and Philip had broken up, and then Sarah had started going out with him.

He hadn't liked that, either. Maybe he'd acted like a jerk, making Abby pay. He'd assumed they'd make it up.

But then… The tragedy that turned Abby from a girl who'd dreamed of being a dress designer, who lived for colour and life, into a lawyer who represented the likes of Wallace Baxter.

A lawyer who was about to marry Philip Dexter.

No.

He came close to shouting it, to thumping his fist down on the flour-covered table.

He did no such thing. There was no reason why she shouldn't marry Philip. There was nothing Raff could put his finger on against the guy. Philip was a model citizen.

He didn't like him.

Jealous?

Yeah. But something else. A feeling?

A feeling he'd had at nineteen that had never gone away.

'Why did you and Dexter stop going out?' he asked as the pasta went through a third and final time.

She didn't lift her head but he saw the tiny furrow of concentration, the setting of her lips.

'Abby?'

'Just ease it in a little more, Sarah.'

'Ten years ago. After your debut. Why did you break up?'

'That's none of your business. Now we put this attachment on to cut it into ribbons.'

'I know,' Sarah said, crowing in triumph as she found the right attachment. 'This one.'

'It's just I've always wondered,' Raff said as Sarah tried to get the attachment in. They both let her be. It'd be easier to step in and do it for her—her fingers were fumbling badly—but she was a picture of intense concentration and to step in now…

They both knew not to.

'You know I only went out with Debbie Macallroy to get back at you,' he said.

'So you did. Childhood romances, Raff. We were dumb.'

Really dumb. Where had they all ended up?

'We did have fun before the crash,' he said gently. 'We were such good friends. But then Philip… First you and then Sarah. But you didn't fall in love with him then. You ditched him.'

'I've changed. We both have.'

'People don't change.'

'Of course they do.'

Of course people changed. She had, and so had Philip.

She didn't look up at Raff; she focused on the sheets of pasta, making sure they were dusted so they wouldn't stick in the final cutting process.

She thought back to Philip at nineteen.

He'd been rich, or rich compared to every other kid in Banksia Bay. He had his own car and it was a far cry from the bomb Ben and Raff were doing up. A purple Monaro V8. Cool.

Every girl in Abby's year group had wanted to go out with him. Abby didn't so much—she was trying hard not to think she was still in love with Raff—but she'd needed a partner for her debut, all Raff thought about was his stupid car, and Sarah had bet her she wouldn't be game to ask him.

For a few weeks she'd preened. Her friends were jealous. Philip danced really well and her debut was lovely.

But what followed…the drive-in movies… Sitting in the dark with Philip… Not so cool. Nothing she could put her finger on, though. It was just he wasn't Raff and that was no reason to break up with him.

But finally…

They'd gone for a drive one afternoon, heading up Black Mountain to the lookout. She hadn't wanted to go, she remembered, and when they'd had a tyre blowout she'd been relieved.

She hadn't been so relieved when they realised Philip's spare tyre was flat. Or when he thought she should walk back into town to fetch his father—because he had to look after the car.

'No way am I trudging back to town while you sit here in comfort,' she retorted. 'You're the dummy who didn't check his spare.'

Not so tactful, even for a seventeen-year-old, but she was reaching the point where she wanted to end it.

Philip left her. Bored, she tried out the sound system. His tapes were boring, top ten stuff, nothing she enjoyed.

She flicked through his tape box—a box just like the one that graced her bedside table, beautiful cedar with slots for every cassette. His grandpa really was great.

Boring cassettes. Boring, boring. But, at the back, some un-marked ones. She slid one in and heard the voice of Christabelle Thomas, a girl in the same class as her at school.

'Philip, we shouldn't. My mum'd kill me. Philip…'

Enough. She met Philip and his father as she stomped down the mountain, fuming.

'You were supposed to stay with the car,' Philip told her.

'I didn't like the music,' she snapped, and held up the tape and threw it at him through his father's car window. 'Put the ripped up tape in my letterbox tomorrow or I'm telling Christabelle.'

Why think of that now?

Because of Raff?

She glanced up and he was watching her. Sarah was watch-ing her.

'What's wrong?' Sarah asked, and she came back to the present and realised Sarah had successfully put the cutting tool in place.

'Hey, fantastic, let's cut,' she said, and the moment had passed. The time had passed. The tapes had been an aberration.

Philip had brought the tape round the next morning, cut to shreds.

'Hey, Abby, I need to tell you I'm sorry. Christabelle and I only went out a couple of times, well before you and me. It's not what you think. I only asked to kiss her. And I hadn't realised the tape was on record. I record stuff in the car all the time on the trip between here and Sydney—I try and recall study notes and then see how accurate I've been. I must have forgotten this was still on. I'm so sorry you found it.'

It was okay, she conceded. It was a mistake. Kids did stupid things.

Like driving on the wrong side of the road?

'What's wrong?' Sarah asked again and Raff's eyes were asking the same question.

'Sorry,' she said. 'I just started thinking about all the things I had to do before the wedding.'

'You want us to go home?' Sarah asked, and Abby winced and got a grip.

'No way. I'm hungry. Pasta, here we come. What setting shall we have it on? Do we want angels' hair or tagliatelle?'

'Angels' hair,' Sarah said.

'My favourite,' Raff said. 'It always has been.'

She glanced up and he was looking straight at her. He wasn't smiling.

Raff…

Don't, she told herself but she wasn't quite sure what she was saying *don't* to.

All she knew was that this man meant trouble. He was surely causing trouble now.

They left at nine, which gave her an hour to clean the kitchen and to get her thoughts in order before Philip arrived.

He arrived promptly at ten. Kleppy met him at the door and growled.

He hadn't growled at Raff and Sarah, but then he knew they were friends.

He didn't yet know Philip was a friend.

'If he bites…' Philip said.

'He won't bite. He's being a watchdog.'

'I thought you had a headache,' Philip said, wary and irritated. 'I hear Finn and his sister have been here.'

She sighed. She lived in Banksia Bay. She should be used to this.

'Sarah brought our wedding present. She wanted to demonstrate.'

'Demonstrate what?'

'Her gran's pasta maker. You need to see it, Philip. It's cool.'

'A second-hand pasta maker?'

'It's an heirloom.'

'Pasta makers aren't heirlooms.'

'This one is.' She gestured to the battered silver pasta maker taking pride of place on her bench. 'We'll make pasta once a week for the rest of our lives. When we're finally in our nursing home we'll discuss the virtues of each of our children and decide who most deserves our fantastic antique pasta maker. If our children are unworthy we'll donate it to the State Gallery as a National Treasure.'

He didn't even smile. 'You said you had a headache.'

'I did have a headache.'

'But you let them in.'

'It was Sarah,' she said, losing patience. 'Her gran's pasta maker means a lot to her. She was desperate to see me using it.'

'You weren't well enough to come out to dinner.'

'If it was necessary I would have come,' she snapped. 'It wasn't. It was, however, absolutely necessary for me to show Sarah that her grandmother's pasta maker will be appreciated.'

'And Finn?'

'You mean Raff?'

'Of course I mean Raff. Finn.'

'He brought Sarah here. He watched.'

'I don't see how you can bear that man to be in the house.'

'I can bear a lot for Sarah.'

'Even having a dog foisted onto you.'

Kleppy growled again and Abby felt like growling herself. 'Philip…'

And, just like that, he caved. He put his hands up in mock surrender, tossed his jacket over the back of a kitchen chair and hugged her. Kissed her on the forehead.

'Sorry. Sorry, sorry. I know you had no choice. I know you wouldn't let Finn in unless you had no choice.'

Of course she wouldn't.

'Tell me about tonight,' she said, and he sat and she made him coffee and he told her all about the fantastic business opportunities they'd discussed—projects of mutual benefit that needed careful legal input if they were to get past council.

And all the while… Things were changing.

Some time in the last twenty-four hours the buried question had surfaced in her head and it was getting louder and louder until it was almost a drumbeat.

Why am I marrying this man?

The question was making her feel dizzy.

A week on Saturday she'd be married to Philip.

Uh-oh.

This was Raff's fault, she thought, feeling desperate. Raff asking her…

Why did you and Dexter stop going out?

She'd shoved that memory away ten years ago, not to be thought of again. Remembering it now… How she'd felt…

Underneath the logic, did she still feel like that?

This was like waking from a coma. A million emotions were crowding in. Memories. Stupid childhood snatches. Laughter, trouble, tears, adventure, fun…

Always with Raff.

'Philip, I…'

'You need to go to bed,' he said, immediately contrite. He

rose. 'I'm sorry, I forgot the headache. You should have said. Just because Finn barges his way in, welcome or not... I have a bit more finesse. You sleep well and I'll see you in the morning. Breakfast at the yacht club? You want to come sailing afterwards?'

'Mum's organised the girls' lunch at midday.'

'Of course. So much to plan...'

So much to plan? This wedding had been organised for years.

'Sleep well, sweetheart,' he told her and stooped and kissed her. Dry. Dusty. He reached for his jacket...

And paused. Frowned. Felt the pockets. 'My wallet.'

'Your wallet?'

'It was in my side pocket.'

'Could you have dropped it?'

'It was there when I got out of the car.' He opened the front door and stared out at the path. The front light showed the path smooth and bare. 'I always check I have my phone and my wallet when I get in and out of the car.'

Of course. Caution was Philip's middle name.

'I'm sure I didn't drop it,' he said.

Which left... She swivelled and looked for Kleppy.

Kleppy was at her bedroom door. He had something on the floor in front of him.

A wallet? Too big?

She walked over to see and he wagged his tail and beamed up at her. She was sure it was a beam. It might be the stupidest beam on the planet but it was strangely adorable.

'What have you got?'

It wasn't the wallet. It was her jewellery box, the cedar box Philip's grandfather had given her. Her heart sank. If he'd chewed it...

He hadn't.

How had he got it down from the bedside table?

There wasn't a mark on it. He had his paw resting proprietorially on its lid but when she bent down and took it he quivered all over with that stupid canine beam. *Aren't I fantastic? Look what I found for you!*

'That dog…' Philip said in a voice full of foreboding.

'He doesn't have it,' she said. 'But…'

She looked more closely at Kleppy. Then she looked at her bed.

Kleppy had retrieved the box via the bed. She had a pale green quilt on her bed. The coverlet was now patterned with footprints.

She bent down and looked at Kleppy's paws.

Dirt.

Uh-oh, uh-oh, uh-oh.

She looked out through the glass doors to the garden. To the fence. To where she'd dug in netting all the way along.

Lots of lovely loose soil. A great place to bury something.

Loose dirt was scattered over the grass in half a dozen places. Kleppy, it seemed, had been a little indecisive in his burial location.

'You're kidding me,' Philip said, guessing exactly what had happened.

'Uh-oh.' What else was a girl to say?

'You expect me to dig?'

'No.' She'd had enough. She was waking from a bad dream and this was part of it.

'I'll find it,' she told him. 'I'll give it to you in the morning.'

'Clean.'

'Clean,' she snapped. 'Of course.'

'It's not my fault the stupid…'

'It's not your fault,' she said, cutting him off. It never was. Of all the childish…

No. She was being petulant herself. She needed to get a grip. She needed to find the wallet and then think through what was important here. She needed to decide how she could do the unimaginable.

'Of course it's not your fault,' she said more gently and

she headed outside to start sifting dirt. 'I took Kleppy on. I'm responsible. Go home, Philip, and let me sort the damage my way.'

'I can help…' he started, suddenly unsure, but she shook her head.

'My headache's come back,' she said. 'I can use a bit of quiet digging. And thinking.'

'What do you need to think about?'

'Weddings,' she said. 'And pasta makers. And dogs.'

And other stuff she wasn't even prepared to let into the corners of her mind until Philip was out of the door.

She dug.

She should have thought and dug, but she just dug. Her mind felt as if it had been washed clear, emptied of everything.

What was happening? Everything she'd worked for over the last ten years was suddenly…nothing.

Stupid, stupid, stupid.

This is just pre-wedding nerves, she told herself. But she knew it was more.

She dug.

It was strangely soothing, delving into the soft loam, methodically sifting. She should be wearing gardening gloves. She'd worn gardening gloves this afternoon when she'd laid the netting, but that was when it mattered that she kept her nails nice. That was when she was going to get married.

There was a scary thought. She sat back on her heels and thought, *Did I just think that?*

How could she not get married?

Her dress. Two years in the making. Approximately two thousand beads.

Two hundred and thirty guests.

People were coming from England. People had already come from England.

Her spare room was already filling with gifts.

She'd have to give back the pasta maker.

And that was the thing that made her eyes suddenly fill with tears. It made her realise the impossibility of doing what she was thinking of.

Handing Raff Finn back the pasta maker and saying, *Here, I can't accept it—I'm not getting married.*

Why Raff? Why was his gift so special?

She knew why. She knew…

The impossibility of what she was thinking made her choke. This was stupid. Nostalgia. Childhood memories.

Not all childhood memories. Raff yesterday at the scene of the accident, standing in front of her car, giving orders.

Raff, caring about old Mrs Ford.

Raff…

'We always wish for what we can't have,' she muttered to herself and shoved her hand deep into the loam so hard she hit the wire netting and scraped her knuckles.

She hauled her hand out and an edge of leather came with it.

She stared down at her skinned knuckle and Philip's wallet.

She needed a hug.

'Kleppy,' she called. 'I found it. You want to come lick it clean?'

Fat chance. It was a joke. She should be smiling.

She wasn't smiling.

'Kleppy?'

He'd be back on her bed, she thought. How long till he came when she called?

'Kleppy?' She really did want a hug. She wiped away the dirt and headed inside.

No Kleppy.

How many hiding places were there? Where was he?

Not here.

Not in the house.

The front door was closed. He could hardly have opened it and walked out. He was clever but not…

Memory flooded back. Philip, throwing open the door to stare at the front path. She'd gone to look for Kleppy, then she'd headed straight out to the garden.

Philip leaving. Slamming the door behind him.

The door had been open all the time they'd talked.

Her heart sank. She should have checked. She'd been too caught up with her own stupid crisis, her own stupid pre-wedding jitters.

Kleppy was gone.

CHAPTER EIGHT

ABBY searched block by block, first on foot and then fetching the car and broadening her search area.

How far could one dog get in what—half an hour? More? How long had she sat out in the garden angsting about what she should or shouldn't be doing with her life?

How had one dog made her question herself?

Where was he?

She wanted to wake up the town and make them search, but even her friends… To wake them at midnight and say, *Please, can you help me find a stray dog?* was unthinkable.

They'd think she was nuts.

Sarah wouldn't think she was nuts. Or Raff.

Her friends…

She thought of the kids she'd messed around with when she was a kid. They'd dropped away as she was seen as Philip's girl. Philip's partner. Philip's wife?

Those who remained… She winced, wondering how she'd isolated herself. She'd done it without thinking. How many years had she simply been moving forward with no direction? Or in Philip's direction. So now, who did she call when she was in the kind of trouble Philip disapproved of?

She knew who.

No.

She searched for another hour.

One o'clock.

This was crazy. She couldn't do it by herself.

Do not go near Raff Finn. That man is trouble. It had been a mantra in her head for years but now it had changed. Trouble had taken on a new dimension—a dimension she wasn't brave enough to think about.

She pushed the thought of Raff away and kept searching. Wider and wider circles. A small dog. He'd be safe until morning, she told herself. He had street smarts. He was a stray.

He wasn't a stray. He was Isaac Abrahams' loved dog. He wore his owner's medal of valour on his collar.

He was *her* Kleppy.

She drove on. Round the town. She walked through the deserted mall. She walked out onto the wharves at the harbour.

And then? There was only one place left to search. Isaac's.

Up the mountain in the dark? To Isaac's? She hated that place. She couldn't.

He had to be somewhere. After this time, logic said that was where he'd be.

She couldn't make herself go alone. She just…couldn't.

Don't do it.

Do it.

At two in the morning she phoned the police. The police singular.

Raff's patrol car pulled up outside her front door ten minutes after she called. He had the lights flashing.

He swung out of the car, six feet two inches of lethal cop. Ready for action.

She'd been parked, waiting for him. In the dark. Not wanting to wake the neighbours. His flashing lights lit the street and curtains were being pulled.

'Turn the lights off,' she begged.

'This is Kleppy,' he said seriously. 'I thought about sirens.'

'You want to wake the town?'

'How much do you want to find him?'

'A lot,' she snapped and then caught herself. 'I mean… please.'

'So how did you lose him? You let him out?'

'I…yes.'

He looked at her face and got an answer. 'Dexter let him out.'

'By mistake.'

'I'm sure.'

'By mistake,' she snapped.

'How long ago?'

'Three hours.'

'Three hours? You've only just discovered he's missing?' There was a whole gamut of accusation in his tone. Like what had she and Philip been doing for three hours that they hadn't noticed they'd lost a dog?

'I've been searching,' she said through gritted teeth. 'Can we just… I don't know…'

'Find him?' he suggested, and suddenly his voice was gentle. The switch was nearly her undoing. She was so close to tears.

'Yes. Please.'

'Where have you looked?'

'Everywhere.'

'That just about covers it. You sure he's not under your bed?'

'I'm sure.'

'That's where we find most missing kids,' he said. 'Within two hundred yards of the family refrigerator.'

'You want to look again?'

'I trust you. Is Dexter out hunting?'

Silence. She wasn't going to answer. She didn't need to answer.

'I'm…I'm sorry to call you out,' she ventured.

'This is what I do.'

'Hunt for lost dogs when you should be home with Sarah?'

'Sarah's used to me being out in the night. She has her dogs.'

'Are you on duty?'

'This is a two cop town. When there's an emergency, Keith and I are both on.'

'This is an emergency?'

'Kleppy's definitely an emergency,' he said. 'He's a loved dog with an owner. I was never more relieved than when you said you'd take him on. For all sorts of reasons,' he said enigmatically, but then kept right on. 'You want to ride with me? We'll check out Main Street. Morrisy Drapers is his favourite spot.'

'I've been there. It's all locked up. The bargain bins are inside. No Kleppy.'

'You've what?' he demanded, brow snapping. 'You walked the mall alone?'

'This is Kleppy.'

'At two on a Saturday morning? There's the odd drunk and nothing else in the mall.'

'Yeah, and no Kleppy.'

His mouth tightened but he said nothing, turning the car towards the waterfront. 'He likes the harbour, our Kleppy. Isaac's been presented with a live lobster before now. Isaac had to get Kleppy's nose stitched but he got him home, live and fighting.'

'Oh,' she said and choked on a bubble of laughter that was close to hysteria. 'A lobster?'

'Almost bigger than he was. Cost Isaac a hundred and thirty dollars for the lobster and another three hundred at the vet's. They had a great dinner that night.'

He had his flashing lights on again now. He hit another switch and floodlights lit both sides of the road.

The law on the hunt.

'I've checked the harbour,' she said in a small voice, already knowing the reaction she'd get.

And she did.

'Also by yourself.' His tone was suddenly angry. 'Hell, woman, you know the dropkicks go down there at night.'

'They haven't seen Kleppy.'

'You asked?'

'This is Kleppy.'

'You asked. You approached the low life that crawl round that place at night? Where the hell is Dexter?'

'In bed,' she snapped. She caught herself, fighting back anger in response. 'I know I should have phoned him but he's not…he's not quite reconciled to having a dog.'

'Which is why he left the door open.'

'He did not do it deliberately.'

'You make one stubborn defence lawyer,' he said more mildly and went back to concentrating on the sides of the road.

She fumed. Or she tried to fume. She was too tired and too worried to fume.

'Have you tried up the mountain?' Raff asked and she caught her breath.

The mountain.

Isaac's place.

'N… No.' She swallowed. Time to confess. 'That's why… that's why I called you.'

'You didn't go up there?'

'I haven't. Not since…' She paused. Tried to go on. Couldn't.

Tonight she'd walked a deserted shopping mall. Tonight she'd fronted a group of very drunk youths down at the harbour to ask if they'd seen her dog.

But the place with the most fears was Kleppy's home. Isaac's place.

Up the mountain where Ben had been killed. To go there at night…

The last night she'd been there would stay in her mind for ever. The phone call. The rain, the dark, the smell of spilled gasoline, the sight of…

'It's just a place, Abby,' Raff said gently. 'You want to stay home while I check?'

'I…no.' She had to get over this. Ten years. She was stuck in a time warp, an aching void of loss. 'I'm sorry. You must hate going up there, too.'

'There's lots of things I hate,' he said softly. 'But going up the mountain's not one of them. It's Isaac's home. He was a great old guy.'

He was. She remembered Isaac the night of the accident. Of course he'd heard the crash; he'd been first on the scene. He'd been cradling Ben when she'd got there.

All the more reason to love his dog. All the more reason to face down her hatred of the place.

'You know, you can't block it out for ever,' Raff said. 'Work it through and move on.'

'Like you have.' She heard the anger in her words and flinched.

'Like I try to,' Raff said evenly. 'It always hurts but limbo's not my idea of a great time. You want to spend the rest of your life there?'

'What's that supposed to mean?'

'Meaning you've never come back,' he said. 'You're as damaged as Sarah is in your own way.'

She shook her head. 'No. No, I'm not. I'm fine. Just find my dog, Raff.'

'I'll do my best,' he said gravely. 'You know, taking Kleppy's a great start. Kleppy's forcing chinks in your lawyerish armour and I'm not so sure you can seal them up again. Let's see if we can find him so he can go the whole way.'

Isaac's place was locked and deserted, a ramshackle homestead hidden in bushland. Through the fence, they could see Isaac's garden, beautiful in the moonlight, but they couldn't get in the front gate. The gate was padlocked and a cyclone fence had been erected around the rickety pickets.

'Isaac's daughter's worried about vandalism before she can get the place on the market,' Raff said. 'She sacked the gardener, hired a security firm and put the fence up.' Raff headed off, striding around the boundary, searching the ground with his flashlight as well as through the fence. Abby had to run to catch up with him.

The ground was unsteady. Raff's hand was suddenly holding hers. She should pull away—but she didn't.

'Call him,' Raff said.

She called, her voice ringing out across the bushland, eerie in the dark.

'Keep calling.' Raff's hand held hers, strong and warm and pushing her to keep going.

'We'll call from the other side,' he said. 'If he's down nearer the road...'

Near the road where Ben was killed?

Move on. She did move on, and Raff's hand gave her the strength to do it. How inappropriate was that?

But she called. And she called. And then, unbelievably...

Out through the bush, tearing like his life depended on it, Kleppy came flying. Straight to her.

She gasped and stooped to catch him and the little dog was in her arms, wriggling with joy. She was on her knees in the undergrowth, hugging. Maybe even weeping.

'Hey, Klep,' Raff said, and she could hear his relief. 'Where have you been hiding?'

She hugged him tight and he licked her...then suddenly he wrenched out of her arms, backed off and barked—and tore back into the bush.

Raff made a lunge for him but he was too fast.

He disappeared back into the darkness.

'You could have held his collar,' Raff said, but he didn't sound annoyed. He sounded resigned.

'Oh, my...' She started to run, but Raff put his hand out and stopped her.

'We walk. We don't run. Wombat holes, logs, all sorts of traps for the unwary in the dark.'

'But Kleppy...'

'Won't have gone far,' he said, taking her hand firmly back into his. 'You saw him—he was joyful to see you. This is Isaac's place, Kleppy's territory, but I reckon you're his now. It seems you're his person to replace Isaac. That's a fair responsibility, Abby Callahan. I hope you're up to it.'

'Just find him for me,' she muttered.

Kleppy's person?

She didn't want to think about where that was taking her.

She didn't actually want to think at all.

Kleppy had headed back down the hill. Towards the road. They were now within two hundred yards of where the cars had crashed.

It had rained this week. The undergrowth smelled of wet eucalypt, scents of the night, scents she hated.

She'd never wanted to come back here.

'Move on,' Raff said, holding her hand tightly. 'You can.'

She couldn't.

The thought that it had been Raff, the man holding her hand right now...

Raff...

She could not depend on this man. This man was dangerous; he always had been. He'd been dangerous to Ben. Now suddenly he seemed dangerous in an entirely different way.

But he was the one searching for Kleppy, not Philip.

That would have to be thought about tomorrow. For now... just get through tonight.

'If he's gone back down to the town...'

'Why would he do that? This is Isaac's place. You're here. Everything he knows is here.' And then, before she could respond, his flashlight stopped moving and focused.

Kleppy was fifty yards from the road. Digging? He was nosing his way through the undergrowth, pawing at the damp earth, wagging, wriggling, digging...

'Kleppy...' she called and started towards him.

Kleppy looked up at her—and headed back in the direction he'd come from. Back to Isaac's.

Raff sighed.

'You don't make a very good cop,' he said. 'Letting the suspect go. Sneaking up and then breaking into a run at the last minute.'

'What's he doing?' They were following him again, back

through the undergrowth. Once more, Raff had her hand. She absolutely should let it go.

She didn't.

'I suspect he's one very confused dog,' Raff said. 'He knows where Isaac lived but he can't get in. He's forming new bonds to you but his allegiance will be torn—he'll still want Isaac. And what's back there buried...who knows? Some long hidden loot, or a wombat hole, or something he sniffed on the way past and thought was worth investigating. But now... He's weighed everything up—you, wombats, Isaac—and decided he needs to go back to his first love.'

And Raff was right. They emerged from the bush and Kleppy was waiting for them—or rather he was waiting for someone to open the gate.

His nose was pressed hard against the cyclone fencing and he whimpered as they approached. He was no longer running. He was no longer joyful to see them.

Abby knelt and scooped him up and he looked longingly at the darkened house.

'He's not there any more,' she whispered, burying her nose into his scruffy coat. 'I'm sorry, Kleppy, but I'm it. Will I do?'

'He'll grow accustomed,' Raff said, and his voice was a bit rough—a bit emotional? 'You want me to take you both home?'

She looked at the darkened house, then turned and looked out towards the road, to where Ben had been snatched from her.

He'll grow accustomed.

Ten years...

Her parents would never forgive Raff Finn. How could she?

'It's okay, Kleppy,' she whispered. 'We'll manage, you and I. Thank you, Raff. We'd appreciate it if you took us home.'

He drove them down from the mountain, a woman and her dog, and he felt closer to her tonight than he had for ten years.

Maybe it was what she was wearing. The normally immaculate lawyer-cum-Abby was wearing old jeans, a faded sweatshirt and her hair had long come loose from its normally elegant chignon. She still had flour on her face from pasta making. There were twigs in her hair.

Her face was tear-streaked and she was holding her dog as if she were drowning.

She made him feel…

Like he'd felt at nineteen, when Abby had started dating Philip.

He and Abby had been girlfriend and boyfriend since they were fourteen and sixteen. Kid stuff. Not serious.

She hung round with Sarah so she was always in and out of the house. She was pretty and she laughed at his jokes. She was always…there.

Then he'd come home and she was dating Philip and the sense of loss had him gutted.

He should have told her how he felt then, only he'd been too proud to say, *Okay, Abby, wise choice, I know at seventeen you need to date a few people, see the world.*

He'd been too proud to say that seeing her and Philip together had made him wake up to himself. Had made him realise that the sexiest, loveliest, funniest, happiest, most desirable woman in the world was Abby.

He had known it. It was just… He thought he'd punish her a little. He and Ben had even been a bit cool to her—Ben had hated her dating Dexter as well.

They'd backed off. The night of the crash, where was Abby? Home, washing her hair?

Home, being angry with all of them.

That probably saved her life, but what was left afterwards…?

The sexiest, loveliest, funniest, happiest, most desirable woman in the entire world had been hidden under a load of grief so great it overwhelmed them all. Then she was hidden by layers of her parents' hopes, their fixation that Abby could make up for Ben, and their belief that Philip was the Ben they couldn't have.

He'd watched for ten years as the layers had built up, until the Abby he'd once known, once loved, had been almost totally subsumed.

And there was nothing he could do about it because he was the one who'd caused it.

He felt his fists harden on the steering wheel, so tight his knuckles showed white. One stupid moment and so many worlds shot to pieces. Ben and Sarah. And Abby, condemned to live for the rest of her life making up for his criminal stupidity.

'You know I once loved you,' he said into the night and she gasped and hugged Kleppy tighter.

'Don't.'

'I won't,' he said gently. 'I can't. But, Abby, if I could wipe away that night…'

'As if anyone could do that.'

'No,' he said grimly. 'And I know I have to live with it for the rest of my life. But you don't.'

'I don't know what you mean.'

'I mean you lost Ben that night,' he said. 'For which I'm responsible and I'll live with that for ever. But Ben was my mate and if he could see what's happening to you now he'd be sick at heart.'

There was a long silence. She wasn't talking. He was trying to figure out what exactly to say.

He had no right to say anything. He'd forfeited that for sure, but then…

Forget himself, he thought. Forget everything except the fact that Ben had been his best friend and maybe he needed to put what he was feeling himself aside.

Make it about Ben, he told himself. Abby hated him already. Saying what he thought Ben would say couldn't make things worse.

'Abby, your parents and Dexter's parents are thick as thieves,' he told her. 'They always have been. After the accident, your families practically combined. The Dexters had Philip. The

Callahans were left only with Abby. Two families, a son and a daughter. When Ben died you were about to go to university and study creative arts. Afterwards, Philip told you how sensible law was. Your mother told you how happy it'd make her to see you at the same law school as Philip. Philip's dad told you he'd welcome you into his law firm. And you just…rolled.'

'I did not roll,' she said but it was a whisper he knew didn't even convince herself.

'You used to wear sweaters with stripes. You used to wear purple leggings. I loved those purple leggings.'

Silence.

'I never saw you wear purple leggings after Ben died.'

'So I grew up.'

'We all did that night,' he said gravely. 'But, Abby, you didn't just leave behind childhood. You left behind…Abby.'

'If you mean I left behind stupidity, yes, I did,' she snapped. 'How could I not? All those years… *Keep away from the Finn boy. He's trouble.* That's what my mother said but I never listened. Not once did I listen and neither did Ben, and now he's dead.'

He couldn't answer that.

The car nosed its way down the mountain. He could drive faster. He didn't.

Keep away from the Finn boy.

He knew Ben and Abby had been given those orders. He even knew why.

His grandfather's drunkenness. His mother's lack of a wedding ring. His family's poverty.

The prissiness of Abby's parents, secure in their middle class home, with their neat front lawn and their nice children.

'I dunno about the Callahan kids.' He remembered Gran saying it when he was small as she tucked him into bed. 'You be careful, Raff, love. They don't fit with the likes of us.'

'They're my friends.'

'And they're nice kids,' his gran had said. 'But one day they'll move on. Don't let 'em break your heart.'

As a kid, he didn't have a clue what she was talking about.

He'd figured it out as he got older, but Ben and Abby never let it happen. They simply ignored their parents' disapproval and he was a friend regardless.

But for how long? If Ben hadn't died...would Abby have gone out with him again?

And now she was a defence lawyer and he was a cop. Never the twain shall meet.

Except she was staring ahead with eyes that were blind with misery and she was heading into a marriage with Dexter and he couldn't bear it.

'I'm not talking about us now,' he said, and it was hard to keep his voice even. 'As you say, we've both grown up and there's so much baggage between us there's never going to be a bridge to friendship. But I'm not talking about me either, Abby. I'm talking about you. You and Dexter. He's burying you.'

'He's not.'

'Mrs Philip Dexter. Where's the Abby in that equation?'

'Leave it.'

'You know it's true. Would Mrs Philip Dexter ever spend the night trawling Banksia Bay looking for a dog?'

'Of course she would.' She gulped. 'No. That is...I'll hang onto Kleppy from now on.'

'And if Dexter leaves the door open?'

'He won't.'

'Don't do it, Abby.'

'Butt out.' They were pulling up outside her house. She shoved the door open and hauled Kleppy out. She staggered a little, but straight away he was beside her, steadying her.

She was so...so...

She was Abby. All he wanted to do was fold her into his arms and hold her. Dog and all.

He'd had ten years to stop feeling like this. He thought he had.

One stupid night hunting a kleptomaniac dog and he was feeling just what he'd felt ten years ago. As if here was the half to his whole. As if something had been ripped out of him ten years back and this woman was the key to getting his life back.

This wasn't about him. It couldn't be.

'There are lots of guys out there, Abby,' he said in a voice that was none too steady. 'Guys who'd marry you in a heartbeat. Guys who'd love Kleppy. Don't marry Dexter.'

'Get out of my way.'

'You're better than this, Abby.'

'We've had this conversation before. Philip's better than any of us. He wasn't stupid. He's dependable.'

'He's boring. He doesn't like this town.'

'How can you say that? He lives for this town.'

'He spends his life criticising it. Making reasons why he should go to conferences far away. Where are you going on your honeymoon?'

'You're suggesting we should honeymoon at Mrs Mac's Banksia Bay's Big Breakfast?'

'No, but...'

'That's what I'd have done if I'd married you.'

Her words shocked them both.

If I'd married you...

The unsayable had just been said.

The unthinkable had just been put out there.

'Abby...'

'Don't,' she said and pushed and Kleppy got caught in the middle and yelped his indignation. 'Now see what you've done.'

Kleppy wagged his tail. Wounded to the core.

'Think about it,' he said, but softly, knowing he'd gone too far; he'd pushed into places neither of them could contemplate going.

'I've thought about it. Thank you very much for your help tonight.'

'Any time, Abby, and I mean that.'

'I've accepted all the help from you I'll ever accept.'

'You can't say that. What if you need help over the street in your old age? There I'll be in my fading cop uniform, all ready to hold up the traffic, and there you'll be with your pride and your walking frame. *Don't you stop the traffic for me, young man…*'

She gasped and choked, laughter suddenly surfacing at the image.

'That's better,' he said. 'Abby, can we be friends?'

Friends. She looked at him and the laughter faded. Her eyes were indescribably bleak.

'No.'

'Because of Ben?'

'Because of much, much more than that.'

'Don't go near the Finn boy. He's trouble?' he said.

'More than that, too,' she whispered. 'You know I… You know we…'

He didn't know anything, and he couldn't bear it. She was looking at him with eyes that were so bleak the end of the world must be around the corner, not the marriage of the year, Banksia Bay's answer to a royal couple—a wedding that had been planned almost since she was a baby.

She hesitated for just a fraction of a second too long and logic and reason and everything else he should be thinking flew straight out of the window.

He took her shoulders in his hands. He tugged her to him—dog included—and he kissed her.

One minute she was angry and confused, intending to wheel away and stalk into the house, dignity intact.

The next minute she was being kissed by Raff Finn and her dignity was nowhere.

Second time in two days? She felt as if her body had opened to this two days ago and she'd been waiting for a repeat performance ever since.

Only this wasn't a repeat performance. Tonight she'd been scared and lonely and emotional, remembering so much stuff that her head was close to exploding even before Raff's mouth met hers.

It was no wonder that when it did she couldn't handle it.

She liked control. She was a control girl. Her emotional wiring was neat and orderly.

His mouth touched hers and every single fuse blew, just like that.

Her circuits closed down and every one of the emotions she'd been feeling during the night was replaced, overridden by one gigantic wire that sizzled and sparked and threatened to blow her tidy existence right out of the water.

Raff Finn was kissing her.

She was kissing Raff Finn.

Or…maybe she wasn't kissing. She was simply dissolving into him.

Ten long years of control, ten years of carefully recreating her life, was forgotten. All she could feel was this man. His hands. His mouth. The taste of him, the smell, the sheer testosterone-laden charge of him.

Raff. The man who was kissing her totally, unutterably, mind-blowingly senseless.

She had sensations within her right now that she didn't know existed. She didn't know feeling like this was possible. If she had…

If she had, she'd have gone hunting for them with elephant guns.

Oh…

Did she gasp? Did she moan?

Who knew? All she knew was that her mouth was locked on his and the kiss went on and on and she didn't care. She didn't care that it was three in the morning and she was engaged to Philip Dexter and Raff Finn was a man her family hated. Raff Finn, six foot two, was holding her and kissing her until her toes curled, until her mind was empty of anything but the taste of him.

This was a pure primeval need. It had nothing to do with logic. It had everything to do with here and now. And Raff—a man she'd wanted since she was eight years old.

Here, now and…and…

'Is that you? Abigail?'

Uh-oh.

This was Banksia Bay.

It was three in the morning.

She lived next door to Ambrose Kittelty and Ambrose watched American sports television all night on Pay TV—as well as watching out of his front window.

Banksia Bay. Where her life was never her own. Could never be her own.

'It's Abby all right.' Somehow, Finn was putting her away from him and she could have wept. To have him so close… To know she could never… Must never…

'Is she kissing you?' Mr Kittelty sounded almost apoplectic.

'Bit of trouble with a dog,' Raff said smoothly. 'I'm helping the lady get him under control.'

'You looked like…'

'Took two of us to get him settled. Seems okay now. You right, ma'am?'

'That's Abrahams' dog,' Ambrose said.

'Yes, sir, the same dog that took your boot from the bowling club,' Finn said. 'Still causing trouble.'

'Get him put down,' Ambrose said and slammed down the window.

'I didn't know Ambrose and Phil were related,' Raff said and any last vestige of passion disappeared, just like that.

She felt cold and tired and stupid. Very, very stupid.

'Thank you for tonight,' she said, and she couldn't keep the weariness from her voice. 'Don't…'

'Come near you any more?'

'That's right,' she whispered. 'There's too much at stake.'

'Your marriage to Philip?'

'You know it's much more than that.'

'First things first, Abby,' he said softly. 'Figure the marriage thing out and everything else can come later.'

'Not with you, it can't.'

'I know that.'

'So goodnight,' she said and she hugged her dog close—a

wild dog this, he hadn't even wriggled while her brain had been short-circuiting—and she walked inside with as much dignity as she could muster.

She closed the door as if she was trying not to wake a household.

There was no household. Just Abby and Kleppy and one magnificent wedding dress.

'What will I do?' she whispered and she leaned back against the closed door. 'Kleppy, help me out here.'

Kleppy's butt wriggled until she set him on the floor. He headed into the bedroom while she stood motionless, trying not to think.

Kleppy headed straight back to her. Carrying her jewellery box.

He set it down at her feet and wriggled all over.

See? She had a guy who'd steal for her.

What more did a girl want?

Raff drove half a mile before he pulled over to the side of the road. He needed time to think.

He didn't have the head space to think.

Abby, Abby, Abby.

Ten years…

He'd been busy telling Abby she should move on. Could he?

He'd dated other women—of course he had. He'd set himself up with a life, of sorts. Living in this town. Keith, his partner, was getting long in the tooth. Keith was senior sergeant but, for all intents and purposes, Raff was in charge of the policing in this town. When Keith retired, Raff would be it.

Not bad for a Boy Who Meant Trouble.

He was still judged by some in this town, but only as someone whose background made people sniff, who'd been stupid in his youth. He was accepted as a decent cop. Sarah had friends, support groups, the farm she loved.

He had everything he needed in life, right there.

Except Abby.

How did you tell a woman you loved her?

He couldn't. To lay that on her... There was no way she could take it anywhere. They both knew that.

This thing between them...

He shouldn't have kissed her. It reminded him that it was more than a kid's dreaming. It was as real today as it had been the first time he'd kissed her. Life had been ahead of them, exciting, wonderful. Anything had been possible.

But to love Abby now...

She'd closed herself off. After Ben's death she'd simply shut down, retired into her parents' world, into Philip's world, and she'd never emerged. She was junior partner in Banksia Bay's legal firm. She was Philip's fiancée. Next Saturday she'd be Philip's wife.

The waste...

Do you want to marry her yourself?

The thought was enough to make him smile, only it wasn't a happy smile. He'd faced facts years ago. Even if she could shake off the past, to live with her parents' condemnation, with the knowledge that every time she looked at him she was seeing Ben...

They'd destroy each other.

A couple of kids drove past—Lexy Netherland driving his dad's new Ford. He bet Old Man Netherland didn't know Lexy was out on the tear. He had Milly Parker in the passenger seat. They'd be going up the mountain, to the lookout. Only not to look out.

Kids, falling in love.

He could put the sirens on, pull 'em over, send 'em home with their tails between their legs.

No way could he do that. It wasn't long before they'd be adults. The world would catch up with them and they'd be accepting life as it had to be.

As he had.

Loving Abby. Then Ben's death. Then the other side, where the woman he loved could never find the courage to move on.

He knew she was having doubts—how could he kiss her

and not sense it? Maybe if he pushed harder he could stop this marriage. But then what? What would he be doing to her?

He'd pushed her already to look seriously at the life she was facing. There was nothing else he could do. For Ben. For himself.

He put his head on the steering wheel and thumped it. Hard. Three times.

The third time he hit the horn and the dogs in Muriel Blake's backyard started barking to wake the dead.

Time to move on, then?

Back to Sarah.

Back home.

Where to move forward in this town?

There was never a forward.

CHAPTER NINE

How to sleep after a night like this? She did at last, but not until dawn. She woke and it was ten o'clock and she'd been meant to meet Philip for breakfast at the yacht club.

She phoned and he was fine.

'No problem. I have three newspapers and Don's here with his plans for the new supermarket. As long as it's safe and clean, I can do without my wallet until later. I've hardly realised you weren't here.'

That was supposed to make her feel better?

She showered slowly, washed her hair, took a long time drying it.

Kleppy watched, looking anxious.

'I'm not going anywhere today where I can't take you,' she told him. 'It's the weekend.'

He still looked anxious. He climbed onto her bed, and then onto the dressing table. Wriggled himself a spot next to her cedar box. His new favourite thing.

'I guess last night upset you,' she told him, abandoning her hairdryer to give him a hug. 'I'm so sorry about Isaac. It's horrid loving someone and losing them.'

Like she had.

Like Raff had.

It was Raff's fault.

But that mantra, said over and over in her head for ten years, sounded hollow and sad and bleak as death—a sentence stretched into the future as far as the horizon.

Could she put it away? Find the Raff she'd once loved?

Whoa. What was she thinking?

'It's wedding nerves,' she told Kleppy and on impulse she carried him into her spare room where her wedding gown hung in all its glory.

Two years of love had gone into making this dress.

She set Kleppy down. The little dog nosed his way around the hem, ducked under the full-circle skirt, poked his nose out again and headed back to her. She smiled and held him and stared at her dress some more.

She'd loved making this dress. Loved, loved, loved.

Once upon a time, this was what she was going to do. Sew for a living. Make beautiful things. Make people happy.

Now she was employed getting a low life off the hook. She was going to be Philip's wife.

But to draw back now…

The morning stretched on. She sat on the floor of her second bedroom and thought and thought and thought.

Her mother rang close to midday. 'You ready, darling?'

'Ready?'

'Sweetheart, don't joke,' her mother said sharply. 'This is your afternoon, like Thursday night was Philip's night. Philip's mother and I will be by to collect you in half an hour. Don't wear any of your silly dresses now, will you, dear. You know I hate them.'

Her silly dresses.

She meant the ones she'd made herself. The ones that weren't grey or black or cream.

This was a wedding celebration. Why not wear something silly? Polka dots. Her gorgeous swing skirt with Elvis prints all over?

'I'll drive myself,' she told her mother. 'I'll meet you at the golf club.'

'You won't be late?'

'When am I ever? Oh, and Mum?'

'What?'

'I'm bringing my dog.'

There was a moment's grim silence. Her mother would know what she was talking about. The whole town would know. She'd expected her mother to have vented her disapproval by now.

'Hasn't Philip talked some sense into you about that yet?'

'About that?'

'Abrahams' dog. Of all the stupid…'

'I'm keeping him.'

'Well.' Her mother's breath hissed in and Abby waited for the eruption. But then suddenly Abby could hear her smile. There was even a tinkling laugh. 'That's okay,' she said and Abby realised she was on speaker phone, and her mother was also talking to her father. 'Philip will cope with this.' Then, back to her… 'They don't let dogs in the club house.'

'They do on the terrace as long as I keep him leashed. It's a gorgeous day. I'm bringing him.'

'This is between you and Philip, not you and us,' her mother said serenely. 'Philip will talk you into sense, and we can cope with a dog for one afternoon. But don't be late. Isn't this exciting? So many plans, finally come together.'

She disconnected.

So many plans, finally come together.

Abby stood and stared at the phone. How could she do the unthinkable?

How could she not?

'I'm ready.'

Sarah looked beautiful. Hippy beautiful. There was a shop behind the main street catering for little girls who wanted to be fairies or butterflies and adults who wanted to be colourful. It suited Sarah exactly.

The woman who ran it thought Sarah was lovely. She rang Raff whenever a new consignment arrived and he'd wave goodbye to half his weekly salary. It was worth it. Sarah's joy in her pretty dresses and scarves and her psychedelic boots made up…well, made up in some measure for the rest.

She'd woken with another of her appalling headaches. It had

finally eased but she was still looking wan, despite her smile. Pretty clothes were the least he could give her.

'Can you drive me to the golf club now? I don't want to be late,' she said, anxious. She'd been looking forward to this week for months. Abby's pre-wedding parties. Abby's wedding itself.

'My car is at your disposal,' he said and pulled on his policeman's cap, tipping it like a chauffeur. She smiled.

'Tell me again why you're not coming.'

At least that was easy. 'It's girls only. I'd look a bit silly in a skirt.'

Sarah giggled, but her smile was fleeting. 'If it wasn't only girls, would you want to come?'

Sometimes she did this, shooting him serious, insightful questions, right when he didn't need them.

'Abby's mother doesn't like me,' he said, deciding to be honest. 'It makes things uncomfortable.'

'Because of the accident?'

'Yes.'

'Oh, Raff,' she said and walked over and hugged him. 'It's not fair.'

'There's not a lot we can do about it, Sares,' he told her and kissed her and put her away from him. 'Except be happy ourselves. Which we are. How can we help but be happy when you're wearing a bright pink and yellow and purple and blue skirt—and your purple boots have tassels?'

'Do you like them?' she said, giggling and twirling.

'I love them.'

He was making Sarah happy, he thought as they headed to the golf club to Abby's pre-wedding party. At least he could do that.

No one else?

No one else.

Philip was sailing. He'd gone out with his supermarket-planning mates. Even now he was cruising round Banksia Bay, discussing the pros and cons of investment opportunities.

How did you tell a guy you'd made the biggest mistake of your life when he was out at sea?

How did you go calmly to your pre-wedding party when you'd made a decision like this?

How did you call it off—when you hadn't told your fiancé first?

All those wedding gifts, coming her way. She'd be expected to unwrap them. Aargh.

But by now the gifts would already be in cars heading towards the golf club. It didn't make any difference if she said, *Don't give them to me today,* or if on Monday she re-wrapped them and sent them all back.

That'd be her penance. Sending gifts back.

That and a whole lot else.

She drove towards the golf club slowly. Very slowly. Kleppy lay beside her and even he seemed subdued. She turned into the car park. She sat and stared out through the windscreen, seeing nothing.

Someone tapped on her window. She raised her head and dredged up a smile. Sarah was peering in at her, looking worried.

'What's wrong? You look sad. Do you have another headache? Oh, Abby, and on your party day.'

Raff was right behind his sister. In civvies. Faded jeans and black T-shirt, stretched a bit too tight.

'No, I… I just didn't want to be the first to arrive.' She climbed from the car and sent Raff what she hoped was a bright smile, a smile that said she knew exactly what she was doing.

'Collywobbles?' he asked and it was just what she needed. It was the sort of word that made a woman gird her loins and stiffen her spine and send him a look that was pure defiance.

'Why on earth would I have collywobbles?'

'I'd have collywobbles if I was marrying Philip.'

'Go jump.'

'Philip's really handsome,' Sarah said. 'Almost as handsome as Lionel.'

'Lionel?' They said it in unison, distracted. They looked at each other. Looked back at Sarah.

'Lionel's cute,' Sarah said. 'So's your dress, Abby. I love the Elvises.'

'So do I,' Abby said, thinking she had one vote at least. She loved this dress—a tiny bustier, a full-circle skirt covered with Elvises—black and white print with crimson tulle underneath to make it flare. It was a party dress. A celebration dress.

What was she celebrating?

'And you've made Kleppy a matching bow.' Sarah scooped up the little dog and hugged him. 'He's adorable. He's even more adorable than Lionel.'

'Who's Lionel?' Abby asked.

'Kleppy's friend,' Sarah said simply. 'Ooh, there's Margy.' Abby's next door neighbour was pulling up on the far side of the car park, a dumpy little woman whose looks belied the fact that she ran the most efficient disability services organisation in the State. 'Hi, Margy. Can I sit next to you?' And she dived off, carrying Kleppy, leaving Abby and Raff together.

'Lionel?' she said, because that seemed the safest way to go.

'There's Lionel who was Isaac's gardener,' Raff said, frowning. 'I didn't realise he and Sarah knew each other, but Sarah gets around more than I think. Okay, have a great hen's party. I'll pick Sarah up at four.'

'Raff?'

'Yes?' He sounded testy.

She'd said his name. She needed to add something on the back of it. Something sensible.

But how to say what she needed to say? How to think about saying what she needed to say? How to get over the impossibility of even thinking about thinking about...?

Maybe she should stop thinking. Her head was about to fall off.

People were arriving all around them. Her friends. Her

mother's friends. Every woman in this little community who'd come into contact with her over the years seemed to be getting out of cars, carrying gifts into the golf club.

How many women had her mother invited?

How many gifts would she need to return?

'Abigail?' That was her mother calling. She was standing on the terrace, shielding her eyes from the sun, trying to see who her daughter was talking to. 'Your guests are here. You should be receiving them.'

'There you go,' Raff said and eased himself back into his car. 'By the way, I'm with Sarah. That's a cute dress. Really cute. You should try wearing that in court some time.'

'Raff?' She didn't want him to go. She didn't want…

'See you later,' he said.

He drove away. She stood there in her Elvis dress, staring after him like a dummy.

'Abigail.' Her mother's voice was sharp. 'What are you thinking? You're being discourteous to our guests. And what on earth are you wearing?'

A cute dress, she thought, as she headed up to her mother, to her waiting guests.

Abigail, what are you thinking?

What was he thinking?

Nothing. He'd better not think anything because if he did there was a chasm yawning and it was so big he couldn't see the bottom.

He needed some work. He needed a few kids to do something stupid so he could lay down the law, vent a bit of spleen, feel in control.

Abby in an Elvis dress.

Abby, who was marrying Philip.

Any minute now the steering wheel was going to break.

'Raff?' His radio crackled into life and he grabbed it as if it were a lifeline.

It was Keith. 'Yeah?'

'There's a bit of trouble down on the wharf. Couple of kids chucking craypots into the water, and Joe Paxton's threatening to do 'em damage. I'm stuck up on the ridge 'cos John Anderson's locked himself out. Can you deal?'

'Absolutely,' Raff said, feeling a whole heap better.

Trouble, he could deal with.

Just not how he was feeling about Abby.

The afternoon was interminable. She smiled and smiled, and thought she should have run. What was she thinking, letting this afternoon go ahead? Just because she needed to tell Philip first.

'You'll make such a lovely couple. A credit to the town.' That was Mrs Alderson, one of her mother's bridge partners. 'We're so looking forward to next Saturday.'

'Thank you,' she said and then realised that Mrs Alderson was carrying a rather long shoulder bag and something had peeped from the edge and Kleppy had just…just…

He was heading under the table, to the full length of his lead, looking satisfied.

She stooped to retrieve it. It was a romance novel, a brand she recognised. A really… Goodness, what was that on the front? She snatched it from her dog and handed it back, apologising.

Margot Alderson turned beet-red and stuffed it back into her bag.

'I don't know what you're doing with that dog,' she snapped. 'He's trouble. If you must get yourself a dog, get a nice one. I have a friend who breeds pekes.'

Kleppy looked up at her from under the table and wagged his tail. He'd done what he wanted. He'd had his snatch and he'd given it to his mistress.

'I kinda like Kleppy,' Abby said. 'And you know…I don't even mind a bit of trouble.'

Her mother's friend departed, still indignant. Abby stared after her, thinking—of all things—about the cover of the romance novel. The cover showed a truly fabulous hero, bare from the waist up.

I don't mind pecs, either, she added silently. *Or a bit of hot romance.*

He had two kids in the cells waiting for their parents to come and collect them. 'Take your time,' he'd told them. 'It'll do 'em good to sweat.'

Which meant he was stuck at the station, babysitting two drunken adolescents. Forced to do nothing but think.

Abby.

A man could go quietly nuts.

It wasn't fair to interfere more than he already had.

He wasn't feeling fair.

'If I was a Neanderthal I'd go find me a club and a cave,' he muttered.

He wasn't. He was Banksia Bay's cop and Abby was a modern non-Neanderthal woman who knew her own mind. He had to respect it.

'I miss the old days,' he said morosely. 'It'd be so much easier to go set up a cave.'

It was over. The last gift was in her father's van, being taken home to their spare room, Abby's old bedroom, pink, pretty.

'I wish you'd come home for your last week,' her mother said, hugging her. 'It's where you belong.'

Abby said no, as she always said no. They left, leaving Abby sitting on the terrace with Kleppy.

Philip was coming by to meet her. She had to tell him.

Her mother's words... *It's where you belong.*

Where did she belong?

She didn't know.

'What do you mean you don't want to get married?'

To say Philip was gobsmacked would be an understatement. He was staring at her as if she'd lost her mind.

Maybe she had.

'I can't,' she muttered, miserable. She'd tried to get him to go for a walk with her, to get away from the people in the bar. He wouldn't. They were out on the terrace but they were still in full view.

Philip was tired from sailing. He didn't want a walk. He wanted to go home, have a shower, take a nap, then take his fiancée out to Banksia Bay's newest restaurant. That was what he'd planned.

He hadn't planned on Abby being difficult.

He hadn't planned on a broken engagement.

'It's just… Kleppy,' she said in a small voice and Philip stared at her as if she were demented.

'The dog.'

'He's made me…'

'What?'

What, indeed? She hardly understood it herself. How one dog could wake her from a ten-year fog. 'You don't like him,' she said.

'Of course I don't like him,' Philip snapped. 'He's a mutt. But I'm prepared to put up with him.'

'I don't want you to put up with him.' She took a deep breath. Tried to say what she scarcely understood herself. The thing in the middle of the fog. 'I don't want you to put up with me.'

'What are you saying?'

'You don't like me, Philip.'

He looked at her as if she'd lost her mind. 'Of course I like you. I love you. Haven't I shown you that, over and over? This is craziness. Pre-wedding nerves. To say…'

'You don't like this dress, do you?'

He stared down at the Elvises and he couldn't quite repress a wince. 'No, but…'

'And you painted your living room…our living room when I move in…beige. I don't like beige.'

'Then we'll paint it something else. I can cope.'

'See, that's exactly what I mean. You'll put up with something else. Like you put up with me.'

'This is nonsense.'

They were sitting at the table right on the edge of the terrace, with a view running all the way down the valley to the coast below. It was the most beautiful view in the world. If anyone looked out from the bar right now they'd see a man and a woman having a tête à tête, she flashing a diamond almost as wide as her finger, he taking her hand in his. Visibly calming down.

'Mum said this was bound to happen,' Philip said. 'She felt like this when she married my father. A week before the wedding. Pre-wedding jitters.'

Philip's mother. A mouse, totally dominated by Philip's father—and by Philip himself.

She'd seen Philip's mother looking at her dress today. Not brave enough to say she liked it. But just…looking.

'I don't want to be beige,' she whispered.

'You won't be beige. You'll be very happy. There's nothing you want that I can't give you.'

'I want you to like my dog.' She felt as if she was backed into a corner, trying to find reasons for the unreasonable. Trying to explain the unexplainable.

'I'll try and like your dog.'

'But why?' she said. 'There are women out there who like beige. There are women out there who don't like mutts. Why do you want to marry me?'

'I was always going to marry you.'

'That's just it,' she said and it was practically a wail. 'We've just drifted into this.'

'We did not drift. I made a decision ten years ago…'

'You wanted to marry me ten years ago?'

'Of course I did.' He sighed, exasperated. 'It's okay. I understand. One week of pre-wedding nerves isn't going to mess with ten years of plans.'

'Philip, I don't want to,' she said and, before she could think about being sensible, she hauled the diamond from her finger and laid it on the table in front of him. 'I can't. I know…I know it's sensible to marry you. You're a good man. I know you've been unfailingly good to me. I know you'll even put up with my dog and paint your living room sunbeam-yellow if I really want. But, you know what? I want someone who likes sunbeam-yellow.'

'What the…? Is there someone else?'

Someone else. At the thought of who that someone else was…at the sheer impossibility of saying his name, voicing the thought, her courage failed her. Her courage to say *Raff*.

But not her courage to do what she must, right now.

'I can't,' she said quietly. 'No matter what. This isn't about someone else, Philip. It's about what I'm feeling. Finding Kleppy… Yeah, it's crazy, but he makes me laugh. He's a little bit nuts and I love it. I wish you loved it. You don't, and it's made me see that I don't want to be Mrs Philip Dexter. You've been wonderful to me, Philip. You deserve a woman who thinks you're wonderful in return. You deserve a woman who'll love the life you want to live instead of putting up with it, and you deserve a woman who you'll think is wonderful instead of putting up with her.'

'Abby…' He was truly shocked now, ashen, and she felt dreadful. Appalling.

She had to do this.

She pushed the diamond closer to him, so close it nearly fell off the edge of the table.

Philip was a sensible man. This diamond was worth a fortune. He didn't let it fall. He took it, looked down at it for a long moment and then carefully zipped it into the pocket of his sailing anorak.

He rose.

'I'm damp in these clothes,' he said, pale and angry. 'I need to get changed. And you… You need to think about what you're throwing away. You're being foolish beyond belief. Insulting, even. I know it's pre-wedding nerves and I'll make allowances. Think about it overnight. I'll come and see you in the morning when you've had time to reconsider.'

'I won't reconsider.'

'You have twenty-four hours to see sense,' he snapped. 'After all I've done for you… I can't believe you'd be so ungrateful.

To walk away from me… Of all the crazy… Why don't you just get on a slow boat to China and be done with it?'

A slow boat to China? Right now, the concept had enormous merit, but she wasn't going anywhere.

She couldn't move. She sat and stared sightlessly over the golf course and she thought…nothing.

Someone came and cleared her glass. Asked if she'd like another drink. Asked if she and Philip were going to China for their honeymoon.

Finally let her be.

They'd be muttering in the bar. Wondering what she was doing, just sitting.

Expecting Philip to come back?

Maybe they'd seen his anger, his tight lips, his rigid stance as he'd stalked to his car.

Maybe the town already knew.

She wouldn't tell anyone. She couldn't. Philip had given her twenty-four hours to come to her senses. She owed it to him to wait, to make him see it was a measured, sensible decision.

Is there someone else?

She thought of Philip's demand. Was there?

Raff had kissed her. Twice. He'd made her feel…

She couldn't afford to acknowledge how he made her feel.

'Klep!' The call jolted her out of her misery, an unfamiliar voice filled with joy. It was one of the golf course groundsmen, striding up from the first tee. She looked closer and recognised him.

Lionel. Isaac's gardener. A big, burly man in his mid-thirties. Slow and sleepy and quiet.

He reached her and knelt on the terrace and Kleppy was licking his face with joy. 'Klep!'

'Lionel,' she said, hauling herself out of her introspection. 'What are you doing here?'

'Working,' he said, briefly extricating himself from Kleppy's licking. 'Gotta job mowing. Not as good as Mr Abrahams'. S'okay.'

'You and Kleppy are friends?'

'Yeah.'

Oh, help. She looked at the two of them and thought…and thought…

Thought they were greeting each other with a joy born of love.

'Did you want him?' It nearly killed her to say it. To lose Kleppy and Philip in the one afternoon…

She knew what would hurt most.

But… 'Can't,' Lionel said briefly. 'I live in a rooming house now. I had to sell the house when Baxter pinched Mum's money. Lost the house, then lost me job when Mr Abrahams died. Someone said the Finns had Klep. Went up there to see and Sarah said he were yours. Sarah said he were happy. You're looking after 'im?'

'I…yes.'

'He's a great dog, Klep,' Lionel said. 'Makes a man happy.'

'I… He'll make me happy.'

'Goodo,' Lionel said. 'That man… Dexter… They said you're getting married.'

'I…'

'He's the lawyer.' It wasn't a question.

'Yes.'

'He don't like dogs,' Lionel said. 'He come up to Mr Abrahams' when he made a will. Kleppy jumped up and it were like he was touching dirt. You and he…' He stopped, the question unasked. *You and he…*

'We'll sort it out,' Abby said. 'I love Kleppy enough for both of us.'

'That's good,' Lionel said. 'You've made me feel better. And you're a lucky woman. Kleppy's the best mate you could have.' He gave Kleppy a farewell hug and went back to mowing.

Abby kept on staring at nothing.

Like he was touching dirt…

She'd done the right thing. She didn't need twenty-four hours. *She was a lucky woman?*

Maybe she was. She had Kleppy and she was...*free?*

CHAPTER TEN

ABBY told no one but it was all over town by morning.

Abigail Callahan and Philip Dexter had had a row. She'd flung his ring back in his face. He'd accused her of having an affair. She'd accused him of having an affair. The wedding would cost squillions to cancel. Abby was threatening to go to China.

Abby was threatening to take the dog to China.

Why, oh, why, did she live in a small town?

The phone rang at seven-thirty and it was her mother. Hysterical.

'Sam Bolte said he saw you at the golf club and you weren't wearing your ring. I've just had a call from Ingrid. Ingrid says Sam says Philip was rigid with anger, and he said it's all about that stupid dog. Are you out of your mind?'

She laid back on the pillows and listened to her mother's hysteria and thought about it.

Was she out of her mind?

Kleppy was asleep on her feet.

She could sleep with Kleppy for ever. If she didn't do something about Raff.

She couldn't do something about Raff. There was nothing to do.

'It's okay, Mum, I'll sort it,' she said.

'Sort it? Tell Philip it's a ghastly mistake? You know, if it means the difference between whether you marry or not, your father and I will even keep the creature.'

The creature nuzzled her left foot and she scratched his ear with her toe.

'That's really generous, but…'

'You can't cancel the wedding. It'll cost…'

'No, it won't.' This, at least, she could do. She'd figured it out, looked at the contract with the golf club, had it nailed. 'I lose my deposit, which is tiny. None of the food's been ordered. Nothing's final. I can do this.'

'You're never serious?'

'Mum, I don't want to marry Philip.'

There was a long, long silence. Then… 'Why not?' It was practically a wail.

'Because I don't want to be sensible. I like being a dog owner. I like that my dog's a thief.' She thought about it and decided, why not go for broke; her mother could hardly be any more upset than she was now. 'I might as well tell you… I don't think I want to be a lawyer, either.'

'You've lost your mind,' her mother moaned. 'John, come and tell your daughter she's lost her mind. Darling, we'll take you to the doctor. Dr Paterson's known you since you were little. He can give you something.'

'I'm not sure he can give me what I want.'

'What do you want?'

'My dog, for now,' she said, shoving another thought firmly away. 'My independence. My life.'

'Abigail…'

'I'm hanging up now, Mum,' she said. 'I love you very much, but I'm not marrying Philip and I'm not mad. Or I don't think I'm mad. I'm not actually sure who I am any more, but I think I need to find out, and I can't do that as Mrs Philip Dexter.'

'Rumour is she's thrown him over. Rumour is she met some guy at that conference she went to in Sydney last month. Chinese. Millionaire. Loaded. Couple of kids by a past marriage but that's not worrying her. Rumour is she wants to take the dog…'

Raff spent the morning feeling…
Surprised?

'Go away. I'm not home.'

She was pretending not to be home. The first couple of times the doorbell rang Kleppy barked, which might be a giveaway, but she fixed that. She tucked him firmly under the duvet, and she put her jewellery box down there with him. Which reminded her…

Should she give the box back to Philip's grandfather? He'd given it to her as a labour of love, on the premise she was marrying his grandson.

Maybe he was one of those out there ringing her doorbell, sent by her mother to tell her to be sensible.

It couldn't matter. Go away, go away, go away.

How long could she stay under the duvet? She started working out how much food she had in the place; when she'd be forced to do a grocery run. She thought of the impossibility of facing shopping in Banksia Bay. Maybe she and Kleppy could leave town for a bit.

Where could she go?

Somewhere Raff could find her. If he wanted to find her.

Don't think of that. Don't think of Raff. Get this awfulness out of the way, and then look forward. Please…

The doorbell rang again.

Go away.

It rang again, more insistent, and it was followed by a knock, too loud to be her mother. Philip?

Go away!

'Abigail Callahan?' The voice was stern with authority and it made her jump.

Raff.

Raff was right outside her front door.

Panic.

What did he think he was doing, hiking up to her front door as bold as brass? She peeked past the curtains and his patrol car was parked out front. With its lights flashing.

She practically moaned. This was all she needed. Who knew what the town was saying about her, but she did not need Raff in the mix. It was all too complicated.

Kleppy whined, sensing her confusion, and she hugged him and held her breath and willed Raff to go away.

But Raff Finn wasn't a man to calmly turn away.

'Abigail Callahan, I know you're in there. Answer the door, please, or I'll be forced to come back with a warrant.'

A warrant? What the...?

'Go away.' She yelled it to the front door and there was a moment's silence. And then a response, deep and serious, and only someone who knew him well could hear the laughter behind it.

'Miss Callahan, I'm here to inform you that your dog is suspected of petty larceny. I have information that stolen property may be being stored on your premises. Open the door now, please, or I'll be forced to take further action.'

Her dog...

Petty larceny...

She lifted the duvet and stared at Kleppy. Who gazed back, innocent as you please. What the...? He hadn't been out. How could he have stolen anything?

She'd given back her mother's friend's romance novel. Kleppy was clean.

'He hasn't done anything,' she yelled, and then had to try again because the first yell came out more like a squeak. 'Go find some other dog to pin it to. Kleppy's innocent.'

'There speaks a defence lawyer. Sorry, ma'am, but the evidence points to Kleppy.'

'What evidence?'

'Mrs Fryer's diamanté glasses case, given to her by her late husband. It's said to be worth a fortune, plus it has sentimental value. It's alleged it was stolen from her bag, which was parked underneath the table you were sitting at yesterday. I have reason to believe your dog was tied under that very table. Circumstantial, I'll grant you, but evidence enough for a warrant.'

Uh-oh.

She thought about it. Kleppy lying innocently at her feet through yesterday's lunch. A big table, twelve or so women. Twelve or so handbags at their respective owners' feet.

Uh-oh, uh-oh, uh-oh.

'I have more serious things to think about this morning than glasses cases,' she managed and she heard the laughter intensify.

'You're saying there's something more serious than grand theft?'

'I thought it was petty larceny.'

'That depends whether the diamantés are real. Mrs Fryer swears they are. I knew old Jack Fryer and I'm thinking otherwise but I need to give the lady the benefit of the doubt.'

'He hasn't got them,' she wailed. 'He'd have given them to me by now.'

'I need to search.'

'Go away.'

'Let me in, Abigail,' he said, stern again. 'The neighbours are looking.'

Oh, for heaven's sake. Raff walking in here… If anyone in this town got even the vaguest sniff of what she was feeling…of why she'd been jerked out of her miserable life into something resembling a future…

Her future.

The word somehow steadied her. She wasn't marrying Philip. She had a future. Okay, maybe she needed to step into it rather than hiding under the duvet.

She climbed out of bed and shrugged on her brand new honeymoon wrap. Where was her shabby pink chenille? She'd got rid of it. Of course she had. That was what a girl did when she was getting married.

So now she was stuck with pure silk. Pure silk and Raff. She shoved her toes into elegant white slippers, pasted a glower on her face and stomped through to the front door. Hauled it open.

Raff was there in his cop uniform. He looked...he looked...

Maybe how *he* looked wasn't the issue. 'Whoa,' he said, his gaze raking her from the toes up, and she felt herself start to burn. She'd had fun buying herself wedding lingerie. She'd never owned silk before. It was making her body feel...

Well, something was making her body feel—as if it had been a really bad idea to give all her shabby stuff to the welfare store. The way Raff was looking...

Stop it. She practically stamped her foot. Raff was a cop. He was here to search the place. What she was thinking?

She knew what she was thinking, and she'd better stop thinking it right now. Instead, she concentrated on keeping her glower at high beam and stood aside as he came in.

'I don't want you here.' What a lie.

'Needs must. You say you don't have a glasses case, ma'am?'

'If you say *ma'am* once more I may be up for copicide.'

'Copicide?'

'Whatever. Justifiable homicide. Kleppy didn't pinch anything.'

'Are you sure?'

She winced at that. 'Um... No.'

He grinned. 'Not such a good defence lawyer, then. So what's with the millionaire?'

'The millionaire?'

'The guy you've thrown Philip over for.'

The millionaire. If he only knew. 'I hate this town,' she muttered, and she didn't need to try and glower.

'So it's all a lie.'

'What's a lie?'

'That you've tossed Philip aside and found another.'

'Yes. No. I mean...'

He caught her hand and held it up for them both to see. She'd been wearing Philip's ring for two years now. A stark white band showed where the ring had been.

'Proof?' Raff said softly.

'If I ran off with someone else I wouldn't be here now,' she snapped. 'And if he was a millionaire I'd have a rock to match.'

'But you've given Philip the flick.'

'Philip and I are taking time to reassess our positions.'

He surveyed her thoughtfully, once more taking in the silk. 'That's lawyer speak for a ripper of a fight and no one's speaking. Does this mean Sarah and I get our pasta maker back?'

That was a punch below the belt. But still… The pasta maker and Philip, or no pasta maker and no Philip.

No choice.

How had she changed so much? This time last week she'd been the perfect bride. Now, here she was, standing in the hall with her criminal dog behind her, with Raff right here. Right in her hall. Big, sexy, smiling.

Raff.

'I'll check my bag,' she muttered but he put her aside quite gently.

'No, ma'am. I'll check your bag. I don't want evidence tampered with.'

'You're thinking of taking paw prints?'

He chuckled, a lovely rich sound that filled the hall; that made her feel…like there might be something on the far side of this awfulness.

Her bag was by the front door where she'd tossed it when she'd come in yesterday. Big, bright, covered with Elvises. She'd made it as a picnic bag, thinking wistfully her Elvis dress would look cute on picnics. As if Mrs Philip Dexter would ever go on picnics.

Now the bag was stuffed with legally gathered loot—all the small gifts she'd been given yesterday. These were the gifts she'd have to sort and send back, with a note saying very sorry, she wasn't marrying Philip.

She'd have to reword that. She wasn't sorry at all. Especially now Raff was here.

He squatted beside the bag and started laying gifts out on the floor.

'Candle holders—very tasteful. Place mats—a girl can't have too many place mats. What's with the Scent-O-Pine Air Freshener? Oh, that's from Mrs Fryer. She really doesn't like your Kleppy. Hey, His and Her key rings—very useful. Oh, and what's this?'

This was a glasses case. Exceedingly tasteful. Pink and purple, studded with huge diamantés.

'Worth a billion,' Raff said appreciatively. 'Every diamond over a carat, but not a one out of place. Lovely soft mouth, our villain.'

The villain had come to investigate, pushing his way through the crack in the bedroom door, nosing his way to the crime scene. Checking out the glasses case. Putting his paw on it, then looking back to Abby and wagging his tail.

'Don't say a thing, Klep,' Abby said. 'No admissions.'

'His DNA's all over it.'

'He put it on just now. He's as horrified as I am. And you… you've let the suspect himself contaminate the crime scene. I'm appalled.'

He grinned and rubbed Kleppy under the ear and Kleppy wriggled his tail, lifted the glasses case delicately from his hand and headed back into the bedroom. Straight under the duvet with the rest of his loot.

Raff looked through to the bedroom, thoughtful. 'Maybe I should search in there, too.'

'Don't you dare,' she said, suddenly panicking, and he straightened and his smile faded.

'I won't. You okay?'

'I'll live.'

'You have a hard few days ahead. I hope your millionaire's going to take care of you.'

'Raff…'

'Mmm?' He was watching her. Just…watching. The laughter had gone now. He was intense and caring and big and male and… and…

'I think I can put Ben behind me,' she said and his face stilled.

'Sorry?'

'I…'

How to say the unsayable? How to get it out? She'd never intended… In a few months, maybe, when the dust had settled… But now? Here?

'I think I might love you,' she whispered and the thought was out there—huge, filling the house with its danger.

Danger? That was what it felt like, she thought. A sword, hanging over her head, threatening to fall.

Falling in love with the bad boy.

'I know…this is dumb.' She was stammering, stupid with confusion. 'It's not the time to say it. I shouldn't… I mean, I don't know whether you want it. I'm not sure even that I want it, but I fell in love with you twenty years ago, Raff Finn, and I can't stop. This week…it's jolted me out of everything. It's made me see… Your craziness broke my heart but it hasn't changed anything. I can't… I can't stop loving you. If I can forgive what happened with Ben, is there a chance for us?'

'For us?' His face was emotionless. Still. Wary?

'Once upon a time we were boyfriend and girlfriend.' She hadn't got this right. She knew it but she didn't know how to get it right. 'I was hoping…'

'We might get together again?'

'Yes.'

'Now you've forgiven me.'

'I…yes. But…'

'There's no chance at all,' he said and suddenly there was no trace of laughter, no trace of gentleness, nothing at all. His voice was rough and cold and harsh. He looked stunned—and, unbelievably, he looked as if she'd just struck him. '*If I can forgive what happened to Ben*… What sort of statement is that?'

'It's what I need to do.'

'What do you mean?' he demanded.

'If I'm to love you. I need to forgive you if I'm to love you. All I'm saying is that I can. All I'm saying is that I think I have.'

Silence. Silence, silence and more silence.

She couldn't bear it. She wanted to dive back under the duvet and hide. Hide from the look on Raff's face.

But there was no escaping that look. There was such pain…

'There's no such thing as forgiveness for Ben,' he said at last, and the harshness was gone. It had been replaced with an emptiness that was even more dreadful. 'If you have to say it… It's still there.'

'Of course it's still there.'

'Of course,' he repeated. 'How can it not? And it always will be.' He took a deep breath. Another.

The silence was killing her.

She had this wrong. She didn't know how. She didn't know what she could do to repair it.

Would it ever be possible to repair it?

'Abby, ten years ago, I was crazily, criminally stupid,' he said at last, speaking slowly, emphasising each word as if it were being dragged out of him. 'I can't think about it without hating myself. But you know what? I've moved on.'

'You've…'

'If I hadn't, then I'd go insane,' he said. 'How do you think I felt? My best friend dead, my sister irreparably injured, and me with no memory of it at all. I was gutted by Ben's death—I still am. To lose such a friend… To inflict such pain on everyone who loved him… And more, every time I look at Sarah I know what I've done. But after ten years…'

Another deep breath. Another silence.

'After ten years, I have it in perspective,' he said. 'I've seen a lot of stupid kids. A lot of appalling accidents. There's always a driver; it's always someone's fault. But in those situations, you know what? There are other things, too. Kids egging other kids on. Being dumb themselves. That night Ben wasn't wearing a seat belt. We had 'em fitted—my gran insisted on it. Sarah wasn't wearing a seat belt, either—she was wearing a cute new dress she knew would crush. None of us should have been up there on that track in the rain. It was totally dumb. Yes, I was driving. Yes, I must have veered to the wrong side of the road and Philip says I was speeding. I've taken that on board. I've convicted myself and I've received my sentence. I've lost Ben as you've lost Ben. I've lost parts of Sarah, and my actions hurt so many, had so many repercussions, they can never be repaired. That's what I live with, Abby, every day of my life, and I'm not adding to it.'

'I don't…I don't know what you mean.'

'If we took this further… Waking up every morning beside a woman who says she forgives me? What sort of sentence it that? This week…okay, I've kissed you and yes, I've wanted you. I've given you a hard time about marrying Philip. And you know what? Last night, when the whispers went round that you'd given back his ring, for one breathtaking moment I thought maybe we could figure out some sort of future. But now… You forgive me? Graciously? Lovingly? Thanks, but no thanks. I can't live with that, Abby. You do what you need to do, but don't factor me in. Fetch Mrs Fryer's glasses case, please. I need to go.'

'Raff…'

'Don't push this any further,' he snapped. 'Figure it out for yourself. It's your life. I've done what I need to survive and forgiveness doesn't come into it. Acceptance…that's a much harder call.'

She stared up at him, confused. Shattered. Knowing, though…knowing in the back of her mind that he was right.

She forgave him?

Where was a future in that?

Raff returned the glasses case to Mrs Fryer, who took it with suspicion and examined it from all angles for damage. She glared at him and he thought that if it had been his dog that had taken the case, he'd be up on charges by now. Even though the case was worth zip.

Diamonds? He'd seen a diamond that big and he knew what a real one looked like. That diamond was sitting in Philip's security safe by now, he thought. That it wasn't sitting on Abby's finger...

He couldn't afford to go there.

'Did you see her?' Mrs Fryer hissed.

'See who, ma'am?'

'Abigail.'

'I did. She's extremely apologetic. I believe she may come round later and apologise in person.'

'Was there anyone with her?'

'Her dog,' Raff said neutrally and Mrs Fryer sighed in exasperation.

'No, dummy. I mean a man. Is there anyone else?'

'I believe the crime was the dog's own work,' Raff said, and turned and left before Mrs Fryer could slap him.

Anyone else...

No. Only him. She'd tossed Philip's ring back at him because she loved...*him?*

I think I might love you.

The words echoed over and over in his head. Where did a man go with that?

Without thinking, he found himself driving past his little farm, further up the mountain, up near Isaac's place, to the road where one night ten years ago his world had been blasted to bits.

How long did a man suffer for one moment's stupidity?

He'd stopped suffering. Almost. He'd almost found peace. Until Abby had said...

I think I might love you.

He couldn't afford to let her words rip him apart. He had his life to get on with and she had hers.

It might be a good idea if she did go to China.

CHAPTER ELEVEN

ON SUNDAY afternoon Abby decided that she did need to speak to Philip. It was only fair. What followed was a very stilted phone call. Philip sounded appalled and angry and confused. She crept back under her duvet and hugged Kleppy and decided she didn't need milk or bread; she could live on baked beans for a while.

The whole town was judging her.

On Monday she decided she couldn't hide under her duvet for ever. She had to pull herself together. She was not a whimpering mess. She was not hiding a millionaire under her bed. She needed to get on with her life.

That meant getting out of bed, dressing as she always dressed, smart and corporate for the last time. Today she'd wind up this court case with Philip and then she'd resign. She'd talk reasonably to her parents. She'd start sending gifts back and then figure, slowly and sensibly, where she wanted to take her life from here.

She did need to be sensible. She no longer wanted to be a lawyer, but that didn't mean stranding Philip or stranding her clients without reasonable notice. That was the sort of thing an hysterical ex-bride would do—the sort of woman who'd throw Philip over for some crazy, unreasonable love.

She wasn't that woman. She'd ended an unsuitable engagement for totally sensible reasons and she was totally in control. She entered court with her head held high. She sat in court and concentrated on looking…normal.

She was aware that the courthouse held more people than it had on Friday. That'd be because people were looking at her. The woman who ditched Philip Dexter.

No matter. She was in control. Kleppy was safely locked up. She looked neat and respectable, and her court notes were beautifully filed in her lovely Italian briefcase in the order they were needed.

As the morning stretched on, she decided she hated her briefcase. She'd give it back to Philip, she thought. That was sensible. He might find a use for a matching pair.

Back home, her wedding dress was packed in tissue, waiting for someone to make another sensible decision.

What to do with two thousand beads?

Decisions, decisions, decisions.

She concentrated on taking notes for Philip, handing him the papers he needed, keeping on her sensible face—but it was really hard, and when Raff entered the courtroom she thought her face might crack. Quite soon.

Philip had called Raff back on a point of law. Just clarifying the prosecution case. Just decimating the case Raff had put together with such care.

Raff wasn't a lawyer and he had no help. The Crown Prosecutor was hopeless. She wanted to cross the room and shake him, but Malcolm was eighty and he looked like if she shook him his teeth would fall out or he'd die of a coronary.

Wallace Baxter would get off. She could hear it in Philip's voice.

Philip might not have had a very good weekend—yes, his fiancée had jilted him—but there was nothing of the destroyed lover in his bearing. As the morning wore on he started sounding smug.

He was winning.

He sat down beside her after pulling the last of Raff's evidence apart and he gave her a conspiratorial smile.

He didn't mind, she thought incredulously. He didn't mind that she'd thrown back his ring—or not so much that it stopped him enjoying winning.

Her sensible face was slipping.

'This is brilliant,' Wallace hissed beside her. 'Philip's great. The stuff he's done to get me off… But what's this I hear about your engagement being off? You'd be a fool to walk away from a guy this great.'

A guy this great. Wallace was beaming.

She felt sick.

She stared around to the back of the court where Bert and Gwen Mackervale looked close to tears. Because of Wallace Baxter's deception they'd had to sell their house. They were living in their daughter's spare bedroom.

She thought of Lionel, a lovely, gentle man who'd live in a rooming house for ever. Because of Wallace.

And because of Philip's skill in defending him.

She looked at Wallace and Philip and the smile between them was almost conspiratorial. The vague suspicions she'd been having about this case cemented into a tight knot of certainty. *The stuff he's done to get me off…*

She was lawyer for the defence. Sensible defence lawyers did not question their own cases.

She'd stopped being sensible on Saturday afternoon. Or she thought she had. Maybe there was more *sensible* she had to discard.

She looked at Wallace—a guy who'd systematically cheated for all his life. She looked at Philip, smug and sure.

She looked at Raff, who'd lost control of a car one dark night when he was nineteen years old.

Forgive?

'It's nailed,' Philip said. 'Let's see Finn get out of this.'

Finn get out of this?

Wallace, surely.

But she looked at Philip and she knew he hadn't made a mistake. Morality didn't come into it. Raff was on the other side, therefore Raff had to be defeated.

How could she ever have thought she could marry Philip? How could her life have ended up here?

Her head was spinning. Define sensible? Sitting in a Banksia Bay courtroom defending Wallace Baxter?

Wallace and Philip…smug. Winning.

Wallace and Philip… *The stuff he's done to get me off…*

Her thoughts were racing, suspicions surfacing everywhere. She didn't know for sure, but in Philip's briefcase… The briefcase that matched hers…

What was she thinking?

Raff was leaving now, his evidence finished. She could see by the set of his shoulders that he knew exactly what would happen.

He'd done his best for the town—for a town that judged him.

Wallace was smiling. Philip was smiling. There were only a couple of minor defence witnesses to go and then summing up. Unless…unless…

She couldn't bear it.

Philip. Smiling. The model citizen.

Raff. Grim and stoic. The bad boy.

She was a mess of conflicting emotion. She was trying to get things clear but it was like wading into custard. All she knew was that she couldn't stay here a moment longer.

'Excuse me,' she said to the men beside her. 'I need to go.'

'Where?' Philip said, astounded.

'To check on Kleppy. He gets into trouble alone.'

'You can't walk out—to check on a dog.'

'No,' she said. 'Not just to check a dog. Much, much more.'

She rose and the eyes of the court were on her. Too bad. She wasn't sure what she was doing, but there was no way in the world she could sit here any longer.

'Bye,' she said, to the courtroom in general.

'Don't be stupid,' Philip snapped, and she looked at him for a long moment and then she shook her head.

'I won't. Not any more. Bye, Philip.'

She lifted up the glossy Italian briefcase from under the desk, swiftly checking she had the right discreet initials, and she strode out of the court. Her pert black shoes clicked on the floor as she walked, and she didn't look back once.

Raff paused in the entrance, to take a few deep breaths, to think there was no one to punch.

He'd wanted to punch Dexter for maybe ten years. He couldn't. Good cops didn't punch defence lawyers. Dexter was just doing his job.

Another deep breath.

'Raff.'

He turned and Abby was closing the courtroom door. Leaning against it. Closing her eyes.

'Hey,' he said and she opened her eyes and met his gaze. Full on.

'Hey.' She sounded like someone just waking up.

'You taking a break?'

'I need to go home and check Kleppy.'

'Fair enough.' He hesitated. Thought about offering her a ride. Thought that might be a bad idea.

Her sports car was close, in the place marked *Abigail Callahan, Solicitor*. Her spot was closer than the one marked *Police*. It wasn't as close as Dexter's though. Dexter and the Judge had parking spaces side by side.

Dexter's Porsche was the most expensive car in the car park.

Get through the other side of anger, he told himself harshly. Was there another side?

Abby had passed him now, walking into the sunlight to her car. She raised her briefcase to lay it in the passenger seat.

Hesitated.

She lowered her briefcase. Fiddled with the catch.

Raised it again. Tipped.

Papers went everywhere, a sprawl of legal paperwork fluttering in the sunlight. And tapes. A score of tiny audio cassettes.

'Whoops,' she said as tapes went flying.

The Abigail Callahan he'd known for the last ten years would never say *whoops*.

But she didn't look fussed. She didn't move. She didn't begin to pick anything up.

He didn't move either. He wasn't sure what was going on.

'You know, these should probably be picked up,' she said. 'They might be important.'

Might they?

'I'm sorry to trouble you, but I seem to have taken the wrong briefcase,' she said, sounding carefully neutral. 'But I'm in such a hurry… Would you mind putting the stuff back in and returning it to Philip?'

What the…?

'There's no rush,' she continued. 'Philip has his notes on the desk so he won't miss these for a while. Maybe you could go back to the station to sort them into order before you give them back. I'm sure Philip would think that was a kindness.'

She sighed then, looking at the mess of tapes and paperwork. 'This is what comes of having matching briefcases,' she said. 'They're so easy to mix up. I told Philip it was a bad idea—I did want a blue one. But at least I do know this is Philip's—because of the tapes. Philip always records his client appointments. He's a stickler for recording…everything. He always has. My briefcase holds files for submission to court. Philip's files and tapes are always in much more detail.'

They stood staring at each other in the sunlight. Abby…

'The tapes, Raff,' she said gently, and she gave him a wide, impudent smile. It was a smile he hadn't seen for years. It made him feel… It made him feel…

As if Abby was back.

'You'll take care of them?' she asked.

'I…yes.' What else was a man to say?

'Have fun, then,' she said and she climbed into her car. 'I'm sure you will.'

He collected the tapes with speed—something told him it might be important to have them collected and be gone before Dexter realised the mix-up.

He thought about Abby.

He headed back to the station thinking about Abby.

Life was getting…interesting.

Have fun?

He should be thinking about tapes.

He was, but he was also thinking about Abby.

She went home, but only briefly. She changed into jeans, collected Kleppy and headed up the mountain.

She had some hard thinking to do, and it seemed the mountain was the place to do it. For a little bit she thought about Philip's briefcase but by the time she reached the mountain she'd forgotten all about Philip. She'd moved on.

She parked out the front of Isaac's place—the safest place to park. Kleppy whined against the fence and she cuddled him and thought…

Ben was here.

That was why she'd come. Ben had died up here, in the thick bushland on the mountain, a place that had magically been spared logging, where the gums were vast and the scenery was breathtaking. After all these years, suddenly it felt right that she was here with him. Her brother.

For the last ten years Ben had been lost, and she'd been empty.

With Kleppy carefully on the lead—who knew what he'd find here?—she walked along the side of the road where the crash had happened. The smells were driving Kleppy wild. He tugged to the place he'd been digging the night she and Raff had been here, but she pulled him away.

'No wombat holes,' she told him. 'Sorry, Klep, but this trip is about me.'

She reached the foot of the crest. The road was incredibly narrow. The trees were huge—they were so close to the road.

Two cars colliding at speed… They'd never stood a chance.

She thought of that night. Of how they'd been before. Five kids. Fledgling love affairs. The things they'd all done.

Stupid kids, trying their wings. They'd been so sure they could fly. The only unknown was how far.

They'd been kids who thought they were invincible.

One stupid night.

She sank onto the verge at the side of the road and hugged her dog. 'Raff's right,' she whispered, the emotions of the past two days kaleidoscoping and merging into one clear vision. 'To forgive… That means he was wrong; the rest of us were right. That's how we've acted and that's what he's worn. He's accepted total blame.'

How hard must that have been?

A truck was approaching, slowly, a rattler. It came over the crest and slowed and stopped.

Lionel. Climbing out. Looking worried. 'Are you okay?' he asked.

Then he saw Kleppy and Kleppy saw him. It was hard to say who was most delighted and it took a while before Lionel finally told her why he was here.

'I keep coming up hoping she's left the gate open,' Lionel told her. 'Mr Isaac's daughter. She's locked the place and I can't water the spuds. We were growing blue ones this year, just to see what they're like.'

'It's a lovely garden.'

'It was a lovely garden,' he said, sad again, and he gave Kleppy a final hug and rose. 'The gate's still shut?'

'Yes.'

'I'd better slope off then,' he said sadly. 'Back to the golf course.' He sighed and glanced towards the garden. 'You gotta put stuff behind you. I'll be good at growing grass.'

'You will, too.'

'I might go out to see Sarah some time,' he said diffidently. 'You be out there, too?'

'I…probably not. I'm not sure.'

'You're Sarah's friend?'

'I am.'

'And the copper's friend? Raff?'

'I hope so.'

'He's good,' Lionel said. 'When I wanted to keep Kleppy he came to see my landlady; told her how much I wanted him. Didn't make any difference but he tried. I reckon a man like that's a friend.'

'He…he is.'

'And I bet he's pleased Kleppy's found you,' Lionel said, and he hugged Kleppy one last time and headed off back to his golf course.

She sat on the verge with her dog for a while longer. Letting her thoughts go where they willed.

She fiddled with the medal on Kleppy's collar. Thought about Lionel. Thought about Isaac.

Isaac Abrahams was a brave man, she thought. He'd been through so much—and he'd gone through more for his dog.

And Raff?

He'd faced condemnation from this community from the time he was a kid, and after Ben's death it had been overwhelming. He'd been based in Sydney at the Police Training College when the accident happened. All he'd needed to do to escape censure was move Sarah into a Sydney apartment and never come back.

He'd come back and faced condemnation because this was the place Sarah loved.

What you did for love…

She hugged her dog and looked at his collar and thought about what brave meant.

And what forgiveness was.

Tears were slipping down her cheeks now and she didn't care. These tears should have been cried out years ago, only she'd shut them out, shut herself down, turned into someone who couldn't face pain.

Turned into someone she didn't like.

Could Raff like her?

In time. Maybe. If she changed and waited for a while.

But then she thought about the expression on his face as she'd told him.

If I can forgive what happened with Ben…

How could she have said it? How could she be so hurtful?

Kleppy whined and squirmed and she hugged him tighter than he approved. She let him loose a little and he licked her from throat to chin. She chuckled.

'Oh, Kleppy, I love you.'

Love.

The word hung out there, four letters, a concept huge in what it meant.

Love.

She whispered it again, trying it out for size. Thinking of all its implications.

Love.

'I love Raff,' she told Kleppy, and Kleppy tried the tongue thing again.

'No.' She set him down and rose, staring along the track where Ben had died. 'I love you, Kleppy, but I love Raff more. Ben, I love Raff.'

Was it stupid to talk to a brother who'd been dead for ten years? Who knew, and it was probably her imagination that a breeze rustled through the trees right then, a soft, embracing breeze that warmed her, that told her it was okay, that told her to follow her heart.

'Just as well,' she told her big brother in a tone she hadn't used for ten years. 'You always were bossy but you can't boss me out of this one. I love Rafferty Finn. I love Banksia Bay's bad boy, and there's nothing you or anyone else can do to change my mind.'

CHAPTER TWELVE

THE sight of Wallace Baxter's face as the Crown Prosecutor asked a seemingly insignificant question about a bank account in the Seychelles was priceless.

As Crown Prosecutor, Malcolm might be too tired to do hard research, but when something was handed to him on a plate he shed twenty years in twenty seconds. Raff slipped him a question with a matching document, and suddenly Malcolm was the incisive legal machine he'd once been.

Wallace Baxter was heading for jail. The people he'd ripped off might even be headed for compensation.

And there'd be more, Raff thought with grim satisfaction. Raff had spent half an hour with Keith, poring through documents, listening to snatches of conversation, before Raff found the Seychelles document and they knew they had enough to pin Baxter.

They also suspected this was the tip of an iceberg. Philip's tapes might have been intended for blackmail, or maybe they were simply a product of an obsessive mind, but they covered this case only, and there'd been murky cases in the past. By the time Philip finished in court there'd be forensic investigators on his doorstep, Raff thought with satisfaction. With search warrants.

Keith, though, was in charge at that end. He was calling for backup. Raff's role was to return to court, focusing on this case only. So he listened to Malcolm ask his question and wave bank statements. He saw the moment Philip realised Abby had taken the wrong briefcase, and he watched his face turn ashen.

What had Philip been thinking, to record everything? Who knew? All he knew was that he was very, very pleased Abby was no longer marrying him.

He wanted to find her, but that was stupid. Wanting Abby had been stupid last night and it was stupid now.

He could leave the case to Malcolm now. He left. He should go back to help Keith—but he didn't. Instead, he stopped at the baker's to buy lamingtons. Sarah's favourite. They'd sit in the sun and eat them, he thought. He needed to settle.

But when he got home he remembered Sarah was at the sheltered workshop on Mondays. What was he thinking, to forget that?

Maybe he'd been thinking about why he couldn't go find Abby.

Stupid, stupid, stupid.

Should he go back and help Keith?

Keith would do just fine without him—and for some reason he didn't want to see the grubby details of Philip's profit-making. He didn't want to think about Philip.

Instead, he turned his attention to the garden. There was plenty here that needed doing. His grandmother would break her heart if she could see how he'd let it run down.

This was a gorgeous old house, but huge. There were four bedrooms in the main house and there was another smaller house at the rear where he and Sarah had lived with their mother before her death, to give them some measure of independence.

Sarah would like to live there now. She hankered for independence but she couldn't quite manage. She loved it here, though. To move away…

He couldn't, even if it meant spending his spare time mending and mowing and tending animals and feeling guilty because his grandmother's garden was now mostly grass.

And he was too close to Abby.

Do not go there, he told himself. He started tugging weeds, but then…

The sound of a car approaching tugged him out of his introspection.

Abby.

The car door opened and Kleppy flew to greet him as if he was his long lost friend, missing at sea for years, feared dead, miraculously restored to life. This was the new, renewed Kleppy, sure again of his importance in the world, greeting friends as they ought to be greeted.

He grinned and scratched Kleppy's stomach as he rolled, and Kleppy moaned and wriggled and moaned some more.

'I wish someone was that pleased to see me,' Abby said.

She was right by her car. She was smiling.

He couldn't roll on his back and wriggle but the feeling was similar.

She'd been crying. He could see it. He wanted…he wanted…

To back off. What she'd said… *If I can forgive what happened with Ben*… He'd gone over it in his mind a hundred times and he couldn't get away from it.

He could not afford to love this woman.

'I came to apologise,' she said.

He stilled. Thought about it. Thought where it might be going and thought a man would be wise to be cautious.

'Why would you want to apologise?' He rose. Kleppy gave a yelp of indignation. He grinned and scooped Kleppy up with him. Got his face licked. Didn't mind.

Abby was apologising?

'The forgiveness thing,' she said, and he could see it was an effort to make her voice steady. 'I didn't get it.'

'And now you do?'

She was standing beside her little red sports car and she wasn't moving. He didn't move either. He held her dog and he didn't go near.

Neutral territory between them. A chasm…

'I've…changed,' she said.

He nodded, still cautious. 'You got rid of the diamond. That's got to be a start.'

'It wasn't the diamond. It was Kleppy. One dog and my life turns upside down.'

'He hasn't ended you in jail.'

'Not yet.'

'How much did you know about what was in Dexter's briefcase?'

'Was there anything?' She couldn't disguise the eagerness. She didn't know, he thought with a rush of relief, though he'd already felt it. The Abby he once knew could never have collaborated with dishonesty. She hadn't changed so much.

Maybe she hadn't changed very much at all. This was the Abby he once knew, right here.

'There's enough to convict Baxter,' he said mildly—there was no need to go into the rest of it yet—and he watched the rush of relief.

'I'm so glad.'

'So are a lot of people. Me included. Is that why you're here? To find out?'

'No. I told you. I came to say sorry.'

Sorry. What did that mean?

He couldn't help her. He knew she was struggling, but she had to figure for herself where she was going.

Abby.

He wanted to walk towards her and gather her up and claim her, right now. He ached to kiss away the tracks of those tears.

But he had to wait, to see if the figuring would come out on his side.

'Kleppy and I have been up at Isaac's,' she said. 'We've been sitting on the road where Ben was killed.'

'Mmm.' Nothing more was possible.

'We were all dumb that night.'

'We were.' Still he was neutral. He was having trouble getting a breath here. Abby took a deep breath for him.

'Sarah and I were seventeen. You and Ben and Philip were

nineteen. I'd made my debut with Philip and you were mad at me. Sarah was mad at you, so she accepted a date with Philip to make you madder still. Ben was fed up with all of us—I think he wanted to go out with Sarah so he was fuming. Then the car… The rain… It would have been far more sensible to wait till the next weekend but Ben had to go back to uni so he was aching to try the car.'

'Abby…'

'Let me say it,' she said. 'I'm still trying to figure this out for myself so let me say it as I see it now.'

'Okay.' What else was a man to say?

'My dad came up here that afternoon and he was angry with Ben for spending the weekend here and not sitting in our living room giving Mum and Dad a minute by minute description of life at uni. So Dad didn't take any interest. He should have said, *Don't try the car until next weekend.* Or even offered to go with you and watch. And Sarah… I remember her trying on the dress I'd just finished making for her, and your gran saying, "Don't you crush that dress, Sarah, after all the time I spent ironing it." And I was home, fed up with the lot of you.'

'So…'

'So it was all just…there,' she said. 'Pressure on you to drive on a night that wasn't safe. Excitement. Knowledge that no one used that track except loggers and no loggers worked over the weekend. Stupid kids and unsafe decisions and a slippery road, and pure bad luck. Sarah not wanting to crush her dress. Ben being too macho to wear a seat belt. Philip wanting to show off his car, his girlfriend. You weren't charged with culpable driving, Raff, and there was a reason. My parents took their grief out in anger. Their anger soured…lots of things. It enveloped me and I've been too much of a wuss to fight my way out the other side.'

'And now you have?' It was a hard question to ask. It was a hard question to wait for an answer.

But it seemed she had an answer ready. 'You kissed me,' she said simply. 'And it made me realise that I want you. I always have. That want, that need, got all mixed up, buried, subsumed by grief, by shock, by obligation. I've been a king-sized dope, Raff. It took one crazy dog to shake me out of it.'

The dog in question was passive now, shrugged against Raff's chest. Raff set him down with care. It seemed suddenly important to have his arms free. 'So you're saying…'

'I'm saying I love you,' she said, steadily and surely. 'I know it seems fast. We've been apart for ten years so maybe I should gradually show you I've changed. But you know what? I can't wait. I've messed the last ten years up. Do I need to mess any more?'

He didn't move. He didn't let himself move. Not yet. There were things that needed to be said.

'Your parents hate me,' he said at last, because it was important. Hate always was.

'They have a choice,' she said steadily now, and certain. Her eyes not leaving his. 'They can accept the man I love or not. It's up to them but it won't stop me loving you. I'll try and explain but if they won't listen…' She took a deep breath. 'I can't live with hate any more, Raff, or with grief. I can't live under the shadow of a ten-year-old tragedy. You and me…' She gazed round the disreputable farmyard. 'You and me, and Sarah…'

And Sarah? She was going there?

She'd accept Sarah. He knew she would.

He could never leave Sarah. That fact had coloured every relationship he'd had since the accident, but this was the old Abby emerging, and it was no longer an issue. This was the Abby who held to her friendships no matter what, who'd never stopped loving Sarah, the Abby with a heart so big…

So big she could ignore her parents' hatred?

So big she could take on the Finn boy?

And then he paused. Another vehicle was approaching, travelling fast. Its speed gave it a sense of urgency and he and Abby paused and waited.

It was a silver Porsche.

Philip.

* * *

For ten years Abby had never seen Philip angry. She'd seen him irritated, frustrated, condescending. She'd always felt there was an edge of anger held back but she'd never seen it.

She was seeing it now. His car skidded to a halt in a spray of gravel, and the hens clucking round the yard squawked and flew for cover. Kleppy dived behind her legs and stayed there.

Philip didn't notice the hens or Kleppy. He was out of the car, crashing the door closed, staring at her as if she were an alien species.

Raff was suddenly beside her. Taking her hand in his. Holding her against him.

Uh-oh.

She should pull away. Holding hands with Raff would inflame the situation.

She tugged but Raff didn't let her go. Instead, he tugged her tighter. His body language was unmistakable. *My woman, Dexter. Threaten her at your peril.*

How had it come to this?

'So that's it,' Philip snarled, staring at the pair of them as if they'd crawled from under Raff's pile of weeds. 'You slut.'

'It's not polite to call a lady a slut,' Raff said and his body shifted imperceptibly between them. 'You want to take a cold shower and come back when you're cooler?'

'You sabotaged the case,' Philip said incredulously, ignoring Raff. 'The bank accounts... Suddenly you leave, and my briefcase's gone and in comes Finn and the Prosecutor has a whole list of new evidence. *You gave it to Finn.*'

'Baxter's a maw-worm,' Abby said, trying to shove Raff aside so she could face him. This was her business, not Raff's. 'I didn't know there was anything in your briefcase to convict him, but if there was we shouldn't have been defending him.'

'It's what we do. Do you know how much his fee was?'

'We can afford to lose it.'

'You might.' He was practically apoplectic, and she knew why. She'd had the temerity to get between him and his money. Philip and his reputation. Philip and his carefully planned life.

'So what about this?' He hauled the diamond out of his top pocket and thrust it towards her, but he was holding it tight at the same time. 'Do you know how much this cost? Do you know how much I've done for you?'

'You've been…' How to say he'd been wonderful? He had, but right now it didn't seem like it.

'I've sacrificed everything,' he yelled. 'Everything. Do you think I wanted to practice in a dump like Banksia Bay? Do you know how much money I could have earned if I'd stayed in Sydney? But here I am, doing the books of the Banksia Bay yacht club, stuck here, seeing the same people over and over, even mowing your parents' lawn.'

'I could never figure out why you offered to do that,' she whispered, but he wasn't listening.

'I've done everything, and you throw it all away. For this?' His tone was incredulous. He was staring at Raff as if he were pond scum. 'A Finn.'

'There's some pretty nice Finns,' she said mildly and Raff grinned and tugged her a little closer. Just a little, but Philip noticed.

'You'd leave me for this…this…'

'For Raff,' she said and she gazed steadily at Philip and she even found it in her to feel sorry for him. 'I'm sorry, Philip, but I'm not who you think I am. I've tried…really hard…to be what everyone wants me to be, but I've figured it out. I'm not that person. I'm Abby and I love bright clothes and sleeping in on Sunday and I hate business dinners and I don't like spending my whole life in legal chambers. I like dogs and…'

'Dogs,' Philip snarled. The new, brave Kleppy with his brave new life had emerged from behind Abby's legs and was nosing round Philip's feet, checking him out for smells. Philip looked down at him with loathing. 'That's what this is about. A dog.'

'I know you don't like dogs,' Abby said. 'It was generous of you to say you'd take him…'

'Generous?' He gave a laugh that made her wince. 'Yeah.

I'd even put up with *that*.' The word made her know exactly what he thought of Kleppy.

'Because you love me?' she asked in a small voice and Raff's hand tightened around hers.

'Love.' Philip was staring at her as if she'd lost her mind. 'What's love got to do with it?'

'I…everything.'

'You have no clue. Not one single clue. Enough. You and your parents have messed with my life for ten years. That's it. I've paid a thousandfold. I'm out of here, and if I never see this place again I'll be delighted.'

He turned away, fast, only Kleppy was in the way. He tripped and almost fell. Kleppy yelped.

Philip regained his feet but Kleppy was still between him and his car. And suddenly…

'No,' Raff snapped, but it was too late. They were both too late.

Philip's foot swung back and he kicked. All the frustration and rage of the last two days was in that kick and Kleppy copped it all.

The little dog flew about eight feet, squealing in pain and shock.

'Kleppy!' Abby screamed and ran for him, but Philip moved, too, heading for another kick. Abby launched herself at him, throwing herself down between boot and dog.

Philip grabbed her by the hair and hauled her back… And then suddenly he wasn't there any more. Raff's body was between hers and Philip's. Raff's fist came into contact with Philip—she didn't know where; she couldn't see—but she heard a sickening thud, she saw Philip lurch backwards, stumble, and she saw Raff follow him down.

He had him on the ground, on his stomach, his arm twisted up behind his back, and Philip was screaming…

'Lie still or I'll really hurt you,' Raff said in a voice she didn't recognise. 'Abby, the dog…'

She turned back to Kleppy but Kleppy was no longer there.

He'd backed away in terror. Whining. Horrified, she saw him bolt under the fence and into the undergrowth beyond.

He was yelping in pain and fear and he ran until he was out of sight.

She couldn't catch him. Beyond Raff's fence was Black Mountain. Wilderness.

'Kleppy,' she yelled uselessly into the bushland, but he was gone.

She turned and stared back at Philip with loathing and distress. 'You kicked him.'

'He's a stray.'

'He's mine. I can't believe...' She gulped and turned back to the fence, knowing to try and follow the little dog into the bush would be futile.

'He was running,' Raff said. He was hauling Philip to his feet, none too gentle. 'If he's running, he can't be too badly injured.'

'More's the pity,' Philip snarled, and Raff wrenched him over to the Porsche with a ruthlessness Abby had never seen before. He shoved him into his driver's seat like she'd seen cops put villains into squad cars, only this was Philip's car and he was sending him away.

Or not. Before Philip could guess what he intended, Raff grabbed the keys to Philip's car and tossed them as far as he could, out into the bush.

'You've lost your keys,' he said conversationally. 'Abby, get the handcuffs. They're in the compartment on the passenger side of the patrol car.'

'What...?' she said, and Raff sighed.

'You want to hold your fiancé or get the cuffs.'

'He's not my fiancé.' It seemed important.

'Sorry,' he said. 'Get the cuffs, Abby.' Then, as she glanced despairingly at the fence, he softened. 'Cuffs first. Kleppy second. Move.'

She moved and thirty seconds later Philip was cuffed to his own steering wheel.

'You can't do this,' he snarled.

'Watch me,' Raff said. Then he lifted his radio. 'Keith? You know we were getting a search warrant for Dexter, thinking it might be better to do it when he wasn't home? I have another suggestion. You come up to my place and pick him up. He's cuffed to the car in the driveway. He kicked a dog, pulled Abby's hair. Take him to the station, charge him with aggravated cruelty to animals, plus assault. I'll be there with details when I can but meanwhile he stays in the cells. The paperwork could take quite some time.'

'You…'

'Talk among yourself, Dexter,' he said. 'Abby and I have things to do. Dogs to rescue. And if I find he's badly hurt…' His look said it all. 'Come on, Abby, let's go. He'll be headed for Isaac's and I hope for all our sakes we find him.'

They drove in silence. There was so much to say. On top of her fear for Kleppy, there was so much to think about. Philip's invective…

Philip's words.

I've paid a thousandfold. It was a statement that made her foundations shift from under her.

She cast a look at Raff and his face was set and grim. Had he heard? Was he thinking about it?

Philip… But her thoughts kaleidoscoped back to Kleppy.

'He can't be too badly hurt.'

'No,' Raff said. 'He can't be. He's a dog who's given me my life back. I owe him more than putting Dexter behind bars.'

Where? Where?

They reached Isaac's place and it was fenced and padlocked as it had been fenced and padlocked since Isaac's death.

All the way up the mountain she'd held her breath, hoping Kleppy would be standing at the gate, his nose pressed against the wire. He wasn't.

She called. They both called.

No Kleppy.

'We've come fast on the track,' Raff said. 'Kleppy's having to manage undergrowth.'

'He could be lost.'

'Not Kleppy. Our farm is on his route down to town from here, his route to his source of stolen goods. He'll know every inch.'

'If he's hurt he could creep into the undergrowth and...'

Raff tugged her tight and held her close. 'He was running,' he said. 'If he's not here in ten minutes I'll start bush bashing.' He tugged her tighter still and kissed her, hard and fast. Enormously comforting. Enormously...right. 'If we don't have him in an hour I'll organise a posse,' he said. 'We'll have an army of volunteers up here before nightfall.'

'For Kleppy?'

'We have two things going for us,' Raff said, and his smile was designed to reassure. 'First, Kleppy's one of Henrietta's dogs. She hates having them put down. She's over the moon that you're taking him, and she has a team of volunteers she'll have searching in a heartbeat. Second, if I happen to mention to about half this town that if we find an injured dog we'll put Dexter behind bars... How many raised hands do you reckon we'd get?'

'Is he that bad?' she said in a small voice.

'You know he is.'

She did know it. The thought made her feel...appalled.

What had she been thinking, to drift towards marriage? She'd been in a bad dream that had lasted for years. Of all the stupid...

'Don't kick yourself,' Raff said. 'We all have dumb youthful romances.'

She tried to laugh. She couldn't. A youthful romance that lasted for ten years?

'I seem to remember I did have a youthful romance.'

'Yeah,' he said. They were walking the perimeter now, checking. 'I should have come home and been your partner at the deb ball.'

She did choke on that one. Her debutante ball. The source of all the trouble.

She'd been seventeen years old. A girl had to have a really cool partner for that.

Raff had been in Sydney. She'd been annoyed that he couldn't drive home twice a week to practice, two hours here, two hours back, just to be her partner. Of all the selfish…

'Don't kick yourself,' he said again. 'Dexter does the kicking. Not us.'

'But why?' It was practically a wail. Why?

She'd always assumed Philip loved her. He'd given up Sydney, he'd come home, he'd been the devoted boyfriend, the devoted fiancé for ten years.

Why, if he didn't love her?

'Let's walk down to the road,' Raff said, taking her hand. He held her close, not letting her go for a moment as they walked down the driveway to the gravel road where their world had turned upside down ten years ago.

'Kleppy?' she yelled and then paused. 'Did you hear?'

'Call again.'

She did and there was no mistaking it. A tiny yelp, and then the sound of scuffling.

She was off the road and into the bush, with Raff close behind. Through the undergrowth. Pushing through…

And there he was. Kleppy.

Digging.

Philip's kick had hit his side. She could see grazed skin and blood on his wiry coat.

He looked up from where he'd been digging and wagged his tail and she came close to bursting into tears.

'Klep…'

But he was back digging, dirt going in all directions. His whole body was practically disappearing into the hole he was creating.

'You don't need a wombat,' she told him, feeling almost ill with relief. She reached him and knelt, not caring about the spray of dirt that showered her. 'Klep…'

He tugged back from inside his hole. He had something. He was trying to hold it in his mouth and front paws, tugging it up as he tried to find purchase with his back legs.

She didn't care if it was a dead wombat, buried for years. She gathered him into her arms, mindful of his injured side, and lifted him from the hole.

He snuffled against her, a grubby, bleeding rapscallion of a dog, quivering with delight that she'd found him and, better still, he had something to give her. He wiggled around in her arms and dropped his treasure onto the ground in front of her.

Raff was with her then, ruffling Kleppy's head, smiling his gorgeous, loving smile that made her heart twist inside. How could she have ever walked away from this man for Philip? Like Kleppy's buried treasure, his smile had been waiting for her to rediscover it.

She had rediscovered it.

She wasn't going to marry Philip. Raff was smiling at her. The thought made her feel giddy with happiness.

'Hey,' Raff said in a voice that was none too steady and he gathered them both into his arms. He held them, just held them. His woman, with dog in between.

Happiness was right now.

But there was only so much happiness a small dog could submit to. He submitted for a whole minute before wriggling his nose free and then the rest of him. He started barking, indignation personified, because Abby hadn't taken any interest in his treasure.

Too bad. Raff was kissing her. She had treasure of her own to be finding.

But Kleppy was nothing if not insistent. He was hauling his loot up onto her knees. It was a dirt-covered box, a little damaged at one corner, but not much. It was pencil-box sized, or maybe a little bigger.

She took it and brushed the worst of the dirt off—and then she stilled.

This box.

Philip's box.

No. Philip's grandfather's box. He made boxes like this for all his relations, for all his friends.

This one, though… The shape…

Slowly now, with a lot more care, she dusted the thing off. It was almost totally intact. Cedar did that. It lasted for generations. Something had nibbled at the corner but had given up in disgust.

Cedar was pretty much bug-proof. Obviously it tasted bad. Except to Kleppy.

It would have been the smell, she thought, the distinctive scent, showing him that something was buried here, something like the box he loved back at her place.

'What is it?' Raff was watching her face, figuring this was important.

'I'm not sure,' she said, hardly daring to breathe. A box. Made by Philip's grandfather. Buried not fifty yards from where Ben had been killed.

A box she might just know.

Her fingers were suddenly trembling. Raff took the box from her. 'A bomb?' There was the beginning of a smile in his voice.

'No,' she whispered and then thought about it. 'Maybe.'

'You want me to open it?'

'I think we must.'

There were four brass clips holding it sealed. Raff flicked open each clip in turn.

He opened the box, but she knew before she saw it what its contents would be. And she was right. She'd seen it before. It held cassette tapes, filed neatly, slotted against each other in the ridged sections of Huon pine that Philip's grandpa had carved with such skill.

She didn't need to take them out to know what they were. Music tapes, with a couple of blank ones at the back.

There was an odd one. Not slotted into place. The ribbon had been ripped from its base and the tape looked as if it had been tossed into the box in a hurry. It wasn't labelled.

Her mind was in overdrive.

What do you do when you're panicking?

You grab the tape from the player, rip the ribbon out, throw it into the box with the others that might point to the fact that this tape might exist, and then you head into the bush. You bury it fast, deep in the undergrowth.

And then you come back to the car and you face the fact that a friend is dead and two others injured...

Even if you tried to find it later, you might not. It'd take Kleppy's sense of smell...

But why?

'I'm guessing what this might be,' she said bleakly, and she knew she had to take this further. She was feeling sick. 'Do you think we could still play it?'

'It looks like it's just a matter of reattaching the ribbon. Is it important?'

'I think it might be.'

CHAPTER THIRTEEN

THEY took Kleppy to the vet and Fred declared he'd live. While he did, Raff made a quick call to Keith.

'Dexter's nicely locked up and he's staying that way,' Keith said. 'I have a team organised to swarm through his files. You look after Abby.'

'How did he know you and I...?' Abby said and Raff grinned and shook his head.

'Banksia Bay. Don't ask.'

With his wound cleaned and dressed, they took Kleppy back to Raff's. An hour later, a hearty meal demolished, Kleppy was watching television with Sarah. Lionel was with them. He'd just sort of turned up.

'Heard Kleppy got kicked,' he muttered, and Abby thought, *How does this town do it?*

Abby and Raff were in the back room, standing over Gran's ancient tape player. Waiting for a repaired cassette to start.

Abby felt sick.

Raff was curious. Worried. Watching her. She hadn't told him what to expect. It might not be anything.

But why was it buried there if it wasn't anything?

And as soon as it started she knew she was right, at least in thinking she knew what it was.

She'd watched Philip over the years as he'd recorded his client discussions—'in case I miss something'. She'd attributed it to his meticulous preparation.

She'd believed him, all those years ago when she'd found

the Christabelle tape. She'd used it as a reason to break up with him, but had hardly thought any more of it. But in the box buried by the roadside where Ben died…there was more evidence.

Maybe Philip taped all his girlfriends.

For this was Sarah, ten years younger but still unmistakably herself. Young and excited and a little bit nervous.

It had been set to record as soon as Philip picked her up, and they knew immediately it was the night of the crash. They listened to Sarah asking if they could go up the mountain and see if the boys had their car going.

'Sure.' Philip was amenable. 'I wouldn't count on it going, though. Let's show 'em what a real car can do. You like my wheels?'

'Your car's great.' But even from the distance of ten years they could hear Sarah's increasing nervousness, from almost as soon as they started driving. 'Philip, slow down. These curves are dangerous.'

'I can handle them. It's Raff and Ben who should worry. They can hardly drive.'

More talk. Sarah asked if he liked her dress. Even then, Philip wasn't into bright dresses.

'Not so much. Why'd it have to be red?'

A terse response. Sarah sounded peeved.

'Movies afterwards?' Philip asked.

'I'm not sure. If you don't like my dress sense…'

'There's no need to be touchy.'

Silence. An offended huff? Then Sarah again…

'Phil, be careful. That was a wallaby.'

'It's fine. Wallabies are practically plague round here, anyway. Why are they using the fire track?'

'They can't go on the roads. Their car isn't registered.'

'That hunk of junk'll never get registered. Not like this baby. Watch it go.'

'Philip, no. Slow down. You're scaring me. There'll be more wallabies—it's getting dark.'

'There's nothing to be scared of. You reckon they're on this track?'

'Philip… Philip, no. You nearly hit it…' And then… 'You're on the wrong side of the…'

'There's ruts on the other side. No one uses this.'

'But it's a crest.' Her voice rose. 'Philip, it's a crest. No…'

Then…awfulness.

Then nothing. Nothing, nothing and nothing.

The tape spun on into silence.

Dear God…

Raff changed colour. Held onto the back of the nearest chair.

She moved then, closing the distance between them in a heartbeat, linking her arms around his chest and tugging him to her. She held him and held him and held him. She'd had some inkling, the moment she'd seen the buried box. But Raff… This was a lightning bolt.

Raff…

He'd been her hero since she was eight years old. He was her wonderful Raff.

Her love.

'I didn't…' he said, and it was as if he was waking from a nightmare. 'I believed Philip. He said I was on the wrong side.'

'That's why there was never a court case,' she whispered. 'The storm hit just as the crash happened. There was only Philip's word.'

They'd believed him. They'd all believed him. It had been so hard—so unthinkable—to do anything else.

She saw it all.

Philip's stupidity had killed Ben; had desperately injured Sarah. He couldn't admit it, but what followed…

Some part of Philip was still decent. He was a kid raised in Banksia Bay, and he'd been their friend in childhood. His parents were friends with her parents. They'd loved Ben to bits.

He'd have been truly appalled.

So a part of him had obviously decided to do the 'right

thing', and in his eyes he had. He'd come back here to practice law, playing the son to her parents, devoting himself to Banksia Bay as Ben would have.

'He's been making amends for Ben,' she said, and she was trying hard to hold back the anger. Raff didn't need her anger now. He just needed...her? 'He came back and tried to make amends to us all.'

And then, despite what she'd intended, anger hit, a wave so great it threatened to overwhelm her. 'No. Not to us all. He tried to make amends to me and to my parents. He would have married me, as if that somehow made up for Ben's life. But to you... For ten years he's let you think you were responsible. For ten years he's let you hold the blame.'

Tears were coursing down her cheeks now. She'd thought she was comforting Raff but her rage was so great there was no comfort she could give. If Philip walked in the door right now...

'I'll tear his heart out,' she stammered. 'If he has a heart. I can't bear it. He's lost you years.'

'No.'

Raff put her back from him then, holding her hard by each shoulder. He'd regained his colour and, unbelievably, he was smiling. 'I believe you told me you loved me before you found this tape.'

'Yes, but...'

'Then it's Philip who's lost the ten years. I've faced it and come out the other side.' He took a deep breath. 'Whew. This takes some getting used to.'

'We can tell the world. Oh, Raff... I can't bear anyone thinking a moment longer that you...'

'That I was dumb as a teenager? I *was* dumb,' he said gently. 'I shouldn't have been up there that night. None of us should. I believe I might even cut Philip slack on this one.'

'No!'

'He's lost you,' Raff said and he tugged her against him and let his chin rest on her hair. 'Winner takes all. That'd be me. And I need to think things through before I do anything rash—like spreading this far and wide.'

She stared at him as if he were out of his mind. 'Why on earth…?'

'You know, my reputation does no end of good for my street cred,' he said, thoughtful now. 'How many local kids know the local cop was dumb and someone died because of it? You get experts lecturing kids on speed and they shrug it off. They see how Mrs Fryer treats me? For a cop, that's gold. I reckon it's even saved lives.'

'Raff…'

'Don't think it's not important,' he said, laughter fading. He was holding her at arm's length and meeting her gaze with gravity and truth. 'To look at Sarah now and know I wasn't responsible for her pain… To look at you and know it wasn't me who hurt you… I can't tell you what that means. But Philip has some pretty heavy stuff coming to him anyway. I can cope without my own pound of flesh. Believe me, I can cope.

'All I need I have right here. This tape is a great gift, Abby, but the greatest gift of all is you.'

He tugged her to him then, and he held her, close enough so their heartbeats merged. She was dissolving into him, she thought. She loved this man with all her heart. No matter what he decided to do about this tape, they could go forward from this moment.

'Marry me,' he said and the world stood still.

'Marry?' She could barely get the word out.

'I hear on the grapevine you have a perfectly good wedding dress. I'm a man who hates waste.'

'Raff…'

'Don't quibble,' he said sternly. 'Just say yes.'

'You're in shock. You're emotional. You need time to think.'

He put her away from him again. Held her at arm's length. Smiled.

'I've thought,' he said. 'Marry me.'

'Okay.'

* * *

Okay? As an acceptance of a marriage proposal it lacked a certain finesse but it was a great start. For a lawyer. He found himself laughing, a great explosion of happiness that came from so far within he'd never known that place existed. He lifted her up in his arms and whirled her round as if she weighed nothing.

She did weigh nothing. She was part of him—his Abby, his love.

His...wife?

He set her down, laughter fading. Joy was taking its place, a joy so great he felt he was shedding an old skin and bursting into something new.

She tilted her chin and he kissed her, so slowly, so thoroughly satisfactorily, that words weren't possible. Words weren't needed for a very long time.

She held him tight, she kissed him and she placed her future in his hands. She loved him so much she felt her heart could burst.

He was Banksia Bay's bad boy no longer. He was just... Raff.

If he insisted, then maybe she wouldn't tell the town about Philip, she conceded—but she would tell her parents. And she would tell Philip that she knew. And then... This was Banksia Bay. If things got around... Things always got around.

But right now it was becoming incredibly hard to care. All she cared about was that Raff was holding her as if he'd never let her go. He was kissing her as he'd kissed her when she was sixteen, only more so. A lot more so. He was grown into her man. He was her love, for ever and ever.

'I can't believe this is happening,' he said at last in a voice that was changed, different. It was the voice of a man who was walking into a future he'd never dreamed of. 'Abby, are you sure?' And then he hesitated. 'I do need to care for Sarah.' There was sudden doubt.

'I believe there's room enough here for all of us,' she said, deeply contented. She pulled back enough to peep through to the next room, where Lionel and Sarah were watching television. They were covered in three dogs, two cats and a vast bowl of popcorn. They were looking…self-conscious. On closer inspection… They were holding hands.

'There must be something in the water,' she said and grinned, and Raff tugged her close again, smiling wide enough to make her dissolve in the happiness of his smile.

'So you'd take us all on? This place. And Sarah's dogs and guinea pigs and hens and ponies and…'

'And whoever else comes along,' she said, and chuckled at the look on his face.

He caught his breath. 'You'd…'

'I think I would,' she said, a bubble of joy rising so fast it was threatening to overwhelm her. 'It might be fun.'

'You're talking babies,' he said, feeling his way.

'I believe I am. You know,' she said thoughtfully, 'if we sold my place we could even do up your other house as well as this one.'

He took a deep breath. Looked through to the sitting room. Saw what she was seeing. Sarah and Lionel…

'We might just have found ourselves a gardener,' Abby said, smiling and smiling.

Enough. This was going so fast he was being left behind. A man had to take a stand some time, so he took his stand right there. Right then. A simple *okay* was not satisfactory for what he had in mind. He dropped to one knee. 'Abigail Callahan, will you marry me?'

'I've already said…' she started.

'You said *okay*. I don't think *okay*'s legally binding.'

'You want me to prepare contracts?'

'In triplicate.'

She smiled down at him, for how could she help it? She smiled and smiled. And then she thought this moment called for gravitas. It was a Very Serious Moment. It was the beginning of the rest of her life.

She stepped back and stood a little way away, looking down at him. At all of him.

At this man who'd be her husband.

She could still see him, she thought. The spiky-haired ten-year-old who her eight-year-old self had fallen in love with. That dangerous twinkle...

Her bad boy.

Her love.

'If I turn out to be a sewing mistress instead of a lawyer...' she ventured.

'Suits me.'

'If I'm not struck off the professional roll for this morning's unprofessional conduct I might help out the Crown Prosecutor from time to time.'

'You can't get struck off for dropping a briefcase—and Malcolm surely needs some help. You know, I'm feeling a bit dumb, kneeling over here when you're over there.'

She hadn't finished. 'I do want babies.'

'How many?' he asked and there was a trace of unease in his voice.

'Six,' she said, and laughed at the look on his face.

'Can we try one out for size first?'

'Sounds a plan. Raff...'

'Yes, my love?'

'That's just it,' she said, feeling suddenly...shy. 'My love. Let me say... I need to explain. Only once and then it's over, but I do need to get it out. Raff, I've loved you all the time without stopping but my pain stopped me thinking with my heart. I forced myself to think with my head. That's done. I'm so, so sorry that I can't take back those ten years.'

'Hush,' he said.

'I have to say it.'

'You've said it,' he murmured. 'I don't like to mention it but there's no carpet here. I'm kneeling on wood. I didn't have the forethought to use a cushion. Any more quibbles?'

'No, but...'

He sighed. 'Then how about saying you'll marry me and taking me out of my pain?'

'Okay.'

'Abigail!'

She laughed, and she hardly felt herself cross the distance between them. She knelt to join him and he tugged her close.

He kissed her again, so thoroughly, so wonderfully that doubts, unhappiness, emptiness were gone and she knew they were gone for ever.

'We can't take back those ten years,' he whispered into her hair as the kiss paused before restarting. 'How about we give ourselves the next ten instead?'

'Ten…'

'And the ten after that. And after that, too. Decades and decades of love and family and…'

And something was bumping against her leg.

Kleppy. He was tugging the popcorn bowl to his mistress with care.

She giggled and lifted him up and popcorn went flying. He'd tugged it with such care and she'd spilled it.

Who cared? A lawyer might. Not Abigail Callahan. Not the wife of Banksia Bay's Bad Boy.

'Decades and decades of love and family and dogs,' she said, and Raff took Kleppy firmly from her and set him down so he could kiss her again.

'Definitely, my love. Definitely family, definitely dogs, definitely love. For now and for ever. For as long as we both shall live. So now, Abigail Callahan, for the third and final time, will you marry me? I want more than *okay*. I want properly, soberly, legally, and with all your heart.'

'Why, yes, Rafferty Finn,' she managed between love and laughter. 'Where would you like me to sign?'

Abby didn't wear two thousand beads to her wedding.

For a start, it didn't seem right that she wear a dress she'd prepared for her marriage to Philip. Almost as soon as Raff put a ring on her finger she was planning an alternative.

Rainbows.

So Sarah wore her dress—Sarah, who'd looked at her dress of

two thousand beads and burst into tears. 'It's the most beautiful thing I've ever seen.' And Sarah needed a wedding gown.

For: 'Lionel's not staying in that horrid boarding house a minute longer,' she declared, but Lionel was old-fashioned. He was delighted to move to Raff's farm; he was incredibly happy to start renovating the little house at the rear, but he'd marry his Sarah first.

They were even thinking…if Lionel got his money back from Philip…Isaac's place wasn't so far from the farm. Maybe they could be even more independent.

So Raff gave his sister away. Abby was maid of honour and if she was as weepy as any mother of the bride then who could blame her? Her gown of two thousand beads had found a use she could hardly have dreamed of.

And then it was Abby's turn for her wedding, a month later, but on a day just as wonderful. They were to be married in the church—the church she'd been baptised in, the church Ben had been buried from.

Half Banksia Bay came to see. Even Mrs Fryer.

For things had shifted for the town's bad boy.

Rumours were flying. True to his word, Raff refused to make public the contents of the tape, but the people of Banksia Bay never let lack of evidence get in the way of a good rumour. And there were plenty of pointers saying Raff might well have been misjudged.

For a start, Abby's parents were trying their best to get to know Raff, and suddenly they wouldn't hear a bad word against him. They even offered to move into Raff's house while Raff and Abby went on their honeymoon, in case Lionel needed help with Sarah.

And people remembered. Raff had been judged on Philip's word and nothing else. But now… Philip had abandoned the town and moved to Sydney. He was facing malpractice charges and more.

Philip's parents were appalled. They owned an apartment in Bondi and rumour said they were thinking of moving themselves, leaving Banksia Bay to be with their son.

They were the only ones behind Philip, though. Even Philip's grandpa was right here at the wedding. What was more, at Abby's tentative request he'd made a beautiful box for the ring bearer.

The ring bearer…

Raff stood before the altar waiting for his bride and he couldn't help thinking the choice of ring bearer might be a mistake.

Abby swore it'd be okay. She'd spent hours training him. The plan was for her mother to hold Kleppy, and then, when Raff called, he'd trot across, bearing the ring. What could possibly go wrong?

Who knew, but Raff organised for Keith to carry a backup ring in his pocket. It wasn't that he didn't trust Kleppy.

Um…yes, it was. He stood in the church waiting for his bride and he thought he definitely didn't trust Kleppy.

But suddenly he could no longer focus on Abby's dog. The doors of the church swung open and Abby was right there. Holding her father's hand. Looking along the aisle to find him.

His bride. His Abby.

She'd wanted rainbows, and that was what she was to be married in. She'd made this herself as well, and it was as individual as she was. The gown was soft white silk, almost transparent, floating over panels of pastel hues, every shade a man could imagine. Her tight-fitting bodice clung to her lovely figure and the skirt flared out in clouds of shimmering colour, with the soft-coloured silk shimmering from underneath.

She was so beautiful…

She wore her hair simply, no longer in the elegant chignon he'd hated for years, but dropping in tendrils to her bare shoulders. She wore a simple halo of fresh flowers in her hair—and she took his breath away.

Sarah followed her in, proud fit to burst. Matron of honour. She wore a matching dress, also rainbow-coloured but without the translucent overskirt that made Abby seem to float.

Sarah was also supposed to be wearing a ring of flowers in

her hair, but that had been the one hiccup of the morning. 'It might give me a headache,' she'd said, doubtful.

'Why don't you take it and leave it in the car?' Raff had suggested. 'That way, you can wear it for the official photographs and take it off if it starts hurting.'

She'd approved his suggestion. She was happy now, bare-headed, beautiful, a married woman, fussing over her best friend's gown.

She wasn't as happy as Raff. Not possible. His Abby was smiling at him. His Abby was about to be his wife.

What could be more perfect?

The music filled the church. Abby's father led her forward, beaming with pride, and Raff stepped forward to receive his bride.

His Abby.

What could go wrong with today?

Kleppy could go wrong.

There was a scuffle in the front pew. Abby's mother had retired behind her handkerchief and forgotten her Kleppy-clutching duty. She made a wild grab but it was too late: he was free.

Kleppy was groomed to an inch of his life. He was wearing a bow of the same rainbow-coloured fabric lining Abby's gown.

He was off and running.

He trotted straight up the aisle, tail high, a dog on a mission—and he disappeared out of the door.

Uh-oh. What was a cop supposed to do now? What was a groom supposed to do?

'Leave him to me,' Keith growled, setting a hand firmly on Raff's shoulder. 'Lights and sirens. Handcuffs. Padded cell if necessary. I'll pull him in no time.'

'Kleppy,' Abby faltered.

'You two get on with your wedding,' Keith told them, and they looked at each other and knew they must. A hundred people were watching them. These people loved them and they were waiting to see them married.

'But he has the ring,' Abby faltered.

'We have backup,' Keith said and handed Raff the spare.

'Oh, Raff...' He could tell she didn't know whether to be thankful or indignant.

'It's not that I didn't trust him,' Raff said—unconvincingly—and then he paused.

Kleppy was back. With a ring.

He had two rings now, the plain band of gold in the tiny box hanging round his neck—and Sarah's halo of flowers, left on the front seat of the bridal carriage.

It was a ring of fresh flowers to match Abby's.

He carried it straight to Abby and sat and wagged his tail and waited to be told how good he was.

'He's brought us a ring,' Abby said and choked.

The congregation was choking as well—or laughing out loud. Kleppy's reputation had grown considerably in the last couple of months.

But Raff had his priorities in order now. There were things to be done before he acknowledged his soon-to-be wife's dog. He took her hands in his, tugged her to face him and lightly kissed her. 'You,' he told her, 'are the most beautiful woman in the world.'

'You make my toes curl,' she said.

There was a light 'harrumph' from before them. They were, after all, here to get married.

Raff smiled and stooped and held out his hand, and Kleppy laid his ring of flowers into his palm. He lifted it up and gave it to Abby.

'I guess this is Kleppy's wedding gift.'

'I'll treasure it for always,' she managed.

'You should. For with this ring, I thee wed,' he said softly. 'With this dog, I thee marry. Before this community, with these friends, I pledge you my troth.'

There was a murmur of delighted approval.

Abby was looking...in love.

Kleppy, however, was still looking expectant.

Raff knelt and lifted the small gold band from the box

around Kleppy's neck. He pocketed it carefully—and then he placed the ring of flowers around Kleppy's neck.

'Sarah,' he said to his sister. 'Can you hold Kleppy? I have things to do.'

'Sure,' Sarah said, beaming. 'Lionel will help me.'

So Sarah and Lionel held Kleppy. Raff took Abby's hands in his and he faced her—a man facing his woman on their wedding day.

'Enough,' he said softly, for her ears alone. 'Dogs have their place, as do sisters and friends and flowers. But for now… Are you ready to marry me?'

'If you'll take me. And my crazy dog.'

'We'll take whatever comes with both of us,' he told her, strongly and firmly. 'As long as we have each other.'

'Oh, yes.' She smiled at him mistily through tears. He kissed her again, lightly on the lips—and then the ceremony began as it was meant to begin. As Rafferty Finn and Abigail Callahan stood together, in peace and in love, to become one.

MISTY AND THE
SINGLE DAD

BY
MARION LENNOX

All the characters in this book have no existence outside the imagination of
the author, and have no relation whatsoever to anyone bearing the same name
or names. They are not even distantly inspired by any individual known or
unknown to the author, and all the incidents are pure invention.

First published in Great Britain 2011
by Mills & Boon, an imprint of Harlequin (UK) Limited,
Eton House, 18-24 Paradise Road, Richmond, Surrey TW9 1SR

© Marion Lennox 2011

ISBN: 978 0 263 88873 7

23-0411

Harlequin (UK) policy is to use papers that are natural, renewable and
recyclable products and made from wood grown in sustainable forests. The
logging and manufacturing processes conform to the legal environmental
regulations of the country of origin.

Printed and bound in Spain
by Blackprint CPI, Barcelona

Dear Reader,

Many years ago, my mum took my little sister to the doctor. They waited for a long time. Finally my sister, small and cute, went to fetch something she'd left in the car—and she found Buster.

Buster had been thrown from a moving car. He was small and nondescript. He was skeletal. His back leg was broken and he hung from my little sister's arms with huge brown eyes, expecting death.

Thus, back in the doctor's waiting room, ten sets of eyes looked at my mum as my little sister sobbed and quavered... 'Can we keep him?'

Buster gave joy to our family for fourteen years, and I've now reincarnated him as Ketchup. I've smiled as I've rewritten his story. Occasionally I've cried. Follow Ketchup as he brings Misty Lawrence and Nicholas Holt together—and watch as their romance blossoms.

I wish you all a Buster, or a Ketchup, and I wish you all the happiness he gave us.

Welcome to Banksia Bay—where love is unleashed.

Marion Lennox

With grateful thanks to Anne Gracie and her Chloe,
a matched pair of great friends, to Trish Morey,
whose skill with words is awesome, and to the
Maytoners, because we rock.

To Buster Keaton, who loved our family
with all his small heart.

CHAPTER ONE

How many drop-dead gorgeous guys visited Banksia Bay's First Grade classroom? None. Ever. Now, when the heavens finally decreed it was time to right this long-term injustice—it would have to be a *Friday*.

Misty took her class of six-year-olds for swimming lessons before lunch every Friday. Even though swimming had finished an hour ago, her braid of damp chestnut curls still hung limply down her back. She smelled of chlorine. Her nose was shining.

Regardless, a Greek God was standing at her classroom door.

She looked and looked again.

Adonis. God of Desire and Manly Good Looks. Definitely.

Her visitor looked close to his mid-thirties. Nicely mature, she thought. Gorgeously mature. His long, rangy body matched a strongly boned face and almost sculpted good looks. He wore faded jeans and an open-necked shirt with rolled up sleeves. Looking closer—and she *was* looking closer—Misty could see muscles, beautifully delineated.

But…did Adonis have a six-year-old son?

For the man in her doorway was linked by hand to a child, and they matched. They both wore jeans and white shirts. Their black hair waved identically. Their coppery skin was the colour that no amount of fake tan could ever produce, and their identical green eyes looked capable of producing a smile to die for.

But only Adonis was smiling. He was squatting and saying to the child, 'This looks the right place. They're painting. Doesn't this look fun?'

Son-of-Adonis didn't look as if he agreed. He looked terrified.

And, with that, Misty gave herself a mental slap, hauled herself back from thinking about drop-dead gorgeous males and back to where she should be thinking—which was in schoolmarm mode.

'Can I help you?'

Frank, Banksia Bay School Principal, should have intercepted this pair, she thought. If this was a new student she'd have liked some warning. There should be an empty place with the child's name on it, paints with paper waiting to be drawn on, the rest of the class primed to be kind.

'Are you Miss Lawrence?' Adonis asked. 'There's no one in the Principal's office and the woman down the hall said this is Grade One.'

She smiled her agreement, but directed her smile to Son-of-Adonis. 'Yes, it is, and yes, I am. I'm Misty Lawrence, the Grade One teacher.'

The child's hand tightened convulsively in his father's. This definitely wasn't a social visit, then; this was deathly important.

'I'm sorry we're messy, but we're in the middle of painting cows,' she told the little boy, keeping her smile on high beam. She was standing next to Natalie Scotter's table. Natalie was the most motherly six-year-old in Banksia Bay. 'Natalie, can you shift across so our visitors can see the cow you're painting?'

Natalie beamed and slid sideways. Misty could see what she was thinking. Hooray, excitement. And the way this guy was smiling…Misty felt exactly the same.

Um…focus. Get rid of this little boy's fear.

'Yesterday we went to see Strawberry the cow,' she told him. 'Strawberry belongs to Natalie's dad. She's really fat because she's about to have calves. See what Natalie's done.'

The little boy's terror lessened, just a little. He gazed nervously at Natalie's picture—at Natalie's awesomely pregnant cow.

'Is she really that fat?' he whispered.

'Fatter,' Natalie said, rising to the occasion with aplomb. 'My dad says it's twins and that means he'll have to stay up all night 'cos it's always a b…' She caught herself and gave Misty a guilty grin. 'I mean, sometimes he needs to call the vet and then he swears.' She beamed, proud of how she'd handled herself.

'Here's her picture,' Misty said, delving into the pocket of her overalls for a photograph. She glanced at Adonis, asking a silent question, and got a nod in response. This, then, was the way to go. 'Would you like to sit by Natalie and see if you can paint as well?' she asked. 'If it's okay with your dad.'

'Of course it is,' Adonis said.

'You can share my paints,' Natalie declared expansively, and Misty gave a tiny prayer of thankfulness that Natalie's current best friend was at home with a head cold.

'Thank you,' Son-of-Adonis whispered and Misty warmed to him. He was polite as well as cute. If he *was* a new student…

'We're here to enrol Bailey for school,' Adonis said, and she smiled her pleasure, but she was also thinking, *Where is Frank?* And why did this pair have to arrive now when she felt like a chlorinated wet sheep?

'I know I should have made an appointment,' Adonis said, answering her unspoken question. 'But we only arrived in town an hour ago. The closer we got, the more nervous Bailey was, so we thought the sensible thing would be to show him that school's not a scary place. Otherwise, Bailey might get more nervous over the weekend.'

'What a good idea. It's not scary at all,' she said, warming to the man as well as to the son. 'We like new friends, don't we, girls and boys?'

'Yes.' It was a shout, and it made Misty smile. In this sequestered town, any newcomer was welcomed with open arms.

'Are you here for long?' she asked. 'You and your… family?' Was Mrs Adonis introducing another child to another class?

'There's only Bailey and me, and we're intending to live here,' he said, stooping to load Bailey's paintbrush with brown paint. Being helpful. But Bailey checked Strawberry's photograph again, then looked at his father as if he'd missed the point. He dipped his brush in the water jar and went for red.

His father grinned and straightened, and held out his hand. 'I'm Nicholas Holt,' he said, and Misty found her hand enveloped in one much larger, much stronger. It was a truly excellent handshake. And his smile…

Manly Good Looks didn't begin to cut it, she thought. Wow! Forget Greek Gods. Adonis was promptly replaced with Nicholas.

She was absurdly aware of her braid, still dripping down her back. She wanted, quite suddenly, to kill Frank. It was his job to give warning of new parents. Why wasn't he in his office when he should be?

She didn't have so much as powder on her nose. It was freckled and it glowed; she knew it did. Her nose was one of the glowingest in the district. And five feet four inches was too short. Where were six inches when she needed them? If Frank had warned her, she might have worn heels.

Or maybe not.

'Miss…' a child called.

'I'm sorry; we shouldn't be disturbing your class,' Nicholas said and she managed to retrieve her hand and force herself to think schoolteacherly thoughts. Or mostly schoolteacherly thoughts.

'If Bailey's to be my student, then you're not interrupting at all,' she said and turned to the child who'd called. 'Yes, Laurie, what do you need?'

'There's a dog, miss,' Laurie said from across the room, sounding agitated. 'He's bleeding.'

'A dog…' She turned to the window.

'He's under my table, miss, in the corner,' Laurie said, standing up and pointing. 'He came in with the man. He's bleeding everywhere.'

Help.

There were twenty-four children looking towards Laurie's table. Plus Nicholas Holt.

A bleeding dog…

There were kids here who'd make this up but Laurie wasn't one of them. He wasn't a child with imagination.

Laurie's table was in the far back corner, and the row of shelving behind it made for a small, dark recess. If a dog was under there…it couldn't be a very big dog.

'Then we need to investigate,' she said, as brightly as she could. 'Laurie, can you go and sit in my teacher's chair, please, while I see what's happening?'

Laurie was there like a shot—the best treat in the world was to be allowed to sit in his teacher's big rotating chair. With the way clear, Misty would be able to see…

Or not. She stooped, then knelt. It was dark under the table. Her hands met something wet on the floor—something warm.

Blood.

Her eyes grew accustomed to the gloom. Yes, there was a dog, cowering right back into the unused shelves.

She could see him clearly now, cringing as far back as he could get.

An injured dog could snap. She couldn't just pull him out.

'Can I help?'

He was Adonis. Hero material. Of course he'd help.

'We have an injured dog,' she said, telling the children as well as Ad…as well as Nicholas. 'He seems frightened. We all need to stay very quiet so we don't frighten him even more. Daisy, can you fetch me two towels from the swimming cupboard?'

'Do you know the dog?' Nicholas asked as Daisy importantly fetched towels. He was standing right over her, and then he was kneeling. His body was disconcertingly solid. Disconcertingly male.

He was peering underneath Laurie's table as if he had no idea in the world what his presence was doing to her.

What, exactly, was his presence doing to her?

Well, helping. That was a rarity all by itself. Misty was the fixer, the one who coped, the practical one. She did things by herself, from necessity rather than choice.

She didn't often have a large attractive male kneeling to help.

Often? Um…never.

'Do you know the dog?' he asked again and she got a grip on the situation. Sort of.

'No.'

'But he's injured?'

'There's blood on the floor. Once I have the towels, I can reach in…'

'It'll be safer if I lift the table so we can see what we're dealing with. Tell you what. If we move the kids back, it'll give him a clear run to the entrance. If he wants to bolt, then he can.'

'I need to see what's wrong.'

'But you don't want a child getting in the way of an injured animal.'

'No,' she said. Of course not.

'I left the outside door open from the porch,' he said. 'I'm sorry; that's how he must have come in. I can shut it now. That means if I lift the table and he bolts we have a neat little space to hold him.'

She thought that through and approved. Yes. If the dog was scared he'd run the way he'd come. They could close the classroom door into the porch and they'd have him safe.

But to trap an injured dog...

This was NYP. Not Your Problem. That was what Frank would say. The School Principal was big on what was or wasn't his problem. He'd let the dog go, close the door after it and forget it.

But this wasn't Frank. It was Nicholas Holt and she just knew Nicholas wasn't a NYP sort of guy.

And in the end there wasn't a choice—the dog didn't give her one. She knelt, towels at the ready. Nicholas lifted the desk, but the dog didn't rush anywhere. The little creature simply shook and shook. He backed harder into the corner, as if trying to melt into the wall, and Misty's heart twisted.

'Oh, hush. Oh, sweetheart, it's okay, no one's going to hurt you.'

This little one wasn't thinking of snapping—he was well past it. She slipped the towels around him carefully, not covering his head, simply wrapping him so she could propel him forward without doing more damage.

He was a cocker spaniel, or mostly cocker spaniel. Maybe a bit smaller? He was black and white, with black floppy ears. He had huge black eyes. He was ragged, bloodstained and matted and there was the smell of tyre rubber around him. Had he been hit?

He had a blue collar around his neck, plastic, with a number engraved in black. She knew that collar.

A couple of years back, Gran's ancient beagle-cross had slipped his collar and headed off after a scent. Two days later, he'd turned up at the Animal Welfare Centre, with one of these tags around his neck.

This was an impounded dog. A stray.

No matter. All that mattered now was that the dog was in her arms, quivering with fear. There was a mass of fur missing from his hind quarters, as if he'd been dragged along the road, and his left hind leg looked…appalling. He was bleeding, sluggishly but steadily, and his frame was almost skeletal.

He needed help, urgently. She wanted to head out to her car right now and take him to the vet.

She had twenty-four first graders looking at her—and Nicholas was looking at her as well. NYP? She had problems in all directions.

'He's hurt.' It was a quavering query from Bailey. The little boy had sidled back to his father's side and slipped his hand in his. His voice was full of horror. 'Has he been shot?'

Shot? What sort of question was that?

'He looks like he's been hit by a car,' she said, to the class as well as to Bailey. Every first grader was riveted to the little animal's plight now. 'He's hurt his leg.' Anything else? She didn't know.

She looked down at him and he looked up at her, his eyes huge and pain-filled and hopeless. His shivering body pressed against hers, as if desperate for warmth.

She'd owned dogs since childhood. She loved dogs. She'd made a conscious decision not to have another one.

But this one… He was an injured stray and he was looking at her.

Uh oh.

'Do you want me to call someone to deal with him for you?' That was from Nicholas—with that question he surely wasn't Adonis. This wasn't a hero type of question. This the sort of response she'd expect from Frank.

Find someone to deal with him. Who?

Frank himself? If the Principal wasn't in his office, she had no one to turn to. Every other teacher had their own class.

She could make a fast call to Animal Welfare. This was their dog. Their problem. They'd collect him.

That was the sensible solution.

But the dog quivered against her, huddling tight, as if he was desperate for the poor amount of warmth she could provide. His eyes were pools of limpid despair.

He looked at her.

NYP. NYP.

Since when had anything ever been Not Her Problem? There was no way this dog was going back to one of the Welfare cages.

She did not need a dog. She did not!

But in her arms the dog quivered and huddled closer. She felt the silkiness of his ears. She could feel his heart, beating so fast... He was so afraid. He was totally at the mercy of the decision she made right now.

And, with that thought, her vow to leave dogs behind disintegrated to nothing.

What were dreams, anyway?

'Mr Holt, I need your help,' she said, attempting to sound like a teacher in control of the situation.

'Yes,' he said, sounding cautious. As well he might.

'I can't leave the children,' she said. 'This dog needs to go to the vet. That's what happens with sick dogs, doesn't it, boys and girls. You remember Dr Cray? We visited his surgery last month. I'm going to ask Bailey's father if he'll take him to Dr Cray for us. Will you do that for us, sir?'

Then she looked straight at Nicholas, meeting those deep green eyes head on. Not His Problem? Ha. He was asking her to teach his child. Payback happened early in Banksia Bay.

'I don't know about dogs,' he said, sounding stunned.

'That's okay,' she said, wrapping the little dog more tightly in his towels. Before he could demur, she handed him over, simply pressing the dog against his chest and letting her hands fall. She wasn't about to drop him, but he wasn't to know that. He was forced to release Bailey to take the dog.

'Dr Cray does a midday surgery, so he should be there,' she said. Then, as he still looked flabbergasted, she thought maybe a little more explanation might be required. Explanation but no choice. She couldn't afford to give him a choice.

She so wanted to take this dog herself, but some things weren't possible. Nicholas would have to do.

'I'm not sure where our Principal is,' she said. 'These children are mostly country kids. We know about injured animals. We know the vet can help, only first we need to get him there. We ask our parents to help all the time—four of our mums and dads helped with swimming lessons this morning. I know Bailey's only just joined the class but we know you'll want to help as well. So please, can you take this dog to the vet? Tell Dr Cray I'll be there after work and I'll take care of the expenses.'

And she mustn't forget Bailey, she told herself. She was asking a lot here—of both father and son.

She looked down at Bailey and something in his expression caught her. Made her remember…

Her mother, walking into her classroom on one of her fleeting visits. Misty might have been as old as Bailey, or maybe a little younger.

Her mother staying for all of two minutes—'just to see my kid'. Speaking gaily to her teacher as she walked out. 'You look after my Misty; she's such a good girl.' Then leaving. As she always left. Sending postcards from a life that didn't include Misty.

Whoa. In the midst of this drama, where had that thought come from? But the memory of it was there, in Bailey's eyes. She knew instinctively that his world wasn't certain, and she was asking more of him.

But, unfair or not, she had no choice. She couldn't leave the classroom and she could hardly toss the dog outside untended. What to do?

Give him the choice, as she'd never been given the choice.

She stooped. 'Bailey, we need your father's help to take this dog to where he can get bandages on his cut leg. Will you go with your dad to the vet's, or will you stay here with us and paint cows? Your dad will come back after he's left the dog with the vet. Won't you, sir? Is that okay with you, Bailey?'

Big breath. She was asking so much. And if she was right in what she sensed...if this little boy had been left in the past...

But it seemed Bailey trusted his father far more than she'd trusted her mother. He thought about it for a moment, looked up at the little dog wrapped in towels and then he gave a solemn nod, answering for both of them.

'My dad can take the dog to the vet.'

'That's wonderful.' It was indeed wonderful. 'Aren't dads great? Will you stay with us or will you go with him?'

'Stay with us,' Natalie said urgently, and Misty blessed Natalie's bossy little boots. 'I have heaps of paint.'

'I'll stay,' Bailey said, giving a cautious smile to Natalie.

'That's excellent.' She straightened and the look she gave Bailey's father was pure pleading. This was outrageous. If Frank could hear what she was doing he'd sack her on the spot. But what choice did she have?

'So will you do it for us?' she asked, and the dog looked hopelessly out at her from where it was cradled against his chest and she knew she was pleading for all of them. For the kids in her classroom, too. Every single one of them wanted a happy outcome for this dog.

'Please?'

CHAPTER TWO

WHAT had just happened?

One minute he had been a father intent on enrolling his son in his new school. He'd been ready to fill in forms, reassure Bailey, do all the things a responsible dad did.

The next he was standing in the sunshine, his arms full of bleeding dog, with a worried schoolteacher watching his rear. Making sure he followed directions.

An army commander couldn't have done it better.

Bailey would be safe with her.

That was a dumb thing to think at such a time—after all, what risk was there in leaving his son in a country primary school, in Australia, in a tiny seaside town where the most exciting thing to happen was…was…

Well, a dog being run over, for a start. Even that was more excitement than Nick wanted.

And it was a whole lot more excitement than this dog wanted. As Nick felt the dog tremble he put the *me* angle aside and focused on the creature he was carrying.

There'd been no time to examine him in the classroom. Miss Lawrence had wanted him out of there.

That was unfair. Her first responsibility must be to the children in her class and she'd put them first. If she'd taken the time to see exactly what was wrong, then the children, too, would have seen. Maybe that would have been distressing.

So he did what he was told. He turned his back on the school and headed for the car.

To the vet?

That, at least, was easy. Banksia Bay's commercial centre consisted of the one High Street running down to the harbour. Right on the town's edge was a brick building set back from the road. There was a big tree out front, a large blue sign saying 'Vet' and a picture of a dog with a cocked leg, pointing to the tree.

He and Bailey had smiled at it when they'd arrived in town. It was barely a block and a half from the house he'd rented.

'We could get a dog,' Bailey had said, but tentatively because maybe he'd already known the answer.

The answer would be no. Nick wanted nothing else that would tear their hearts. He was totally responsible for Bailey now, and for Bailey to have any more tragedy…

Look at this dog, for instance—running away, being hit by a car. He didn't know how badly it was injured. In all probability, there was still a tragedy here.

If there was then he'd lie to Bailey, he decided. This dog obviously belonged to a nice farmer who lived a long way out of town. The farmer would come and collect him. No, it'd be too far to visit…

The dog in question quivered again in his arms—the trembling was coming in waves—and he stopped thinking of difficulties. The sensible thing would be to set the dog on the car seat beside him but when he went to put him down he shook so much he thought okay, if it's body warmth he needs, then why not give it to him?

If Miss Lawrence was here she'd hold him. She'd expect him to hold him too.

She was one bossy woman.

Strong? Independent? Like Isabelle?

Not like Isabelle. She was a country schoolteacher. She wasn't a risk-taker.

She was…cute?

Now there was a dumb thing to think. He'd come here to set himself and Bailey up as safe and immune from any more risk—from any more tragedy.

From any more complications.

Isabelle had been dead for little more than a year. Even though their marriage had been on the rocks well before that, it hadn't made her death less shocking. Less gut-wrenching. It was far too soon to think that anyone, much less Bailey's new schoolteacher, was cute.

Hard not to think it, though. And maybe it was okay. Normal, even. She was a country schoolteacher and her ability to intrude on his life would be limited to teaching his son.

And asking him to take a dog to the vet.

It took two minutes to drive the short distance to the vet's. When he carried the dog in, an elderly guy with heavy spectacles and a grizzled beard emerged from the swing doors behind Reception. His glance at Nick was only fleeting; he focused straight away on the blood-stained towel.

'What's happened?'

A man after my own heart, Nick thought. Straight to the core of the problem.

'Miss Lawrence from the local school asked me to bring this dog in,' he said as the vet folded back an edge of the towel so he could see what he was dealing with.

'Misty?' The vet was touching the dog's face, running his fingers down his neck. Feeling for his pulse. 'Misty doesn't have a dog.'

'No, he ran into the schoolroom while…'

But the vet had found the collar. He fingered the nylon—checked the number, winced.

'It's the second.'

'Sorry?'

'From our local Animal Welfare Centre.' The vet took the dog from him, holding him with practised ease. 'Henrietta gives dogs every chance, only there are never enough homes. When the dogs have stayed there for...well, it's supposed to be ten days but she stretches it as long as she has room... she brings them to me. Three months after Christmas, cute pups turn into unwanted dogs. Yesterday morning she had a van full and some driver ran into the back of her. Dogs went everywhere. This is one of them.'

'So...' Nick said, and paused.

'So,' the vet said heavily. 'Thank you for bringing him in.' He paused and then craggy eyebrows raised. 'It's okay,' he said gently. 'I promise it'll be painless.' And then, as Nick still hesitated, 'Unless you want a dog?'

'I...no.'

'You're not a local.' It was a statement.

'My son and I have just moved here.'

'Have you just? Got a house with a yard?'

'Yes, but...'

'Every kid needs a dog.' It was said neutrally, probing a possible reprieve.

'No.' Yet still he hesitated.

'No pressure,' the vet said. 'The last thing this guy needs is another place that doesn't want him.'

'Miss Lawrence says she'll pay,' Nick said. 'For you to treat him.'

'Misty said that?'

'Yes.'

'She wants to keep him?'

'I'm not sure.'

The vet seemed confused. 'Misty's dog died last year. She's sworn she won't get another.'

'I'm sorry. I don't know any more than you do.'

'She won't have realised he's due to be put down. Or maybe she has.' The vet sighed. 'Trust Misty. Talk about a soft touch...' He glanced at his watch. Grimaced. 'I need to talk to her, but I won't be able to catch her until after school.

That's almost three hours.' He looked at the dog again and Nick could see what he was thinking—that three hours was too long to make a dog suffer if the end was inevitable.

This wasn't Nick's problem. He should walk away. But…

But he had to face Misty, the bossy little schoolteacher with the pleading eyes. Did she see this as her dog?

She'd said she'd cover the expenses. He had to give her the choice.

'I'm going back to the school anyway,' he said diffidently. 'I was enrolling my son when we found the dog. I could talk to her and phone you back.'

The vet's face cleared. 'Excellent. Let's do a fast assessment of this guy's condition so Misty knows what we're dealing with. She's not a girl to mess me around—it'll be yes or no. Can you give me a hand? I'll give him some pain relief and we'll tell her exactly what she is or isn't letting herself in for.'

Bailey drew a great cow. Misty gazed down at the child's drawing with something akin to awe. He was six years old, and his cow even looked like a cow.

'Wow,' she said as she stamped his picture with her gold elephant stamp—gold for Effort, elephant for Enormous. 'You must really like drawing, Bailey.'

'My dad can draw,' Bailey said. 'People pay him to draw pictures of boats.'

His father was an artist?

'Then you've come to the right place,' she said, glancing out of the window towards the distant harbour.

Nicholas Holt didn't look like an artist, she thought, but then, what did she know of artists? What did she know of anything beyond the confines of this town?

Don't think it. There was no point going down that road. For now, Banksia Bay was her life.

And for how much longer? She'd just offered to pay for a dog.

How long did dogs live?

'Story time,' she said determinedly. 'Tell you what, Bailey, as you're the new boy today, you can choose the story. Any book from the rack. Take a look.'

Bailey looked at her dubiously but he'd obviously decided this was an okay environment—this was somewhere to be trusted. And chubby little Natalie was right beside him, his new Friend For Life.

'Choose *Poky Little Puppy*,' Natalie whispered as only a six-year-old could whisper. "'Cos it's all about a puppy getting into trouble, like your new dog.'

Like your new dog...

Uh oh.

'He's not Bailey's new dog,' Misty said as she settled on the reading stool with the kids around her.

'Then whose is he, miss?' Natalie asked, and she knew the answer. She'd known it as soon as she'd seen the plastic collar.

She sighed. She was stuck here anyway. Why keep fighting the odds? Her dreams had already stretched a lifetime and it seemed they needed to be stretched a while longer.

'I guess he's mine.'

And ten minutes later when Nick walked back into the classroom the thing was settled. He entered the room, Natalie's hand shot up and she asked before Misty could give permission.

'Please, sir, how's Miss Lawrence's dog?'

Miss Lawrence's dog. He flashed a look at Misty and she met his gaze with every evidence of serenity. As if she picked up stray dogs all the time.

Why? Dogs must give her heartache upon heartache, he thought. The lifespan for a dog was what? Sixteen years? The mutt in question was around ten years old already and battered, which meant he was sliding towards grief for all concerned. He had six years, at most—if he made it through the next twenty-four hours.

'He has a broken leg,' he said, aware of a classroom of eyes, but aware most acutely of Bailey. Bailey, who'd seen far too much horror already. Because of his father's stupidity...

'Is Dr Cray fixing him?' Misty asked from the front of the room, and his gaze locked on hers. He could reply without speaking; he knew this woman was intelligent enough to get it.

'It's an extremely expensive operation to fix his leg,' he said, trying for a neutral tone. 'He's already an elderly dog, so there may be complications. Apparently he's from the Animal Welfare Centre—a stray—but Dr Cray says he's willing to take care of him for us. All he needs is your permission. I can phone him now and let him know it's okay.'

She got the message. He saw her wince.

The vet was letting her off the hook. All she had to do was nod and go back to reading to the children. Nicholas would relay her decision and the problem would be solved.

But this woman didn't work like that. He sensed it already and her response was no surprise.

'How expensive?'

So she couldn't save the dog at any cost. She was a school-teacher, after all.

What to say? He ran over the options fast.

Could they talk outside? Could he say, *Let's talk without the children hearing.* Let's give you the cold facts—that this dog's going to cost a mint; he's a stray with a limited lifespan. No one wants him; the kindest thing is to let Dr Cray do what he thinks best, which is to put him down.

He'd come to Banksia Bay to be sensible. He had to be sensible.

But then...Bailey was looking up at him with huge eyes.

Bailey would want details about what happened to the dog. Could he tell him the story about the distant farmer?

Could he lie?

All the children were looking at him. And their teacher?

Their teacher was looking trapped.

She had a dog.

The dog had trembled and cringed against her. He'd looked up at her, and she'd disappeared into those limpid eyes. His despair had twisted her heart.

But reality had now raised its ugly head and was staring her down.

How much was *extremely expensive*?

Becky, her best friend from school days, had just spent twelve thousand dollars on her Labrador's hip. But then, Becky had a property developer husband. Money was no problem. How badly was this dog's leg damaged?

Was she being totally stupid?

She thought of her wish list—twelve lovely things for her to dream about. To replace her list with a dog...

'I might not be able to aff...' But she faltered, knowing already that she would afford—how could she not? The moment she'd seen those eyes she knew she was hooked.

But then, amazingly, Nick stopped her before she could say the unsayable.

'He's a stray,' he said gently. 'But if you're offering to keep him, then Bailey and I will pay for his operation. We left the school door open. It may even have been our fault that he was run over—maybe he saw the open door from across the street and ran here for shelter. You tell me that in Banksia Bay parents are asked to volunteer for jobs? This, then, is our job. If he's your dog, then we'll pay.'

Misty stared up at him, astounded. Her thoughts were whirling.

Extremely expensive was suddenly no cost at all.

No cost except putting her dreams on hold yet again.

How could she not?

Nicholas was looking at her. Her whole class was looking at her.

'Fine,' she said weakly. 'I do need a dog.'

Dreams were just that—dreams.

Frank arrived then, blustering away his absence, playing the School Principal to Nicholas and to Bailey. Misty used the time to excuse herself and phone Dr Cray to say she was accepting Nicholas's very kind offer.

'Misty, love, are you out of your mind?' the vet demanded. 'You need this dog like a hole in the head. He's old, neglected and he'll need ongoing treatment for the rest of his life.'

'He's got lovely eyes. His ears… He's a sweetheart, I know he is.'

'You can't save them all. You swore you didn't want another dog. What about your list?'

'You know that's just a dream.'

Of course he did. This was Banksia Bay. The whole town knew everyone else's brand of toothpaste. So the town knew about her list, and they'd know her chances of achieving it had just taken another nosedive.

She cringed, but she couldn't back down now. It'd be like tearing away a part of herself—the part that said, *Good old Misty; you can always depend on her.* The part where her heart was. 'I've fallen for him,' she said, softly but determinedly. 'Now that Mr Holt's paying…'

'And that's something else I don't understand. Who is this guy?'

'I don't know. A painter. New to the town.'

A pause. Then… 'A painter. I wonder how he'd go painting props.'

Fred Cray was head of Banksia Bay Repertory Society.

There was a lot more to moving to Banksia Bay than just emptying a moving van. Did Nicholas realise it?

Maybe he already had.

'Give him a day or so before you ask,' she pleaded. 'Just save my dog.'

'You're sure?'

'Yes.'

So she had a dog again. At one time she'd been responsible for Gran, for Grandpa and for four dogs. Her heart had been stretched six ways. Now she was down to just Gran.

But who was wishing Gran away? She never would, and maybe taking this dog was simply accepting life as it was.

Banksia Bay. What more could a girl want?

New blood, at least, she thought, moving her thoughts determinedly to a future. With a dog.

And, with that, she decided she wouldn't mind a chance to get to know Nicholas Holt. She at least needed to thank him properly. But when she returned to the classroom Frank ushered Nicholas straight out to his office, and that was the last she saw of him for the day.

Bailey stayed happily until the end of school—any hint of early terror had dissipated in the face of Natalie's maternal care—and then Frank declared himself on gate duty, probably so he'd be seen by this new parent to be doing the right thing.

For there was something about Nicholas…

See, that was the problem. There was something about Nicholas Holt that made Frank think maybe he ought to stick around, be seen, just in case Nicholas turned out to be someone important.

He had the air of someone important.

A painter?

It didn't seem…right, Misty thought. He had an air of quiet authority, of strength. And he also had money. She knew now what the little dog's operation would cost and he hadn't hesitated. This was no struggling single dad.

She cleared up the classroom and headed out to find a deserted playground. What did she expect? That he'd stick around and wait for her?

He'd made one generous gesture and he'd moved on. He had a house to move into. A future to organise.

Boats to paint?

She headed for the car and then to where she always went after school, every day without fail. Banksia Bay's nursing home.

Gran was in the same bed, in practically the same position she'd been in for years. One stroke had robbed her of movement. The last stroke had robbed her of almost everything else. Misty greeted her with a kiss and settled back and told her about her day.

Was it her imagination or could she sense approval? Gran would have rescued the little dog. She'd probably even have accepted money from a stranger to do it.

'It's not like I'm accepting welfare,' she told Gran. 'I mean, he's saving the dog—not paying me or anything. It's me who has to pay for the dog's ongoing care.'

Silence.

'So what shall we call him?'

More silence. Nothing new there. There'd been nothing but silence from Gran for years.

'What about Nicholas?' she asked. 'After the guy who saved him.'

But it didn't seem right. Nicholas seemed suddenly…singular. Taken.

'How about Ketchup, then?' she asked. 'On account of his broken leg. He'll spend the next few months ketching up.'

That was better. They both approved of that. She just knew Gran was smiling inside.

'Then I'd best go see how Ketchup's getting on,' she told

her grandmother. 'He's with Dr Cray. I'm sorry it's a short visit tonight, but I'm a bit worried…'

She gave her grandmother's hand a squeeze. No response. There never was.

But dogs had been her grandmother's life. She'd like Ketchup, she thought, imagining herself bringing a recuperating Ketchup in to see her. Who knew what Gran could feel or sense or see, but maybe a dog on her bed would be good.

It had to be good for someone, Misty thought. Another dog…

Another love?

Who needed freedom, after all?

Nick and Bailey had the house sorted in remarkably short time, probably because they owned little more than the contents of their car. The house was only just suitable, Nick thought as they worked. Maybe it hadn't been such a good idea to rent via the Internet. The photographs he'd seen appeared to have been doctored. The doors and windows didn't quite seal. The advertised view to the sea was a view *towards* the sea—there'd been a failure to mention a fishermen's co-op in between. There were no curtains, bare light bulbs, sparse floor coverings.

But at least it was a base to start with. They could make it better, and if the town worked out they'd buy something of their own. 'It's like camping,' he told Bailey. 'We'll pretend we're explorers, living rough. All we need is a campfire in the backyard.'

Bailey gave him a polite smile. Right. But the school experience had made them both more optimistic about the future. They set up two camp beds in the front room, organised the rudiments of a kitchen so they could make breakfast, then meandered down to the harbour to buy fish and chips for tea.

They walked for a little afterwards, past the boats, through the main street, then somehow they ended up walking past the vet's.

Misty had just pulled up. She was about to go in.

He should stay clear, he thought. Paying for the dog was one thing, but he had no intention of getting personally involved.

But Bailey had already seen her. 'Miss Lawrence,' he called, and Misty waved. She smiled.

She smiled at Bailey, Nick told himself sharply, because a man had to do something to defend himself in the face of a smile like that.

He didn't have any intention of smiling back. Distance, he told himself harshly. He'd made that resolution. Stay clear of any complication at all. The only thing—the only one—who mattered was his son.

He'd messed things up so badly already. How many chances did a man have to make things right?

But Misty was still smiling. 'Hi,' she said. 'Are you here to see how Ketchup is?'

'Ketchup?' Bailey was beaming, and Nick thought back to the scared little boy of this morning and thought, *What a difference a day makes.* 'Is that what his name is?'

'Absolutely.'

'Why?'

'He's a hopalong. He'll spend his life ketching up.'

Bailey frowned, his serious little brow furrowing as he considered this from all angles. Then his face changed, lit from within as he got it. 'Ketchup,' he said and he giggled.

Nick had no intention of smiling, but somehow… This felt good, he thought. More. It felt great that Bailey giggled. Maybe he could afford to unbend a little.

'Great name,' he told her.

'He'll be a great dog,' Misty said.

'How is he?'

'He was still under anaesthesia last time I rang. Did you know his leg was broken in three places?'

'That's bad,' Bailey said, his giggle disappearing. 'When I got shot my arm was only broken in one place.'

Misty stilled. 'You were shot?'

'I'm better now,' Bailey said and tugged up his sleeve, revealing a long angry scar running from his wrist to his shoulder. 'I had plaster and bandages on for ages and it hurt a lot. Dad and I stayed at the hospital for ages and ages while the doctors made my fingers wiggle again but now I'm better. So we came here. Can we see Ketchup?'

'Of course,' she said, but her voice had changed. He could well imagine why. She'd have visions of drug deals, underworld stuff, gangsters… For a small boy to calmly say he'd been shot…

So maybe that was okay, he thought. Maybe it'd make her step back and it suddenly seemed important that she did step back.

Why did he think this woman might want to get close?

What was he thinking? *He wanted her to think he was a gangster?* What sort of future was he building for his son? Maybe he needed to loosen up.

'Now?' Bailey was asking.

Misty glanced at Nick. Okay, he didn't want to be a gangster, and he had to allow Bailey to form a relationship with his teacher. He nodded. Reluctantly.

And, even if she was thinking he might be carrying a sawn-off shotgun under his jacket, despite his curt, not particularly friendly nod, Misty smiled down at his son and her face showed nothing but pleasure.

'Wow, wait until we tell Ketchup you've had a broken arm,' she said. 'You'll be able to compare wounds.' She took Bailey's hand and tugged open the screen door. 'Let's see how he's doing.'

And she didn't even care if he was a gangster, Nick thought, feeling ashamed. All she cared about was his son.

Ketchup had looked bad this morning but he looked a lot worse now. He lay on towels in an open cage. His hind quarters were shaved, splinted and bandaged. He had a soft collar around his neck, presumably to stop him chewing his bandages, but he wasn't about to chew any time soon. He looked deeply asleep. The tubes attached to his foreleg looked scary.

'I have him heavily sedated,' Dr Cray said. 'Pain relief as well as something to calm him down. He's been deeply traumatised.'

'Do we know anything about him?' Misty looked down at the wretched little dog and she felt the same heart twist she'd felt this morning. Yes, it was stupid, taking him on, but there was no way she could help herself. This dog had come through so much… He had to have a second chance.

'He was at the Shelter for two weeks,' Fred Cray said, glancing at his card. 'No one's enquired about him. Rolf Enwhistle found him and another dog prowling round his poultry pen but they weren't exactly a threat to the hens. This one rolled over and whimpered when Rolf went near. They were both starving—no collars. They looked like they'd been dumped in the bush and been doing it tough for weeks.'

'Oh, Ketchup,' Misty breathed. She looked back to Nick then, and she smiled at him. Doubts about the wisdom of keeping this dog had flown. How could she consider anything else? 'And you've saved him for me.'

'It's okay,' Nicholas said, sounding uncomfortable.

'Will he be your dog now?' Bailey asked.

'He certainly will,' she said, still smiling, though her eyes were misting. 'I have the world's biggest couch. Ketchup and I can watch television together every night. I wonder if he likes popcorn.'

'He's a lucky dog to have found you lot,' Fred said—but Bailey was suddenly distracted.

'We don't have a couch,' he said urgently to his father. 'We need one.'

'We'll buy a couch,' Nicholas said. 'On Monday.'

'Can we buy a couch big enough for dogs?'

'We'll buy a couch big enough for you and me.'

'Can Miss Lawrence and Ketchup come over and sit on our couch?'

'There won't be room.'

'Then we need to buy a bigger couch,' Bailey said firmly. 'For visitors.'

'I suspect Ketchup might want to stick around home for a while,' Misty said, seeing conflicting emotions on Nicholas's face and deciding he'd paid for Ketchup's vet's fees—the least she could do was take the pressure off. 'Ketchup needs to get used to having a home.'

'That's what Dad says we need to do,' Bailey said.

'I hear you're moving into Don Samuelson's old place,' Fred said neutrally. 'That's a bit of a barn. You could fit a fair few couches in there.'

'We don't have anything except two camp beds and a kitchen table,' Bailey said, suddenly desolate, using the same voice he used when he said he really, really needed a hamburger. 'Our new house is empty. It's horrid. We don't have pictures or anything.'

'Hey, then Misty's your girl,' the vet said, nudging Misty. 'Give 'em your spiel, Mist.'

'No, I…'

'She wanted to be an interior designer, our Misty,' the vet said before she could stop him. 'Sat the exams, got great marks, she was off and flying. Only then her gran had the first of her strokes. Misty stayed home, did teaching by correspondence and here she is, ten years later. But we all know she does a little interior decorating on the side. Part-time, of course. There's not enough interior decorating in Banksia Bay to keep a girl fed, eh, Mist? But if you're in Don Samuelson's place... There's a challenge. A man'd need a good interior designer there.'

'I'm a schoolteacher,' Misty said stiffly.

'But the man needs a couch.' Fred could be insistent when he wanted to be, and something had got into him now. 'New to town, money to spend and an empty house. It's not exactly appealing, that place, but Misty knows how to make a home.'

'You could come and see and tell us what to buy,' Bailey said, excited.

'Excellent idea. Why don't you do it straight away?' the vet said. He glanced down at the little dog and his eyes softened. Like Misty, Fred fell in love with them all. That Nick had appeared from nowhere with the wherewithal to pay...and that Misty had offered the dog a home...

Uh oh. Misty saw his train of thought and decided she needed to back off, fast. Fred Cray had been a friend of her Grandpa's. He was a lovely vet but he was also an interfering old busybody.

'I need to go home,' she said.

'You've visited your gran and you ate a hamburger at Eddie's half an hour ago,' Fred said, and she groaned inside. There was nothing the whole town didn't know in Banksia Bay. 'The little guy and his dad had fish and chips on the wharf, so they've eaten, too. So why don't you go by his place now and give him a few hints?'

'There's no rush,' Nicholas said, sounding trapped.

'Yes, there is. We need a couch.' Bailey was definite.

'See,' Fred said. 'There is a rush. Misty, I'm keeping this little guy overnight. Come back in the morning and we'll see how he is. Nine tomorrow?'

'Yes,' she said, feeling helpless. She turned to Nicholas. 'But there's no need...I'm not really an interior decorator.'

'Bailey and I could do with some advice,' he admitted,

looking as bulldozed as she felt. 'Not just on what couch to buy but where to buy it. Plus a fridge and beds and a proper kitchen table. Oh, and curtains. We need curtains.'

'And a television,' Bailey said.

'You really have nothing?' Misty asked, astonished.

'I really have nothing. But I don't want to intrude…'

'You're not intruding. You're the answer to her dreams,' the vet said, chortling. 'A man with a blank canvas. Go with him, Misty, fast, before some other woman snaffles him.'

'I don't…' She could feel herself blush.

'To give him advice, I mean,' Fred said, grinning. 'You'll get that round here,' he told Nicholas. 'Advice, whether you ask for it or not. Like me advising you to use Misty. But that's good advice, sir. Take it or leave it, but our Misty's good, in more ways than one.'

CHAPTER THREE

PICK a quiet town in rural Australia, the safest place you can imagine to raise a child. Rent a neat house on a small block without any trees to climb and with fences all around. Organise your work so you can be a stay-at-home dad, so you can take care of your son from dawn to dusk. Hunker down and block out the world.

His plan did not include inviting a strange woman home on day one.

The vet had obviously embarrassed her half to death. She emerged from the clinic, laughing but half horrified.

'Fred's the world's worst busybody,' she said. 'You go home and choose your own couch.'

That was good advice—only Bailey's face fell.

If she was old and plain it'd be fine, he told himself, but her blush was incredibly cute and when she laughed she had this kind of dimple... Danger signs for someone who wished to stay strictly isolated.

But maybe he was being dumb. Paranoid, even. Yes, she was as cute as a button, but in a girl-next-door way. She was Bailey's schoolteacher.

Maybe they needed a couch, he told himself, and found himself reassuring her that, yes, he would like some advice. There were so many decisions to be made and he didn't know where to start.

All of which was true, so he ushered her in the front door

of their new home and watched her eyes light up with interest. Challenge. It was the way he felt when he had a blank sheet of paper and a yacht to design.

For Fred was right. This place was one giant canvas. They'd set up camp beds in the front room and slung a sheet over the windows for privacy. They had a camp table and a couple of stools in the kitchen. They'd picked up basic kitchen essentials.

They had not a lot else.

'You travel light,' she said, awed.

'Not any more, we don't.'

'We're staying here,' Bailey said, sounding scared again. The minute they'd walked in the door he'd grabbed his teddy from his camp bed and he was clutching it to him as if it were a lifeline. The house was big and echoey and empty. This was a huge deal for both of them.

Bailey had spent most of his short life on boats of one description or another, either on his father's classic clinker-built yacht or on his grandparents' more ostentatious cruiser. The last year or so had been spent in and out of hospital, then in a hospital apartment provided so Bailey could get the rehabilitation he needed. He had two points of stability—his father and his teddy. He needed more.

But where to start? To have a home...to own furniture... Nick needed help, so it was entirely sensible to ask advice of Bailey's schoolteacher.

He wasn't crossing personal boundaries at all.

'You really have nothing?' she asked.

'We've been living on boats.'

'Is that where Bailey was hurt?'

'Yes. It's also where Bailey's mother was killed,' he said briefly. She had to know that—as Bailey's teacher, there was no way he could keep it from her.

'I'm so sorry,' she said, sounding appalled.

'Yeah, well, we've come to a safer part of the world now,' he said. 'All we need to make us happy is a couch.'

'And a dog?'

'No!'

'No?' she said, and she smiled.

She smiled ten seconds after he'd told her his wife had died. This wasn't the normal reaction. But then he realised Bailey was still within hearing. She'd put the appalled face away.

Bailey had had enough appalled women weeping on him to last a lifetime. This woman was smart enough not to join their ranks.

'A girl can always try,' she said, moving right on. 'Do you want all new stuff?'

'I don't mind.'

'Old stuff's more comfortable,' she said, standing in the doorway of the empty living room and considering. 'It'd look better, too. This isn't exactly a new house.' She stared around her, considering. 'You know, there are better houses to rent. This place is a bit draughty.'

'It'll do for now.' He didn't have the energy to go house-hunting yet. 'Do you have any old stuff in mind?'

She hesitated. 'You might not stay here for long.'

'We need to stay here until we're certain Banksia Bay works out.'

'Banksia Bay's a great place to live,' she said, but she was still looking at the house. 'You know, if you just wanted to borrow stuff until you've made up your mind, I have a homestead full of furniture. I could lend you what you need, which would give you space to gradually buy your own later. If you like, we could make this place homelike this weekend.'

'You have a homestead full of old stuff?'

'My place is practically two houses joined together. My grandparents threw nothing out. I have dust covers over two living rooms and five bedrooms. If you want, you can come out tomorrow morning to take a look.'

'Your grandparents are no longer there?'

'Grandpa died years ago and Gran's in a nursing home. There's only me and I'm trying to downsize. You're settling as I'm trying to get myself unsettled.'

He shouldn't ask. He shouldn't be interested. It wasn't in his new mantra—*focus only on Bailey*. But, despite his vow, she had him intrigued. 'By getting a new dog? That doesn't sound unsettled.'

'There is that,' she said, brightness fading a little. 'I can't help myself. But it'll sort itself out. Who knows? Ketchup might not like living with me. He might prefer a younger owner. If I could talk you into a really big couch…'

'No,' Nick said, seeing where she was heading.

'Worth a try,' she said and grinned and stooped to talk to Bailey. Bailey had been watching them with some anxiety, clutching his teddy like a talisman. 'Bailey, tomorrow I'm coming into town to pick up Ketchup. If I spend the morning settling him into his new home, would you and your dad like to come to my house in the afternoon to see if you can use some of my furniture?'

'Yes,' Bailey said. No hesitation. 'Teddy will come, too.'

'Excellent,' Misty said and rose. 'Teddy will be very welcome.' She smiled at Nick then. It was a truly excellent smile. It was a smile that could…

That couldn't. No.

'Straight through the town, three miles along the coast, the big white place with the huge veranda,' she was saying. 'You can't miss it. Any time after noon.'

'I'm not sure…'

'Oh, sorry.' Her face fell. 'You probably want all new furniture straight away. I got carried away. I'm very bossy.'

And at the look on her face—appalled at her assertiveness but still…hopeful?—he was lost.

Independence at all costs. He'd had enough emotion, enough

commitment and drama to last a lifetime. There were reasons for his vows.

But this was his son's schoolteacher. She was someone who'd be a stalwart in their lives. He could be friendly without getting close, he told himself, and the idea of getting furniture fast, getting this place looking like home for Bailey, was hugely appealing.

And visiting Misty tomorrow afternoon? Seeing her smile again?

He could bear it, he thought. Just.

'We'll be extremely grateful,' he said, and Bailey smiled and then yawned, as big a yawn as he'd ever seen his son give.

'Bedtime,' he said, and Bailey looked through to the little camp bed and then looked at Misty and produced another of the smiles that had been far too rare in the last year.

'Can Miss Lawrence read me a bedtime story? She reads really good stories.'

'I'd love to,' Misty said, smiling back at him. 'If it's okay with your dad.'

It was okay, he conceded, but…

Uh oh.

There were all sorts of gaps in their lives right now, and this was only a small one, but suddenly it seemed important—and he didn't like to admit it. Not in front of a schoolteacher. In front of *this* schoolteacher.

'We don't have any story books,' he conceded.

What sort of an admission was that? He'd be hauled away to be disciplined by…who knew? Was there a Bad Parents Board in Banksia Bay? He felt about six inches tall.

They did own books, but they'd been put in storage in England until he was sure he was settled. Containers took months to arrive. Meanwhile… 'We'll buy some tomorrow,' he'd told Bailey.

'I have story books,' Misty said, seemingly unaware of his embarrassment.

'We've been living in a hospital apartment. Story books were provided.'

'You don't need to explain,' she said, cutting through his discomfort. 'My car's loaded with school work—there'll be all sorts to choose from. If you would like me to read to Bailey...'

They both would.

Forget vows, he told himself. He watched Bailey's face and he felt the tension that he hadn't known he had ease from his shoulders.

For the last twelve months the responsibility for the care of his little son had been like a giant clamp around his heart. He'd failed him so dramatically... How could Bailey depend on him again?

Over the last year he'd been attempting to patch their lives back together and for most of that time he'd had professional help. But today they'd left behind the hospital and all it represented. This was day one of their new life together.

To admit that he needed help...to have Bailey want help and to have it offered... It should feel bad, but instead it made his world suddenly lighter; it made what lay ahead more bearable.

'We'd love you to read to Bailey,' he admitted, and it didn't even feel wrong.

'Then that's settled,' she said, beaming down at Bailey. 'I'm so glad you started school today. All weekend I'll know I have a new friend. Right, you get into your pyjamas and clean your teeth and I'll fetch a story book. I have my favourite in the car. It's about bears who live in a house just like this one, but every night they have adventures.'

'Ooh, yes, please,' Bailey said and the thing was settled.

* * *

So Nick sat on the front step, watched the sunset and listened to Misty telling his son a story about bears and adventures—and he found himself smiling. Unlike the bears, they'd come to the end of their adventures. The house was terrible but they could do something about it. This place was safe. This place could work.

He'd chosen Banksia Bay because it was a couple of hours drive to Sydney. It had a good harbour, a great boat building industry and it was quiet. He should have come and checked the house before he'd signed the lease but to leave Bailey for the four hours it'd take to get here and back, or explain what he was doing... He'd have had to come during office hours, and those hours he spent with his son.

Choosing this house was the price he'd paid, but even this wasn't so bad.

He couldn't see the sea from here but he could hear it. That was good. To be totally out of touch with the ocean would be unthinkable.

He'd set up his office over the weekend. On Monday Bailey would start regular school hours. He'd be able to get back to work.

Work the new way.

The bear story was drawing to its dramatic conclusion. He glanced in the open window and Bailey's eyes were almost shut.

He'd sleep well in his new home—because of this woman.

She was so not his type of woman, he thought. She was a country mouse.

No. That was unjust and uncalled for. He accepted she was intelligent and she was kind. But her jeans were faded and her clothes were unpretentious. Her braid was now a ponytail. She'd changed since she'd cradled the dog this morning. She'd lost the bloodstains, but she must have changed at school because this shirt had paint on it already.

She was stooping now to give his son a kiss goodnight, and her ponytail looked sort of…perky? Actually, it was more sexy than perky, he thought, and he was aware of a stab of something as unexpected as it was unwanted.

The thought of those curls… He'd like to run his fingers through…

Whoa. How to complicate a life, he thought—have an affair with the local schoolteacher. He had no intention of having an affair with anyone. Let's just keep the hormones out of this, he told himself savagely, so when Misty came outside he thanked her with just a touch too much formality.

And he saw her stiffen. Withdraw. She'd got his unspoken message, and more.

'I'm sorry. I should have given you the book and left. I didn't mean to intrude.'

She was smart. She'd picked up on signals when he'd hardly sent them.

'You didn't intrude,' he said, and this time he went the other way—he put more warmth into his tone than he intended. He gripped her hand, and that was a mistake. The warmth…

How long since he'd touched a woman?

And there was another dumb thought. He'd been shaking hands with nurses, doctors, therapists every day. Why was Misty different?

He couldn't permit her to be different.

'You want to tell me about Bailey?' she asked and he did the withdrawal thing again. Released her hand, fast.

'It's on his medical form at school.'

'Of course it is,' she said, backing off again. 'I left school in a hurry because I wanted to get to the vet's, so I haven't caught up with the forms yet. I'll read them on Monday.' She turned away, heading out of his life.

She'd see the forms on Monday…

Of course she would, he thought, and he'd been frank in what he'd written. He'd had no choice. There were a thousand ways that keeping what happened to Bailey from his classroom teacher could cause problems. *Okay, boys and girls, let's pretend to be pirates...*

She had to know, and to force her to read the forms on Monday rather than telling her now... What was he trying to prove?

'I can tell you now,' he said.

He was all over the place.

He felt all over the place.

'There's no need...'

'There is a need.'

Why did it feel as if he were stepping on eggshells? This was Bailey's teacher. Treat her as such, he told himself harshly. Treat her professionally, with cool acceptance and with an admission that she needed to know things he'd rather not talk about.

'I'm not handling this well,' he admitted. 'Today's been stressful. In truth, the last year's been stressful. Or maybe that's an understatement. The last year's been appalling.' He paused then, wanting to retreat, but he had to say it.

'I don't want to interrupt your evening any more than I already have, but if you have the time... You're Bailey's teacher. You need to know what he's been through.'

'I guess I do,' she said equably. 'We both want what's best for Bailey.'

That was good. It took the personal out of it. He was telling her—for Bailey.

He paused then and looked at her. She was a woman without guile, his kid's teacher. She was standing on the veranda of the home he was preparing for his son. She was a warm, comforting presence. Sensible. Solid. *Safe*.

His parents would approve of her, he thought, and the idea sent a wave of emotion running through him so strongly that he felt ill. If he'd chosen a woman like this rather than Isabelle...

Someone safe.

Someone he could trust if he let his guard down.

When had he last let his guard down?

'So tell me, then,' she said—and he did.

There was no reason not to.

It took a while to start. Nick fetched lemonade. He said he'd rather be drinking beer but he hadn't yet made it further than the supermarket. He apologised for there being no food but cornflakes. She said she didn't need beer and she wasn't hungry. She waited.

It was as if he had to find his mindset, as well as his place on the veranda.

Nick didn't look like a man who spent a lot of time in an easy chair, Misty thought, and when he finally leaned his rangy frame on the veranda rail she wasn't surprised. She was sitting on the veranda steps. The width of Bailey's window was between them. Maybe that was deliberate.

For a while he didn't say anything, but she was content to wait. She'd been teaching kids for years. Parents often needed to tell her things about their children; about their families. A lot of it wasn't easy. But what Nick had to say…

'Bailey's mother was shot off the coast of Africa,' he said at last, and the words were such a shock she almost dropped her lemonade.

No one ever got shot in Banksia Bay. And…*off the coast of Africa?*

If this was one of her students, she'd give them a sheet of art paper and say, 'Paint it for me.' Dreams needed expression.

But one look at this man's face told her this was no dream. It might not happen in her world, but it did happen.

'She was killed instantly,' he said, and he was no longer looking at her. He was staring out at the blank wall of the fisherman's co-op, but she knew he was seeing somewhere far off. Somewhere dreadful. 'Bailey was shot as well,' he told her. 'It's taken almost a year to get him this far. To see him safe.'

What to say after a statement like that? She tried not to blurt out a hundred questions, but she couldn't think of the first one.

'It's a grim story,' he said at last. 'Stupidity at its finest. I've needed to tell so many people over the last year, but telling never gets easier.'

'You're not compelled to tell me.'

'You're Bailey's teacher. You need to know.'

'There is that,' she said cautiously. If she didn't know a child's history, it was like walking through a minefield. 'Oh, Nicholas…'

'Nick,' he said savagely, as if the name was important.

'Nick,' she said—and waited. 'It's okay,' she said gently. 'Just tell me as much as I need to know.'

He shrugged at that, a derisory gesture, half mocking. 'Right. As much as you need to know. I was working on a contract in South Africa, Bailey and Isabelle were with Isabelle's parents. They were on a boat coming to meet me, they were robbed and Isabelle and Bailey were shot.'

'Oh, Nick…'

His face stopped her going any further. There was such emptiness.

'What's not obvious in that version is my stupidity,' he said, and she sensed that she was about to get a story that he hadn't told over and over. He no longer seemed to be talking to her. He seemed somewhere in his head, hating himself, feeding his hatred.

The hatred made her feel ill. She wanted to stop him, but there was no way she could.

If this man needed to talk, ugly or not, maybe she had to listen.

'As a kid I was…overprotected,' he said at last into the silence, and the impression that he wasn't talking to her grew stronger. 'Only child. Protected at every turn. So I rebelled. I did the modern day equivalent of running away to sea. I studied marine architecture. I designed boats, won prizes, made serious money. I built a series of experimental boats, and I took risks.'

'Good for you,' she murmured. Then she added, before she could help herself, 'Half your luck.'

'No,' he said flatly. 'Risks are stupid.'

'It depends on the risks,' she said, and thought of how many risks she'd ever encountered. Approximately none.

But then…this wasn't about her, she reminded herself sharply. Listen.

'My kind of risks were definitely the stupid kind,' he said and, despite her interjection, she still had the impression he was talking to himself. 'Black run skiing, ocean racing in boats built for speed rather than safety, scuba-diving, underwater caving… Fantastic stuff, but the more dangerous the better. And then I met Isabelle. She was like me but more so. Risks were like breathing to her. The stuff we did… Her parents were wealthy so she could indulge any whim, and Isabelle surely had whims. In time, I learned she was a little bit crazy. If I skied the hardest runs, she didn't ski runs at all. She skied into the unknown. Together, we did crazy stuff.'

'But you had fun?' She was trying to keep the wistfulness from her voice, not sure if she was succeeding. Nick glanced at her as if he'd forgotten she was there, but he managed a wry nod.

'We did. We built *Mahelkee*, our gorgeous yacht, and we sailed everywhere. I designed as I went. We had an amazing life. And then we had Bailey, and that was the most amazing thing of all. Our son.'

He hesitated then, and she saw where memories of good times ended and the pain began. 'But when I held him…' he said softly, 'for the first time I could see where my parents were coming from. Not as much, of course, but a bit.'

'So no black ski runs for Bailey?'

He was back staring at the side of the co-op. No longer talking to her. 'There were no ski runs where we lived but there was no way Isabelle was living in a house. We kept living on the boat. It caused conflict between us but we kept travelling. We kept doing stuff we loved. Only…when I saw the risky stuff I thought of Bailey. We started being careful.'

'Sensible.'

'Isabelle didn't see it like that.'

Silence.

This wasn't her business, she thought; she also wasn't sure whether he'd continue. She wasn't sure she wanted him to continue.

'You want to finish this another day?' she ventured, and he shook his head, still not looking at her.

'Not much more to tell, really. I'd married a risk-taker, and Isabelle was never going to change. Bailey and I just held her back. We were in England when I got a contract to design a new yacht. She was to be built in South Africa. I needed to consult with the builders.'

'So you went.'

'We were docked at a pretty English port. Isabelle's parents own the world's most ostentatious cruiser and they were docked nearby. Isabelle was taking flying lessons and they were keeping her happy. Everyone seemed settled; we were even talking about enrolling Bailey in kindergarten. So I flew across to South Africa. But Isabelle was never settled for long. She got bored with her flying lessons and persuaded her parents to bring their boat out to surprise me.'

'To Africa?'

'In a boat that screamed money.' There was no mistaking the bitterness in his voice now. The pain. 'To one of the poorest places on the planet. When I found out they were on their way I was appalled. I knew the risks. I had security people give them advice. I sent people out to meet them, only they were hit before they arrived.'

'Hit?'

He shrugged. 'What do you expect? Poverty everywhere, then along comes a boat with a swimming pool, crew in uniform, dollar signs practically painted on the sides. But they'd had good advice. If you're robbed, once you're boarded, just hand over everything. Isabelle's father carried so much cash it'd make your head swim. He thought he could buy himself out of any trouble. Maybe he could, but Isabelle…she decided to defend,' he said savagely.

Misty knew she didn't exist for him right now. There was no disguising the loathing in his voice and it was directed only at himself. 'I knew she owned a gun before we were married, but she told me she'd got rid of it. And I believed her. Of all the stupid…' He shook his head as if trying to clear a nightmare but there was no way he could clear what he was going through. 'So, as her father tried to negotiate, she came up from below deck, firing. At men who made their living from piracy. Two shots—that's all it took. Two shots and she was dead and Bailey was close to it.'

She closed her eyes, appalled. 'So that's why you're here,' she whispered.

'That's why we're here. Bailey's spent a year in and out of hospital while I've researched the safest place in the world to be. I can design boats from here. Most of my designs are built internationally. I've hired an off-sider who can do the travelling for me. I can be a stay-at-home dad. I can keep Bailey safe.'

'You'll wrap him in cotton wool?' She felt suddenly, dreadfully anxious. 'Small risks can be exciting,' she ventured. 'I can make my bike stand on its front wheel. That's meant the odd bruise and graze. There's risks and risks.'

'I will not take risks with my son's life.'

The pain behind that statement… It was almost over-whelming.

What to do?

Nothing.

'No one's asking you to,' she said, deciding brisk and prac-tical was the way to go. 'You have a house to organise, a child to care for and boats to design. Our vet, Fred, has plans for your painting, and I might even persuade you to get a dog. You can settle down and live happily ever after. But if you'd never had those adventures…'

What was she talking about? Don't go there, she told her-self, confused at where her mind was taking her. If he'd never had those adventures…like she hadn't?

This was not about her.

She made herself step down from the veranda. This man's life, his past, was nothing to do with her. She needed to return to the nursing home to make sure Gran was settled for the night. She needed to go home.

Home… The home she'd never left.

Nick didn't stop her. He'd withdrawn again, into his isolation, where risks weren't allowed. He seemed as if he was hardly seeing her. 'Thank you for listening,' he said formally.

'You're welcome,' she said, just as formally, and she turned and left before she could ask him—totally inappropriately—to tell her about Africa.

What was he about, telling a total stranger the story of his life? It was so out of character he felt he'd shed a skin—and not in a good way. He felt stupid and naive and exposed.

He'd never done personal. Even with Isabelle… He'd hardly talked to her about his closeted childhood.

So why let it all out tonight? *To his son's schoolteacher?*

Maybe it was because that was all she was, he decided.

Bailey's teacher. Someone whose focus was purely on his son. Someone prepared to listen when he needed to let it all out.

Why let it out tonight?

Justification?

He stared around at the shabby house, the empty walls, the lack of anything as basic as a storybook, and he thought that was where it had come from. A need to justify himself in the eyes of Misty Lawrence.

Why did he need to justify himself?

He didn't want her to judge him.

That was stupid, all by itself. She was a country hick schoolteacher. Her opinion didn't matter at all.

If it did... If it did, then it'd come under the category of taking risks, and Nicholas Holt no longer took risks.

Ever.

She went home, to her big house, where there was only herself and the sound of the sea.

Africa.

She'd just got herself a dog.

Africa.

Nick's story should have appalled her. It did.

But Africa...

Since Gran's stroke, she'd started keeping her scrapbooks in the kitchen where recipes were supposed to be. Dreams instead of recipes? It worked for her. She tugged the books down now and set them on the kitchen table.

She had almost half a book on Africa. Pictures of safaris. Lying at dawn in a hide, watching a pride of lions. The markets of Marrakesh.

Africa was number eight on her list.

She had a new dog. How long would Ketchup live?

She picked up a second scrapbook and it fell open at the Scottish Highlands. She'd pasted in a picture of a girl in a floaty white dress lying in a field of purple heather. Behind her was a mass of purple mountains.

She'd pasted this page when she was twelve. She'd put a bagpiper in the background, and a castle. Later, she'd moved to finer details. Somewhere she'd seen a documentary on snow buntings and they had her entranced—small birds with their snow-white chests and rippling whistle. Tiny travellers. Exquisite.

Birds who travelled where she never could. She had pictures of snow buntings now, superimposed on her castle.

She flicked on, through her childhood dreams. Another scrapbook. The Greek islands. Whitewashed houses clinging to cliff faces, sapphire seas, caiques, fishermen at dawn…

These scrapbooks represented a lifetime of dreaming. The older she was, the more organised she'd become, going through and through, figuring what she might be able to afford, what was feasible.

She'd divided the books, the cuttings, into months. She now had a list of twelve.

Exploring the north of England, the Yorkshire Dales, a train journey up through Scotland, Skara Brae, the Orkneys… Bagpipers in the mist. Snow buntings. Number ten.

Greece. Number two.

Africa.

Risks.

Bailey.

She closed the book with a snap. Nicholas was right. You didn't take risks. You stayed safe.

She'd just agreed to keep another dog. She had no choice.

Her computer was on the bench. On impulse, she typed in *Nicholas Holt, Marine Architect* and waited for it to load.

And then gasped.

The man had his own Online Encyclopaedia entry. His

website was amazing. There were boats and boats, each more wonderful than the last. Each designed by Nicholas Holt.

This man was seriously famous.

And seriously rich? You didn't get to design boats like these without having money.

That a man like this could decide Banksia Bay was the right place to be…a safe place to be…

'It makes sense,' she told herself, and she flicked off the Internet before she could do what she wanted to do—which was to research a little more about Africa.

'I have a dog now,' she told herself. 'Black runs are probably cold and wet. Doesn't Scotland have fog and midges? Who knows what risks are out there? So gird your loins, accept that dreams belong in childhood and do what Nick Holt has done. Decide Banksia Bay is the best place in the world.'

But dreams didn't disintegrate on demand.

Dogs don't live for ever, she told herself. Her list money was still intact. She could hold onto her dream a while longer.

One day she'd complete her list. In her retirement?

Maybe.

Just not one day soon.

CHAPTER FOUR

KETCHUP decided to live.

At nine the next morning Misty was gazing down at the little dog with something akin to awe. He was still hooked up to drips. His back leg was splinted and bandaged. He had cuts and grazes everywhere, made more gruesome by the truly horrid-coloured antiseptic wash, but he was looking up at her with his huge black eyes and…his tail was wagging.

It had lost half its fur and it had probably been a pretty scrappy tail to start with, but it was definitely wagging. The eyes that looked at her were huge with hope, and she fell in love all over again.

'How can he have been at the shelter for two weeks and no one claimed him?' she demanded of Fred, and the old vet smiled, took out the drips, bundled the little dog up and handed him over.

'Not everyone has a heart as big as yours, Misty. Not everyone accepts responsibilities like you do.'

'What's one more responsibility?' she said and, yes, she felt a little bitter but, as she carried Ketchup out to her car, she wondered how she could feel bad about giving this dog a home.

There was no way she could leave Banksia Bay with Gran like she was. Ketchup would make life better—not worse.

She settled him onto the passenger seat and she talked to him the whole way home.

'You're going to like it with me. I have a great house. It's old and comfy and close to the beach, where you'll be able to run and run as soon as your leg's better. And there's so many interesting smells...' Then she couldn't stop herself adding a bit more exciting stuff because, for some reason, it was front and centre. 'And this afternoon we have two friends coming out to visit. Bailey and Nick. Nick's the one who saved you.'

He really had saved him. Fred had given her the facts.

'He's left his credit card imprint. Every cost associated with this dog, long-term, goes to Mr Holt. There's nothing for you to take care of. Yeah, he'll need ongoing care, but it's sorted.'

'He's a real hero,' she said, thinking of the website, of Nick's image, and of Nicholas last night. His care of his little son. His willingness to pay for Ketchup. The fact that he was haunted by his perceived failure to protect Bailey.

He was in such pain...

Ketchup wriggled forward and put his nose on her knee. Yes, he should be in a crate in the back but she figured this guy had had enough of crates to last a lifetime.

She was still thinking of Nick.

'He's our hero,' she told him. 'He's come to Banksia Bay to be safe, not heroic, but he's saved you. So maybe there's a little bit of hero left in him.'

A little bit of Adonis?

No. He was done with adventure. He was done with risk-taking.

He wanted to settle in Banksia Bay and live happily ever after.

Maybe even marry the local schoolteacher?

Where had that idea come from? A guy like that... She felt herself blush from the toes up.

But you need to settle as well, she told herself as she took her dog home. You have a great life here. A comfortable existence. All you need is a hero to settle with.

And put another rocker on the front porch so you can rock into old age together? I don't think so.

So what is it you want? she asked herself, and she knew the answer.

Life.

'Life's here,' she told herself out loud. 'Life's Banksia Bay and a new dog and a new pupil in my class. Woohoo.'

Ketchup pawed her knee and she felt the familiar stab of guilt.

'Sorry,' she told him. 'I love it here. Of course I do. I'd never do anything to upset you or Gran or anyone else in this place. You can come home and be safe with me.'

Safe with Misty.

A flash of remembered pain shafted through her thoughts. Her grandfather's first heart attack. Her grandmother, crippled with arthritis, terrified. Misty had been thirteen, already starting to understand how much lay on her shoulders.

And then her hippy mother had turned up, as unexpectedly and as briefly as she'd turned up less than half a dozen times in Misty's life. Misty remembered standing beside her grandfather's bedside, watching her grandmother's face drawn in fear. She remembered the mother she barely recognised hugging her grandmother, then backing out, to friends who never introduced themselves, to a psychedelic combi-van waiting to take her to who knew where? To one of the places the postcards came from.

'You'll be fine,' her mother had said to her grandmother, and she'd waved inappropriately gaily. 'I'm glad I could fit this visit in. I know Dadda will be okay. He's strong as a horse, and I know you'll both be safe with Misty.'

'See,' she told the little dog. 'My mother was right all along.'

* * *

There was no way he could miss Misty's house. It was three miles out of town, set well back from the road. There were paddocks all round it, undulating pastures with cattle grazing peacefully in the midday sun. The sea was its glittering backdrop, and Nick, who'd been to some of the most beautiful places on the earth, felt that this was one of them.

Here was a sanctuary, he thought. A place for a man to come home to.

Misty was on the veranda, easy to spot as they pulled up. She was curled up on a vast cane rocker surrounded by faded cushions. There was a rug over her knee.

Ketchup was somewhere under that rug. As they climbed from the car, Nick could see his nose.

Once again, that pang. Of what? Want? Of the thought that here was home? This place...

This woman.

He'd bared his soul to this woman last night. It should feel bad. Somehow, though, it didn't feel threatening.

'I can't get up,' she called, her voice lilting in a way he was coming to recognize, beginning to like. 'We've just gone to sleep.'

As if in denial, a tail emerged and gave a sleepy wag.

Bailey scooted up the steps to meet her, but Nick took his time, watching his son check the dog, smile at Misty, then clamber up onto the rocker to join them.

Something was happening in his chest.

This was like a scene out of *Little House on the Prairie*, he told himself, at the same time telling the lump in his throat to go down and stay down. The way he was feeling was kitsch. Corny.

Any minute now, Misty would invite them inside for home-baked cookies and lemonade. Or maybe she'd have a picnic to take down to the beach. She'd have prepared it lovingly beforehand, with freshly baked cakes, fragrant pies, home-made preserves. They'd be packed in a cute wicker basket with a red gingham cover…

'It's about time you got here,' she called, interrupting his domestic vision. 'I'm stuck.'

'Stuck?'

'I've been aching for lunch but Ketchup gets shivery every time I put him down. So I'm hoping I can stay here while you make me a sandwich.' She peeped up at him—cheeky. 'Cheese and tomato?'

'I could do that,' he said, waving goodbye to schmaltz and deciding cheeky was better. Much better.

'The bread's on the kitchen table. Cheese is in the fridge and tomatoes are out the back in the veggie garden. I like my cheese thick.'

Mama in *Little House on the Prairie* would never demand her man make a sandwich, Nick thought, and he grinned. Misty saw it.

'What?'

'I was expecting the table to be laid, Dresden china and all.'

'I have Dresden china,' she said, waving an airy hand. 'It's in the sideboard in the dining room. You're right, Ketchup and I would like our sandwich on Dresden china.'

'You're kidding.'

'Why would we kid about sandwiches on Dresden china?' She was helping Bailey snuggle down beside her. 'Important things, sandwiches. Would you like a sandwich, Bailey?'

'We've had lunch,' Bailey said shyly.

'Since when did that make a difference?' she asked, astonished. 'It's not a school day. We can eat sandwiches all afternoon if we want. Will we ask your daddy to make you a sandwich as well? Is he a good cook?'

'He cooks good spaghetti.'

'Not sandwiches?'

'I can make sandwiches,' Nick said, offended.

'Wonderful.' She beamed. 'Bailey, what sort of sandwich would you like?'

'Honey.' That was definite.

'We have honey. Can I add that to our order?' Misty asked and smiled happily up at Nick. 'Please?'

So he made sandwiches in Misty's farmhouse kitchen over-looking the sea, while Bailey and Misty chatted just outside the window.

He felt as if he'd been transported into another universe. He was making sandwiches while Bailey and Misty admired Ketchup's progress and compared Ketchup's bandaged leg to Bailey's ex-bandaged arm.

'My dad drew pictures on my plaster cast. Of boats.'

'Ketchup's more into bones. We'll ask him to draw bones on Ketchup's bandages.'

Bailey was giggling. *Giggling.*

This was too good to be true. His son was giggling on the veranda of a woman who was a part of his future.

His future?

Surely he meant Bailey's future. Misty was Bailey's teacher.

But his treacherous mind said *his* future.

He stabbed the butter and lifted a chunk on his knife, con-sidering it with care. Where to take this?

This did not fit in with his plans.

He'd come to this place with a clear path in view. A steady future. Nothing to rock the boat.

Misty wouldn't mess with that.

So maybe he could just…see. He could let his barriers down a little. He'd let them down last night and there was no issue.

There were no risks down this road.

'Are you planning to hoist that butter on a flagpole or put it on our bread?' Misty called through the window and he saw what he'd been doing and chuckled—and that in itself was amazing. When was the last time he'd felt like chuckling?

He made his sandwiches. He carried them outside, plus a bottle of not home-made lemonade, and he watched as Misty and Bailey munched and Ketchup woke a little and accepted a quarter of a sandwich and retired again.

'This is the best place for a dog,' Nick said. He'd settled himself on the veranda steps, not bothering so much about distance now but thinking more of view. If he leaned back at the top of the stairs he got a full view—of Misty.

And of Bailey and Ketchup, he reminded himself, but he was forgetting to remind himself so often,

'It's the best place for anyone,' Bailey declared. He'd eaten two more sandwiches on top of his lunch. For a child who'd needed to be coaxed to eat for a year, this was another thing to be amazed at.

Teddy, Nick noticed, had been set aside.

'It's pretty nice,' Misty said, but suddenly her voice sounded strained.

'Don't you like it?' Bailey asked.

'Yes.' But she didn't sound sure.

'Where else would you like to live?' Nick asked.

'In a yurt.'

He and Bailey both stared. 'A yurt?'

'Yep.'

'What's a yurt?' Bailey asked.

'My mother sent me a postcard of one once. It's a portable house. It's round and cosy and it packs up so I can put it on the back of my camel. Or my yak.'

Bailey was intrigued. 'What's a yak?'

'It's a sort of horse. Or maybe it's more like a sheep but it carries things. The yurt on my postcard had a camel in the foreground but I've been reading that camels bite. And yaks seem to be more common in Kazakhstan,' she said. 'That's where yurts are found. Probably in lots of other places, too, but

I've never been there to find out. Yaks seem pretty friendly, or at least I think they are. I've never met one, but some day I will. That's my dream. Me and my yak will take our yurt and head into the unknown.'

'In term vacations?' Nick asked before he could help himself. Bailey did not need his new-found teacher to be heading off into the unknown.

'I'd need more than term vacation,' she retorted. 'To follow the dreams I have…' The lightness in her voice faded a little and she gave a wry smile. 'But of course you're right. Term vacations aren't long enough. It's only a dream.'

'And you have a really nice house,' Bailey said placatingly. 'It's big and comfy.' Then he looked at Misty's face and maybe he could see something there that Nick was sensing—something that was messing with his domestic harmony as well. 'Could you buy a little yurt and put it in the backyard?' he asked. 'Like a tent?'

'Maybe I could.' The lightness returned but it was determined lightness. 'Maybe I could buy a yurt on the Internet—or maybe we could build one as a school project.'

Bailey's eyes widened with interest. 'My dad could help you build one. He's good at building.'

'Could he?' Misty smiled, but Nick saw a wash of emotions put aside and thought there were things here he didn't understand. But then… Why should he want to understand this woman?

He did. There was something about her… Something…

'Can you, Dad?' Bailey asked.

'I'm not sure…' he started.

'Well, I am,' Misty declared. She tossed off her blankets in decision. 'I think Ketchup needs to stand on the grass for a bit and then we need to remember why you came. We need to look at spare beds—I counted them last night and we have ten. Then I'm going to make a list of everything else you need in your house while you and your dad draw me a picture of a little yurt we could build in the school yard.' She rose and hugged her little dog tight against her. 'A little yurt would be fun and we can do without yaks. We don't need anything but what's in Banksia Bay, and why would a woman want anything but what's right here?'

They searched the Internet and learned about yurts. They drew more and more extravagant plans and then Nick got serious and sat down and designed one they really might be able to construct in the school yard. Then they explored the muddle of furniture in the largely unused house.

Misty was right—the place was huge. It had been a big house to start with, and she told him her great-grandparents had built an extension when her grandparents married. She had two kitchens and three living rooms. She owned enough furniture to cater for a small army, and she was offering him whatever he liked.

With Bailey's approval, Nick chose two beds, two couches, a table and chairs. He chose wardrobes, sideboards, armchairs. So much...

'Why don't you want it?' Bailey asked, intrigued.

'There's only me,' Misty said. 'And Ketchup,' she added. She was carrying the dog along with her. He seemed content in her arms, snuggled against her, snoozing as he chose, but taking comfort from her body heat. 'I've tried to rent out the other half but no one wants to live this far out of town. So now I'm closing rooms so I won't need to dust.'

'Won't it feel creepy when it's empty?' Bailey asked. 'Like our place does?'

'Ah, but you've forgotten, I have a watchdog now. Ketchup's messed with my plans but now he's here I can make use of him.'

'Were you thinking of moving somewhere smaller?' Nick asked, and she gave him a look that said he didn't get it.

'I told you. I want a yurt. But I'm amenable. Is this all you want? If we're done, then how about tea?'

'You can't be hungry again.'

'How can you doubt it? It's four hours since my sandwich.'

Four hours! Where had the time gone? In drawing yurts. In exploring. In just…talking.

'I'd like a picnic on the beach,' she said and visions of gingham baskets rose again—to be squashed before they hit knee height.

'There's a great pizza place in town,' she said. 'I bribe them to deliver all the way out here.'

'Pizza,' Bailey said with joy, and Ketchup's ears attempted to rise.

'We've hit a nerve.' She grinned. 'Picnic pizza it is. If that's okay with you, Mr Holt?'

'Nick,' he said and it was almost savage.

She made him take three trips to her favourite spot on the sand dunes, carrying cushions, rugs and food, because she was carrying Ketchup.

They ate pizza until it was coming out of their ears. Ketchup ate pizza, too.

'I have a feeling Ketchup's met pizza in a former life,' Misty said, watching in satisfaction as he nibbled round the edges of a Capriccioso.

'He looks like he might be a nice dog,' Nick said—cautiously. He was feeling cautious.

He was feeling strange.

Ketchup and Bailey were lying full length on the rug. They were playing a gentle boy-dog game that had them touching noses, touching finger to paw, touching paw to finger, then nose to nose again. They were totally absorbed in each other. Bailey was giggling and Ketchup seemed at peace.

The evening was warm and still. The sun was sinking low

behind the sand hills and the outgoing tide sent a soft hush-hush of surf over the wet sand. Sandpipers were sweeping up the beach as the water washed in, then scuttling out after the waves to see what had been washed bare.

Misty's house looked out over paradise.

How could a man want adventure when he had this?

And this woman… She was watching Bailey with contentment. She seemed secure in herself, a woman at peace.

She was so different from Isabelle. A woman like this would never need adrenalin rush, danger.

A woman like this…

'Why don't you have a dog already?' he asked and Misty stopped squashing pizza boxes, glanced at Ketchup and looked rueful.

'We had a surfeit of dogs.'

'Who's we?'

'My grandparents and me.'

He thought about that. It seemed safer than the other direction his thoughts were taking. Actually, he wasn't sure where his thoughts were taking him, only that it seemed wise to deflect them. 'Not your parents?'

'My mother didn't live here.'

'Never?'

'Not since she was eighteen. She left to see the world, then turned up only for brief visits, bringing things home. Weird people, artwork, dream-catchers. One day she brought me home. She didn't stay any longer than the time she brought the dream-catchers, but she left me for good. Gran and Grandpa kept the dream-catchers and they kept me.'

'That sounds dreadful.'

'Does it?' She smiled and ran her fingers the length of Ketchup's spine, causing the little dog to roll his eyes in pleasure. 'It never seemed dreadful. Sad, yes, but not dreadful. We saw her world through postcards, and that gave me a presence to cling to. An identity. And, as for needing her…I wasn't deserted. Gran and Grandpa did everything they could for their daughter, and they did everything they could for me.'

'But you stayed, while your mother left.'

'I loved my grandparents, and they loved me,' she said, sounding suddenly uncompromising. 'That's something I don't think my mother's capable of. It took me a while to figure it out but I know it now.' Her smile faded. 'It's her loss. Loving's fine. Like I fell in love with Ketchup yesterday. I'm a soft touch.'

'You've never fallen in love before?'

'With other dogs?' That wasn't what he'd meant but maybe she'd purposely misunderstood. 'Of course I have. Five years ago we had four. The last one died six months ago. He's buried under Gran's Peace rose in the back garden. And now Gran herself...'

But something there gave her pause. She gave herself a shake, regrouped, obviously changed direction. 'No. Gran's okay. She's had a couple of strokes. She's in a nursing home but she's only seventy-three. I thought... When she had the second stroke and our last dog died I thought...'

Pause. Another shake.

'Well, it doesn't matter what I thought,' she said, almost to herself. 'It's right to get another dog. When you fall in love, what choice do you have?'

'There's always a choice.'

'Like you could walk away from Bailey?' Bailey looked up at that, and she grinned. 'See? I defy you not to love that look.'

'My son's look?'

'Your son.'

'How can you compare a dog...?'

'Love's love,' she said simply. 'You take it where you find it.'

Where he found it? He'd thought he had it with Isabelle. He'd been out of his mind.

Bailey stretched out and yawned. The sun was sinking low in the evening sky.

Misty sat and watched the sandpipers, and he thought she was such a peaceful woman. She was also beautiful. And the more he looked… She was quite astonishingly beautiful.

He wanted, quite badly, to kiss her.

And that was a really bad idea. This was his son's school-teacher. His son was two feet away.

But not to touch her seemed impossible.

Her hand was on the rug, only inches from his. How could he not? He reached out and ran his fingers gently over the back of her hand and she didn't flinch.

Her skin wasn't silk-smooth like Isabelle's had been. There were tiny scars. Life lines.

The world was still. Maybe…

'No,' she told him and tugged her hand away.

'No?' The contact had been a feather touch, no more. But she'd said no, and even now he knew her well enough to realise that she meant it. And for him? No was sensible. What was he thinking of?

'Parent-teacher relationships are disasters,' she said.

'Always?' The word was out before he could stop it.

'Always.'

'You've tried a few?'

'That's my business.'

He smiled but it was an effort, and that was a puzzle on its own. What was happening here? He had to get this back on a lighter note.

'I've told you about Isabelle,' he said, in a dare you tone.

'You want me to tell you about Roger Proudy kissing me behind the shelter sheds when I was eight?'

'Did he?'

'Yes, and it was sloppy.' She was also striving to make this light, he thought. That was good. She had a handle on things, which was more than he did.

'When Grandma kisses me it's sloppy,' Bailey said dreamily from where he was snoozing against Ketchup, and the conversation suddenly lost its intensity. They were back on a plane where he could keep his balance.

'Do you have one grandma or two?' Misty asked Bailey.

'Two, but Grandma Holt cries, and she gets lipstick all over me.'

'That sounds yuck,' Misty said. 'Do you see your grandmas often?'

'Gran Rose and Papa Bill live on a boat like we used to,' Bailey said. 'They came to see me in hospital lots of times. They gave me computer games and stuff. But Grandma and Grandpa Holt only came once. Grandma said computer games are the work of the devil, and Grandpa yelled at Dad when he said we weren't going back to Pen...Pennsylvania. Then Grandma Holt cried, and kissed me too hard, and it was really, really sloppy.'

'Double yuck.' Misty smiled, then turned to Nick, her eyes lighting with laughter. 'Would Grandma Holt be the no risk grandma? Someone should tell her you can share germs with sloppy kisses.'

And suddenly Nick found himself grinning.

The decision to bring Bailey to Australia had been made under all sorts of constraints. If he'd returned to the States, his parents would have given him a hard time. They'd give Bailey a hard time. But if he'd stayed in England...

Isabelle's parents were based in England. They loved Bailey desperately, but loving had its own challenges. They'd smother Bailey, he thought, and maybe Bailey would react as Isabelle had reacted.

Since Isabelle's death, he'd been in a haze of grief and self-blame. Banksia Bay offered a new start. Here, they were away from Isabelle's parents, with their indulgence. They were away from his own parents saying the things they'd always said, only this time with the rider: 'I told you so.'

Moving to Banksia Bay meant Bailey was spared sloppy kisses.

He looked at Misty and he thought…kisses equal germs? His grin faded.

'We need to go home,' he said, and he knew he sounded harsh but he couldn't help himself. What he was feeling was suddenly pushing him right out of his comfort zone. This was his kid's schoolteacher. He'd touched her. He shouldn't have touched her.

He shouldn't want to touch her.

But she was right beside him, and she was warm, open and loving in a way he could only sense. She was smiling a question at him now, wondering at the sudden change in his tone.

She wouldn't react with anger, he thought, flashing back to Isabelle's moments of fury, of unreasonable temper. Here was a woman who saw everything on an equable plane. Who moved through life with serenity and peace.

And beauty. She really was beautiful, he thought. Those eyes…those curls…

No. He had to leave.

'We need to get moving,' he told his son, rising too fast. 'Let's get this gear up to the house and go.'

'I don't want to go home.' Bailey's voice was slurred by sleep. He was nestled against Ketchup, peaceful now as he hadn't been peaceful for a year. Or more. Maybe never? 'Why can't we stay here?'

'We can't sleep on the beach.'

'I mean in Miss Lawrence's house.' It was as if Bailey was dreaming, drifting into fantasy. 'I could sleep in one of her big, big beds. Me and Ketchup. I could see Ketchup every morning.'

What the…? The idea took his breath away. 'Miss Lawrence doesn't want us here.'

'Ketchup wants us here.'

'No,' Misty said, sounding strange. She also rose, and she looked just as taken aback as he was. 'That's not a good idea, Bailey. You have a house.'

But suddenly Bailey was fully awake, sitting up, considering his suggestion with care. 'Our house is horrid. And we could help look after Ketchup.'

'I can look after Ketchup on my own.'

'He likes me.'

'I know he does,' she said. She stooped and hugged Bailey, then lifted Ketchup into her arms. 'But Ketchup's my dog. Your dad's paid his bills and that's all the help I'll ask. I look after Gran and I look after Ketchup. I can't look after anyone else. I'm sorry, but you and your dad are on your own.'

CHAPTER FIVE

SHE needed to visit Gran. She needed to find her balance.

Once Nick and Bailey were out of sight she settled Ketchup back into her car. He'd be best off sleeping in his basket at home, but every time she walked away he started shaking.

She could worry about Ketchup. She couldn't worry about Bailey and his father.

She couldn't think about Bailey's father.

Was it only yesterday she'd been celebrating Adonis arriving in her classroom? One touch and her equilibrium was shattered.

Think about the dog. Much, much safer.

'You've sucked me in,' she murmured. 'Where did you come from, and how exposed have you made me? Oh, Ketchup.'

But he hadn't made her exposed—he'd simply shown her what life was. Yurts were fantasy. Ketchup was real.

Bailey was real.

She was a total sucker.

'I'm sorry, but you and your dad are on your own.' She'd watched Bailey's face as she'd said it and she'd seen him become…stoical.

She'd been stoical at six. For all her bravado about not needing her mother…surviving on postcards had hardly been survival at all.

She'd ached to go with her. Other kids had mothers. She'd got postcards in the mail.

Bailey got nothing.

He had his dad. It was more than she'd ever had.

No, she told herself sharply. She'd had grandparents who loved her. But grandparents never, ever made up for what a mother was supposed to be. She had a clear idea of what was right, even at six.

'So you're thinking you can possibly turn yourself into a substitute mother for Bailey? Take them in and coddle them?

'Of course I can't.' She was talking to herself, out loud, the habit of a woman who lived alone.

'Why not? The place they're in is awful. You've been looking for tenants for months. Bailey would love living with Ketchup. Why reject them out of hand?

'Because Nicholas scares me.'

Think about it.

She did think.

She couldn't stop thinking.

She was out of her mind.

'Why can't we live with Miss Lawrence?'

There were a million reasons. He couldn't tell his son any of them.

Except one.

'You heard her. She said no. I think Miss Lawrence likes living alone.'

'She doesn't. She said she tried to rent part of her house. And we wouldn't have to move furniture.'

Why was he blessed with a smart kid with big ears?

'Maybe she wants a single person. Maybe another lady.'

'We're better than a lady.' Bailey wriggled down into his seat and thought about it. 'It'd be good. I really like Ketchup.'

Nick thought Ketchup was okay, too. Ketchup and Bailey

touching noses. Bailey truly happy for the first time since his mother died. Ketchup had made him smile.

'Maybe we could get our own dog,' he said and then he heard what he'd said and couldn't believe it.

Here was a perfect example of mouth operating before head. Was he out of his mind? Where were his resolutions?

But he'd said it, and it was too late to haul it back. Bailey's face lit like a Christmas tree. 'We can get a dog?' he breathed.

'Maybe we can,' he said, feeling winded. 'Seeing as we can't live with Miss Lawrence.'

But Bailey had moved past Miss Lawrence. He was only seeing four legs and a tail. 'I can have a dog of my own?'

Miss Lawrence had a lot to answer for, he decided. His plans had *not* included a dog. 'A young dog,' he said. That, at least, was sensible. A young healthy dog wouldn't cause grief. A young dog *probably* wouldn't cause grief.

He'd have to reinforce fences, he thought. He'd have to keep the dog safe, too.

'He'll be able to play with Ketchup,' Bailey said, not hearing his reservations. He was almost rigid with excitement. 'Do you think we can find a dog who'll touch noses? Me and Ketchup touch noses. Like you and Miss Lawrence touch hands.'

'That's got nothing to do…'

But Bailey wasn't listening. The touching hands thing was simply a passing fact. 'Dogs are great,' he said, breathless and wondering. This was turning into a very good day in the World According to Bailey, and he was starting to plan. 'We'll be able to take our dog to visit Ketchup. We'll all have picnics on the beach. We'll all still be able to touch.'

What was a man to say to that?

'Can we build a kennel?'

'I…yes.'

'I can't wait to tell Miss Lawrence,' Bailey said.

'We may not see Miss Lawrence until Monday.'

'We need to get our furniture,' Bailey said happily. 'We'll see her tomorrow. Can we get a dog tomorrow?'

'Do you think having Nicholas Holt and his son as tenants is a bad idea?'

It *was* a bad idea. There were complications on every side. She shouldn't even think it but Bailey's expression wouldn't go away. Bailey's need.

What was it in him that had touched such a chord within?

Other kids lost mothers.

It was the way he'd touched noses with Ketchup, she thought. She'd watched him find huge pleasure in that simple contact, and she remembered how important dogs had been to her as a child. Bailey couldn't go his whole life without a mother—and without a dog.

If they became her tenants he'd share Ketchup. Ketchup would be on Bailey's bed in no time. Kid and dog. Perfect fit.

Their house was truly appalling. Bailey's suggestion was even sensible.

If only she could ignore Nicholas.

She was a grown woman. Could a grown woman get her hormones under control enough to consider a sensible plan?

Surely she could.

Misty set the whole thing in front of Gran, and Gran considered it. Misty knew she did. Gran did a lot of considering these days.

Gran's eyes were closed tonight but, when Misty settled Ketchup on her bedclothes, against Gran's hand, she saw Gran's fingers move against his furry coat. Just a little, convulsively, as if she was remembering something she'd forgotten.

Gran loved dogs.

Love was a dangerous concept, Misty thought. She'd fallen for Ketchup, she was falling for Bailey, and where were her plans now? In a muddle, that was where.

'I shouldn't have agreed to keep Ketchup.'

Gran's fingers moved again.

'You're a soft touch, too. We both are.' She lifted Gran's spare hand to her cheek. 'Oh, Gran, this is dumb. I have fallen for Ketchup, and I would like someone living in the other side of my house. Bailey needs a good place to live and it's sensible. It's just…Nick touched me. I'm scared I'll get involved and I want to be free. But free's not an option. I'm being dumb.'

She had to let her plans go.

She already had, she thought, or she almost had, the moment she'd fallen for Ketchup. And maybe letting her plans go was her only option.

Six months ago, the doctors had told her Gran had weeks to live. But Gran was still here, and there was no thought of her dying. And in the end… How could Misty possibly dream of a future with Gran not here?

Ketchup was deeply asleep now. He'd had a huge day for an injured dog. She should have him at home, right now.

'It's okay to live alone,' she told her grandmother. 'I don't need anyone to help me care for Ketchup, and I don't need complications.'

Gran's hand slid sideways. The tiny moment of awareness was gone.

Misty's thoughts telescoped, out of frame. To a future without Gran?

She'd thought of what she'd do when Gran was gone, but now…Gran was here but not here, and she could well be like this for years.

The future looked terrifying. Living in that great house alone. Never leaving this town.

What to do?

Since Gran's first stroke she'd been trying to plan, trying

to figure her future. But in truth she'd been planning since before she could remember. Making lists.

Maybe she should stop planning and just…be.

She wouldn't mind Nicholas and his little son living next door. It wasn't exactly a bleak thought.

She wouldn't need to rush home to feed Ketchup on nights when she had to stay back at school.

That was a sensible thought.

And then… Another sensible thought. The resurgence of the dream.

'You know, if anything happened to Gran,' she told Ketchup as she settled him back into her car. 'Just saying… If it did, and if Nicholas and Bailey were living in my house… They could look after you while I tried out a yurt. Just for a while.'

Yes. Her dream re-emerged, dusted itself off, settled back into the corner of her mind, where it had been a comfort for years.

'You're making me realign my existence,' she told Ketchup. 'Two days ago, I was alone. What are you doing with my life?'

Ketchup looked at her and shifted his tail, just a little, but enough to make her smile. She did want this dog.

'Maybe you're my nemesis,' she told him. 'I thought Gran's death would be the thing that changed my life. Maybe it's you.'

She bent over to hug him and got a lick for her pains.

'Enough.' She chuckled. 'I'm not used to kisses.'

A kiss. A touch? She was thinking again of Nick's hand on hers. The strength of his fingers. The warmth of skin against skin.

Ketchup wasn't her only nemesis. There was something about Nicholas that was messing with her plans in a far bigger way. In a way that was much more threatening.

She had to be sensible, she told herself. She had a dog and

a grandmother and a house that was too big for her. And if there was something about Nicholas that scared her…

Yep, she just had to be sensible.

He'd agreed to get a dog.

Bailey had gone to sleep planning dog kennels. Tomorrow they'd build a kennel and they'd start to make this place habitable. They were settled. Here.

He'd leased this place for three months. He'd find somewhere else after that, maybe near the school. It'd be okay.

He and Bailey and dog—a young healthy dog—could live happily ever after.

So what was there in that to make him stare up at the ceiling and think…and think…?

And think of Misty.

She tossed the concept around all night and in the morning there was only one answer.

So ask him. Now, before she chickened out.

She didn't have Nick's cellphone number. She could go into school and fetch his parent file, only she'd have to drive past his house to get it. Which was stupid. Cowardly, even.

Ketchup was deeply asleep. She'd had him in a basket beside her bed all night. At dawn he'd stirred. She'd taken him outside and he'd smelled the sea and sniffed the grass. He looked a hundred per cent on yesterday. She'd cuddled him and cooked them both breakfast. He'd eaten two bacon rashers and half a cup of dog food and returned to his basket.

He was now fast asleep on Gran's old woollen cardigan and he didn't look as if he'd stir any time soon.

Unlike Misty, who was stirring so much she felt as if she was going nuts.

It was eight o'clock. The world must surely be awake.

So ask him *now*.

* * *

He heard the knock as he stood under the shower. Which was cold. The hot water service gave exactly thirty seconds of tepid water. 'Bailey...'

'I heard,' Bailey yelled, sounding excited, which was pretty much how he'd sounded since Nick had said the D word last night.

'Don't answer it.' He groped for his towel, swearing under his breath. It could be anyone out there. *Do not take risks.*

'Bailey, don't...' he yelled again but it was too late. There was a whoop of pleasure from the hall.

'It's Miss Lawrence. Dad, it's Miss Lawrence. She's come to visit.'

Bailey was still in his pyjamas, clutching his teddy, rumpled from sleep. He was beaming with pleasure to see her. He looked adorable.

He also looked big with news. He was jiggling up and down, stammering with excitement.

'I'm getting a dog,' he told her before she could say a word, and she blinked in astonishment.

'A what?'

'A dog.' He did another jig. 'We've talked about it. I think we should look at the lost dogs' home 'cos Dad says Ketchup was from the dogs' home and he's good. But I want a dog who can run. Dad says I can choose but he can't be old. And he can't be sick. We're going to build a dog kennel, only Dad says he doesn't know if we can buy wood and stuff on Sunday.'

His joy was enough to make the hardest heart melt, and Misty's wasn't all that hard to start with. A dog of his own...

This little boy had lost his mother in dreadful circumstances. His only friend was his father. But now... To have his own dog...

'That's...' But she never got to answer.

Nick strode from the bathroom, snapping orders. 'Bailey, don't answer the door to strangers…'

He was wearing nothing but boxers.

Misty was a woman with sound feminist principles. She didn't gasp. She didn't even let her knees buckle, which she discovered they were more than willing to do. Women with feminist principles did not gasp at the sight of near naked men. Nor did they allow their knees to buckle, even if they wanted to.

Nick had towelled in a hurry and he wasn't quite dry. His bare tanned chest was still wet. More, it sort of glistened under the hall light. This was a male body which belonged…which belonged somewhere else but in her universe.

'H…hi,' she managed, and was inordinately proud she'd made her voice work.

'It's Miss Lawrence,' Bailey told Nick unnecessarily. He was still jiggling. 'I told her we're getting a dog.'

'Why are you here?' There was a pause, and Nick seemed to collect himself. It was possible he hadn't intended to sound as if she might be a child-snatcher. He took a deep breath, started again. 'Sorry. Obviously I need to get used to country hours. So…' He hesitated and tried a smile. 'You've already milked the cows, churned the butter…'

'Swilled the pigs and chewed the buttercups,' she agreed, managing to smile back. She might be disconcerted, but Nick looked even more disconcerted. Which was kind of…nice. To have such a body disconcerted because of her…

Get serious, she told herself, but it was really hard to be serious in the face of those pecs.

'It's me who should be sorry,' she managed. 'Ketchup woke me at dawn and I've been thinking. Actually, I was even thinking last night.'

'Thinking?'

'That maybe I was wrong to knock Bailey back so fast.

'That maybe it's not a bad idea at all. That maybe it might suit us all if you share my house.'

Silence.

More silence.

Whatever reaction she'd expected, it wasn't this. Nick was staring at her as if he wasn't quite sure who—or what—she was.

As well he might. He'd only met her yesterday. What sort of offer was this?

But they didn't need to be friends to be a landlady and tenant, she reminded herself. They hardly needed to know each other. This was business.

Still there was silence. She wasn't quite sure how to break it, and finally Bailey did it for her. 'We can live with you?' he breathed, and his question hauled her straight down to earth.

Uh oh. Stupid, stupid, stupid. This was not strictly business. Here was the first complication. A basic principle of teaching: don't make children excited before plans are definite. She and Nick should have had this conversation out of Bailey's hearing.

What had she been thinking, just to blurt it out?

She knew what she'd been thinking about. This was all about Nicholas Holt's wet, glistening body. It had knocked the sense right out of her. Understandably, she decided. There was something about Nicholas Holt that was enough to throw any right-minded woman off balance.

'If your father thinks it's a good idea,' she managed, struggling to make it good. She allowed herself to glance again at that glistening body and she thought maybe she'd made a king-sized fool of herself.

He was still looking at her as if she'd grown two heads. That was what she felt like, she decided. As if there was the one-headed Miss Lawrence, the woman who made sense. And the two-headed one who was making all sorts of mistakes.

No matter. She'd made her offer.

If he wanted to live with a two-headed twit then she'd left herself open for it to happen.

She was asking him to live with her?

No. She was asking if he'd like to rent the spare side of her gorgeous house.

Nick was cold. This house was cold.

He'd tried to make toast and the fuse had blown. Half the house was now without electricity. He'd checked the fuse box and what he saw there made him wince. This house wasn't just bad, it was teetering on unsafe.

There were possums—or rats—in the roof. He'd lain awake all night trying to decide which.

A breeze was coming up through the floorboards.

This was not a suitable house for Bailey. He'd made that decision at about four o'clock this morning in between muttering invective at possums. He needed to go find the letting agent, throw back his keys, threaten to sue him for false advertising, find somewhere else…

Before tonight?

But here was Misty, warm and smiling and friendly, saying come and live in her house, with her squishy old furniture, with a veranda that looked over the sea, with Misty herself…

Um…take Misty out of the equation fast, he told himself. This was a business proposition. A good one?

Maybe it was. It'd get him out of immediate trouble. To have his son warm and comfortable and safe…

He wouldn't need to get a dog.

He looked down at Bailey. Bailey looked up at him with eyes that were pure pleading.

A comfortable house by the sea. No dog. Misty.

This was a very sensible plan.

* * *

'We accept.'

He accepted? Just like that? The two words seemed to make Misty's insides jolt. What had she just done?

But Nick was sounding cautious, as well he might. *She* was feeling cautious. What sort of crazy impulse had led her here?

For, as soon as he accepted, complications crowded in. Or maybe as soon as she'd seen his wet body complications had crowded in, but she'd been so overwhelmed she'd made the offer before she thought.

And now...

Now he'd accepted. Warily. So where to take it from here?

This was still sensible, she told herself. Stick to business. She needed to avoid looking at his body and remember what she'd planned to say.

'You might need to think about it,' she managed. 'You... you'll need to agree to my rent. And we'd need to set up rules. We'd live on opposite sides of the house. You'd look after yourselves. No shared cooking or housework. Separate households. I'm not turning into your housekeeper.'

'I wouldn't expect you to.' He raked his fingers through his damp hair, looking flummoxed. 'You're serious?'

'I think I am.' Was she serious? She was probably seriously nuts—but how did a girl back out now?

She couldn't.

A sudden gust of wind hit the outside of the house and blew straight through the floorboards. This house was colder inside than out, she thought. Bailey shouldn't be here and Nick knew it.

'Would there be gossip?' he asked.

So he knew how small towns worked. He was right. In most small towns, gossip would be an issue.

But there was never gossip about *her*, Misty thought, feeling suddenly bitter. She was Banksia Bay's good girl. It'd take more than one man and his son to mess with the stereotype the locals had created for her.

'It'll be fine,' she told him. 'The town knows I'm respectable and they know I've been looking for a tenant for months. And people already know about Bailey. Believe it or not, I've had four phone calls already saying how can you—*you*, Nicholas Holt—take care of a recuperating child in this house, and why don't I take pity on you and ask you to move into my place?'

And every one of those calls had been engineered by Fred. The old vet was a Machiavellian busybody.

She loved him to bits.

'So all I need to do is tell the people who've suggested it how brilliant they are,' she added.

And keep this businesslike, she added to herself, because, respectable or not, any sniff of anything else would get around so fast…

But, in truth, Banksia Bay might decide *anything else* was a good thing, she thought, letting herself wallow in bitterness a bit longer. The locals knew of her dreams, but they flatly rejected the idea she could ever leave. They'd approve of anything that kept her here.

Despite that, she was still fighting to get herself free. And this could help. Having people share her house. Share Ketchup.

Businesslike was the way to go, she told herself again. Adonis or not, involvement messed with her dreams.

As did the sight of Nicholas Holt's bare chest.

But in her silence Nick had been thinking. 'It could work well,' he said slowly. 'We can share Ketchup.'

Here was an echo of her thoughts. 'Share?'

'I told Bailey if we didn't move into your house we'd get a dog.'

'Dad…' Bailey said, unsure.

'We don't need our own dog if we have Ketchup,' Nick said.

And all the colour went from Bailey's face, just like that. All the joy. He'd opened the door for Misty looking puffed up like a peacock, a six-year-old with all the pleasure in the world before him.

Right now, he looked as if he'd been slapped.

'But you said,' Bailey whispered. Nick had seen Bailey's colour fade. In two strides he was beside him, lifting him up into his arms. Holding him close. 'Don't you want to stay with Miss Lawrence and Ketchup?' he asked.

'Yes, but I want a dog of my very own,' Bailey whispered.

'We don't need...' Nick started but Misty shook her head. She'd looked at Bailey and thought yes, he does. He does need a dog of his own.

Sharing wouldn't cut it.

Misty had had a solitary childhood, living out of town with her elderly, invalid grandparents. Her dogs had meant everything to her.

Last night she'd seen an echo of that. Noses on the beach. Ketchup.

Bailey was a great kid. She knew him well enough to realise he'd take great care of a dog.

So say it.

'What if I give you Ketchup?' she said, and both guys looked at her as if she'd just declared she was selling her grandmother.

'But Ketchup's yours,' Bailey whispered, appalled. 'He knows he is. He told me.'

'I've only just got him,' Misty said gently. 'He doesn't really know me. You and Ketchup had a wonderful game on the beach last night.'

'I want my dog and Ketchup to be friends.'

And Nick obviously had qualms as well, but they were different qualms. 'The vet says Ketchup's close to ten years old,' he said.

Now it was Misty's turn to look at Nick as if he was selling *his* grandmother.

'So?'

'So he'll…'

'He'll what?' she said dangerously.

'If we must get a dog, we'll get a young one. Ketchup will cause you grief.'

'Everyone causes you grief,' she said. 'That's what loving's about. Like you. You love Bailey so you promised him a dog.'

'I didn't actually promise.'

'You did,' Bailey said and buried his face in his father's shoulder.

'I believe I said if we didn't live with Miss Lawrence.'

His explanation didn't help at all. Bailey's sob was truly heart-rending—and Nicholas looked at her as if she'd personally caused this.

Enough. This was crazy. She was starting to feel as if she was causing nothing but heartache.

The sight of Nick hugging Bailey was doing weird things to her. Nick with his gorgeous body. Nick with the way he loved his son.

And Bailey? Somehow this small boy had managed to twist his way right around her heart.

Bailey's pyjama sleeve was hitched up as he clung round his father's neck. She could see the savage mark of the bullet, and the scars from the surgery after.

She was messing with Bailey by being here, she decided. Nick had had this sorted, and now she'd come in with an offer that was messing with Bailey's dreams.

Nick would find somewhere else to live. She didn't actually need these two guys in her house. Not if it messed with dreams.

'I believe I need to rescind,' she said before she could think it through any further.

'Sorry?' Nick sounded stunned.

'My offer is withdrawn.' She took a deep breath and met his gaze square on. 'Bailey needs a dog.'

'Not if he gets to share yours.'

'He's not sharing mine. I no longer want you as tenants. Not if it means Bailey misses out on a dog of his own.'

Once again, that look as if she had two heads. 'This is ridiculous.'

'It is,' she said, but then she thought that it wasn't. She thought of the white-faced little boy on Friday night, grabbing his teddy as soon as he got home. She thought of him last night on the beach, touching noses with Ketchup.

A dog of his own would be perfect.

But Nick's face…

How had this happened? He was stuck if he did, and stuck if he didn't.

So help him out. Make his decision for him. She'd always fought for her students' needs. For Bailey, there was never going to be a better time to fight than right now.

'So you're saying…' Nicholas said slowly.

'That I'm no longer offering you my house. Unless,' she said softly, watching Bailey, 'Bailey has his own dog.'

Nick's face turned to thunder.

'Henrietta Farnsworth runs the Animal Welfare,' she said, briskly efficient now she saw her way. Or Nick's way. 'It's only open weekdays, but on Sundays she feeds and cleans at eleven. You could go choose a dog and then accept my very kind offer by midday.'

'This is blackmail.' Nick's growl was truly menacing, but Bailey had turned to look at her and his look strengthened her resolve. She grinned at Bailey and she winked.

'I agree with Bailey. He needs his own dog.'

'Dogs cause you grief. I don't want Bailey to face that kind of hurt.'

'You're saying you won't get a dog because eventually you

might lose him? What sort of argument is that? You're living in the country now. Country kids know about birth and death. Natalie's dad's cow lost one of her twins yesterday. Natalie will tell everyone all the gory details on Monday morning. It's sad but it happens. You can't shield Bailey for ever. Choose a young dog and take your chances.'

Silence. She let the silence run.

Nick set Bailey down and Bailey had the sense to remain silent. Nick raked his fingers through his hair again. She'd first noticed him doing it yesterday, when he was drawing his plans for her yurt. His long strong fingers, running through thick wavy hair, had made her feel… Was making her feel…

Uh oh. Let's not go there.

But she was there. Maybe this man was going to live just through the wall from her.

She shivered, but not with cold.

But he was still coming at her with arguments. 'I didn't mean to promise Bailey a dog,' he started.

She was ready for him this time, growing firmer. 'Yes, you did or you wouldn't have said it.'

'It was a rash moment.'

'You'll love a dog. You saw Ketchup and Bailey together. You'll both love a dog.'

'But Ketchup's recuperating.' He was starting to sound helpless. Helpless and sexy. It seemed an incredibly appealing, incredibly masculine combination.

Stop it. She was a respectable schoolteacher, she told herself. She was a potential landlady. Listen to what he's saying.

'Ketchup doesn't need company.' His arguments were getting weaker.

'Ketchup doesn't need a rough companion,' she agreed. 'Or not at first. But we can keep them separate. Like you and I will be separate. I want tenants, not friends.'

'Really?'

She drew her breath in on that one. *Really?*

'We can meet on the veranda occasionally,' she conceded.

'And Bailey can play with Ketchup,' he said, fast. 'See, he doesn't need a dog of his own.'

'I do,' Bailey said.

'He does,' she said. 'But this is no longer my call. Talk to your son about it. I'm happy to welcome you, your son and your dog into my house, or I'm happy to continue living alone. I need to check on Ketchup. Let me know.'

Enough. She'd thrown her hat into the ring.

Now it was up to him.

'Up to you,' she said and she turned and walked back down the veranda steps and drove away.

What had she done?

Nicholas Holt had just backed himself into a very small corner.

Maybe he'd be angry. Maybe he'd decide that yes, he'd buy a dog, but they wouldn't move into her place. If he thought she was a blackmailer, they just might.

Maybe he'd tell Bailey that yes, he'd buy him a dog, but not till, say, Christmas. Or when he reached twenty-one.

Ketchup was awake and watching for her. He hopped stiffly out of his basket, balancing on three legs as he nudged her ankles. He had a world of worry in his eyes.

'That makes two of us worried. But I don't know why I am,' she told him. 'I don't want them to move here. It'd cause complications.'

But she was lying. She did want them to move here. She wanted complications.

'Only because I can't have my yurt for a while longer,' she muttered. 'I need to let it go.'

She had let it go. And maybe she'd just let prospective tenants go.

'I've pushed him too far,' she told Ketchup.

Maybe he wasn't as wealthy as the Internet suggested. She

knew the guy who owned the house he was in. He'd have demanded rent in advance.

Nick was already paying an expensive veterinary bill. He hadn't asked her how much she intended charging. Maybe... Maybe...

Maybe she was a complete fool. And the way he made her feel... What was she doing, hoping the phone would ring?

The phone rang.

She let it ring five times. It wouldn't do to be eager.

On the sixth ring she lifted it. 'Yes?' She was gearing herself for a blunt refusal. Anger. Maybe he had the right to be angry.

'You need to help me,' Nick said, sounding goaded.

'How can I do that?'

'You need to help my son choose a dog,' he said. 'What time did you say this woman will be at the Shelter? And then you need to give me a key to your front door. I believe you have two new tenants. Three, if you count our new dog.'

CHAPTER SIX

NICK drove towards the Animal Shelter and beside him Bailey's face glowed. He held his teddy, but he was looking forward, all eagerness, to what lay ahead.

'A dog of my own,' he whispered as if he couldn't believe what was happening. 'And living with Miss Lawrence...'

'*Next door* to Miss Lawrence.'

'I know,' he said. 'I'm getting a dog.'

Dogs had germs. Nick could still hear the echo of his mother's horrified response when he'd asked for a dog thirty years ago.

Germs. Heartbreak. Loss. This was a risk—but Misty was right. He couldn't protect his son from everything. He needed to loosen up.

And his son would be safe with Misty. The sensation that caused was wonderful. It was like going into freefall, but knowing the landing was assured. And maybe the landing was more wonderful than the fall itself.

For, dog or not, once he'd agreed to her conditions, he felt as if he was landing. He was finding a home for his son—with Misty.

He was finding a home *beside* Misty, he reminded himself, but that wasn't how his body was thinking.

She'd teased him this morning. She'd backed him into a corner and she'd enjoyed doing it.

He'd been angry, frustrated, baffled—but he'd loved her doing it.

He turned the corner and she was already parked outside the Shelter. She was standing in the dappled sunlight under a vast gum tree, in her faded jeans, a sleeveless gingham shirt and old trainers. Her hair was caught back with a red ribbon and the sunlight was making her chestnut curls shine.

'Isn't she pretty?' Bailey whispered and he could only agree.

Beautiful.

'She has Ketchup,' his son added, and Bailey was right. She had her dog in her arms. Why did she have him here?

'We need Ketchup's approval,' she explained. 'If these dogs are to live next door, we can't have them growling at each other.'

'I want a running dog,' Bailey said.

'Fast is good,' Misty agreed. She wasn't looking at Nick. Her attention was totally on Bailey and he was caught by the fact that he was sidelined.

From the time he'd won his first design prize, aged all of nineteen, Nick had moved among some of the wealthiest women in the world. His boat owners had money to burn and the boats he designed meant he had money to match them.

Women reacted to him. Even when he'd been married, women had taken notice of him. But now it was clear he came a poor second to his son and he thought the better of her for it.

More than that, the sensation had him feeling... Feeling...

Now's hardly the time to think about how you're feeling, he told himself. Not when you're about to move next door to her. You're here to choose a dog for your son.

'Let's get this over with,' he muttered, and Misty looked at him in astonishment.

'Don't sound so severe. This isn't a trip to the dentist.'

'It might as well be.'

She'd started walking towards the Shelter but his words stopped her. She turned and met his gaze full on. Carefully, she set Ketchup down on the grass and she disengaged her hand from Bailey's.

'If you really don't want a dog, then stop right now,' she said, her voice suddenly steely. 'The dogs in the Shelter have had a tough time—they've been abandoned already. They don't want a half-hearted owner. Bailey, if your daddy doesn't really want a dog, then of course I won't insist. You can still share my house, and you and I can share Ketchup.'

She was angry?

She was definitely angry.

'I got it wrong,' she told him, still in that cold voice. 'I thought it was just your stupid qualms about germs and risks. But if it's more…say it now, Nicholas, and we'll all go home. Bailey, if your father doesn't really want a dog, honestly, could you be happy with Ketchup?'

Bailey stared up at her, surprised. He looked down at Ketchup, who looked back at him. Kid and dog.

'Dad says we can have a dog,' he whispered.

'He needs to prove it. Why don't we leave it for a bit so he can make up his mind? Owning your own dog is a big thing. I'm not sure your dad's ready for it.'

He was a bright kid, was Bailey, and he knew the odds. He looked up at Nick and he tilted his chin. And then, surprisingly, he tucked his hand into Misty's.

'It's okay,' he told his father. He swallowed manfully. 'Miss Lawrence and I can share looking after Ketchup.' He sounded as if he was placating someone the same age as he was—or younger. 'If you really, really, really don't want a dog just for us, then it's okay, Dad.' He gulped and clutched his teddy.

It only needed this. Nick closed his eyes. When he opened them, they were still looking at him. Misty and Bailey. And Ketchup. Even Teddy.

If you really, really, really don't want a dog just for us...

Misty's gaze had lost its cool. Now she looked totally non-judgmental. She'd backed right off. She'd given him a way out.

Behind them, a woman was emerging from the Shelter. Glancing across at them. Starting to lock up.

Was this Henrietta, finishing early? She was letting him off the hook as well.

He felt about six inches high.

What had he got himself into?

He glanced once more, at his son and his son's teacher, and suddenly he knew exactly what he was getting into.

'You want to go home?' Misty asked and he shook his head.

'I'm an idiot,' he told her. And then... 'Are you Henrietta?' he called before any more of his stupid scruples could get in the way of what was looking more and more...he didn't know what, but he surely intended to find out.

'Yes,' the woman called back, cautious.

'Can you wait a moment before you lock up?' he asked her. 'If it's okay with you... My son and I are here to see if we can choose a dog. We both want a dog and we're hoping we can find one, right now. A dog that's fast. A dog that's young and a dog who can belong just to Bailey.'

And in the end it was easy.

Misty and Nick left things to Henrietta and Bailey. 'Henrietta knows her dogs,' Misty told Nick. 'She won't introduce him to one that's unsuitable.'

Bailey walked along the pens, looking worried. He looked at each dog in turn. They barked, they whined or they ignored him, and Bailey looked increasingly unsure.

But then he came to a pen near the end, and he stopped.

'This one's a whippet,' Henrietta said. 'She's fast. She's hardly more than a pup and she's a sweetheart.'

'She's hurt her face,' Bailey whispered.

'Most dogs in here have scars,' Henrietta told him and she was talking to him as if he was an equal and not six years old.

Bailey looked back along the lines of pens—then, as if he'd made some sort of decision, he sat beside the pen with the whippet. The whippet was lying prone on the concrete floor, her nose against the bars, misery personified.

Bailey put his nose against the dog's nose. Testing?

Nick started forward, worried, but Misty put her hand on his arm.

'Trust Henrietta. If she thinks a dog's safe with kids, she'll be right. And did you know kids from farms have twenty per cent fewer allergies than city kids? What's a nose rub between friends?'

Bailey looked back to them, his little face serious. 'She's skinny,' he said cautiously. 'Can I pat her?'

'Sure you can,' Henrietta said, and Nick and Misty walked forward to see. They reached the cage—and something amazing happened. Ketchup stared down at the whippet from the safety of Misty's arms. He whined—and then suddenly he was a different dog. He was squirming, barking, desperate to get down.

The whippet was stick-thin, fawn with a soft white face, and she was carrying the scars of mistreatment or neglect. She'd been flattened on the floor of the pen, shivering, but as Misty knelt with Ketchup in her arms she lunged forward and hit the bars—and she went wild.

Both dogs did.

They were practically delirious in their excitement. Two dogs with cold bars between them… That these dogs had a shared history was obvious.

'Hey, I'd forgotten. You've brought her friend back.' Henrietta grinned and stooped to scratch Ketchup behind his ears, only Ketchup wasn't noticing. He was too intent on the whippet.

'These two were found together,' Henrietta told them. 'I reckon they were dumped together. We put 'em in pens side by side but they seemed inseparable so they ended up together. Your little guy...' She motioned to Ketchup. 'He's cute and normally we'd have had no problem rehousing him, but no one's wanted the skinny one. And somehow no one wanted to separate them.'

'He's ugly,' Nicholas said, looking at the whippet, appalled, and the Shelter worker looked at him as if she wasn't sure where to place him.

'I like whippets,' she said neutrally. 'They're great dogs, intelligent and gentle and fun. Whippets always look skinny, but you're right, this one's ribs practically cross over. She's a she, by the way. She'll feed up, given time, but, of course, they ran out of time. They were both in the van when it crashed on Thursday. Dotty Ludeman found this one in her yard last night and brought her in. So here they are, together again.'

She smiled then, the tentative smile of a true animal-lover who thought she scented a happy ending. 'So Misty's saved one—and your little boy wants the other?'

'I'm not sure.' Nick had visions of something cute. Surely Bailey had visions of something cute.

'Whippets can run,' Bailey breathed.

'How do you know?'

'There was a book about dogs at the hospital,' Bailey told him. '*Whippy the Whippet.* Faster'n a speeding bullet.'

'I know that book,' Misty said. 'Ooh, I bet she could run on our beach.'

Our beach. That sounded okay. Nick crouched to get a better view of the...whippet? He knew zip about dogs.

'She's really skinny,' Bailey said.

'Are you sure she's safe with kids?' Misty asked, and Henrietta chuckled and nodded and opened the cage. The skinny dog wriggled out and wormed ecstatically around Ketchup. Misty and Bailey were sitting on the concrete floor now and the whippet wound round them and back, round them and back. Ketchup whimpered but it was a whimper of delight.

'Uh oh,' Misty said.

'Uh oh?' Nick queried.

'I need to tell you.' She smiled and sighed, letting the whippet nose her way into her arms along with Ketchup. 'What are lists, anyway? If you don't want this little girl, then I do.'

'Do you want her to live on your side of the wall?' Bailey demanded, watching the skinny dog with fascination.

'If you and your dad don't want her,' she said. 'But if you do…these two are obviously meant to be together.'

'So could we cut a hole straight away?'

'I guess we could,' she said, glancing at Nick. Who was glancing at her. Only he was more than glancing.

She'd take on the world, he thought. She'd taken on Ketchup. She'd take on this skinny runt of a dog as well.

Would she take on…?

No. Or…way too soon.

Or way too stupid.

'You want her?' Henrietta was clearly delighted. She checked out Nick, clearly figuring if she could go for more. 'If Misty wants hers plus the whippet, and your little boy wants another, then we have plenty…'

'No,' Misty and Nick said as one, and then they grinned at each other. Grinning felt great, Nick thought. Even if it involved a whippet.

'Do you think she'll let me pick her up?' Bailey asked.

'Try her out, sweetheart,' Henrietta said and Bailey scooped her up and the whippet licked his face like Ketchup had licked Misty's.

'There's been kids in these dogs' background,' Henrietta said, surveying the scene in satisfaction.

'And pizza,' Misty said. 'I bet this little girl likes pizza.'

'That means we need to have pizza tonight,' Bailey said. 'On the beach again. Or on the veranda. We're going to live together,' he told Henrietta. 'Can we take her, Dad?'

'I guess…'

'Then she's Took.'

'Took?' Nick said, bemused.

'Yes,' Bailey said in satisfaction, cuddling one scrawny dog and one battered teddy. But then he glanced along the row of dogs and looked momentarily subdued. 'But… Only one?'

'Only one.' That was Misty and Nick together again.

'Okay,' Bailey said, with a last regretful look at the rest of the inmates. He hugged his new dog closer, as if somehow loving this one could rub off on the rest. 'She's mine. I'm calling her Took 'cos that's what she is.' He smiled shyly up at Henrietta. 'Me and Dad and Ketchup and Took are going to live on both sides of Miss Lawrence's house and we're going to cut a hole in the wall.'

'Why not just open the door?' Henrietta said, and chuckled, and went to do the paperwork.

They took the two dogs back out to the farm and left them in the laundry while they shifted Nick and Bailey's gear.

That took less than an hour.

The laundry was shared by both sections of the house. In theory, they could put the dogs there to sleep. During the day Misty could take Ketchup to her side of the house and Bailey could take Took to his side. But it was never going to happen. Bailey was in and out of Misty's side about six times in the first fifteen minutes.

'I need to go see Gran,' Misty decreed at last, so both dogs settled in the sun on the veranda. Together. When Misty came home, both dogs and Nick and Bailey were on the veranda. Together.

Two days ago, this veranda had been all hers. Now…

Now she had emotions running every which way.

But why quibble? If she had to put her dreams on hold, maybe this was the next best thing.

They ate pizza again—'Just to show Took we can,' Bailey explained. Then Nick read his son a bedtime story on his side of the house and he came outside again as Misty was thinking she ought to go into her side of the house. But Took had left her now-sleeping owner and come back to join Ketchup. Both dogs were at her feet. Why disturb them?

Rockers on the veranda? Any minute now, Nick would offer to make her cocoa.

'Can I make you cocoa?' Nick asked and she choked.

'What?' he demanded.

'It needed only that.'

'It is…cosy,' he ventured and she grinned and shook her head.

'Ma and Pa and Kid and Dogs. It's not the image I want to take to bed with me.' She rose and picked up her dogs. Her *dog*, she reminded herself. And Bailey's dog. In time, they might teach Took to sleep on Bailey's bed. But she had a very clear idea of exactly what would happen. Ketchup and Took would both be on Bailey's bed. Two dogs on a child's bed…

It was the same as cocoa.

She'd settle them in the laundry and go do some school-work, she told herself and turned to the door. But Nick was before her, opening the door, and then, as she struggled to keep Took's long legs under control, he lifted Took from her and followed her.

They'd set up two dog beds. They put a dog in each, side by side. Ketchup whimpered and Took sidled from her basket into Ketchup's. She sort of sprawled her long legs around Ketchup so Ketchup was wrapped in a cocoon of whippet.

'These guys are great,' Nick said, smiling and rising, and Misty smiled and rose, too, only she rose too fast and Nick was just…there.

His face was right by hers. His hands were steadying her.
Back away fast.

She couldn't.

There was something between them she didn't recognise.
There'd been no guy in Banksia Bay who made her feel…like
she felt like she was feeling now.

She didn't want him to let her go.

They were standing in her grandmother's laundry. How
romantic was that? The dogs were snuffling at their feet. That
was hardly romantic, either.

She didn't feel romantic. She didn't feel…

She felt…

She was tying herself in knots. She had to step away, but
his hold on her was tightening. He was looking down at her,
his eyes questioning. If she tugged then he'd let her go. She
knew it.

How could a girl tug?

She smiled up at him, a silly quavery smile that said she
was being a fool. A sensible adult would step away and close
the doors between them and treat this as just…as just him
steadying her because she'd risen too fast.

But one of his hands had released her shoulder, and now
his fingers were under her chin, tilting her face to meet his.

Yes.

No?

Um…yes. Yes, and yes and yes. Her face was definitely
tilting and there was no need for his fingers to propel. She was
propelling all by herself. Her bare toes were rising so she was
on tiptoe, so he could hold her tighter, so she could meet…

His mouth.

Her whole world centred on his mouth.

Her lips parted involuntarily, and why wouldn't they?
She was being kissed by a man who'd made her body melt
practically the first time she'd seen him. *See a man across
a crowded room and your world turns to fire…* She'd read

that somewhere, in a romance novel or a short story or even a poem. She'd thought it was nuts.

Nicholas Holt had walked into her classroom and she'd thought he was Adonis. Only he wasn't. He was just... Nicholas.

He was pressuring her mouth to open, gently, wondrously, and her lips were responding. She seemed to be melting. Her mouth seemed to be merging with his. His hands were tugging her up to him. Her breasts were moulding to his chest. The world was dissolving into a mist of desire and wonder and white-hot heat.

He tasted of salt, of warmth, of wonder. He tasted of... Nicholas.

Her body no longer belonged to her. It felt strange, different, as if she were flying.

She let her tongue explore his. Oh, the heat...

Oh, but he felt good.

'Misty...'

It was his voice, but she scarcely recognised it. He'd put her a little away from him and his voice was husky, with passion and with desire. He wanted her.

It felt powerful to be wanted by a man like this. It felt amazing.

'Mmm?' Their mouths were apart, but only just. She let her feet touch the floor again, grounding herself a little with bare toes on bare boards. Cooling off.

'It's too soon,' he whispered into her hair, but he didn't let her go.

'To take me to bed, you mean?' she whispered back and she surprised herself by managing a trace of laughter. 'Indeed it is. So if you think...'

'I'm not thinking.'

Only of course he was. They both knew what they were both thinking.

And why not? She was twenty-nine years old, Misty thought with sudden asperity. If they both wanted it…

Um…she'd known the guy for two days. He was right. It was too soon.

'So back on your side of the door, tenant,' she managed and he smiled and put her further away, but he was still holding her. They were a whole six inches apart but his hands were on her shoulders and if he tugged…

He wouldn't tug. They were both too sensible for that.

'Let's just see where this goes,' he said and she nodded.

'Yes.'

'But not tonight.'

'No.'

'So different doors?'

'Yes,' she said.

'And a small hole in the wall for dogs and Bailey. But not for us.'

'But rockers on the veranda?' she said, trying to smile.

'Not cocoa?' He was laughing at her.

'No!'

'Dangerous thing, cocoa.'

'It is,' she said with asperity. 'Even cocoa has risks.'

Risks. She thought suddenly, inexplicably, of her list. Her scrapbooks.

Her scrapbooks were dreams. Maybe fate had sent her Nicholas instead.

CHAPTER SEVEN

How could a girl sleep soundly after that? She managed a little, but she slept thinking Nick was just through the wall and she woke up thinking the same.

Nick was her tenant, but their worlds were already intertwined.

Was that a good thing?

Monday. School. No matter how muddled her thoughts, she needed to get going.

She went to check the dogs and found them already on the back lawn, with Nick supervising. He was wearing his boxers again, and nothing else. *Get dressed before you leave your side of the house,* she wanted to say, but she didn't because that'd tell him she'd noticed. And she didn't want to make a big deal of it.

Besides…she was absurdly aware that she wasn't dressed either, or she was, but just in her nightie that was a bit too short and her pink fluffy slippers that were just a bit too silly.

'Cute,' Nick said, surveying her from the toes up, and her toes were where her blush started.

'Inappropriate,' she said, flustered. 'Go get your son ready for school.'

'Yes, ma'am.' He hesitated and she felt like fleeing and finding a bathrobe.

She didn't have a bathrobe.

She'd buy one in her lunch hour this very day.

'If you take Bailey to school I'll look after the dogs,' he said.

'Okay,' she said cautiously, wondering what she was getting herself into. Suddenly she was committed to a school run? 'You'll need to pick him up, though,' she warned. 'I visit Gran after school.'

'Of course,' he said. 'The dogs can come with me.'

'They'll be okay by themselves if you need to leave.'

'Mostly I'll stay,' he told her. 'I have my desk set up overlooking the sea. My son's safe. I'll have dogs at my feet. What more could a man want?'

'A pipe and slippers,' she said, and she caught herself sounding waspish. What was wrong with a pipe and slippers?

'You'll need to think about shopping,' she told him. 'You can't live on pizza for ever.'

'Would you like to eat together tonight?'

'No!' It was a response of pure panic.

'No?'

'I...I may need to stay longer with Gran. Sometimes I grab a takeaway burger and eat with her.'

'Is she very ill?'

'She's not aware...' she started and then her voice trailed off at the impossibility of explaining the unexplainable. 'Or maybe she is. I'm not sure.'

'I'm sorry.'

'No, but sometimes I think she is. And then I stay.' She hesitated. 'Maybe she'd like to meet Bailey. I'll tell her about him. If you think Bailey...'

'We could do that,' he said gravely. 'Tell me when.'

When I'm ready, she thought as he retreated to his side of the house and closed the door behind him. When I'm ready to admit that these doors might stay open.

'That was fast.'

Playtime. She was on yard duty. Frank hardly ever graced the grounds with his presence, but today the Principal of

Banksia Bay Primary wandered out as she supervised play and nudged her, grinning with a leer she hated. 'I didn't think you had it in you.'

'What?' Frank could be obnoxious, and she suspected he was about to give a display.

'Nicholas Holt. Taking him home to bed already?'

Great. She might have known Frank would make it into a big deal. Most locals wouldn't think less of her for taking Nick and Bailey in as tenants, but the school Principal had a grubby mind.

'And you've got a dog,' Frank said. 'I thought you were clearing the decks.'

'What do you mean?'

'So you could get out of here after your grandmother dies.'

No one else would say it to her face, Misty thought. No one else was so horrible.

But she'd known Frank for a long time, and she was well past the stage where he could upset her. 'Leave it, Frank.'

'Don't do it, Mist.'

'Sorry?'

Suddenly Frank's voice was serious. Once upon a time she and Frank had been friends. He was the same age as she was. At fifteen...well, they hadn't dated but they'd hung out together and they'd shared dreams.

'I'm going to be a politician,' he'd said. 'I'll go to Canberra, do Political Science. I can make a difference, Mist.'

And then he'd fallen head over heels with Rebecca Steinway and Rebecca had eyes for only one thing—marriage and babies and not necessarily in that order. So, instead of going to Canberra, at eighteen Frank had become a father, struggling to do the same teacher's course Misty was doing.

Their qualifications were the same. Misty could have applied for the top teaching spot when it became vacant—she'd done a lot better in the course than Frank—but, by the time the old Principal had retired, Frank had three babies and was desperate for the extra money.

And now...

'You'll be stuck in this dump with a stepkid,' he said, almost roughly.

'I'm taking in tenants, not getting engaged. And it's not a dump. It's a great place...'

'To raise a family? Is that what you want?' Then he laughed and turned away. 'But of course it is,' he said. 'The only one who ever really wanted to get out of here was me. So much for your list, Misty. One dose of hormones and it's shot to pieces.'

She watched him go, his shoulders slumped. She didn't feel sorry for him, or not very. He could change what he was. Rebecca was nice, bubbly, cuddly. They had good kids. But staying here...being trapped...

It had changed him, destroyed something in him that was fundamental to who he was, she conceded. Frank was no longer faithful to Rebecca. He was no longer committed to this school.

Your list is fundamental to who you are, a voice whispered. *It's why you've got up in the morning for years.*

She closed her eyes. Her list wasn't important. Was it?

When she opened her eyes, Bailey was being towed to the sandpit by Natalie, the two of them giggling.

Bailey looked like his dad. Nicholas was gorgeous. Nicholas made her feel...

As Rebecca had once made Frank feel?

Stop it, she told herself harshly. Don't even go there. One day at a time, Misty Lawrence, and don't you dare pull back because of Frank, or a stupid, unattainable list. If you do, then you risk ending up with nothing.

But, decision or not, she didn't eat with them that night. Deliberately. Gran was more deeply asleep than usual when she visited her after school but she decided she'd stay on anyway. She did her schoolwork by Gran's bedside and at eight she finally went home.

Nick was on the veranda, by himself.

Her heart did this queer little twist at the sight of him. Stupid.

He wasn't by himself, she saw as she got nearer. The two dogs were at his feet and for some reason that made her heart twist all over again.

They looked up and wagged their tails and settled again.

'Is your gran okay?' Nick asked, and smiled, and her stupid heart did its stupid back flip with pike. Stop it, stop it, stop it.

'She's okay,' she managed. 'The dogs?'

'They've been missing you.'

'Really?' They'd done their tail wagging. Their eyes closed again. 'They're ecstatic to see me?'

'I'm ecstatic to see you.'

'At least they wagged their tails,' she retorted, deciding to treat that remark very lightly indeed.

'I don't do a good wag.'

'Neither do I. Especially when I'm tired.'

Was she tired? No, but it seemed the sensible thing to say. It was a precursor to walking right by him, going inside, closing the door.

'There's wine in my refrigerator,' he said, motioning to the glass in his hand. 'I'm only one glass down. It's good wine. I was hoping you'd join me.'

'I…' She gathered herself, her books, her resolution. 'Thank you, no. I need to do some work.'

'Really?'

'Really.'

'Scared, Misty?'

Scared? Maybe she was, but she wasn't admitting it. Last night's kiss had done things to her she didn't want to admit, even to herself. 'It's you who's scared of risks,' she managed.

'I'm not fearful here,' he told her. 'And I'm not fearful for me. I'll do whatever it takes to make my son safe, and he's safe here.'

She didn't like that. The tiny sizzle inside her faded, cooled.

Last night's kiss had started something in her heart that she wasn't sure what to do with. There was a warmth, the promise of fire, the promise of things to come.

My son's safe here.

That was the statement of a man who loved his child above all else. As a teacher, she should have warmed to him saying it. She did.

But had last night's kiss been more of the same? Part of a strategy to make his son safe?

'I do need to work,' she said, trying desperately to tighten things inside that needed to be tightened. To sit on the veranda and drink wine with this man…to plan on doing it again tomorrow and the night after…

No. She would not be part of his safety strategy, or no more than she already was.

'Are the dogs okay?' she asked, managing to make her voice brisk.

'They're great,' he said. 'We carried Ketchup down to the beach after school. Took ran about ten miles in wider and wider circles until we all felt dizzy. Ketchup lay on the rug and watched Took and quivered all over. He'll be running in no time.'

She bit her lip. If she'd come straight home she could have joined them. Maybe Nick and Bailey had been expecting her to come home in time to join them.

It was just as well she hadn't. Be practical.

'They're fed?'

'They're both fed. Ketchup's had his painkillers and his antibiotics. Would you like to take him inside with you?'

She looked down at her dog. He was nestled at Nick's feet, warm against Took. Took was so thin; she needed Ketchup's body warmth. And Ketchup would still be hurting. With Took...

With Nicholas...

'They need each other,' she said. 'They're fine with you.'

'Ketchup's supposed to be your dog.'

'Yours, mine, this is just home.'

'My thoughts exactly,' Nick said and rose. 'Are you sure you don't want wine?'

'No.'

'Cocoa?'

'No!'

'That got a reaction,' he said, and grinned. 'You don't see yourself as a cocoa girl?'

'I have some living to do before then.'

'This is a great spot to do some living,' he said contentedly.

'No,' she said, and she remembered Frank's words. They weren't about her, she thought. It shouldn't matter that one man had been trapped and turned bitter.

But, oh, the bitterness...

'This might be a place for you to retreat to and live the rest of your life after danger,' she whispered, bending to give Ketchup a pat, a scratch behind his ears, before she made her escape. 'But for me it's a place to come home to between living.'

He frowned. 'What do you mean?'

'Meaning I've never had danger at all,' she told him. 'Not... not that I want it. Of course I don't. But I would have liked one little adventure before I retired to my rocker and cocoa.'

He was looking confused. As well he might, she thought. Her dreams were nothing to do with this man.

'Sorry, I'm being dumb,' she managed. 'But I do need to do some work. Enjoy your evening.' And she bolted through the screen door onto her side of the house before he could probe any more.

I've never had danger at all... What sort of stupid statement was that? But she knew what she meant.

'Your list is hopeless,' she whispered to herself as she closed the door on man and dogs. So stop rabbiting on about danger. About adventures.

Deep breath. 'Okay,' she told herself. 'Let's get this in perspective. Yes, I kissed him and yes, I liked it. Or more than liked it,' she conceded. 'But I won't be kissed because I'm a safe haven. Nicholas Holt and his son are gorgeous but I'm not stupid. At least—please don't let me be stupid. Please let me keep my head. Please don't let me turn into Frank.

'And please give me strength to stay on my side of the door.'

How could she live in the house and avoid him? She tried, but in the mornings when Bailey bounced through to be taken to school she couldn't miss him.

She dressed early now—there was no way he was catching her in her nightwear again—but even when she was ready for them...

Nick leaned his long body against the kitchen bench while she finished her coffee and Bailey gave her a full report on all that had happened since she'd last seen him.

Seeing that was only since school finished the night before, it was hardly momentous but there was still a lot to tell—how many seagulls Took had chased, or that Dad had cooked sausages for them the night before—she'd smelled them and it had almost killed her not to dump her pasta and head next door—and how Dad's sketches of his new boat were almost finished and it was going to be beeyootiful and it was going to be built in England but Dad said they couldn't go and see it.'

'Why not?' She couldn't help herself asking. She could be polite. She just couldn't be involved.

She was not a safe haven.

But it seemed she was, like it or not. 'This is where we live now,' Bailey said happily. He hesitated. 'Gran Rose and Papa Bill still live in England but Dad says they might come out and see us soon.'

'Isabelle's parents,' Nick explained.

'Dad's Mom and Papa don't like us very much,' Bailey confided. 'When I was in hospital they told Dad, "Reap as you sow". I don't exactly know what it means but Dad got angry and Gran Rose started to cry and then they went away. And they think Australia's dangerous.'

'Oh, dear,' Misty said and abandoned the rest of her coffee and bundled Bailey to school. Feeling ill for Nick.

Ill or not, she could not afford sympathy. It was important not to get caught up in his shadows.

Yeah, and pigs might fly but she didn't have to hang round the kitchen one minute longer than she must.

She didn't need to hang round Nicholas Holt.

She was not safe.

She arrived home the next night and Nick was in the laundry, inside her washing machine. Bits were spread everywhere. He was wearing greasy overalls and she couldn't see his head.

'So how long's it been taking itself on tours all over the laundry?' he asked, muffled by washing machine. 'And ripping the odd shirt.'

'I had someone look at it last week.' Indeed she had, and last month as well. 'Buy a new one,' the mechanic had said. 'It's well past its use-by date.'

Nick inflicted a couple of satisfactory thumps and a final one for good measure before hauling himself out from underneath. 'I'm thinking she'll be right now,' he said. 'I just need to put her back together.'

There was a long line of grease running down the side of his nose. He had grease in his hair. He looked…he looked…

She didn't want to think how he looked.

He put the washing machine back together. It purred like a kitten. She and Bailey watched the first load in respectful awe.

Nick tried not to look smug. Misty thought she wouldn't need to use her list money to pay for a new washing machine. Misty thought there was a man in greasy overalls in her laundry.

She was having trouble not purring herself.

Which just went to show, she thought, as she retreated hastily to her side of the house.

She wasn't the least bit safe—and Nicholas Holt was starting to look downright dangerous.

'I don't want it to be the weekend.' Bailey announced to the world on Friday morning, and she wasn't surprised. Bailey had taken to school with joy, and the thought of no school tomorrow seemed more than Bailey could bear.

'You'll have the dogs to play with, and it'll do you good to sleep in,' Nick told his son, delivering him to Misty's kitchen for the ride to school. 'It'll do us all good. Miss Lawrence works too hard.'

Um…she didn't need to, Miss Lawrence admitted to herself. There wasn't a huge amount of correction to be done for Grade One, and she'd created so many lesson plans over the last few evenings she could rest on her laurels for a month.

But she wasn't about to admit that out loud. If only he wouldn't wear those jeans in her kitchen. If only he wouldn't lean against her bench. If only he'd stop fixing things. If only he'd stop smiling. If only he wasn't so long, so rangy. So… Nicholas

No.

'I work no harder than I must,' she said primly and bustled Bailey out to the car with speed, but she was aware of him watching her as she drove away.

He was amused?

He knew she was attracted to him, she thought. But did he know just how afraid she was? Of being kissed.

No. She wasn't the least afraid of being kissed.

She was afraid of being safe.

She was afraid, he thought, and he wasn't sure why. Had she been burned in the past? Roger Proudy and his sloppy kisses?

Why was it important to figure it out?

It wasn't important. It couldn't be important. He'd known Misty Lawrence for less than a week. He'd made an absolute commitment to his son, to do what he must to give him the stability he needed. That did not include getting involved with any woman.

Only this wasn't any woman. This was Misty and she made him feel...different.

Yeah, she was warm, funny, loving. She didn't threaten his plans for the future in any way—rather she augmented them.

But what he was feeling was more than that.

He was working on plans for a seriously large yacht. She was being built in England. He should be there now, but this new way—delegating responsibility to a partner—was working fine. He sat in the big front room with his plans spread out over two tables. He was consulting via Skype. He could see what was happening every step of the way.

He should be excited by this project. He *was* excited, but undercutting his excitement was...Misty.

The vision of Misty was always there, in front of him.

The dogs were sleeping on his feet as he worked. Misty

and Bailey were both at school. He should be knee-deep in boat plans.

He was, but...

'But tomorrow's Saturday,' he told the dogs. 'Tomorrow we get to take a day off. We'll all take a day off. Together?'

Separate houses. Separate lives.

He looked at the two dogs. Separate lives? Yeah, right. They'd figured it out.

Misty.

He needed to do a bit of figuring himself.

Saturday morning, and Misty had every intention in the world of keeping the door between the sides of the house firmly shut.

She could use some extra sleep, she told herself, so she didn't set her alarm, and when she heard a door slam and a child giggle on the other side of the house she closed her eyes again and wished she'd closed the curtains.

Only when had she ever? Her almost floor-length windows opened out to the veranda, to the sea. The breeze was making the net curtains flutter outward. It'd be a great day, Misty thought, and yawned and stretched—and a dog landed on her chest.

Any dog but Took might have winded her, but Took was a very slight dog and she barely packed a whumph.

'Yikes,' she said and Took quivered and licked. It was good to have dogs back here, she thought. It was great.

And more. Bailey's head poked though the window, peering around the net curtains. 'Took! Dad said we're not allowed to wake up Miss Lawrence.'

Took, it seemed, wasn't following instructions. She stood on Misty's chest and continued quivering, but not with fear. This was excitement.

So much for separate. Misty chuckled and moved sideways in the bed so Bailey could join them. Then she realised

Ketchup was at the window, whining at being left out. With one gammy leg, he couldn't manage the twelve-inch sill, so she had to climb out of bed, scoop Ketchup up and scoot back to bed before anyone…anyone in particular…came looking for his son.

She tugged the covers to her chin. She was covered in two dogs and Bailey. She was respectable.

'Where's your father?' she asked, trying to sound… uninterested.

'In the shower. He takes ages. What will we do today?'

'I'm not sure what you're doing,' Misty said cautiously. 'This morning I'll visit my gran, and this afternoon I'm sailing.'

'Sailing.' Bailey lit with excitement. 'I like sailing. Can Dad and I come?'

'Come where?' And it was Nick—of course it was Nick— speaking from right outside the window. So much for showers taking ages. He did have the decency not to stick his head in, though. 'What are you two planning?'

'Sailing,' Bailey said and flew to the window to tug the curtains wide. 'Miss Lawrence and I are going sailing.'

Nick was wearing jeans again and a T-shirt, a bit too tight. His hair was wet. He looked… He looked…

Like it was totally inappropriate for him to be looking through her bedroom window.

At first glance he'd been smiling—his killer smile—but Bailey's words had driven the smile away.

'You're not sailing,' he told his son.

Misty thought that was his prerogative, but his voice was so hard, so definite, so unexpectedly angry that, before she could help herself, she heard herself say, 'Why not?'

'We don't sail.'

'You design yachts,' she said in astonishment. 'You built a yacht.'

'I design yachts, yes, but that's all. Bailey doesn't sail.'

It was a grim snap, and somehow it was impossible not to respond.

'Says your mother.'

His face froze. Uh oh, she thought grimly. That was out of line. She'd overstepped the boundaries—of what was wise, of what was kind. This was not her business.

But she'd said it. The words hung. It was the second time she'd goaded him about his paranoia, and his smile wasn't coming back.

'I beg your pardon?' he said, icy with anger.

Should she apologise? Part of her said yes. The other part wasn't having a bar of it.

'Ooh, who's cross?' she ventured, thinking there was no unsaying what she'd said. It might even be a good thing that she had said it, she decided. Someone had to fight for Bailey. Maybe they should have this out when Bailey wasn't around, but Bailey looked interested rather than worried.

'Dad fusses,' he said and she nodded.

'I guess if I had a little boy who'd just come out of hospital I might fuss, too.' She peeped Bailey a conspiratorial smile, a smile of mischief. 'But the sailing I do is pussycat. I have a Sharpie, a tiny yacht, I'd guess it's far smaller than anything you guys have ever sailed. The bay's safe as houses. Bailey, if your dad lets you try *Mudlark* out—that's the name of my boat, by the way, because the first time I tried her out I got stuck in mud—we could stay in shallow water. And of course we'd wear life vests.'

'You got stuck in mud?' Bailey said, entranced.

'It was very embarrassing,' she told him. 'Philip Dexter, the town's lawyer, had to tow me off. I'm a better sailor now.'

'Dad…' Bailey said.

'No,' Nick said, refusing to be deflected.

'I can swim,' Bailey said, jutting his jaw at his father. They really were amazingly alike.

'No.'

'I'll wear a life vest.'

'Life vests are great,' Misty said. 'They take all the worry out of tipping over.'

'You tip over?' Bailey said, casting a dubious glance at his father.

'Sometimes,' she admitted, being honest. In truth, there was nothing she loved more than setting her little boat into the wind, riding out conditions that had more experienced yachtsmen retire to the clubhouse. Tipping was part of the fun. 'But today's really calm—not a tipping day at all. If your dad did decide to let you come I'd be very careful.'

She ventured a cautious peek at Nick then and thought, *Uh oh.* She wasn't making headway. Nick looked close to explosion. But if he was about to explode…Why not take it all the way?

'You know, if your father was on board, too…' she ventured. 'I'm thinking your dad knows yachts better than I do. I bet he'd never let it tip over.'

'No!' Nick said, and it was a blast of pure icy rage.

Should she leave it? She glanced at Bailey and she thought Nick had brought him here, to this house, because he thought it was safe. Because he thought she was safe.

And something inside her matched his fury. She was *not* going to stick to his rules.

'So what else do you intend to forbid?' she demanded. 'Every kid in Banksia Bay plays in a boat of some sort. Canoes, dinghies, sailboards, surf-kites, water-skis. This is a harbour town.'

'Will you butt out?'

'No,' she said. 'Not when you're being ridiculous.'

'Ridiculous,' Bailey said and finally—and probably too late—Misty decided she'd gone too far. Nick's face was almost rigid. His own child calling him ridiculous…

A woman might just have to back off.

'Maybe your dad's right,' she told Bailey, and she hugged

him against her. She was still in bed, with Bailey and dogs crowded in with her. Nick seemed suddenly an outsider.

She looked at his face and she saw pain behind his anger. Worse, she saw fear. He'd been to hell and back over the last year, she thought. What was she doing, adding to it because she was angry?

'Maybe ridiculous is the wrong word,' she conceded. 'Maybe I'm not being fair. Your dad worries because of what happened to you and your mum, because he knows bad things happen. He brought you to Banksia Bay because it's safe, and it is, but maybe he needs time to see it. I tell you what; why don't you and your dad bring the dogs to the beach this afternoon and watch? When your dad sees how safe it is, then maybe next Saturday or the one after that he'll agree.'

'You think I'm being dumb,' Nick said, sounding goaded.

'I do.' She hugged the dogs and she hugged Bailey. 'But that's your right.'

'Being dumb.'

'Being…safe. But let's change the subject,' she said—and the frustration in his eyes said it was high time she did. 'You and Bailey talk about sailing and let me know if you ever want to join me. Meanwhile, I need to go see Gran. So if you gentlemen could give me a little privacy and if you could take the dogs with you it would be appreciated,' she said, and she smiled at Nick and she kept her smile in place until he'd taken his son and their dogs and let her be.

'Why not?' Bailey demanded as soon as Misty's door was shut.

'If anything happened to your arm…'

He was talking to a six-year-old. He should just say no and be done with it. What happened to the good old days when a man was master in his own home?

This was Misty's home. Her rules?

'I can wear my brace,' Bailey said, and he slid his hand into his father's. Beguiling as only a six-year-old could be.

'No.'

'Dad…'

'We'll think about it. Later.'

'Okay,' Bailey said. He really was a good kid. There'd been so many things he couldn't do over the last year that he was used to it. 'Can we make Ketchup and Took bacon for breakfast?'

'Yes,'

'Hooray,' Bailey said and sped away, dogs in pursuit.

How much bacon did he have? Enough for dogs?

He could borrow some from Misty.

The way he was feeling… No.

But then he thought of Misty, her chin tilted, defiant, pushing him to the limit.

And he thought of his son.

There'd been so many things Bailey couldn't do over the last year…

What was he doing, adding more?

Define *safe*, he thought, and he thought of Misty in bed with dogs and Bailey.

Misty was safe.

Misty was gorgeous.

The feeling stilled and settled.

Misty was home.

CHAPTER EIGHT

MISTY visited Gran, who was so deeply asleep she couldn't be roused.

Discomfited, worrying about Gran and worrying almost as much about the guys she'd left at home, she made her way to the yacht club. There was no need for her to go home to change. She kept her gear here.

'Hey, Misty, how's the boyfriend?' someone called, and there was a general chuckle.

She didn't flush. She didn't need to, for the words had been a joke. But inside the joke made her flinch. Was it so funny to think Misty could ever have a boyfriend?

It had been four years since she'd had any sort of relationship, she thought, as she fetched her sailing clothes from her locker. She'd been twenty-five. Luke had been her friend from kindergarten. He'd been away to the city, broken his heart and come home to Misty. He'd wanted to marry, settle on his parents' farm and breed babies and cows.

She'd knocked him back. He'd married Laura Buchanan and they had two babies already and four hundred Aberdeen Angus.

Since then... Misty was twenty-nine and for four years she'd lived alone with her scrapbooks and a list. Miss Havisham in the making?

'What's he like?' someone called, and she tugged herself back to the here and now. 'The boyfriend.'

'Wildly romantic,' she threw back, figuring she might as well go along with it. 'I've seen him in his pyjamas. Sexy as.'

She hadn't seen him in his pyjamas. She'd seen him in his boxers. He was indeed sexy.

Let's not go there.

'Woohoo,' someone called. 'Our Misty has a life!'

Only she hadn't. She changed into her yachting gear and the old frustrations surged back.

Nick had kissed her. *Misty has a life?* Maybe she had. If she wanted it, a relationship was beckoning.

But why had he kissed her? He was attracted to her because she was Misty, the safe one.

Luke had broken his heart and come back to her.

To Misty. To safe.

She glanced out at the bay and saw a gentle breeze rippling the water. It was perfect sailing conditions, but she didn't want perfect. She wanted twenty-foot waves, a howling sou-easterly and trouble.

'My turn to win this time,' someone said and it was Di, the local newsagent. At sixty-five, Di was still one of the town's best sailors. She'd represented Australia in the Olympics. She'd travelled around the world honing her skills.

Misty had stayed home and honed hers.

She and Di were competitive enough. In this bay she could often beat her. But if she ever got out of this bay...

Who knew? She certainly didn't.

Don't think about it, she told herself. Concentrate on beating Di.

And not thinking about Nick?

The race didn't start until two. Mostly the yachties sat round the clubhouse talking, but Misty bought a sandwich and launched *Mudlark*. She sailed out to the entrance to the bay—looking for trouble? But conditions outside weren't any different to inside.

No risks today. Safe as houses.

What was wrong with safe? she demanded of herself. Get over it.

Thoroughly unsettled, she sailed her little boat back inside and spent an hour practising, pushing herself so she had *Mudlark* so tuned to the wind she was flying.

Finally, it was time to make her way to the start line. She'd win today.

There was nothing else to aim for.

Oh, for heaven's sake, what was wrong with her? If Gran could hear her now she'd give her a tongue-lashing. What was the point of complaining about something you couldn't change?

What was wrong with settling for dogs and a lovely tenant—a tenant who'd kissed her…?

The boats were tacking backwards and forwards behind the starting line, trying to gain an edge. There were up to thirty Sharpies who raced each week. The yacht club kept some available for hire, so visitors to the town could join in. That made it more fun; often an out of town yachtie could surprise them. But no out of town yachtie could beat them.

Di had the experience. Misty had the local knowledge. It was Di or Misty, almost every week.

She checked Di's boat. Di was geared up, ready to go.

The starter's gun fired. *Mudlark* flew, streaming across the water, her sails catching the wind at just the right angle.

The wind was in her hair, on her face. She was sailing fast and free. If she couldn't have her list, this was the next best thing.

And Nick? Was he the next best thing?

A boat was edging up on the same tack as *Mudlark*. She saw it out of the corner of her eye and was surprised. She'd expected to be well in front by now.

And then… Startled, she realised it wasn't Di. It was one of the little orange Rentaboats.

Hey, an out-of-towner pushing her. That'd do to keep her mind off things. She tightened the jib, read the wind, tightened still more.

She passed the marker buoy. Brought her round. The Rentaboat was closing in. What the...?

No matter. Just win. Tug those sails in. Go.

Rentaboat was almost to the buoy and, as she caught the wind and sailed back, she passed within ten yards.

'Hey, Miss Lawrence, we're racing you.' The high, excited yell pierced her concentration and Misty came close to letting go of her stays.

Bailey.

Nick.

'Go faster, Dad, we're catching up,' Bailey yelled and Misty saw Nick grin.

Her heart did this stupid crazy leap.

Nick was racing. Nick and Bailey...

Bailey was crouched in the bow, whooping with excitement, bright with life and wonder. Nick was at the helm, intent, a sailor through and through.

'Miss Lawrence!' Bailey yelled across the water. 'Miss Lawrence, we're going to win.'

Maybe they would. Her jib had slackened. She was tightening, tightening. Of all the...

She and Di were competitors with each other. Occasionally something happened and another local took line honours, but to concede honours to a Rentaboat...

Pride was at stake here.

She tuned and tuned, every sense totally focused on the boat, the water, the wind. But no, that was a lie because overriding everything else was the awareness that Nick was in the next boat.

He'd brought his son sailing.

A risk...

Hardly a risk. They were both wearing life vests; of course

they were. They'd not be allowed to race without them. They were surrounded by a fleet of small boats. Even if they capsized, they'd be scooped up so fast there was never a hint of risk

But still…it was a start, Misty thought.

No, she corrected herself. Getting Took had been a start. This was simply the next step.

As finding Ketchup had been her start. Her start of retreating from her list, from her dreams.

What was her next step?

The wind rose, just a little. She should have seen it coming. Maybe she had seen it, but she was away with her lists. The sudden gust caught her unaware, pushed her sideways, dropped her speed.

Nick surged ahead.

'Hurray, we're winning,' Bailey yelled and they would; the finish line was in sight. But then…

Di. Misty hadn't even noticed her coming up on the far side of Nick. Di's Sandpiper edged just ahead. Nosing over the line.

Local pride was intact. Di first. Nick and Bailey second. Misty third.

But a win had never felt as good. It felt fantastic. It was as if she'd been granted the world.

Was it silly to feel like this?

Thoroughly disconcerted, she reduced sail, manoeuvred her little boat back to dock and was inordinately pleased to see Nick had trouble. You needed to know the currents around the clubhouse to get in tight. He didn't know the currents and was having to take an extra run.

Di was calling to him, congratulating him over the water. On the dock, Fred, the vet, was watching. Fred's son sailed. Fred usually watched his son but he was watching Nick now, and she remembered Fred's reaction when he'd heard Nick was a painter.

Nick would be painting for Fred's beloved repertory society in no time.

He'd be a local.

That was great. Wasn't it?

Befuddled, conflicted, she pushed her little boat into shore, then tugged her out onto the hard. Nick needed to go further along, to return his Rentaboat. It gave her time to get her thoughts together, so when Bailey came hurtling through the yard gates and whooped towards her she could laugh and swoop him up into her arms and hug him. And smile over his shoulder to his father.

'You beat me.'

'Your mind must have been on other things,' he said, smiling back, and he looked…fantastic. Faded sweatshirt. Jeans rolled up to his knees. Strong, bare legs. Bare feet. Wind-tousled hair.

He was smiling straight into her eyes, and something was catching in her chest.

Your mind must have been on other things. Really? What could they have been?

'We should have warned you,' he said, and she wondered if she was blushing. She felt as if she was blushing. Was it showing? 'I believe Bailey's yell might have distracted you.'

'You really can sail,' she managed.

'It's what I do,' he said softly. 'It's what I love. I just… needed reminding.'

'That it's safe.'

'That it's still possible to have fun. We've forgotten a bit.'

'And now you have a dog and a sailing club,' she said, a bit more sharply than she intended, and then wondered why she'd snapped. What was wrong with her? She should be pleased for him. She *was* pleased for him. She was delighted that he was starting to loosen up, become part of this community.

But there was something still not right. Something…

'Speaking of dogs… Did you leave them home?'

'What a question,' he said, sounding affronted. He motioned to the clubhouse yard. The dogs were tied under a spreading eucalypt, a water bowl in reach. They were occupied with a bone apiece. A vast bone apiece.

'I didn't do the bones,' he told her. 'But Fred told everyone their story within two minutes of them arriving and your local butcher headed straight back to his shop and brought them one each. Have you ever seen anything happier?'

She hadn't. She felt herself smiling. But then… Tears?

Of all the stupid, emotional…

She did not cry. She didn't. But now…

Dogs with happy endings. Nick and Bailey with happy endings.

And Nick was watching her. Mortification plus. But he wasn't laughing at her. He didn't look like her tears embarrassed him. He lifted his hand and he wiped a tear away before it had the chance to roll down her cheek.

His touch burned. She wanted to catch his hand and hold it against her face—just hold it.

People were watching.

What did it matter? Was this the next step?

'Hey, Nicholas…'

The moment—the danger?—had passed. Fred was bearing down on them, intentions obvious. 'Great sail. Well done. I hear you can paint.'

'Paint?' Nick said cautiously and Misty managed a chuckle as she moved swiftly away.

'Welcome to my world,' she murmured and went to congratulate Di. She hadn't taken his hand, she told herself. She'd stayed self-contained. Good.

But self-contained wasn't actually going to happen. Not if Bailey could help it. She'd taken two steps when he slid his hand into hers.

'When we go home can I come in your car? Dad says we

can have fish and chips for tea. Can we eat tea together? The dogs and I would really like it.'

It seemed surly to refuse, so yes, they ate fish and chips together on the beach. Took bounded a mile or more and then settled beside Ketchup in blissful peace. Apart from looking enquiringly to the chips every now and then, both dogs seemed happy.

Ketchup was looking better every day. The initial pinning of the badly fractured leg needed follow-up. There'd be more surgery later on, but for now he was with Took and he'd found a home.

More, he'd found a boy. And boy had found dogs. The three of them were curing each other, Misty thought, as she watched Bailey tease Took with a chip—tease her, tease her, then shriek as Ketchup whipped in from the side to snatch it. While Bailey was expounding indignation, Took wolfed three more.

Bailey giggled, his father chuckled, Misty went to move the chips out of dog range, Nick did the same and somehow Nick's hand was touching hers again.

They glanced at each other. Nick moved the chips. Then he returned to touch again.

And hold.

'It's been a magical day,' he said softly. 'Thanks to Misty.'

'Thanks to Misty not winning, you mean,' she said with what she hoped was dry humour, but he shook his head and suddenly he had both her hands and he was drawing her closer.

'That's not what I mean at all. Misty…'

What was he doing? Was he planning to kiss her? Now?

'Not in front of Bailey,' she breathed. No!

'Not what in front of Bailey?' Nick asked, smiling down

into her eyes. 'Not thanking his teacher for giving us a lesson in life?'

'How can I have done that?'

'Easy,' he said. 'By being you.' He tugged her closer. 'Misty…'

'No.'

'You mean you don't want me to kiss you?'

'No!'

The laughter was back in his eyes. Laughter should never leave him for long, she thought. He was meant for smiling.

He was meant for smiling at her?

'You mean no, you don't not want me to kiss you?' he asked, his smile widening. Becoming wicked.

'No!' She had to think of something more intelligent to say. She couldn't think of anything but Nick's smile.

'It's very convoluted,' he complained. 'I'm not sure I get it. So if I pulled you closer…'

'Nick…'

'Bailey, close your eyes,' he said. 'I need to give Miss Lawrence a thank you kiss.'

'She doesn't like 'em slurpy,' Bailey said wisely. 'She tells Ketchup that all the time.'

'Not slurpy,' Nick said. 'Got it.'

'And she hates tongues touching,' he added. 'That happened yesterday after Ketchup chewed the liver treat. She went and washed her mouth out with soap.'

'So no tongue kissing—or no liver treats?'

'Nick…' She was trying to tug away. She was trying to be serious. But his eyes were laughing, full of devilry, daring her. Loving her?

'Miss Lawrence has said I mustn't kiss her in front of you,' Nick told his son, and his eyes weren't leaving hers. He was making love to her with his eyes, she thought. How did that happen?

'I mean it,' she whispered.

'So can you take Took down and feed the rest of the chips to the seagulls?'

'Why? It's okay to watch.'

'What would the kids at school say if they saw you kissing a girl?' his father asked.

Bailey considered. 'I guess they'd giggle. And Natalie would say, "Kissie kissie". I think.'

'Exactly,' his father said. 'Miss Lawrence is really scared of giggling and she's even more scared of kissie kissie. So, unless you go away, I can't kiss her.'

'You can't kiss me anyway,' Misty managed and his eyes suddenly lost their laughter.

'Really?'

And how was a girl to respond to that?

'I don't...'

'Know?' he said. 'There's only one answer to that. Bailey, down to the water right now or there's no fish and chips on the beach until the next blue moon. Right?' And then, as Bailey giggled, and he and his dog headed towards the seagulls on the shoreline, he pulled her closer still. 'Ready or not...'

And he kissed her.

Second kiss.

Better.

He knew what he wanted.

His parents considered him insane for being a risk-taker. He'd sworn risk-taking would end.

Was it a risk to believe he was falling in love in little more than a week? Was it a risk to want this woman?

It had been a risk to think he was in love with Isabelle. More—it had been calamity. But this was no risk.

This was Misty. A safe harbour after the storm. A woman to come home to.

She wasn't pulling back. Her lips would feel warm, he thought. Full and generous. Loving and reassuring.

But then his mouth met hers and instead of warmth there was…more. Sizzle. Heat. Want.

Instead of kissing her, he found he was being kissed.

There was nothing safe about this kiss. It asked much more than it told, but it told so much. It told that this woman wanted him, ached for him, came alive at his touch.

It told him that she wanted him as much as he wanted her—and more.

Just a kiss…

Not just a kiss. He was holding a woman in his arms and he was making her feel loved, desired. He knew it because the same thing was happening to him. The awfulness of the last twelve months was slipping away. More—the pain of a failing marriage, the knowledge that he was always walking a tightrope, slipped and faded to nothing, and all there was left was Misty.

He was deepening the kiss and she was as hungry as he was, as desperate to be close. Her hands tugged him closer. Closer still… She was moulding to him and her breathing was almost like part of him.

He wanted her so much…

He was on the beach with two dogs and his son.

Ketchup was nosing between them. Misty's hands were… pushing? She wanted to stop?

They should stop.

Who moved first? He didn't know; all he knew was that they were somehow apart and Misty was looking at him with eyes that were dazed, confused, lost.

'Misty…' Her look touched something deep within. Was she afraid?

She'd wanted him as much as he wanted her. Hadn't she?

Her look changed, the smile returned, but he knew he'd seen it.

'What is it?' he asked, but her smile settled back to the confidence, the certainty he knew. The impudent teasing that he somehow suspected was a mask.

'Entirely inappropriate, that's what it is,' she retorted. 'For me to kiss the parent of one of my students.'

Her student was whooping back to them now, trying to beat Took, who was practically dawdling. 'Can I come back now?' Bailey demanded.

'Yes,' Nick told him. 'And you're not to tell anyone.' His eyes didn't leave Misty's. 'That I kissed Miss Lawrence.'

'Why not?'

'People will tease us,' Nick said and Bailey considered and decided the explanation was reasonable.

'Like saying "kissie kissie".'

'Exactly. And then I wouldn't be able to kiss Miss Lawrence again.'

'I think you need to call me Misty,' she said, no longer looking at him. 'Bailey, when we're on our own, would you call me Misty? Could you remember to call me Miss Lawrence at school?'

'Sure,' Bailey said. 'Do you think you'll marry Dad?'

What sort of question was that?

It was a reminder that fantasy had gone far enough. It was time for reality to kick in.

'Um…no,' Misty managed and the schoolteacher part of her took charge. 'Kissing someone doesn't mean you have to marry them.'

'But it means you like them.'

'Yes,' she admitted, carefully not looking at him. She could feel colour surge from her toes to the tips of her ears. 'But I gave you a kiss goodnight last night. That doesn't mean I'll marry you.'

'It wasn't a kiss like the one you gave Dad.' Bailey sounded satisfied, like things were going according to plan. She cast him a suspicious look—and then turned the same one on his father.

'Have you guys been discussing kissing me?'

'No,' Nick said, but the way he looked…

'Has your father said he wants to kiss me?' she demanded of Bailey and Bailey looked cautiously at his father and then at Misty. Truth and loyalty were wavering.

'I'm your teacher,' Misty said, hauling her blush under control enough to sound stern. 'You don't tell fibs to your teacher.'

'Dad just told you a fib,' Bailey confessed, virtuous.

'Hey,' Nick said. 'Bailey…'

'So you have been talking about me?'

'I saw you kissing in the laundry,' Bailey said. 'I was sort of…up. But I hardly looked.' He grinned. 'But I saw Dad kiss you and later I asked if it was nice to kiss a girl and he said it depends on the girl. And then he said it was very, very nice to kiss you. So I asked if he was going to kiss you again and he said as soon as he possibly can. And tonight he did. Dad, was it okay?'

'Yes,' said Nick.

Misty glared at him. 'You planned…'

'I merely took advantage of an opportunity,' Nick said, trying to look innocent. 'What's wrong with that?'

'How many times do you have to kiss each other before you get married?' Bailey asked.

'Hundreds,' Misty said and then, at the gleam of laughter in Nick's eyes, she added a fast rejoinder. 'So that's why I'm never kissing your father again.'

'Really?' Nick asked and suddenly the laughter was gone.

'R…really.'

'It wasn't just a kiss,' he said softly. 'You know it was much more.'

'It was just a kiss. I'm your landlady.'

'I'm not asking for a reduction in the rent.'

'I'm thinking of putting it up.' She started clearing things, trying to be busy, doing anything but look at him.

'Why the fear?' Nick asked and she shook her head.

'No fear. You're the one who wants to be safe.'

'Hey, we went sailing.'

'I won't be safe,' she muttered.

He frowned. 'What sort of statement is that?'

'Safe as Houses Misty. That's me. Didn't you know? Isn't that why you kissed me? Now, if you'll excuse me, I need to go say goodnight to Gran.'

He was questioning her with his eyes, gently probing parts of her she had no intention of exposing. 'Misty, your Gran's been in a coma for months.'

'And I still need to say goodnight to her,' she snapped.

'Of course. I'm sorry. I'd never imply otherwise. You love her. It's one of the things…'

'Don't,' she said, panicking. 'Nick, please, don't. I need to go.'

'It wasn't just a kiss, Misty,' he said gently, and he rose and took the picnic basket from her and set it down on the sand before she could object. 'Was it?'

And there was only one answer to that. 'No.'

'Then let's not get our knickers in a knot,' he said and his sexy, seductive, heart-stopping smile was back. It was crooked, twisted and gorgeous, as if he was mocking, but there was no mocking about it. His smile was real and wonderful and it turned her knees to jelly.

'Bailey's going too fast for us,' he said. 'There's no rush. There's no need to panic. But still, it wasn't just a kiss. We both know it.' He took her hands and tugged her to him, only he didn't kiss her this time, at least not properly. He kissed her lightly on the tip of her nose.

'Let's take this slowly,' he said. 'We won't mess this up by rushing. But maybe we both know it could be something wonderful. If we play it right—it could be home for both of us.'

* * *

Misty took the dogs with her because she wanted to talk to someone. She left Nick and Bailey sitting on the beach, and they had the sense to let her be.

As they should.

'Because they're my tenants,' she told Ketchup as she carried him. 'I need to be separate.'

But Took was bouncing along beside her. Took was Bailey's dog. Ketchup was her dog.

To separate the two would be cruel.

It felt a little like that now. She was aware of Nick and Bailey watching as she walked away. She was leaving Nick. She was leaving his laughing eyes, his sudden flashes of intuitive sympathy, his sheer arrant sexiness.

'See, that's what I can't resist,' she told Ketchup as she changed out of her sandy clothes to go to the hospital. 'He makes my toes curl but he just thinks I'm safe. If I give into him…if I dissolve like he wants me to dissolve, then I get to stay here for ever. In this house. Mother to Bailey.'

Wife to Nick?

'Maybe I want that,' she said. Ketchup was lying on her bed watching her while Took roamed the bedroom looking for anything deserving of a good sniff. 'Banksia Bay's fabulous, and so's this house. It's the best place in the world.'

As if in response, Took leaped onto the bed and curled up beside Ketchup. Misty looked down at them. Her two dogs, curled on her bed, happy, hopefully for the rest of their lives.

But… There was a scar running the length of Took's face from an unknown awfulness. Ketchup's leg was fixed tight in its brace.

'You guys have had adventures,' she whispered. 'Now you've come home, but I've never left.'

Don't think about it, she told herself. Take your scrapbooks and burn them.

Nicholas had kissed her and he'd touched something deep within. To risk losing what he promised…

For scrapbooks?

The kiss had felt amazing. Her body had responded in ways she'd never felt before.

'I'm a lucky girl,' she told the dogs. 'Yes, I should burn the scrapbooks.'

But she didn't. She slung her bag over her shoulder and she went to see Gran instead.

'Do you want to marry Misty?'

Nick had left enough time for Misty to change and go to the hospital. He was aware he was rushing things. Risking things. Now Bailey tucked his hand into his father's as they set off towards the house and he asked his most important question.

Did he want to marry Misty?

'I've already been married,' he said cautiously. 'It was dreadful when Mama was killed. It takes time for a man to be ready to marry again.'

'Yeah, but we sailed again.'

'So we did.'

'And it was awesome.'

'It was.'

'You marrying Misty would be awesome.'

Would it?

It wasn't his head telling him yes. It was every nerve in his body.

But he wouldn't rush it. He couldn't rush it. There were things he didn't understand.

She didn't want safe?

She must. To come home... He longed for it with all his heart.

And to come home to Misty...

Home and Misty. More and more, the images merged to become the same thing.

CHAPTER NINE

How had they become a couple in the eyes of the town? It had just…happened. There was little gossip, no snide rumours of the Frank variety. There was simply acceptance of the fact that Nick was sharing Misty's house, he was an eligible widower and Bailey needed a mother.

'And he's rich!' Louise, the Grade Five teacher, did an Internet search and discovered a great deal more information than Misty knew. 'He can demand whatever he wants for his designs,' she informed Misty, awed. 'People are queueing for him to work for them. If I'd realised what we had here I'd have kicked Dan and the kids out of the house and invited him home myself. You're so lucky.'

That was the consensus. Misty was popular in the town. A lonely childhood with two ailing, elderly grandparents made the locals regard her with sympathy. They knew of her dream to travel, and they knew she couldn't. This seemed a wonderful solution.

Especially since Nick was just…there. Wherever Misty was.

'So tell me what sort of steak you like for dinner,' he'd ask as he collected Bailey from school, making no secret of the fact that they were eating together. Well, why wouldn't they? The dogs and Bailey insisted the door dividing the house stayed open. Nick was enjoying cooking—'Something I've never been able to try'—and it seemed churlish to eat TV dinners while the most tantalizing smells drifted from the other side.

They settled into a routine. After dinner they'd take the dogs to the beach. They carried Ketchup to the hard sand, set him down, and he sniffed the smells and limped a little way while Bailey and Took bounced and whooped around him.

Then Nick put Bailey to bed while Misty went back to say goodnight to Gran—whose sleep seemed to be growing deeper and deeper—and when she came home Nick was always on the veranda watching for her.

He worked solidly through the day—she knew he did for he showed her his plans—but he always put his work aside to wait for her. So she'd turn into the drive and Nick would be in his rocker, beer in hand. The dogs were on the steps. Bailey was sleeping just beyond.

It was seductive in its sweetness. Like the call of the siren...

Sometimes she'd resist. She did have work to do. When that happened Nick simply smiled and let her go. But, more and more, she'd weaken and sit on the veranda with him. No, she didn't drink cocoa but it was a near thing. He'd talk about the boat he was working on. He'd ask about her day. And then... as the night stretched out, maybe he'd mention a place he'd been to and she couldn't help but ask for details. So he'd tell her. Things he'd done. Places he'd been.

She was living her adventures vicariously, she thought. Nick had had adventures for her.

And then the moon would rise over the horizon and she'd realise the time and she'd rise...

And he'd rise with her and always, now, he'd kiss her. That was okay, for kissing Nick was starting to seem as natural as breathing. It seemed right and wonderful—and after a month she thought it seemed as if he'd always been a part of her life. And part of Banksia Bay.

He was painting for the repertory society. He was repairing

the lifeboat at the yacht club. He was making friends all over town.

And her friends were starting to plan her future.

'You know Doreen's mother's coming from England next term,' Louise said thoughtfully one school lunchtime. 'Doreen would love to get a bit of casual teaching while her mum's here to mind the kids. If you and Nick were wondering when to take a honeymoon…'

Whoa. She tossed a chalkboard duster at Louise. Louise ducked and laughed but Misty suspected she'd go away and plant the same idea in Nick's head.

So what? She should be pleased. Nick warmed parts of her she hadn't known were cold. He held her and he made her feel every inch a woman.

She should embrace this new direction with everything she possessed. She knew she should.

But then Nick would tell her about watching the sunset over the Sahara, or Bailey would say, 'You remember that humungous waterfall we walked under where there was a whole room behind?'

Or Nick would see a picture in the paper and say, 'Bailey, do you remember this? Your mother and I took you there…'

And she'd wait until they'd gone to bed and she'd check the Internet and see what they'd been referring to. The dogs would lie on her feet, a wonderful warm comfort, like a hot-water bottle. Loving her. Holding her safe.

Holding her here.

'So when do you think he'll pop the question?' Louise demanded as term end grew closer, and she blushed and said,

'He hasn't even…I mean we're not…'

'You mean you haven't slept with him yet?' Her friend threw up her hands in mock horror. 'What's keeping you, girl?'

Nothing. Everything. Louise got another duster thrown at her and Misty went to lay the situation before Gran.

'I love him,' she told Gran and wondered why it didn't feel as splendid as it sounded.

Maybe it was sadness that was making her feel ambivalent about this wonderful direction her life was taking. For Gran didn't respond; there was no longer any way she could pretend she did. Her hands didn't move now when Ketchup lay on the bed. There was no response at all.

Oh, Gran…

If she didn't have Nick…

But she did have Nick. She'd go home from the hospital and Nick would hold her, knowing intuitively that things were bad. She'd sink into his embrace and he'd hold her for as long as she needed to be held. He'd kiss her, deeply, lovingly, but he never pushed. He'd prop her into a rocker and make her dinner and threaten her with cocoa if she didn't eat it.

He and Bailey would make her smile again.

What more could a girl want?

'Are you sure he hasn't asked?' Louise demanded a week later.

She shook her head, exasperated. 'No.'

'He looks like a man who's proposed. And been accepted.'

'How could I miss a proposal?'

'You're not encouraging him.' Louise glared. 'Get proactive. Jump his bones. Get pregnant!'

'Oi!'

'He's a hot-blooded male. There must be something holding him back.'

She knew there was. It was her reluctance. He sensed it and he wouldn't push.

All she had to do was smile. All she had to do was accept what he was offering.

She would, she thought. She must.

And then Gran…

* * *

Five in the morning was the witching hour, the hour when defences were down, when everything seemed at its worst. For some reason she woke. She felt strange. Empty.

Something was wrong. She threw back the covers and the phone rang.

Gran.

'She's dead.' She barely knew if she'd said it out loud. She was in the hall, standing by the phone, staring at nothing. And then Nick was there, holding her, kissing her hair, just holding.

'I...I need to go.'

'Of course you do. Put something warm on,' he said, and while she dressed—her fingers didn't work so well—she heard him on the phone. Then someone was at the front door. There was a short bark from Ketchup, quickly silenced, and she went out to find Louise in the hall.

Louise's husband farmed the neighbouring property, and Louise's son was in the same grade as Bailey. Louise and Misty often swapped classes, so Bailey already knew Louise well.

She hugged Misty now, tight. 'Oh, Misty, love, she was a lovely lady, your gran, she'll be missed. Nick says he's going to the hospital with you, so we've agreed that I'll stay here until Bailey wakes. Then I'll scoop him home with me. Is it okay if I tell him what's happened?'

'It's okay,' she said numbly.

'And it's Saturday so there's no pressure,' Louise said. 'If Bailey's okay with it, maybe he can have a sleepover. That'll leave you to get on with things. But we can talk later. You'll be wanting to get to the hospital. Give her a kiss goodbye from me,' she told Misty and she hugged her again and propelled her out of the door.

Nick held her as they walked to the car. She shivered in

the dark and moved closer. She'd known this was coming. It wasn't a shock. But…

'She's all I've had for so long.'

'I wish I'd met her,' Nick said. 'Your gran raised you to be who you are. She must have been wonderful.'

She huddled into the passenger seat while Nick drove and she thought of his words. They were a comfort.

And Nick had known Gran. He lived in Gran's house. He walked on the beach Gran loved. He cooked from her recipe books. And once… She'd needed to stay back late at school. It had been late before she'd made it to the hospital—something she hated. Gran probably no longer knew she came every day but there was a chance…

So she'd rushed in, feeling dreadful, to find Nick beside the bed with Bailey curled up beside him.

Nick was reading aloud, *Anne of Green Gables*, Gran's favourite book of all time. It wouldn't be hard to guess it, for the book had been lying on the bedside table, practically disintegrating with age.

She'd stopped short and Nick had smiled at her, but fleetingly, and he hadn't stopped reading until he reached the end of the chapter.

'I guess that's all we have time for tonight, Mrs Lawrence,' he'd said as he drew to a close. 'Misty'll take over now. Bailey and I will leave you while she says goodnight.'

Who knew what Gran had been able to understand, but Nick had read to her, and for now it felt right that he take her into the hospital to say goodbye.

'Thank you,' she told him as he drove.

'It is my very great honour,' he said. 'This is a privilege.'

The next few days passed in a blur. Too many people, too much organization, too great a bruise on her heart to take in that Gran finally wasn't here. If she'd had to do this by herself…

She didn't. Nick was with her every step of the way. That first night she clung and he held her. If Nick had carried her to his bed she would have gone. But…

'I don't want you to come to me in grief,' he said softly. 'I'll hold you until you sleep.'

'You're stronger than I am.' She tried for a chuckle. 'If you think I can lie beside you and sleep…'

'Okay, maybe it's not possible,' he said and tugged her tight and kissed her, strong, warm, solid. 'So separate bedrooms still.'

'Nick…'

'No,' he said, almost sternly. 'I want all of you, Misty. When you come to me it's not to be because you're raw and vulnerable. It's because you want me.'

'I do want you.'

'For the right reasons?' He set her back, tilted her chin and his smile was rueful. 'Loving you is taking all my strength but I won't go back on what I promised. I won't rush you.'

He was stronger than she was. There was nothing she wanted more than to lie with him, to find peace in his body, to find her home…

And she knew, as he turned away, that he sensed it. That she was torn.

There was still a part of her that wasn't his.

She and Gran had a contact point for her mother—a solicitor in London. A postcard had arrived about five years ago, adding an email address, 'In case anything ever happens'. She emailed her mother the morning Gran died. She left messages with the solicitor but she heard nothing.

So what was new? She went about the funeral arrangements and she could only feel thankful that Nick was with her. He didn't interfere. The decisions were hers to make, but he was just…there. His presence meant that at the end of a gruelling time with the funeral director she could stand in Nick's arms and let his strength and his warmth comfort her. She wasn't alone.

The funeral was huge—Gran had been truly loved. Misty sat in the front pew, and who cared what people thought, Nick sat beside her.

She spoke at the ceremony, for who else was to speak for Gran? When she choked at the end, it was Nick who rose and held her.

This was the end of a life well lived. She couldn't be too sad that Gran was finally gone. But what did make her desperately sad…

Where was her mother?

She remembered her grandfather's death, terrifyingly sudden, her grandmother devastated.

'But your mother will come home now,' Gran had whispered, her voice cracked with anguish, and Misty knew she was searching for something that would lighten this awful grief.

'I expect she will,' she said, but of course she didn't.

So why should she come now?

If Nick hadn't been here…

All through that long day, as neighbours came, hugged her, comforted her, Nick was beside her, ready to step in, ready to say the right thing, ready to touch her hand, to make sure she knew he was there for her.

The locals responded to it. Nick had been here for little more than a month, yet already he was treated as one of them. He was Misty's partner. Misty's man.

If he wanted to marry her she'd say yes, she thought, as the day faded to dusk. It might not be the right thing to think on this day but it steadied her. She had Nick and Bailey and two dogs and a house, and a job she loved and a town full of people who loved her.

Her house was full of food and drink, full of people who'd loved Gran. There was laughter and stories and tears, all about Gran.

'I keep thinking about Paris,' someone said—it was an old lady Misty scarcely recognised. And then she did. This was Marigold, her grandmother's bridesmaid. She remembered Marigold visiting them when she'd been a child. Marigold lived in Melbourne now, with her daughter. That she'd come so far to say goodbye to her friend made her want to cry.

'Paris?'

'Before we were married,' Marigold said. 'Your grandmother and I scraped enough to buy tickets on a ship and just went. Our parents were horrified. Oh, the fun… Not a bean between us. We got jobs waitressing. We taught each other French. We had such adventures. The night we both got bedbugs… There were two lovely English boys who let us use their room. They slept on the floor so we could have clean mattresses but the scandal when Madame found out where we'd slept; you'd have thought we were worse than bedbugs.'

Her old face wrinkled, torn between laughter and tears. 'Such a good friend. Such memories. Memories to last a lifetime.'

'Gran went to Paris?'

'She never let me tell you,' Marigold said. 'She told your mother and look what happened.' Then she glanced at Nick with the unqualified appreciation of a very old lady for a piece of eye candy. 'I can tell you now, though,' she said. 'You wouldn't leave this to racket around the world like your mother. This is lovely.'

For some reason, Misty was finding it hard not to cry. Why now, when she'd held it together all day? 'I…'

'Misty's had enough,' Nick, interceding gently. 'Today's been huge. If you'll excuse her…'

'That's right; you look after her,' Marigold said approvingly. 'She's a good girl, our Misty. She always does the right thing.'

The crowd left. Nick started clearing the mess but he shooed Misty to bed. The dogs were on her bed, warm and comforting, but she felt cold.

Gran had gone to Paris?

And then…the sounds of a car arriving. She glanced at her bedside table—eleven o'clock? What? Bailey had wanted to stay with Natalie tonight. Was something wrong? Had Natalie's parents brought him home?

She heard a car door banging. Nick's greeting was cautious—not the greeting he'd give Bailey. She heard a woman's voice, raised in sharp query.

'Who are you? What are you doing in my house?'

She knew that voice.

It was her mother.

It took her five minutes to get her face in order; to get her thoughts in order, to get dressed and calm enough to face her mother. By that time, Grace was already in the kitchen, drinking coffee, dragging on a cigarette.

She looked older, Misty thought, but then why wouldn't she? How long since she'd seen her? Ten years?

She was wearing tight jeans and black boots to above her knees. The boots were stilettos, their heels digging into the worn wooden floor. She was too thin. Her hair was black—definitely not what Misty remembered. It was pulled up into a too-tight knot and tied with a brilliant scarf that dragged the colour from her face.

This was a new look mother. Grace had a new look every

time she saw her. Not so hard when she left years between visits.

She saw Misty in the doorway, stubbed her cigarette out and rose to embrace her. 'Misty. Sweetheart. You look awful.'

'Mum.' The word was hard to say.

Nick was standing beside the stove, silently watchful. He'd obviously made Grace coffee. He motioned to the kettle but Misty shook her head.

Her mother was here.

'Why have you come?' she asked, maybe not tactfully, but the emotions of the last few days had left her raw and unable to do anything but react instinctively.

'I was in Australia, darling, when the lawyer contacted me. In Perth.' Her mother sat down again and lit another cigarette. 'Wasn't that lucky?'

'How long have you been in Australia?'

'About a year.' A careless wave of the cigarette. Took had emerged from the bedroom to check out this new arrival. The cigarette came within inches of her nose and Took retreated.

Misty felt like doing the same.

A year…

'I let you know about Gran's strokes,' she said. 'I contacted the lawyer every month saying how ill she was.'

'Yes, but there was nothing I could do. Hospitals are not my scene. It was bad enough with Dad.'

'You only visited Grandpa for ten minutes. Once.'

'Don't you get preachy, miss,' her mother said tartly. 'I'm here now.'

'Not for the funeral. They're not your scene, either?'

Nick said nothing. He stood silent, wary.

'No,' her mother said. 'They're not. I can't pretend grief for someone I hardly knew. But I'm here now.' She glanced at Nick, considering. 'You two aren't in my bedroom, are you?'

'No.' Her mother's bedroom was on her side of the house. Beside hers.

'Excellent. No one told me you had a man.'

'I don't have a man. Nick's my tenant.'

'Some tenant.' She yawned. 'Such a long flight. I had to take a cheap seat. Did you know Fivkin and I have split? So boring. The money…you have no idea. But now…' She glanced around the kitchen thoughtfully and Misty suddenly knew exactly why she was here.

'I don't know any Fivkin,' she said, playing for time.

'Lovely man. Oh, we did such things. But now…' Her mother's face hardened. 'Some chit. He married her. Married! And the paltry amount he settled on me makes me feel ill. But that's okay. I'm fine. I've been checking out real estate prices here. We'll make a killing.'

'We?'

'Well, you and I,' Grace said, smiling tenderly at her daughter. 'The lawyer said I may need to give you a portion. You have been doing the caring, after all.'

It took only this. All of a sudden, Misty wanted to be ill. Badly.

'Leave it,' Nick said, and suddenly he was no longer on the sidelines. He was by Misty's side, holding her, his anger vibrating as a tangible thing. 'This is not the time.'

'To speak of money?' Her mother rose, too. 'I suppose you think I'm insensitive. It's just that I need to sort it and get away again. I've been stuck in Perth for too long. I hate keeping still. I talked to Mum years ago about selling this place but she wouldn't. Now…'

'Is there a will?' Nick asked. He was almost holding Misty up.

'I…yes,' Misty said.

'Whatever it says, it doesn't matter,' Grace told her. 'I'm the only daughter. Misty inherits after I go.'

'Misty's going to bed,' Nick said, cutting across her

with brutal protectiveness. 'We'll talk this through in the morning.'

'We?'

'You fight Misty, you fight me,' he said.

'I'm sure Misty doesn't want to fight. She's a good girl.'

She *was* going to be ill. Seriously. If she stayed here…

'We're going,' Nick said, ushering her through the door. 'Look after yourself, Grace. Misty's had a terrible few days and she's exhausted. I need to look after your daughter, and I will.'

She'd thought she was shivering before. Now… She couldn't stop. Her whole body shook. Nick held her and swore. Or she thought he swore. She didn't actually recognise the words but he kept right on until finally what he was saying cut through her shock and misery.

He was definitely cursing—but not in English.

She let it be for a while, letting the string of invective wash over her, finding it weirdly comforting. Being held by Nick and listening to…

'Russian?' she managed at last, and he said a few more carefully chosen terms of obvious invective.

Distracted, she pulled away. 'What are you saying?'

'What do you think I'm saying?'

'Swearing?'

'A nice boy like me?'

It was impossible to keep shaking when he was smiling. 'A nice boy like you,' she said, and she found herself smiling back. 'Definitely swearing.'

He tugged her back again, into his arms. Against his heart. 'Don't stop me,' he said. 'Otherwise I'm going to have to slug your mother and it's already been a black day. Ending up in jail might put the cap on it.' He waited until she was nestled against him again. He rested his chin on her hair and swore again.

'What is that?' she managed.

'Something a good girl shouldn't listen to.'

She choked. 'Language?'

'Tajikistan,' he said. 'It has the best cusses. Uzbekistan's good and so's Peru. Mozambique's not bad and Kazakhstan adds variety but, when I'm really against it, good old Tajikistan comes up trumps every time. Tonight's definitely a Tajikistan night.'

'That's my yurt territory.'

'Yurts and swear words. A truly excellent country.'

How could you not smile at yurts and Tajikistan swear words? She was almost forced to chuckle. Oh, but Grace… 'She's appalling,' she whispered.

'She is appalling. Is there a will?'

'Yes, but…'

'Leaving her the house?'

'Leaving me the house.'

'You want me to evict her tonight? It'd be my pleasure.'

'No.'

'I could set the dogs on her,' he said thoughtfully, and once again shock and sadness gave way to laughter.

'Right. And they'd evict her how?'

'Wind,' he said. 'If you're in a small enclosed place they can clear a room at twenty paces. All we do is ease them into her room and lock the door.'

She smiled again, but absently. 'She'll win,' she said. 'She has the right.'

'To this house? No, she doesn't. But it's okay, Misty. I'll manage this. This is our home.'

Our home.

The words had been swirling round for weeks. Our home.

He held her tight and let the silence soak in his words.

Our home.

Her home and his. And Bailey's and Ketchup's and Took's.

Home.

'It's okay,' he said again, and he stroked her hair and then he kissed her, first on the top of her head and then on her nose—and then more deeply on her mouth. He was tilting her face, holding her to him, but with no pressure. She could step away at any time.

The night was far too bleak to step away.

Nick. What would this day have been without him?

He loved her and she knew it. This man could make her smile when her world was shattered. How lucky was she that he was here?

She wanted him.

And, with that, everything else fell away. The sadness, the shock, the anger. There was only Nicholas, holding her, loving her.

There was only Nick.

'Can you take me to your bed?' she whispered and she felt his body still.

'Misty…'

'My mother will be sleeping next door. I don't want to sleep so close. Please…Nick, tonight I want to sleep with you.'

'I can't…' he said and she knew exactly what he was thinking. He couldn't hold her all night and take it no further.

'Neither can I,' she whispered and somewhere a chuckle came; somehow laughter was reasserting itself. 'Not any more. I want you, I need you and unless you don't have condoms…'

'I have condoms.' He sounded dazed. 'You think I'd enter a house you were in without condoms?'

'I do like a man who's prepared.'

'Misty…'

'You've been wonderful,' she said, but suddenly he was holding her at arm's length.

'No,' he said, suddenly harsh. 'Not that. I'm not accepting an offering, Misty. Do you want me?'

'I...yes.' There was nothing else to say.

'Then this is mutual lovemaking, or not at all. I want you more than life itself, but I won't take you as thanks.'

'I do want you.'

'For love? This needs to be an act of love, Misty, or no matter that it'll tear me in two, it's separate beds. You've had an appalling day. Is this shock and grief talking? Or something else? Something deeper.'

Something deeper?

Her world was changing. It had changed when Gran died, she thought, and it had changed again when her mother walked in. But now... Something was emerging she wasn't aware she had. Herself. Misty. She had rights, she thought. This was her life.

And Nicholas was her man?

She took his hand, lifting it, resting it against her cheek. He let her be, not moving, letting her make her own declaration as to what she wanted. The back of his hand was against her cheek. She loved the feel of it. The strength.

Nicholas.

She did want. She ran her fingers across his face, a wondrous exploration, never letting her eyes move from his.

'Definitely deeper,' she whispered. 'I need to be kissed. More, I need to be loved, and I need to be loved by you.'

He gazed down at her for a long moment. He smiled, that magical heart-twisting smile—and then he kissed her.

Magically, his mouth was merging with hers. His hands were holding her face, brushing her cheeks with his lovely long fingers, loving her.

Loving her with his mouth.

The awfulness of the day disappeared as the kiss deepened, then deepened still more. She clung to him, aching to be held, aching to lose herself in love. Nicholas...

But he wasn't completely done with her. Not yet. He moved back then, just a little, and his eyes were dark with love and desire.

'Misty, love, are you sure?'

She smiled at that, for she'd never been so sure of anything in her life. This moment. Nicholas.

'Yes.'

Definitely yes.

And the word was no sooner formed before she was being kissed again, lifted, held, claimed. Holding her in his arms as if she were a featherweight. A man triumphant with his woman.

'My bedroom,' he said, and she hardly recognised his voice. It was shaken with passion and desire. It was deep and husky and so sexy she wanted to melt.

But not here. Not yet. He walked to the door, still carrying her. Paused. Listened.

They heard a clatter in the kitchen—Grace was still there, then. They could make their way through the darkened passage, through the dividing door, then into Nick's side of the house.

Nick's bedroom was vast. The bed was a big four-poster with too much bedding and too many pillows. It was a bed made for more than one man.

It was a bed made for a man and a woman, and she wanted to be in that bed.

Nick was kissing her as he carried her. Then he was kissing her as he set her down on the bed. As he undid the buttons of her blouse. As he held her and held her and held her, closer and still closer.

She closed her eyes, aching with sensual pleasure. His fingers were tracing the contours of her body, her breasts. Each tiny movement sent shivers of wonder from top to toe.

She clung to him as he kissed her, holding him, glorying in the strength of him, the sheer masculinity, the wonder of his body. This day had seemed unreal. Now she wanted reassurance that this was happening in truth.

Her blouse was gone, and so was her bra. Nick was still clothed, but she could feel the strength of him underneath. In a moment she'd attack the buttons of his shirt, she thought. In a moment. When her body had space between trying to absorb the sensations she was feeling.

They had all the night. They had all the time in the world.

'I think I love you, Nicholas Holt,' she told him. 'Is that scary?'

He pulled away at that, holding her at arm's length. 'You think you love me?' he queried.

'I guess I know.'

'That's very good news.' His voice was grave, serious, husky with passion. 'For I know I love you. I'd marry you tomorrow. I will marry you tomorrow.'

Tomorrow.

The word gave her pause. Tomorrow. Grace. The worries that crowded in.

Nick sensed her withdrawal. He cursed in Tajik. 'Hey, Misty, don't look like that.'

'Tomorrow's tomorrow,' she murmured. 'Can we just take this night?'

A flicker of doubt crossed his face, and she smoothed it away with her fingers. 'No,' she said. 'This is not some one-night stand. I'm not saying that. I'm saying I do love you. I want you. Whether I want to marry you tomorrow…'

'It could be the day after.'

'It could,' she said and chuckled and tugged him close because she didn't want him to see doubt. She didn't want anything to interfere with tonight.

For tonight there was only Nick.

He still had clothes on.

'Not fair,' she said, and started slowly unbuttoning. He was hers, gift packaged, and she was going to take her own sweet time unwrapping.

Only maybe not. For, as she was concentrating—or trying to concentrate—on buttons, he was kissing her. Slowly, sensuously, achingly beautiful. Her neck, her lips, her eyelids.

She felt herself arch up to him and felt his fingers cup the smooth contours of her breasts, tracing the nipples, just touching, feather-soft, making her gasp with need and love and heat.

The night was magic. The moon was full outside, sending ribbons of silver over the ocean, the ribbons finding their way into the bedroom, across the bed, giving two lovers all the light they needed.

Only she had to get these buttons off!

She ripped.

'Uh oh,' he said.

'Was that a good shirt?'

'My best.'

'Sorry,' she said and her mouth found his nipples and suddenly any discussion of the ripped shirt was put aside.

He was hers, she thought. One loving gesture and she had him, putty in her hands. Or in her mouth.

His breathing was ragged, harsh, as her fingers found his belt, unfastened, unzipped. She could hear his breathing deepening. She kissed his neck, tasting the salt of him.

He'd marry her. Her Nick.

Her fingers sought and found. Explored.

Loved.

Enough. One ragged gasp and he surrendered—or not. His hands caught hers, locked them behind her, and suddenly she was his again, and it was she who was surrendering. He kissed each breast in turn, tantalizing, teasing. Savouring. Their heated bodies moulded together.

Skin to skin.

Their mouths were joined again. Of course. It was as if this was their centre—where they needed to be.

Or maybe… Another centre beckoned. His hands were below her waist and she felt her jeans slipping.

As everything else slipped. Doubts. Sadness. Anger.

This night…this time… It was a watershed. Somehow, what was happening right now was firming who she was. A woman who knew what she wanted.

She wanted Nick, and wondrously he wanted her right back. How cool—how magical—how right!

But…

'Wait,' he said, in a voice she no longer recognised. 'Wait, my love.'

She must, but it nearly killed her to wait, until he'd done what he needed to do to keep them safe.

But then there was nothing keeping them apart. The night was theirs.

Outside, the world was waiting but for now, for this night, for this moment, there was only each other.

They were lying against each other, their bodies curved against each other, skin against skin. She'd never felt like this. She'd never dreamed she could feel like this.

A rain of kisses was being bestowed on her neck, her breasts, her belly, while his magical hands caressed and caressed and caressed. The heat…

The French windows were open. The warm night air did its own caressing, and the soft murmur of the surf was more romantic than any violin. She could vaguely hear the distant chatter of the ring-tailed possums who skittered along the eaves. She'd never felt so alive and so aware and so… beautiful?

But…hot? Oh, these kisses. The sounds of the night were receding, giving way to a murmur in her ears that was starting to grow.

He was kissing her low, loving her body, his tongue doing crazy, wondrous things... Amazing things.

'Nick!'

'Hey,' he growled and chuckled his pleasure and did it again. 'You like?'

Did she like? She arched upward, close to crying, aching with need. He was above her, sliding up again so his dark eyes gleamed down at her in the moonlight. He was loving her with his eyes.

'You want me?' he murmured and what was a girl to say to that?

'Like life itself,' she managed and she held him and tugged him down. Down...

But he wasn't sinking. His arms were sailor's arms, muscled, too strong for her to fight him. He was forcing her to wait. She arched and moaned and he kissed her, deeply, more deeply still. Holding the moment. Savouring what was to come.

'My Misty,' he whispered. 'My heart.'

'I need you. Nick, please...' Her thighs were burning; her body was on fire, but still he resisted. He lowered himself, a little but not enough, just so his chest brushed lightly against her breasts. He kissed her neck, behind her ears, her throat, her eyelids, and all the while his body brushed her breasts, over and back until she thought she'd melt with desire and love and need.

No more. What use would she be to this world if she melted into a puddle of aching need, right here on the bed? She took his shoulders and tugged, fierce with want, strong with need, and she rose to meet him.

And he was there.

Her love.

Her Nick.

Her body took rhythm from his. He was reaching so deep inside her, to the point where love and desire and need melted into one and she felt as if she were dissolving, dissolving, flying.

The night and the moonlight and the sounds of the sea, the grief of the day, the shock of the night, the luxury of this bed, the feel of this man's body... There was no separate sensation. No separate thought.

There was only her love.

And when finally they lay back, exhausted, as his arms cradled her and she moulded to his body and she felt his heartbeat, she knew her safe haven—her home—was much more than it had ever seemed.

Nick wanted to marry her. It was a tiny thought at the edge of all the consciousness she had left, but it felt lovely.

Their bodies could merge over and over. She could lie with this man for the rest of her life. She could help him raise his son, a little boy she loved already.

Wife and mother...

It felt... It felt...

'Like a miracle,' Nick said and he kissed her softly, languorously, lovingly. 'My Misty. At last I've come safe home.'

Safe home.

They were the last words she heard as she drifted into sleep.

Safe home.

CHAPTER TEN

MISTY stirred, stretched, opened her eyes. Sunbeams were streaming through the windows, falling across the rainbow quilt on the bed. Morning?

She'd slept spooned in the curve of Nick's body. Now she could no longer feel him. Oh, but she was so warm. Sated. She rolled over to find him. The grief she'd felt for Gran had eased, backed off, taken its rightful place. She was no longer bereft and grey. Nick…

Nick's side of the bed was empty.

The bedside clock said ten. What was she thinking? Her mother had to be faced. Life had to be faced.

Was Nick out there, facing it for her?

She showered fast, in Nick's bathroom because she didn't want to be caught by her mother, tousled by sleep, fresh from lovemaking. Besides, she liked the smell of Nick's soap. It smelled like Nick. Of course it did. So much for distinctive aroma, she thought wryly. Lemon grass? She'd thought it was testosterone.

She chuckled. Feeling absurdly happy even though Grace was out there—and that was a scary thought—she twisted a towel round her hair, donned Nick's dressing gown—a gorgeous crimson robe that looked as if it had come from somewhere exotic—of course it had come from somewhere exotic—and scuttled along the passage, through to the other side of the house to find fresh clothes.

And then she paused. There were voices coming from the kitchen. Her mother. Nick.

She should dress before she faced her mother, but...

She hesitated. The kitchen door was almost closed, but not quite. If she stood silent, she could hear every word.

Why would she want to?

She did.

'How much?' It was Nick's voice, but it was a tone she hadn't heard before. He sounded harsh and angry, trying, she thought, for control.

And her mother named a sum that made her gasp.

What the...? They were discussing...

She knew suddenly, definitely, what they were discussing. Selling her house.

'It's Misty's home,' Nick said. 'Her grandmother left it to her.'

'Misty's grandmother was my mother. This house is my right. I'll take her to court if I must but I won't need to. Misty will do the right thing. She always has.'

'You mean you expect her to walk away and leave you to do what you want?'

'I mean she'll do what's expected of her.' Her mother sounded scornful. 'You don't know her father. I did. He was a doormat. Misty's the same. Useful, though. She's kept this place looking great.' She could almost sense Grace assessing the place, looking around at the warm wood, at the lovely old furnishings. 'It'll get a good price. Much more than you're offering. So tell me again why I should accept?'

'Because Misty and I wish to live here. It's our home.'

'You're marrying her?'

'Yes.'

'Well, good for you. So buy it outright. Give me market value. Save your wife the nasty business of the courts. That'd upset her, fighting me in the courts.'

'It would or I wouldn't suggest it,' Nick snapped. 'You

know she's a soft option. She's had no experience of the real world.'

'Then pay,' her mother said harshly. 'Of course you can't expose her to the courts. My mother always said she had to be protected. Don't tell her about what you're doing,' she said. 'It'll upset her. And here you are, ready to keep on keeping her safe. Excellent. Nasty thing, reality.'

'I'll get an independent valuation…'

'You'll take my price or I'll see Misty in court.'

She almost burst in on them then. Almost. Right at the last, she pulled back.

And here you are, ready to keep on keeping her safe.

Last night hadn't been about keeping her safe. Last night had been about loving her, pure and simple.

Did loving involve keeping her safe?

Last night she'd been so sure, but now…

She's a soft option. She's had no experience of the real world.

Standing in the passage, listening to her mother produce valuations of like properties, listening to Nick become reasonable, as if what her mother was suggesting was reasonable, suddenly certainty gave way to doubt.

Nick was doing this to protect her. She knew it. So why did it seem so wrong?

Her mother's words…

You don't know her father. I did. He was a doormat. Misty's the same.

Anger came to her aid then. She was no doormat. How could Nick simply accept that as fact?

She's had no experience of the real world.

Nick wasn't going to pay for her house. Hard cold fact. She could go in there right now and tell him so. But something inside her was saying, *think. Get this right before you fly in with temper.*

She backed out of the passage, out of the back door to the

veranda. Ketchup and Took were out there in the morning sun, supervising the sea. She sank down beside them and they nosed her hands and wagged their tails.

'Why aren't you in there biting my mother?' she whispered. 'Dogs are supposed to protect their masters.'

But the dogs weren't in the kitchen because they'd found each other. Their security was each other.

As her security was Nick?

The dogs had had their adventures. They'd come home. They weren't doormats.

Nick had had his adventures. Even Bailey…

She's had no experience of the real world.

Even her grandmother, never telling her she'd been to Paris because Misty had to be protected. Protected from herself?

There was a huge muddle of emotion in her mind but it was getting clearer. She stared out over the bay she'd loved all her life. The dogs nestled against her and the knot of confusion in her heart settled to certainty.

A doormat. Safe.

'You guys don't need me,' she whispered. 'When Gran was alive, when Ketchup needed me, and when I met Nick, my list seemed wrong. Stupid. But maybe it's not stupid. Maybe it's important if Nick and I are to build something. I won't have him spending his life thinking I need to be safe.'

Ketchup whimpered a little and put a paw on her knee. She managed to smile, but she didn't feel like smiling. What she was thinking…? It would hurt, and maybe it would hurt for ever.

'You don't really need me, do you?' she told Ketchup. 'You have Took. What's more, you have Nick and Bailey. You have guys who are in the business of keeping everyone safe. That's what they want to do, so they can stay here and do it.'

Okay. She took a deep breath. She girded her loins—as much as a girl could in such a bathrobe. She thought of what she had to do first.

'Nick's keeping this place safe. He can keep doing that, only there's no way he's paying my mother for the privilege,' she told the dogs.

She closed her eyes, searching for courage. What she was going to do seemed appalling. Loving Nick last night had made it so much harder.

She thought back to Frank, to her bitter colleague, regretting for all of his life that he'd never left this town.

'I can't do that to Nick,' she whispered. 'I'd try not to mind, and mostly I wouldn't, but every now and then…'

Every now and then she would mind, and it could hurt them all.

She's had no experience of the real world.

So do it now or do it never.

Deep breath. She stood and wrapped Nick's gown more tightly round her.

'Wish me luck, guys,' she whispered. 'Here goes everything.'

Nick had trouble with his own parents. Grace, though, was unbelievable.

She'd dumped her infant daughter on her parents and walked away. Half an hour with her this morning and he understood why. There was nothing she wouldn't do to get her own way.

If he hadn't been here…Misty would be trampled, he thought. Misty was no match for this… He couldn't find words to describe her. Not even Tajikistan had a good one.

'I have good lawyers,' Grace snarled and he faced her with disgust.

Maybe a fight through the courts would give the house to Misty, but the thought of it not succeeding, and the thought of what Misty would go through to claim it…

She might not even try. Misty was a giver, and he loved her for it.

'We need to get this in writing…' he started but he didn't finish. The back door slammed open. Misty.

She was standing in the doorway, his crimson bathrobe all but enveloping her. The towel around her hair was striped orange and yellow. Her eyes matched her outfit. They were flashing fire.

'What do you think you're doing?' she demanded and she was talking to them both.

Grace stubbed her cigarette out in her saucer and smiled at her daughter, a cat-that-got-the-cream smile that made Nick feel ill.

'We're discussing business,' she said sweetly. 'Your man's being very reasonable. There's no need for you to get involved.'

'Nick's not *my* man.'

Uh oh. Nick sensed trouble. Where was the woman who'd melted into his arms last night, who'd surrendered completely, utterly, magically? The look she gave him now was one of disbelief. 'You're offering to buy *my* house. From my mother.'

'We want to live here.'

'So?'

'It's easier, Misty. I'll just pay her and she'll leave.'

'She's leaving anyway,' Misty snapped. 'Grace, get out of my house. Now.' She picked up the ash-filled saucer and dumped it in the bin. 'You light up one more cigarette in this kitchen and I'll have you arrested for trespass.'

'This is my house.' Grace looked as stunned as Nick felt. This wasn't Misty. This was some flaming virago they'd never seen before.

'You left this house when you were eighteen,' Misty told her, cold as ice. 'You came back only when you needed money—or to dump a baby. What gives you the right to walk in now?'

'They're my parents,' Grace hissed. 'This house has always been waiting…'

'For you to sell it the moment they're dead? I don't think so. Gran left me this house, and its contents.'

'I'll contest…'

'Contest away,' Misty snapped and Nick could hear unutterable sadness behind the anger. 'Gran had macular degeneration for the last fifteen years. That's meant she's been almost blind. Since I was sixteen I've been signing cheques, taking care of all the business. Grandpa left Gran well off but almost all her income has been siphoned to you. You've been sending pleading letters. I've read them to her and every time she'd sigh and say, "What shall we do, Misty?" To deny you would have killed her. So I've sent you cheques, over and over, and every single one was documented. You've had far more than the value of this house, yet you couldn't even find it in you to come to her funeral. I don't know what gene you were handed when you were born, but I thank God I didn't inherit it. Gran loved me. She wanted me to have this house and I will.'

'Misty…' Nick started and she turned on him then.

'And don't you even think of being reasonable. You're doing this to protect me? Thank you but I don't need protecting. I've had no experience of the real world? Maybe not, but I'm not going to get it with you protecting me. So I'm telling you both what's going to happen. First, Grace is going to get out. The cheques have stopped. You're on your own, like it or lump it. And Nick, you want a quiet life? That's what you can have because I'm leaving, too. Oh, not for ever, just for twelve months. I have a list to work through and for the first time in my life I'm free. I had Gran but she's dead. I thought I had Ketchup but he has Took and he has you. You and Bailey will love this house. It's safe…as houses.'

She took a deep breath, holding her arms across her breasts as if she needed warmth. He rose to go to her but she backed away. 'No. Please, Nick…' Her anger was fading a little but she seemed determined to hold onto it. 'This is hard but I have to do it. I know it sounds ungrateful, but…it's what I'm going to do. Now, I need to go and get dressed. Grace, when I get back here I don't want to see you. You'll be gone. Nick will be looking after my house—*my house*—but it's my house in absentia.'

They were left looking at each other. Grace looked…old, Nick thought and, despite the shock of Misty's words, he felt a twinge of pity.

Misty hadn't called her Mom or Mama or Mother. She'd called her Grace. If Bailey ever looked at him as Misty looked at Grace…

She deserved it. She'd been no mother to Misty, but still…

'You'd best go,' he said and Grace looked at him like a wounded dog.

'I don't…I can't. I don't have any money.' It was a defeated whine.

He hesitated. There'd been a resounding crash from Misty's bedroom door. They were safe from her hearing.

Had Misty meant what she said?

Don't think about that now. Just get rid of Grace. Without Misty knowing?

Definitely without Misty knowing.

He tugged out his chequebook and wrote, and handed over a cheque. Grace stared down at it, stunned.

'I want the value of the house.'

'And instead I'm giving you your plane fare back to Perth and enough for approximately six months' rent. If Misty finds out I've done it I'll cancel the cheque. It's the last you'll get off us, Grace, so I suggest you take it and leave.'

'Us?' She dragged herself to her feet and regarded him with loathing. 'It didn't sound to me like there's any *us*. She sounds like she's leaving.'

'That's up to us,' he said evenly. 'But you're leaving first.'

* * *

Misty found him on the veranda, in his normal place, in his rocker, dogs at his feet. She was feeling ill.

She'd yelled at him. He didn't deserve to be yelled at.

'I'm sorry,' she said quickly before he could rise. 'That was dreadful. I sounded like I was a witch. You were only trying to help.'

'I'd like to help,' he said. 'You know I want to marry you.' He rose and came towards her. 'I'll protect you in any way I can.'

'But I don't want to be protected. Nick, I'm sorry, but I don't want to marry you. Or…not yet.'

His face stilled. He'd taken her hands but she wouldn't let her fingers curl around his. She mustn't.

'I've never taken a risk in my life,' she said.

'That's why I love you.'

'You see, that's what I'm afraid of. I won't be loved because I'm safe.'

That he didn't understand was obvious. 'I don't love you just because you're safe,' he told her. 'I love you because you're beautiful and warm and big-hearted and fun and…'

'And safe. I'm someone to share a rocker with.'

'Misty…'

'It's okay,' she said, feeling unutterably weary. She didn't want to say this. It would be so easy to sink into the rocker beside him, to wait until Bailey came home, to live happily ever after.

Was there something of Grace inside her? Some heart-lessness?

No. She felt cold and fearful and sad, but she knew she was doing the right thing. If she didn't go now…She'd seen what bitterness could do.

'If you still want me in a year…' she said.

'A year?'

'I think I can do most of my list in a year.'

'What list?'

'It's a dream,' she said. 'I've had it since I was little. To fly away, to see something other than this town. Occasionally, when I was little, Grace used to send postcards, from one exotic place after another.'

'You were jealous of Grace?'

That was easy. 'I never was. Sometimes I even felt sorry for her. She'd fly in and make Gran cry and Gran would say the house was empty without her. But I kept thinking…why would you want to make Gran cry? That would have made me ill. I couldn't. Until now.'

His face was expressionless. 'So now you'll leave?'

'What's holding me here?'

'Us. Bailey and me.'

She closed her eyes. There was such a depth of meaning in the words—so much. He didn't understand. For her to walk away… To hurt him…

'See, that's the problem,' she said, as gently as she could. 'I'm falling so in love with you that I never want to hurt you. It's borderline now—that I never want to leave. As I could never leave Gran. For a while there I couldn't even leave Ketchup. But I must. Just for a year. Nick, can you try and understand?'

'Understand what? What do you want to do for a year?'

'Adventures,' she said promptly. 'I want to balloon over Paris at dawn. I want to roll down heather-covered hills in Scotland and get bitten by midges. I want to go white-water rafting in the Rockies…'

But she'd already lost him. 'You don't know what you're talking about,' he said coldly, flatly. 'You have everything you need here. It's…'

'Safe,' she threw at him. 'Tell me, if you didn't think I was safe, would you seriously consider marrying me?'

'No, but…'

'There you are, then.'

'But I have Bailey to consider.'

'You're not considering Bailey. You're choosing a wife for yourself. To choose me because top of your list of requirements is safe…Good old dependable Misty, cute as, we'll stay in her lovely house and if anything threatens her like a nasty, mean mother then we'll drive her away; we'll protect Misty because she's little and cute and can't protect herself.'

'This is overreacting.'

'Like paying for a house without even asking me?' she said incredulously. 'I guess I should be grateful, but I'm sorry, I'm not. You see, I want to be independent. Nick, I can't cling to you before I see if I can manage without anything to cling to. I need a year.'

'To go white-water rafting in the Rockies.'

'Yes.'

'You're just like Isabelle.' It was a harsh, cold accusation that left her winded.

She didn't answer. She couldn't. Was she just like Isabelle? Would she put a child's life at risk when she didn't need to?

If he thought that, then there was nothing to defend. He wanted her to marry him and he didn't know the first thing about her.

She looked at him and her heart twisted. How easy would it be to fall into his arms, say sorry, it had all been a mistake and she wanted nothing more than to stay here with him, with Bailey, with Ketchup and Took, for ever and ever?

But he was looking at her with such anger.

Last night meant so much to her. It meant everything. But in a sense it was last night that had given her the courage to do this. For last night she'd accepted that she wanted to spend her life with this man, and she also knew that he deserved all she could give.

All or nothing. She would not marry him feeling like she did right now—knowing she'd dissolve into him and he'd make her safer, safer. She'd fought to get him onto a yacht.

Every tiny risk would be a fight, but it'd be a fight to do what she already had now, and not what she dreamed of.

She couldn't let go of her dreams and marry him. She'd end up bitter and resentful.

She's had no experience of the real world.

It was a line to remember. It was a line to make her go.

'I will not end up in this rocker before I'm thirty,' she said, and suddenly she kicked the rocker with a ferocity that frightened them all. Took yelped and headed down the steps with her tail behind her legs. Ketchup yelped and cowered and cringed behind Nick's legs.

'Enough,' she said wearily. 'Sorry, guys. Sorry to you all. I know you're all very happy here. I hope you'll stay here and be safe and happy while I'm away. And if at the end of twelve months…'

'You expect us to wait for you?' Nick's voice was so cold she cringed. But she'd known this was the risk—the likely outcome. She had to face it.

'Can I ask whatever you do that you'll take care of Ketchup and Took?'

'Misty, after last night…' he said explosively and she nodded sadly.

'Yes. Last night was magic. It made me see how close I am to giving in.'

'Then give in.'

'I won't be married because I'm the opposite of Isabelle,' she said, and she knew it for the truth, the bottom line she couldn't back away from. 'You figure it out, Nick. I think I love you but I'm me. I'm me, lists and all.'

CHAPTER ELEVEN

'WHEN I suggested we get a relief teacher next term I thought you might use the time off for a honeymoon. Not to leave.' Louise was practically beside herself. 'What happened? We were all so sure. A honeymoon with Nick… Oh, Misty, why not?'

'Because our honeymoon would be at Madge Pilkington's Bed and Breakfast out on Banksia Ridge, with tea and scones, a nice dip in the pool every day and bed at nine. We might watch a bit of telly. Wildlife documentaries, maybe, but no lions hunting zebras for us. Nothing to put our blood pressure up.'

'You're nuts,' her friend said frankly. 'Nicholas Holt would put my blood pressure up all on his own.'

'Not if he can help it,' she said. 'Safe and sedate R Us, our Nick.'

'So you're definitely leaving?'

'I'm leaving.'

'Natalie's mother says he wants to marry you.'

'How would Natalie's mother know?'

'Does he?'

'He doesn't want to marry me,' she said. 'He wants to marry who he thinks I am. But, if I'm not careful, that's who I'll be and I suspect I'd hate her.'

'I don't understand.'

'You know something?' Misty muttered. 'Neither do I. But

all I know is that I've fallen in love with him. He deserves everything I'm capable of giving and I don't know what that capability is. I have to leave to find out.'

'For ever?'

'For a year,' she said. 'I've taken a year's leave of absence. I'm not rich enough to walk away for ever. Nor do I want to.'

'He won't wait. You can't expect him to.'

'No,' she said bleakly. 'I can't expect him to.'

'Why is she going away?'

It was about the twentieth time Bailey had asked the question and it never got easier.

'Because her gran's died and she needs a holiday. Because we're here to look after the dogs.'

'We could all go on a holiday.'

'Misty wants to be by herself.'

But did she? He didn't know. He hadn't asked.

He wasn't going to ask. There was no way he was taking Bailey white-water rafting in the Rockies.

'We could go sailing,' Bailey said, verging on tears. 'All of us together.'

'You and I will go sailing. Next Saturday.'

'Misty's leaving on Friday.'

'Then we'll miss her very much,' Nick said as firmly as he could. 'But it's what she wants to do and we can't stop her.'

Friday. At eight Louise was collecting her to drive her to the airport. At dawn Nick went outside and found her crouched on the veranda, hugging two dogs.

'Hi,' he said and she turned to face him and he saw she'd been crying. 'Misty…'

'Hay fever,' she muttered, burying her face in Ketchup's coat. 'I'm allergic to dogs. How lucky I'm leaving.'

'Stay.'

'No.'

'Misty, we love you,' he said, feeling helpless. 'Both of us do. No, all of us,' he added, seeing the two dogs wuffle against her. 'This is craziness.'

'It's not craziness,' she said and swiped her cheeks with the back of her hand. 'It's what I need to do. I'm not Isabelle, Nick, no matter what you think, but I have my reasons. Instead of hating me for what I'm doing…I wish, oh, I wish you'd try to see who I really am.'

'I know who you are.'

'No, you don't,' she said and rose and brushed past him, heading for the door. 'You see what you want to see, and that's not me.'

'So who are you?'

'Heaven knows,' she said bluntly. 'I'm heading off into the unknown to find out.'

Nick watched her go.

He watched until Louise's car was out of sight.

Then he walked inside and slammed the door so hard it fell off its hinges.

Great. Something to do.

Something to do to stop him following her and dragging her back any way he knew how.

Misty was staring down at the receding vision of Sydney and all she could think of was what she'd left behind. What she'd given up.

'But I'm not giving it up,' she muttered. 'I'm leaving for a year. It'll be there waiting for me when I get back.'

'Nick won't be there,' she reminded herself. 'That's up to Nick.'

Oh, but what a risk. She sniffed before she could help herself and the man in the next seat handed over a wad of tissues.

'My wife does this every time we fly,' he said. 'So I'
prepared. She's not with me this time but she sobbed a.
airport. Leaving family then, are you, love?'

'Sort of.' It was all she could manage.

'He'll be there when you get back,' the man said comfort-
ably. 'If he has any sense.'

'That's just the problem,' she told him. 'He has too much
sense.'

'So what will we do without her?'

What, indeed? Move? The idea had appeal—to shift out of
this house where he'd thought he had his life sorted. Only he
had two dogs, and Bailey loved his new school, and to move
out now...

They'd move before she came home, he decided. If she
came home. She'd probably meet someone white-water rafting. Or kill herself in the process.

'Why do you keep looking angry?'

'I'm not angry.'

'So what will we do?'

It was Sunday afternoon. They'd had a whole forty-eight
hours without her. It was raining.

Even the dogs were miserable.

Nick stared round the kitchen, looking for inspiration.
'Maybe we can cook,' he said. 'I've never tried a chocolate
cake. You want to try?'

'It'd be better if Misty was here,' Bailey said, stubborn.

'Yes, but Misty's not here.' He headed for the recipe shelf
and tugged out a few likely books. 'One of these...'

But then he was caught. There was a pile of scrapbooks
wedged behind the recipes. One came out along with Mrs
Beeton's *Family Cookery*.

It was a scrapbook, pasted with pictures. All sorts of
pictures.

the front in childish writing…
Misty Lawrence. My Dreams, Book One.'

didn't quite come up to expectations. Flying over Paris at dawn…

For a start, it was loud. It hadn't looked loud in the pictures. The brochures had made it look still and dreamlike, floating weightlessly above the Seine, maybe sipping a glass of champagne, eating the odd luscious strawberry.

She was cold. Champagne didn't cut it. If she wanted anything it was hot cocoa—where was Nick and his rocker now?—but she was too busy gripping the sides of the basket to even think about drinking or eating. The roar of the gas was making her ears ring. It was so windy… It had been a little windy before they'd started but had promised to settle, but a front had unexpectedly turned. So now they were being hit by gusts which, as well as making the ride bumpy and not calm at all, were also blowing them way off course.

Mind, she couldn't see their course. All she could see was a sea of cloud. The guy in charge was looking worried, barking instructions into his radio, most of which seemed to be about the impossibility of finding a bus to get his passengers back from who knew where they were going to land.

There were three couples in the basket and Misty. The couples were holding each other, giggling, keeping each other warm.

She was clinging to the basket, telling herself, 'Number One on my list, okay, not great, but now I'll get to wander down the Left Bank and take a barge down the Seine and buy Lily of the Valley on the first of May.'

Alone. She glanced across at the giggling couples who were holding each other rather than the basket.

Get a grip, she told herself. This was her list. She'd waited almost thirty years for it.

A month of Paris. Then the Dordogne. The great chateaux of Burgundy.

And then cruising the Greek Islands. It'd be fa[...]
she could just hold on for another hour and she did[...]
to death or burst her eardrums. And maybe the cloud[...]
part for a little so she could see Paris.

She must have started these lists when she was Bailey's ag[...]
They had all the scrapbooks out now, spread across Misty'[...]
kitchen table. Every night they seemed to be drifting back to
Misty's side of the house to read her scrapbooks.

But, in truth, it wasn't just to read her scrapbooks. It felt
better here—on Misty's side.

The dogs seemed more settled in Misty's kitchen. They
slept by the stove, snuggled against each other, but every time
there was a noise their heads came up and they looked towards
the door with hope.

No Misty, and their heads sagged again.

How can they have fallen in love with her in so little
time? Nick thought, but it was a stupid question. He knew
the answer.

He had. And he was still falling…

They were reading the scrapbooks instead of bedtime
stories. There was so much…

She'd been an ordered child, neat and methodical. The first
couple of scrapbooks were exotic photographs cut from old
women's magazines, and the occasional postcard. Some of
the postcards had lost their glue and were loose. They were
tattered at the edges as if they'd been read over and over. As
he and Bailey flipped the pages it was impossible not to read
their simple messages:

In Morocco. Oh, guys, you should be here. I feel so sorry
for you, stuck in Banksia Bay.
Grace.

He thought of an eight-year-old receiving this from her
mother, and he thought of going out and cancelling Grace's

couldn't. It would have been long cashed. Grace

y was gone.

wish she was here,' Bailey said, over and over. He leafed
ough to the third scrapbook. 'This place is number one on
r list.'

Her list…

They'd found it now, carefully typed, annotated, researched.
What she'd done was take her piles of scrapbooks and divided
them into twelve to make her list.

He went from scrapbooks to list, then back to scrapbooks.
Pictures, pictures, pictures. And then, later, articles, research
pieces, names of travel companies.

A child's hand turning into a woman's hand.

These were dreams, a lone child living with ailing grandparents, using her scrapbooks to escape to a world where her
mother lived. Her mother didn't want her, but to know a little
of her world… To dream of a world outside Banksia Bay…

I feel so sorry for you, stuck in Banksia Bay…

She'd been raised with that message ringing in her head.

Bailey found the scrapbooks entrancing but, as Nick
worked his way slowly through them, he found them more
than entrancing.

He began to see what he'd done.

He'd asked her to give up her dreams.

'Twelve months,' she'd said. 'I just want twelve months.'
He hadn't given them to her. He'd reacted with anger.

'You're just like Isabelle.'

It had been said in an instinctive reaction when he hadn't
got his way. Yes, it was born of his need to protect Bailey,
but it had been unfair and untrue. He thought of Misty's face
when he'd said it and he felt appalling.

'We miss her,' Bailey said, looking at pages linked to the
item at the top of her list, at the advertisements for hot air ballooning over Paris, at the lists of castles on the Dordogne, at

photographs of a tiny chateau hotel at Sarlat, at u
cellars, miles and miles of cellars where they kept t
great Burgundies. Paris in springtime. France. 'She'll
now,' he said. 'Is hot air ballooning dangerous?'

Yes, was his instinctive response. After the terrors Ba
had been exposed to...

But he knew it wasn't.

'No,' he told his son. 'It can be uncomfortable. Often
noisy.'

'It doesn't look noisy,' Bailey said doubtfully.

'The gas burners are really loud.'

'I don't think Misty likes noise. Do you think we should
ring her and tell her not to do it?'

He picked up the list and read it. Drinking Kir at sunset
on the Left Bank. Wandering through the Louvre. Standing
on top of the Arc de Triomphe and watching the crazy traffic
underneath.

What was this? Hiring a motor scooter and riding round
the Arc de Triomphe? Should he ring and tell her how crazy
that was?

No.

He thought of her sailing, wearing a life vest. He and Bailey
had watched her from the clubhouse before the race, practising
and practising. Pushing herself to the limit, but her little boat
was fine.

He'd accused her of being just like Isabelle. Was he
mad?

'I think Misty wants to find out all by herself,' he said, and
he knew part of it was true—she did want to find out—but
the rest...

Bailey went to bed and he returned to Misty's side of the
house—with scrapbooks. Misty was here on these pages, a
girl's dreams followed by a woman's serious commitment.

He'd given her a choice. Himself and his son—or her
dreams. Would he want her to give this up?

...ed her to.

...o do?

...ad clients arriving in Banksia Bay now. His interna-
...clients were talking to him about their boats, about
...r dreams. They were finding out where he was based and
...ying, 'You know what? We'll come talk to you in person.'

They loved it. Banksia Bay was beautiful. He never had to
leave.

Bailey was safe.

But these scrapbooks...

Her list...

Twelve months.

The dogs sighed. They lay at his feet but they looked at the
door.

'She'll be back in a year,' he told them.

But if there's someone else in her balloon...some guy who
sees what Misty really is...how beautiful...

How could they not? He flicked through the list, thinking
if she found someone to do these with her...

It was an amazing list.

He hadn't done some of the stuff on this list.

Bailey was asleep. Here. Safe. But maybe...maybe...

He read the list again. Slowly. Thoughtfully.

This was not Isabelle.

Maybe dreams were made to be shared?

He turned to the dogs, considering. It was his responsibility
to care for these two.

Kennels?

No. He knew where they'd come from. If he and Bailey
were to be free...

'Sorry, guys, but I think tomorrow morning we need to go
see Fred.'

Fred the vet.

* * *

She'd been away for six weeks. She was loving e
of it. Sort of.

Number three on her list was cruising the Gree
It'd be magic. She'd pinned pictures up on her stud
at home. Whitewashed villas with blue-painted wind
Caiques bobbing at anchor. Greek fishermen stripped to
waist, hauling in their nets. Santorini, Mykonos, the Cyclade
islands. It was all before her.

She climbed off the bus at the harbour in Athens. Her boat
was due to leave in two hours.

Two emotions…

After so much planning, it was impossible not to feel ex-
hilarated as dreams became real.

It was also impossible to block the thought that back home
was Nick. Nick and Bailey and Ketchup and Took, learning
to live in Banksia Bay without her.

She couldn't think about them now. She mustn't. To follow
her dreams with regret—what sort of compromise was that?
She lifted her back pack and trudged down to the departure
point, telling herself firmly to think ahead.

But the boat at anchor wasn't what she'd expected. In the
pamphlets it had been shown as a graceful old schooner,
wooden planking, sails, lovely.

The boat before her was huge, white, fibreglass. There were
tourists filing up the gangplank already. Many tourists. This
was far bigger than she'd imagined.

Her heart sank—but she was getting used to this. Adjusting
dreams to fit reality. She would *not* be disappointed. She'd
looked forward to this for so long. Sailing on the Aegean…

But still… No sails. So many tourists.

A hand on her shoulder.

'It's not the same as your pictures. Maybe we can offer you
an alternative?

She almost jumped out of her skin.

She whirled—and he was there.

...e to find you,' Nick said before she could even ...er heart. 'Me and Bailey.' He smiled down at her, ...at made her heart stop even trying to kick-start— ...put on the voice of a spruiker, the guys who pushed ...sts to change their minds.

...Madam wishes to sail the Greek islands? On this?' He gestured contemptuously to the fibreglass cruiser. 'My *Mahelkee* is a much smaller boat, but she's infinitely more beautiful. There's four aboard now. A crew of four, whose only wish is to keep madam happy. You come with us, madam, and we will make you happy. You come with us, madam, and we intend to make you happy for the rest of your life.'

CHAPTER TWELVE

You didn't travel alone for long without learning to avoid spruikers. Misty was very good at saying, 'No, thank you,' and walking away without looking back.

But this was some spruiker.

For a start, he wasn't alone. He was working as one of a pair. For as well as Nick with his heart-stopping smile, there was also Bailey. Bailey wasn't smiling. He was a little behind his father, gazing up at her as if he wasn't quite sure he still knew her. Anxious. Pleading?

Nick. Bailey.

How to get her heart beating like it should again? She wasn't sure she could.

'H...How...?' she managed. 'How did...?'

'Lots of work,' Nick said. He'd removed his hand from her shoulder. He was no longer touching her. He was just...smiling. If she wanted to back away and head up the gangplank to her cruiser, she still could.

Turn away? A girl would be mad.

'W...work?' she managed. 'You've worked to get here?'

'We just got on an aeroplane,' Bailey said from behind his father. 'It was easy.'

'So no work.'

'We would have worked if we had to,' Nick said. Virtuous. 'To reach you. And I had to make a whole lot of phone calls.'

slept on the aeroplane,' Bailey said.

class, huh,' she said and somehow she managed a

Of course,' Nick said, and his smile deepened and strength-
ed, a caress all by itself. 'If it's to reach you, then only the
est will do.'

'Nick…'

'We have your list.' Bailey was clutching his father's hand
but his eyes were on Misty. Desperately anxious. 'Dad and I
have your list. We want to do it, too. If you let us.'

There was a statement to take a girl's breath away. *We want
to do it, too…*

'I believe I've made a mistake,' Nick said gravely. Around
them, passengers were streaming up onto the gangplank. They
were having to divert around this couple and child, plus one
very large backpack. Misty didn't notice. 'I believe I made
the biggest mistake of my life. I'm hoping…Bailey and I are
hoping…that it's not too late to fix it.'

She was having trouble breathing. 'I don't know what you
mean,' she whispered.

'We mean your list is part of you,' Nick said, and still he
didn't touch her. He was holding back, leaving her be, outlin-
ing the facts and allowing her space to absorb. 'After you left,
Bailey and I read your scrapbooks.'

'You read…'

'We hope you don't mind.'

'No, but…'

'But they're part of who you are,' he said. 'Part of the
whole. Misty, we tried to love only the part of you that I
wanted. That was so dumb it doesn't bear thinking of. I'm
hoping against hope that it's not too late to let me repair the
damage. I'm hoping it's not too late to tell you that I love all
of you, without reservations. That Bailey and I fell in love
with Misty the schoolteacher, Misty the dog-lover, Misty the

sailor. But we want more. We want Misty the ɩ
the adventurer.' He hesitated. 'And... And Mistʝ

'Oh, Nick...'

'And Misty the mother,' Bailey piped up from
'When we talked about this at home...Dad, you saiɗ
the mother. You said let's come over here and see if we
make Misty love us. Let's come over here and see if we can ǥ
Misty to teach me how to make scrapbooks. But I've already
started,' he said proudly. 'I have a picture of a motorbike on
the first page.'

'A motorbike,' Misty said faintly. 'Aren't they dangerous?'

'Yes,' Bailey said, peeping a smile. 'And they're noisy. Like
balloons.'

She smiled back. She wasn't sure how she managed to smile.
She believed there were tears slipping down her cheeks.

Tears? Who felt like crying now?

'We have a tour mapped out,' Nick said. He reached a hand
towards her and then pulled it back again. As if he was afraid
to touch—as if she might turn and flee if he did. 'Santorini,
Mykonos, the Cyclades Islands.'

'They're the ones on your list but Dad says we can do
more,' Bailey said. ''Cos *Mahelkee* is a smaller boat. She can
go into lots of places big boats can't go. Dad showed me on the
Internet—there's beaches and beaches and beaches. There's
even places where Ketchup and Took can get off. They can't
get off here because of...qu... Dad, what is it?'

'Quarantine,' Nick said, his eyes not leaving Misty's face.
'We had a friend sail *Mahelkee* here, and Ketchup and Took
flew with us. Fred's given them every inoculation they need.
If they stay on the boat when there's any restrictions then they
can go with us wherever we want.'

'You've brought the dogs?'

'Family,' he said diffidently. 'They didn't want to stay at
home.'

ught two stray dogs to Greece?'

culations will cover them for almost every place
. There's a couple of places they can't go, but Rose
will look after them then.'

se and Bill?'

isabelle's parents,' he said, and there was a tension in
s voice that said he wasn't sure if he was stepping over
some invisible line with this. 'They've been desperate to help
since Isabelle died. They love Bailey. We've sort of…I've sort
of backed off from them, but they're lovely people. They're
Bailey's grandparents. I know they'll like you.'

'And they have a really big boat,' Bailey said. 'So they
can look after Took and Ketchup every time we go and have
adventures and then we can come back and get them. And
Took's even learned to swim. Dad went swimming yesterday
and Took jumped right in and swam as well—and they already
know how to use their sand tray.'

'How long have you been here?' she asked faintly.

'Four days,' Nick said. 'Waiting for you.'

'Four days…'

'We'll wait for a year if we must. If you really want to do
your list alone. Only we'd very much like to do it with you.'

'I want to see snow buntings,' Bailey said.

Oh, help. She was really crying now. She was crying and
crying, and an elderly woman cast her a sideways look and
stopped.

'Are you okay, dear?' she said. 'Is this man annoying you?
Can I get my husband to carry your bags aboard?'

'I…' She had to pull herself together. Somehow. She sniffed
and sniffed again. 'I'm fine,' she managed. 'I'm really fine.
This gentleman's not annoying me at all. In fact…' She took
a deep breath. Regrouped. Cast a last look at a big white
fibreglass boat that was no longer about to carry her to her
dreams.

'In fact, I might have found someone to carry my bags

for me,' she managed, and she smiled. And then she
and smiled, and before the elderly lady knew what h
she reached out and hugged her. 'But thank you for offe.
I love it that you offered your husband, but I believe I mi₁
just have found my own.'

'You mean you'll let us join you?' Nick asked and the whole
world held its breath.

Her world settled. Her heart started beating again. She was
standing before the man she loved with all her heart, and her
list was waiting.

'Why, yes,' she said as he reached for her and beside her
an extremely astonished elderly lady started to smile as well.
'Why, yes, I believe I will.'

Sunrise.

Bailey was still in bed, deeply asleep. He'd had a really
big day yesterday, trudging gamely up the sides of the hills
of Tulloch. He'd seen snow buntings. He'd giggled and run
and been every inch the child he should be.

He seemed younger now than he'd been twelve months ago.
That was great. It was how it should be. He was confident and
happy. If he woke now, he had his dogs on his bed and the
lovely lady who ran their bed and breakfast overlooking the
loch would reassure him that Dad and Misty would soon be
home.

But not yet. Bailey might have seen a snow bunting but
Misty wanted to hear them, and there wasn't a lot of listening to be had with a chattering seven-year-old. So they'd
crept away at dawn, rugged up, because even in summer the
Highlands could be cool and misty.

They walked side by side up the scree, sometimes hand
in hand, steadying each other, sometimes coming close, hugging, then clambering the tricky bits apart…and then coming
together again as they intended coming together for the rest
of their lives.

y reached the point the landlady had suggested.
sank into a bed of heather—not so soft as Misty had
_ined—she did need to keep adjusting these dreams—and
y watched the sun rise over the distant peaks.

In silence. Apart from the snow buntings.

It was the best…

Where had she read the words… *'It's not how many breaths you take; it's how often your breath is taken away'*?

Her breath was taken away now. She was lying in heather on a Scottish hillside, listening to the birds she'd read about for so long, beside the man she loved.

Her husband.

They'd married in Greece, on the Isle of Lindos. In an ancient temple overlooking the Aegean Sea. Lindos hadn't been on her list but there'd been a few wonderful additions to her list and there were more to come.

'Does this place come up to scratch?' Nick asked her as the sun rose higher and the tangerine blush faded to the cool, clear grey of the day. 'Can we put a tick beside this one?'

'Yep,' she said and rolled happily into his arms. 'Yes, we can. Definitely a tick. Or maybe a scratch is a better description. Oh, Nick, I love you.'

'I love you, too,' he said and he kissed her long and wondrously and they clung and held—two lovers finding their dreams together. 'You want to go back to bed?' he asked as the kiss finally ended and she knew by the passion in his voice what he wanted—what they both wanted right now.

'Wuss,' she said. 'Just because heather's a bit scratchy.'

'A lot scratchy. Double bed back at the house. Pillows. More pillows. Lovely, soft quilt.'

'Take your coat off,' she ordered. 'Heather. More heather. Lovely soft coat.'

'Wicked woman. Someone might see.'

'We're the only people in the world,' she said and kissed him again. 'Don't you know?'

'We're not, you know,' he said and held her close. 'Misty, it's almost time we went home.'

Home. Banksia Bay. It was waiting for them, a lovely place to come home to.

But maybe not for ever. They'd leave and leave again, she thought. But for now…maybe they did need a bit of stability.

Banksia Bay was a good place to have a baby. Twelve weeks to go… She put her hand on her tummy and she felt her baby move, and she thought life couldn't get any better than it was right now.

'I'm thinking we should get another dog,' Nick said and she pushed herself up on her elbows and looked down at him. Dark and lean and dangerous. Wickedly laughing.

Her Nick.

'Why would we get another dog?'

'I've been thinking…'

'Thinking's risky.'

'Yes, but…' He tugged her down and kissed her nose. 'Ketchup and Took…in a way they brought us together.'

'I guess they did.'

'So to bring this new little person into the family…'

'We need another dog?'

'A pound dog,' he said in satisfaction. 'One who needs a home.'

'We'd have to extend the sand tray on *Mahelkee*.'

'I'm a marine architect,' he said smugly. 'Bigger sand tray? I can handle that.'

'Baby first,' she said. 'Dogs need attention.'

'Home first,' he said, unbuttoning her coat with delicious, languorous ease. 'Banksia Bay.'

'For now,' she said and kissed him and kissed him again, as she intended to kiss him for the rest of her life. 'Banksia Bay's our base. Somewhere Bailey can go to school, where we can work, where we can recoup for the next adventure. But home? Home's where the heart is. Home's number thirteen or number fourteen on our list. Home's wherever we are, my love. Home is where I am, right now.'

Cherish

THE BABY PROJECT by *Susan Meier*

When Whitney's made temporary guardian of tiny baby Gino, there's a problem—the little orphan's new daddy...shockingly gorgeous tycoon Darius and the inconvenient feelings he inspires!

SECOND CHANCE BABY by *Susan Meier*

Hot-shot tycoon Nick's stunned. The woman who broke his heart is his new assistant—and she's pregnant! Can they dare dream of getting back together and having a family the second time around?

RICHES TO RAGS BRIDE by *Myrna Mackenzie*

When her cheating fiancé steals her inheritance, *ex*-heiress Genevieve has to get a job—fast! But her new boss, Lucas McDowell, leaves her tongue-tied and head-over-heels!

THE HEIRESS'S BABY by *Lilian Darcy*

Nate had no desire to babysit a spoilt socialite as she played at having a job. But after one sultry night with the boss's daughter, Atlanta surprises him—now she's *expecting his baby*!

HER BEST FRIEND by *Sarah Mayberry*

Amy got over best friend Quinn when he got married. But now he's single and wants to help her fulfil a childhood dream, is Amy ready to let him back into her life?

Cherish

AND BABIES MAKE FIVE
by Judy Duarte

Despite being single, Samantha's dream of becoming a mother is about to come true—in triplicate! Yet can her handsome neighbour Hector convince Sam that he's her Mr Right?

AT LONG LAST, A BRIDE
by Susan Crosby

Joe knew it was past time for his now ex-fiancée to stand on her own two feet. So why were all roads leading him back into Dixie's arms?

RANCHER'S TWINS: MUM NEEDED
by Barbara Hannay

Nanny Holly has already bonded with her late cousin's gorgeous twins... and she's reluctant to let go when their rough, rugged father Gray claims the precious babies. Yet could their future be together as a family?

Cherish™

RIVA™

Cupcakes and Killer Heels
by Heidi Rice
Ruby Delisantro's usually in the driving seat when it comes to relationships, but after meeting Callum Westmore's bedroom eyes she's in danger of losing control and—worse—of *liking* it!

Sex, Gossip and Rock & Roll
by Nicola Marsh
Charli Chambers has *never* met someone as infuriating—or delectable!—as businessman Luca Petrelli. Can she ever get close enough to the real Luca for their fling to be more than just a one-hit wonder?

The Love Lottery
by Shirley Jump
When her name is unexpectedly drawn in the town's love lottery, uptight Sophie Watson's horrified to be matched with smug-but-sexy Harlan Jones! A week of dating him will be *terrible*—won't it?

Her Moment in the Spotlight
by Nina Harrington
Mimi Ryan's debut fashion show is her dream come true. If she's being bossy then grumpy photographer Hal Langdon will just have to live with it! It's a shame she can't get his strong arms or teasing smile out of her mind...

On sale from 6th May 2011
Don't miss out!

Available at WHSmith, Tesco, ASDA, Eason and all good bookshops

www.millsandboon.co.uk

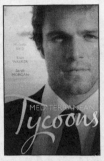

...he three Keyes sisters—in
...usan Mallery's unmissable
family saga

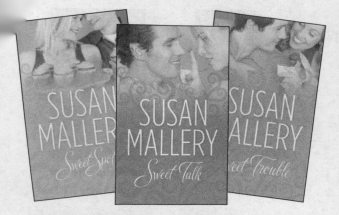

Sweet Talk
Available 18th March 2011

Sweet Spot
Available 15th April 2011

Sweet Trouble
Available 20th May 2011

*For "readers who can't get enough of
Nora Roberts' family series"—Booklist*

www.millsandboon.co.uk

Nora Roberts' *The O*

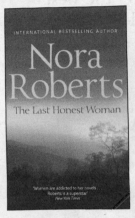

The Last Honest Woman

4th March 2011

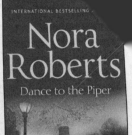

Dance to the Piper

1st April 2011

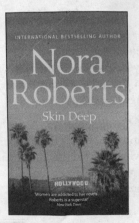

Skin Deep

6th May 2011

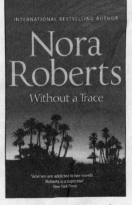

Without a Trace

3rd June 2011

...king children bring
...r mothers the best
gift of all—love!

The Matchmakers

Dori Robertson's eleven-year-old son wants a new father. He's already chosen the guy—Gavin Parker. Dori thinks it's safe enough…until he kisses her!

The Courtship of Carol Sommars

Peter Sommars is fifteen and he needs a little more independence. Which is why he'd like his mum to start dating. He even knows the perfect man— Alex Preston, his best friend's dad…

Make time for friends.
Make time for Debbie Macomber.

One innocent child
A secret that could destroy his life

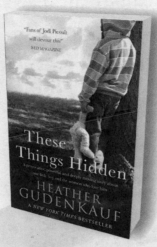

Imprisoned for a heinous crime when she was a just a teenager, Allison Glenn is now free. Desperate for a second chance, Allison discovers that the world has moved on without her…

Shunned by those who once loved her, Allison is determined to make contact with her sister. But Brynn is trapped in her own world of regret and torment.

Their legacy of secrets is focused on one little boy. And if the truth is revealed, the consequences will be unimaginable for the adoptive mother who loves him, the girl who tried to protect him and the two sisters who hold the key to all that is hidden…

"Deeply moving and lyrical…it will haunt you…"
—*Company* magazine on *The Weight of Silence*

www.mirabooks.co.uk

How far would you go to protect your sister?

As teenagers, Maya and Rebecca Ward witnessed
their parents' murder. Now doctors, Rebecca has
become the risk taker whilst her sister Maya lives a
quiet life with her husband Adam, unwilling to deal
with her secrets from the night her parents died.

When a hurricane hits North Carolina, Maya is
feared dead. As hope fades, Adam and Rebecca
face unexpected feelings. And Rebecca finds
some buried secrets of her own.

www.mirabooks.co.uk

2 FREE BOOKS
AND A SURPRISE GIFT

We would like to take this opportunity to thank you for reading this Mills & Boon® book by offering you the chance to take TWO more specially selected books from the Cherish™ series absolutely FREE! We're also making this offer to introduce you to the benefits of the Mills & Boon® Book Club™—

- **FREE home delivery**
- **FREE gifts and competitions**
- **FREE monthly Newsletter**
- **Exclusive Mills & Boon Book Club offers**
- **Books available before they're in the shops**

Accepting these FREE books and gift places you under no obligation to buy, you may cancel at any time, even after receiving your free books. Simply complete your details below and return the entire page to the address below. You don't even need a stamp!

YES Please send me 2 free Cherish books and a surprise gift. I understand that unless you hear from me, I will receive 5 superb new stories every month, including two 2-in-1 books priced at £5.30 each, and a single book priced at £3.30, postage and packing free. I am under no obligation to purchase any books and may cancel my subscription at any time. The free books and gift will be mine to keep in any case.

Ms/Mrs/Miss/Mr _____ Initials _____

_____

Surname _____

Address _____

_____

_____ Postcode _____

E-mail _____

Send this whole page to: Mills & Boon Book Club, Free Book Offer, FREEPOST NAT 10298, Richmond, TW9 1BR